The Left-Handed
FATE

KATE MILFORD

illustrated by
ELIZA WHEELER

Henry Holt and Company
New York

Henry Holt and Company, LLC
Publishers since 1866
175 Fifth Avenue, New York, New York 10010
mackids.com

Henry Holt® is a registered trademark of Henry Holt and Company, LLC.
Text copyright © 2016 by Kate Milford
Illustrations copyright © 2016 by Eliza Wheeler
All rights reserved.

Library of Congress Cataloging-in-Publication Data
Names: Milford, Kate, author. | Wheeler, Eliza, illustrator.
Title: The Left-Handed Fate / Kate Milford ; illustrated by Eliza Wheeler.
Description: First edition. | New York : Henry Holt and Company, 2016. |
Summary: "A quest story to find the three pieces of a magical engine which can either
win the War of 1812 . . . or stop it altogether"—Provided by publisher.
Identifiers: LCCN 2015033437 |
ISBN 9780805098006 (hardback) | ISBN 9781627796569 (e-book)
Subjects: LCSH: United States—History—War of 1812—Juvenile fiction. | CYAC:
United States—History—War of 1812—Fiction. | Magic—Fiction. | Sea stories. |
BISAC: JUVENILE FICTION / Action & Adventure / General. | JUVENILE
FICTION / Science Fiction. | JUVENILE FICTION / Fantasy & Magic.
Classification: LCC PZ7.M594845 Le 2016 | DDC [Fic]—dc23
LC record available at http://lccn.loc.gov/2015033437

Our books may be purchased in bulk for promotional, educational, or business use.
Please contact your local bookseller or the Macmillan Corporate and Premium
Sales Department at (800) 221-7945 ext. 5442 or by e-mail
at MacmillanSpecialMarkets@macmillan.com.

First edition—2016 / Designed by Eileen Savage
Printed in the United States of America by R. R. Donnelley & Sons Company,
Harrisonburg, Virginia

3   5   7   9   10   8   6   4   2

....

To my friends and family in Maryland, but especially to the memory of Bud Chell Sr. and Norma Hauswald Chell;
To the folks of the Chesapeake Bay, the Outer Banks, Topsail Island, and Key West, with gratitude for bringing a certain place to life in my mind and heart;
And, as always, to Nathan and Griffin, with all my love.

— Part One —

CHESAPEAKE

one

THE *LEFT-HANDED FATE*

June 22, 1812

Baltimore was a beautiful, twinkling, probably hostile collection of lights up ahead, half-hidden by two sheltering arms of land and one massive fortress. The topsail schooner *Left-Handed Fate* slid like an elegant knife through the water, trying as hard as ever she could not to look like a British privateer as she passed under the guns of Fort McHenry. The three youngest passengers stood at the port rail, leaning progressively farther out over the water in order to get a view unobstructed by someone else's head until the tallest, a young man in spectacles and a blue velvet coat, shoved the leather portfolio he was holding into the hands of the girl in the middle, pivoted abruptly, and vomited over the side.

"Is Max all right?" asked the smallest, a child with Chinese features, leaning around the girl to give the older boy the briefest of looks.

"Just committing his supper to the sea." After that, other than handing the portfolio back once the boy called Max had composed himself, Lucy Bluecrowne ignored them both. Her eyes were on the fortress, and not all the vomiting landlubbers in the world were going to distract her from the hornet's nest they were sailing into.

"But there isn't even any sea running," the small boy protested. "This river's calm as glass."

"Since when does he need a reason?" Lucy muttered.

"I'm right here," Max said with wounded dignity. "And I'm not seasick, Liao."

"Nerves, then," Liao said sympathetically, patting his arm.

"I'd be an idiot not to be nervous," Max retorted.

"Enough," Lucy said abruptly. The night was far too clear for this sort of adventure. You wanted dirty weather—clouds, mist, a good fierce soaking storm—for sneaking in and out of unfriendly ports. But the weather hadn't chosen to cooperate, so here they were, the *Fate* and all the souls aboard her, waltzing toward the harbor of Fells Point as if it were the most natural thing in the world.

The crew had done what they could to disguise her more distinctive features—detaching and stowing the left-handed figurehead that was sometimes called a Fate and sometimes called a Fury, overpainting and scuffing the beautiful piney green she usually wore on her sides, dirtying up the decorative gilt gingerbread-work that was the bosun's mate's pride and joy. The *Fate* looked drab and nondescript now, except for her sharply back-slanting masts. Fortunately the schooner had been built in Baltimore, so it was perhaps the one place where she would look right at home. And they were headed for a friendly shipyard. Still . . . Lucy forced herself to unclench her jaw.

She also forced herself not to look back. The *Fate* had enemies behind her as well as enemies ahead, but there were already plenty of eyes scanning the dark river behind them for familiar sails.

Or strange lights on the water. Or strange lights *under* it. Or, worst of all, strange lights aboard the *Fate* itself. Lucy shuddered, then reached out and scratched one of the nearby lines of rigging for luck.

"Cutter's ready," came a rough whisper from across the deck. Lucy put one arm—a comforting arm, it was meant to be—around Max. For some incomprehensible reason, this made him flinch, which made her want to give him something to flinch about. Instead she took a deep breath and reminded herself that, yes, he was sure to be terribly nervous, and also he had just thrown up, and she led him across the deck as gently as she thought appropriate. Meaning that to anyone watching, it probably looked more like dragging him for twenty-five feet than leading him, but with effort, she kept herself from shoving him across with a kick in the backside to hurry the process along.

Kendrick and another sailor called Whippett were holding one of the *Fate*'s cutters steady against the starboard side. Max managed not to fall in the water as he climbed down into it. This was uncommon enough to seem like a good omen to Lucy.

Captain Richard Bluecrowne appeared at her side just as she was about to clamber down herself. "Take care, Lucy. You're clear on the rendezvous?"

"Yes, sir."

"And if there's trouble?"

"All clear on that, too, sir."

The captain nodded. "Don't go out of your way—I should prefer you to get Max where he needs to go and back again as quickly as possible—but keep your eyes open and take note of anything that might confirm or disconfirm the rumor."

The rumor. "Yes, sir."

He leaned over the gunwale and tossed a quick "Best of luck, Mr. Ault" to Max, then kissed Lucy's forehead. "See you soon. May no new thing arise."

Liao ducked under one of the captain's arms. "And don't worry, Lucy. I shall look out for our papa and the rest in the meantime." His voice was jaunty enough, but Liao was twisting the end of his long, braided pigtail between the fingers of his right hand. It was a thing he'd done for as long as Lucy had known him, and it meant he was nervous, too.

"I know you will, Liao." She kissed the little boy's cheek, then dropped easily down the side of the *Fate* and joined Max, Kendrick, and Whippett in the waiting cutter.

She and the two sailors piloted the little boat toward a dark stretch of open land to the north of Baltimore proper, just beyond the shipyards that lined the waterfront of the town of Fells Point. Kendrick was her father's coxswain; he was one of the most trusted hands aboard the *Fate* and also the closest thing to an uncle that Lucy had. She'd known him and Whippett most of her life, and the three of them handled the cutter like the practiced team they were, right down to beaching it neatly and getting Max out of it again without him getting his feet wet. Two good omens, that was. Then Lucy, Max, and Kendrick hiked through the open scruff under that awkwardly clear night sky toward Fells Point, leaving Whippett to guard the boat.

"So where is this shop?" Lucy asked as they encountered the beginnings of a packed-dirt road underfoot at last.

"Bond Street," Max said. They walked on, passing the first shipyards and bulkheads, and at last found themselves rather suddenly in town. Max paused under a flickering street lamp, opened his portfolio, and took a hand-drawn map from it. "Let us just find out where we are now. Gough Street? That should intersect with Bond."

"Look," Kendrick said in a grim tone. Lucy followed his pointing finger to a crisp new broadside tacked to the side of a warehouse. Printed upon it in words big enough to read from all the way across the street: WAR WITH BRITAIN HAS COME AGAIN AT LAST.

Lucy sighed. "Well, evidently it's not just a rumor. Mr. Madison has finally made it official."

Max swore. It was so out of character that even Kendrick glanced over in surprise. Max paced a few steps away, still swearing, and came back rubbing his face. "Nothing for it," he said, finally. He consulted his map for a minute, then put it away. "Let's go."

Lucy trailed Max and Kendrick deeper into Fells Point, her insides slowly coiling themselves into knots. She always experienced a sort of mild upheaval when she came ashore, where she constantly suspected she abruptly and obviously didn't belong. But this was worse—now she felt doubly that she must stick out like a sore thumb. There was no reason to suppose anyone who looked at her would know she was British; for the most part Americans and Englishmen looked and sounded basically the same. But it didn't matter. Lucy sensed eyes on all sides. Her feet, so sure and effortless at sea, seemed determined to trip over every cobble in the street, just in case anyone hadn't already noticed this awkward enemy girl in their midst.

Max, on the other hand, appeared to be suddenly, completely, and infuriatingly at ease and in control as he navigated through the early-evening streets. He led them unerringly to a shop with some sort of philosophical device over the door: an assortment of spheres connected by slender metal shafts that gleamed darkly in the moonlight. "This is it."

"It's closed," Lucy observed.

Max nodded up to the second-floor windows, where slivers of yellow light peeked out from behind the curtains. "He lives upstairs." He commenced alternating loud knocks and hard yanks on the pull that rang the bell just inside the door. Lucy glanced around, but even with most of the businesses shuttered for the night, Bond Street was a busy lane. Dozens of people were out, and nobody took any notice of the noise Max was making. A lot of them seemed to be talking about war, though. Lucy caught snippets here and there: "If it takes a second war to finally have independence . . ." "We've been at war for years already, as far as I'm concerned." "What odds New England'll finally secede, the Tory bastards?"

Lucy fidgeted. Kendrick lit a pipe and smoked placidly. Max kept on knocking and ringing, knocking and ringing.

At last an old woman threw open a window on the second floor and leaned out. "What on earth is the meaning of this? The shop is closed!"

Max leapt back into the street and waved. "Good evening! I'm sorry to call so late, but I'm here to see Mr. Jeton. My name is Max Ault. I'm Lawrence Ault's son."

The old woman's eyes popped so wide her spectacles fell right off her nose. She grabbed for them, performed a neat midair catch, and disappeared back into the room above. The window slammed shut.

Lucy, Max, and Kendrick looked at one another. "Good luck," Lucy said.

Max smiled. "What's there to need luck for?"

"Well," Kendrick said around his pipestem, "this Mr. Jeton's country just declared war on ours and you're about to ask him to help you build the most powerful weapon in history. So."

"Not to use against America, obviously," Max grumbled. "*This* war is nothing. Who cares about James Madison's war? It's irrelevant, a distraction. It's Napoleon Bonaparte and his wars that matter."

Kendrick said nothing, just exhaled a mouthful of smoke, but his eyebrow rose nearly to his hairline.

"Obviously," Lucy repeated, trying to keep a straight face. "I'm sure Mr. Jeton will see that. And people love being told their presidents are irrelevant and their wars a distraction, so that'll help."

Max's face began to look a bit green, but before he could vomit again, a light sputtered to life in the shop. The door swung open and the old woman stood there glaring out at them. "Who are these?" she asked, eyeing Lucy and Kendrick.

"Traveling companions," Max said, his gaze flicking past the woman and inside in search of Mr. Jeton. The woman's eyes narrowed even further.

"I'm his wife," she said coldly. "And I'm sorry to tell you Mr. Jeton isn't at home." She didn't look sorry at all.

"Well . . . well, when do you expect him back?"

"Not for a fortnight."

Max's jaw dropped. "He's not coming back for *two weeks*?"

"At least," Mrs. Jeton replied. Was it Lucy's imagination, or did she look a bit smug?

Max pulled himself together and cleared his throat. "Might we come in, madam?"

"No," the old woman snapped.

"Well . . . do you know if perhaps he—Mr. Jeton—left something for me? I did write him to say I was coming."

"He didn't leave anything for you."

"For my father, perhaps? Lawrence Ault?" Lucy restrained herself from kicking Max as the old lady said nothing and he kept on talking. "He was looking for a . . . a mechanical something-or-other, a piece of a larger thing, and Mr. Jeton wrote to tell my father he thought he'd found it, and that Papa should come and get it." Blessedly, Max stopped then, probably because there was no more he could say without getting into uncomfortable details. Still nothing from the old lady. "So my letter didn't arrive?" Max persisted a little desperately. "I did write."

"Oh, it arrived," Mrs. Jeton said frostily. "It certainly did."

"Well, that's good news." The old lady didn't seem to agree, and under her unfriendly stare, Max's face went very confused. "Then . . . well, I imagine we shall just . . . wait?"

"I shouldn't advise that." Then she stepped back into the darkened shop and shut the door right in poor Max's face. Through the window they could see the little light of her candle disappear back up the stairs.

"Not what you'd hoped, then," Kendrick said mildly.

Lucy scanned the street, then nodded at the dark alley between Jeton's shop and the next one over. "The passage there."

"Why?"

"Because if I go to work on *this* lock, people might notice," Lucy said patiently. Then, without waiting to see if Max followed—which took effort, because she knew the horrified expression on his face would be priceless—she walked purposefully down the street until she could sidestep into the shadows.

Taking care not to trip over the lumps and holes and old, rusted buckets that filled the passage, Lucy made her way to the back of the shop. Then she squatted before the rear door and took her folding knife and her marlinespike from the embroidered ditty bag she always carried when she went ashore. The marlinespike, a curved steel spike on an inlaid handle that was mostly useful for splicing rope, had a flattened tip that ought to do nicely for this lock.

A clumsy noise rattled in the passage. "What are you doing?" Max hissed, just barely avoiding landing on top of her as he tripped over a mass of refuse.

"Shut up. I think I can get this open." This wasn't her forte—Liao was the family picklock—but she'd learned enough to pop a door or the lock on a trunk now and then.

"Then what? Are you—" He dropped his voice to a whisper. "Are you proposing we sneak in and just . . . and just *take* the thing?"

"Obviously. I'm a *privateer*. We sneak in and take things. This is what you hired us for." Lucy, like all her shipmates, generally preferred the term *letter-of-marque* to *privateer*. *Letter-of-marque* felt less piratical. Just now, though, she wanted to make a point.

"But—that's stealing!"

Lucy dropped the spike she'd been about to slip into the keyhole and gaped up at him. "As opposed to the way we *acquired* that other *item* for your papa? That thing that's in your cabin as we speak?"

"But you took that from the French. We're at war with—" Lucy made her glare extra-scathing, and Max's voice died away. "Oh."

"Exactly." She went back to work. "We were at war with the French, making our capture of the first part of this project of yours a lawful act of war. Now we're at war with the Americans, too." It was unquestionably true about the French capture, but Lucy didn't go so far as to actually say what she was doing now was also a lawful act of war. She was murkier on the laws governing wartime taking-of-things from civilians on land. Hopefully Max was, too.

Meanwhile, here was a problem: the moment she had the spike

in the keyhole, Lucy knew she wasn't getting the lock open. The keyway was too narrow for her to move the spike even a little bit. She could barely feel any of the interior works, never mind manipulating them at all.

Well, this was embarrassing. Lucy gave the spike a few useless twitches while she tried to figure out how to get out of this situation without admitting her mistake to Max. Liao would have had the thing open ages ago, she thought sourly. "Do you know what you're looking for once I get us inside?" she asked, playing for time. *If I get us inside.*

Max took a deep breath. "No."

Lucy lowered her hands. "What?"

"I don't know what it is."

"You hired us to bring you to Baltimore to retrieve this priceless *thing*, an artifact that you keep saying is part of"—she lowered her voice—"some remarkable arcane *weapon*, and you don't know what this thing *is?*"

Max's face was so red even the shadows couldn't hide the flush on his cheeks. "Jeton's letter to my father just said he thought he'd found 'the thing you were looking for.' I don't have my father's side of the correspondence."

"But your father's notes—"

"Keep your voice down."

"But you have your father's notes, Maxwell," she hissed.

"My father's notes say things like *mechanism, question mark,* and *manna, question mark,* and *clock or similar, question mark.* They aren't what you'd call terribly descriptive."

"So how on earth were—"

"I was expecting Mr. Jeton to be here and to be willing to give me this thing, whatever it is, because he *told my father to come and get it!*" Max exploded. A light flickered to life behind the curtains above them on the second floor of the house. Lucy shoved her tools in her bag, grabbed Max's arm, and dragged him back toward Bond Street.

While they'd been arguing, Lucy had been vaguely aware of noise rising in the street. By the time they reached the mouth of the alley, it had escalated to a proper din: loud voices, hooves, and wheels. Kendrick's broad back barred their way, but Lucy and Max could make out big clumps of shouting people gathering on Bond.

Pipe smoke swirled around Kendrick's head. "Stay there," he murmured. "Something's happened."

Lucy and Max crouched in the shadows, listening. Evidently, somewhere in Baltimore, a printshop that had fiercely denounced the president and his declaration of war in its publications had been put to the torch by a mob. Dispirited, she dropped to a seat against the wall. It was hard to imagine how their timing could possibly be worse.

To distract herself from this fact—which could, she supposed, be interpreted as the fault of the *Fate* and her crew—she turned on Max again. "You don't know what we're looking for," she whispered. "This is unbelievable. All this time you've had us racing after this . . . this remarkable *thing* that's going to change the course of the war, and here we are and you don't know what you're looking for."

"Oh, get over it," Max grumbled, leaning churlishly against the wall with his arms folded. "It isn't as if you could get that lock open, anyhow."

"Another minute, I would have!" He never needed to know the truth.

"No, you would not," Max argued. "We both know it, so let's just move on past this little escapade and figure out what to do next. And anyway, what Jeton has is only a *piece* of the remarkable thing that's going to change the course of the war."

"A piece you can't build the thing without."

"Yes."

"And there are three pieces."

"One of which we already have."

Lucy nodded at the shop to their right. "But you don't know what *this* piece, the one Jeton has, actually is."

"No."

"And the third piece? The one you'll need after we find this one?"

"What about it?"

"Do you know what *that* piece is, Max?"

He pursed his lips and said nothing.

"I thought as much." Lucy shook her head. "Unbelievable."

"It's going to get worse out here before it gets better," Kendrick muttered. "Let's go. Sharply, now."

They ducked out of the alley and onto the street, which was only coming more and more to life as the news of the newspaper's torching spread. Fortunately, with news like that, nobody seemed to have attention to spare for three strangers, and they reached the beach, Whippett, and the cutter without incident.

"Papa's not going to like this," Lucy grumbled as she took her place at the prow of the beached boat.

Max had the gall to actually shrug. "Your father works for me at the moment."

It was that comment, true though it undoubtedly was, that made Lucy give the cutter a sharp shove into the water just as Max reached one foot gingerly over the side to climb in. It was just enough to throw Max's balance off and send him sprawling into the surf. He came up sputtering in perfect time for a wave to smack him neatly in the back of the head and knock him flat again.

two

TRANSLATIONS

Max scrambled onto the weather deck of the *Left-Handed Fate*, then shambled, dripping, toward the forward ladder-way. Somehow he'd managed to have his pocketwatch on him when he'd gone into the cutter. He had to get the thing into oil before all that river water really fouled up the works.

"Max." Lucy grabbed his sleeve. "The captain will want a report."

"He's waiting for you in his cabin," said Mr. Fitch, the first mate, from the low rise at the back of the ship that passed for a quarterdeck. "Voices carry on clear nights."

Max looked down at his dripping clothes, and then, with deep sadness, at his watch. It wouldn't survive too many more dunkings like this.

"I'll take it, sir." Kendrick plucked the watch from his palm.

"Thank you, Kendrick." He squared his sopping shoulders and followed Lucy toward the other ladder, the one at the back of the ship.

They descended to the rear section of the lower deck—the aft platform, the sailors called it, since this deck was interrupted by the open maw of the hold and didn't run the entire length of the schooner. The forward section, the fore platform, was where the galley was. Presumably Kendrick was going there now to get some sweet oil for the watch.

The captain's quarters hunkered beneath the quarterdeck. Max knocked on the door, feeling like an errant child reporting to his father. True, he'd hired the *Left-Handed Fate*, so technically, yes, Captain Bluecrowne worked for him. But even after months together at sea, it still didn't feel that way. Taken together, Captain Bluecrowne, his ship, and his crew—and his daughter—were a force of nature. You didn't *hire* a force of nature. You maybe harnessed it for a while, if you were very lucky and it happened to be going in your direction.

"Come in."

Lucy opened the door and Max followed her into the captain's quarters. Richard Bluecrowne stood beside his desk, brooding over a logbook. He raised his eyes. "Mr. Ault, you are dripping on my floor. Has someone at least seen to your watch?"

Max flushed. Evidently he was both helpless and predictable. "Kendrick is seeing to it, thank you, sir."

"Good. Between wet clothes and a wet watch, I should have seen to the watch first, too. More time-sensitive." Captain Bluecrowne winked at his daughter, who snorted back a mouthful of laughter. Max forced himself not to roll his eyes. Forces of nature the Bluecrownes might be, but they shared a terrible sense of humor.

"Forgive me for not inviting you to sit, Mr. Ault," the captain added, "but I rather like that chair. What news?"

"Mr. Jeton has left town for a fortnight, sir. His wife was not very . . . welcoming. Then Lucy tried to break in, but—"

"But he doesn't know what the thing Jeton has looks like," Lucy finished, shooting him an irritated look.

To Max's surprise, Captain Bluecrowne waved a careless hand. "His father didn't even know what all the components of his device were. We got lucky with the first piece. Doesn't mean we shan't be lucky again, though. As it happens, while I can't say I'm terribly excited about the idea of lingering in an enemy port, we do have allies here who can hide us for that long, and it would give us time for repairs and provisioning that we cannot afford to put off much longer."

"Then we can stay?" Max hadn't dared hope for that.

"I think we must. Hiding in plain sight is dangerous, but sneaking out and back again later would be worse. The Chesapeake will

be full of American ships looking for prizes, and our navy will blockade the bay before long, which won't help us either . . . to say nothing of our particular pursuers."

"I suppose at least we're safe from them while we're in port," Max said. "Even if it is an enemy harbor."

Captain Bluecrowne disagreed. "The French aren't at war with the States, so there's no reason your Frenchman can't sail into Baltimore if he chooses. As for the others . . . well, who on earth knows? Until we discover who they are, we cannot assume any port is safe." He tapped his fingers on the desktop. "I gather you didn't approve of Lucy's plan. Breaking into the shop."

Max very carefully did not look at Lucy. "It felt a bit larcenous, sir."

"I thoroughly agree," the captain said, glancing darkly at his daughter. "But I suggest you take this time and figure out what you plan to do if Mr. Jeton won't hand the thing over after all."

"But he told my father he would keep it for him," Max protested. "Why wouldn't he give it to me?"

"Well, Max, not to offend you, but you are not your father. Jeton doesn't know you. And, which is perhaps the bigger problem, does he know that what he has is part of a weapon?"

"I don't know how much my father told him," Max said a little sullenly.

"Let's assume the worst, then. If he's a patriotic American who's aware that he has a component of a revolutionary weapon, there is not a chance in the world he'll give it to you now that America has declared war on Britain. Larceny may be your only chance, so you'd best reconcile yourself to it."

"It's not for using against America," Max protested for the second time that night. "It's for stopping the French. Why does no one understand that?"

Captain Bluecrowne gave him a pitying look. "We all understand. It just doesn't matter." He clapped Max on the shoulder. "Best figure out what Mr. Jeton has in case you have to go looking for it yourself. Now get some dry clothes on, for heaven's sake."

"Yes, sir."

Max left as quickly as he could and ducked into his own tiny cabin two doors down. He stripped out of his wet garb and pulled on dry things, muttering all the while to the taxidermied puffin that hung from the ceiling, a relic from home called Otto that his father had picked up who knew where. He had barely gotten his breeches on before Lucy burst into the room. Max jumped and attempted unsuccessfully to cover his torso with his hands.

"Oh, good lord, Max, I've seen shirtless chests before." She climbed into Max's hammock and kicked one heel against the copper-bound trunk beneath it. "Right here, for instance." She leaned back against the wall, laughing at her own joke.

"I cannot take two Bluecrowne bons mots in one evening," Max said with exaggerated dignity as he reached out to shut the door.

"Ouch, Max." Liao fended off the closing door with one shoulder and breezed inside carrying a cup in both hands. Max's poor chronometer, still dripping oil and water, hung from a pencil that lay across the top. "I've brought your watch." He sidled past Max to set the cup on the table, then he climbed on the crate that Max used for a chair.

"Get a shirt on," Lucy ordered. "We're here to help you work out what we're after, and I don't want to be distracted."

"Distracted?" Liao said curiously.

"It was sarcasm, Liao."

Max grumbled and blushed as he pulled on a shirt, then joined Liao at the table. He set the cup aside and opened his portfolio on the tiny tabletop. Lucy barely had to lean out of the hammock to be able to look down at the neat stack of paper inside. "Explain."

"All right." Max moved his map of Fells Point and there it was, the text that had spurred this entire mad enterprise. "This is my father's translation of the inscription on the stone." It was full of cross-outs and write-overs, and there were question marks and jotted queries in the margins, but messy though it was, it was his father's handwriting, and the sight of it made Max's chest tighten just a little.

"And the stone came from Egypt," Liao said, tilting his head at an absurd angle to attempt to read the page upside-down.

"Yes. It was an inscribed block, an artifact Britain received as part of the treaty when we helped boot the French out of Egypt. But Papa thought it referenced ideas from somewhere else. The imagery doesn't fit with what little we know of ancient Egyptian beliefs." Max's eyes roved over the text and his father's notes in the margins as the other two read them for the first time. "The three sections of the text correspond to the three pieces of the device." He knew it all, almost by heart, and yet he still had practically no idea what any of it meant.

Say the words:
Of these is the world made, by these is the world contained. From the singularities is built the great engine that in turn builds the vision of the dreamer and rains down upon the others the end of dreaming:

> *the net (fabric?) that encloses*
> *and connects and binds (imprisons?) and buoys*
> *and builds the library (the knowledge? the information?)*
> *and the promises (laws?)*
> *and the prayers and the spells*
> *and the vast unknowns that exist in the ellipses (horizons?)*
> *and the angles and variables,*

for the information (library?) *is the world*
and the world is the information (library?);

the process (mechanism?) *that takes the name and creates the*
work
    and draws creation and destruction from its hidden places,
    from the spokes of the wheel and from between the teeth of
the gears,
    that turns and drives and moves the world by its movement
(clock or similar?)
    and makes of the world a new thing (reality? life?)
    and takes from the world the thing it no longer needs (the
dead? an enemy?);

    the sustenance that feeds the hunger that drives and grows
    and kills and soothes and sustains, and vanishes before day-
break (manna?);
    for without these we cannot create (without what? refers to
sustenance or hunger?)
    and without these we cannot destroy,
    and without these acts we do not live though we breathe.

"Clear as mud," Lucy muttered.

"I imagine that's on purpose. If you're writing up a road map to a weapon, you don't want just anyone to be able to read it. And hieroglyphics aren't literal things anyway. The inscription itself is all paradoxes and riddles and pictures of bread and owls and other birds that apparently you have to know what sounds they make or how they move to understand what they mean in context."

"Oh, I see," Liao said immediately. "Like how *crow* sometimes means a kind of yell. Or *duck* can mean the bird or—what?" he asked as Max gaped at him. "It makes sense to me. But what does all this have to do with a weapon? You all keep talking about this tremendous weapon, but I don't see how this mentions one anywhere." Liao hated weapons.

"It's all the talk of destroying, I imagine," Lucy said, scratching her head. "Raining down the end of dreaming, that sort of thing."

"What about the creating parts?" Liao argued. "It doesn't make sense."

"It means a weapon," Max said. "Both my father and the Frenchman were certain." The Frenchman: Professor Ault's nemesis, the fellow they'd taken the first piece from, and the reason the *Left-Handed Fate* needed so much repairing at the moment. Or one of the reasons, at least.

Max pointed to the bottom of the page, where the professor had written *fabric/library; process; sustenance.* "The first part we know." He nodded at the crate presently holding Liao up. "The net, or the fabric."

Liao scooted off the box. Max opened it, reached into the packing straw, and found a familiar ridged surface interrupted by impossibly soft fabric. With both hands, he lifted out a tall stack of rectangular cards the color of unwashed wool, bound each to the next by very old blue silk ribbon. Each card was punched with a different arrangement of rectangular holes.

"I remember when we took these off the French ship, back when your father first hired us," Lucy said. "Three years ago, I think?" She glanced at Liao. "It was just before you came aboard. But I never saw them. Some sort of weaving thing, no?"

"It was three years ago," Max confirmed, trying not to think about what had come after that. "And yes, they're loom-cards. Weavers use them for making patterns in cloth."

"And cloth fits into this how?" Lucy sounded dubious, which

wasn't surprising. The stacked cards didn't look like they belonged to a war engine, and yet from these and a few other bits would come the last weapon the world would ever need.

How the punched cards could provide both a fabric and a library Max didn't know. Evidently both his father and the Frenchman who was now chasing Max had been in agreement on the matter, though, because the Frenchman had tracked the cards down and Professor Ault had paid a substantial amount for the *Left-Handed Fate* to take them away. Then had come the letter from Franklin Jeton, an old friend Lawrence Ault had asked to be on the lookout for another bit of the engine, the piece corresponding to *the process*, which he believed would be mechanical.

Shortly after that, Max had found his father dead.

That might have been the end of it; as far as Professor Ault's son and wife knew, the old scholar had merely been studying Egyptian artifacts for the British Museum, so they'd packed his notes away in the attic until another scholar took over. But one night a few months after his father's funeral, Max had been woken by voices. He'd tiptoed down the hall in the dark and crouched outside the study to listen to strangers speaking quietly, hurriedly, and in French. Whatever those operatives had been looking for, they hadn't found it, but they searched the study almost until daybreak. Clearly, Max's father had been involved in something more dangerous than the study of antiquities.

For the next year Max studied his father's notes. The specifics weren't clear, but it appeared that the professor had come across an account of an ancient engine of war, something immensely, almost incomprehensibly powerful. Something that could perhaps be made again, something to end the everlasting wars that had been the backdrop of Max's entire life. But the account didn't explain how to build the thing, nor was it even particularly clear about what the thing was. All it did was describe the three pieces that seemed to make up either the device or a schematic for it.

Then a letter of condolence arrived from the master of the ship that had helped Max's father find the first of the three pieces—the laced cards. Six months later, Max hired Captain Bluecrowne again to take him to Baltimore. It had seemed like a fairly simple journey at the time. Yes, they had to avoid the French—every English ship had to avoid the French—but the *Left-Handed Fate* was famously good at that. And for the first month, things had gone fine.

Then the *Marie Colette* had shown up: the Frenchman's ship. Captain Bluecrowne knew her from his voyage with Professor Ault, and Max knew her master from his father's notes. They weren't just going to go away. Still, the *Fate* was faster and a better fighter, and in the end all they had to do was beat the *Marie Colette* to Baltimore. And so for most of the second month, things had gone fine, too, albeit with a few brief but terrifying intervals of battle.

Then one night the lookout had spotted a strange light out on the water.

It had been Liao who'd come and roused Max for a look. On deck, the sailors were murmuring about omens and sea-fire and water-burn and whether anyone knew a man who knew a man who'd seen such a thing before and whether the phenomenon presaged good or ill. "Is it something philosophical?" Liao had asked, pressing a telescope into Max's hand.

It had been some miles off, and all Max could see, even through the glass, was a flat glow, blue-white like lightning. But—strange!—the glow seemed to be coming from *under* the water.

Everyone on deck, including the officer on duty, had been waiting to hear his findings. "Is it not like whatever makes the wake glow in some waters?" Max asked. "Phosphorescent creatures or weeds or some such thing?" His theory was rejected utterly by the deck hands, who had seen *that* plenty of times but nothing like *this*. Before Max could come up with another theory, the bizarre radiance had vanished.

The discussions of what sort of omen the light was continued, but the ship returned to its usual nighttime rhythm. Just as Max had been about to head below again, a number of small violet flames had blinked to life at the tops of the masts. These Max recognized, and so did the sailors: corposants. Saint Elmo's lights.

And with those lights had come the *Left-Handed Fate*'s first encounter with a second ship: a brig that seemed to appear out of nowhere, crewed by men in uniforms of black-upon-black. They had never seen the strange light under the water again, but the ghostly flares at the tops of the masts had appeared again and again, and the brig with them nearly every time.

This ship flew no flag. It confounded the *Fate*'s otherwise excellent lookouts. It flew across the water, Max would come to learn, far faster than a brig had any right to go. It seemed impervious to the *Fate*'s masterful gunnery. And it hounded the *Fate* across the Atlantic. Over and over they would finally fight their way free and leave it behind, only to have it turn up again where it seemed no ship had been a moment before.

Worst of all, those repeated engagements with the brig had slowed the *Fate*'s passage enough for the Frenchman's *Marie Colette* to catch up, and for the United States to declare war on Britain. And now, here they were. Perhaps too late, and by a matter of mere days.

"So the fabric bit is about these cards," Liao said now. "What about the next bit, the *process*?"

"Well, what with all the talk of wheels and gears and turning and driving, my father thought it meant something mechanical, which was why he'd asked Jeton to keep an eye out for it. Mr. Jeton is a mechanical fellow."

"And *the sustenance?*" Lucy asked.

"I'll worry about that later," Max said. "All we need to figure out now is what Jeton has. Whatever *the process* is, my father thought the actual object in question is something like a clock. A *movement* is the name for the mechanism of a timepiece—the working guts of a clock, or a watch. Plus the gears and wheels—that's what a horological movement would be made up of. And it would make sense for a weapon to need some sort of moving parts inside."

Liao shook his head. "But there's no point in trying to figure out what this means from individual words, you know. You can't trust them."

"What do you mean, we can't trust the words?" Max asked, frowning. "The words are all we have."

"But your father translated it," Liao said slowly, "so these are his words. Words *he* chose, not the words of whoever wrote it first." He shook his head. "Did the Egyptians even have clocks and watches?"

Max hesitated. "They certainly had ways of marking time."

"But not the same as ours. *Movement* is your father's word, one he chose because it made sense to him as part of this whole thing, not necessarily because it's the most precise translation of the single word. Because if he did choose it because it's exactly what that word meant, then the original word probably meant *movement*, like this." Liao waggled his hands in the air. "Or, if it's really all written in birds . . ." He flapped his elbows.

Max followed Liao's gesticulations in despair. "What are you saying? That the one thing we have to go on is meaningless?"

"I only know what happens when I have to translate," the boy said apologetically. "If I have to translate something to understand it—or to make someone else understand me—the actual words aren't always enough, Max. They're only clues, signs that point you toward what they're trying to say. You have to pull the meaning out of them by how they all work together. But sometimes you need more hints, like voice and face and where you are in the world and how the wind's blowing."

He looked to Lucy. "It's like omens. Sometimes an albatross means one thing and sometimes it means something else, so you need more to know what it means for *you*. Are you on land or not, is it dead or not, and if it's dead, were you the one who killed it?"

Lucy nodded. "That makes perfect sense, actually."

Perfect sense? Max shook his head. "Then what do I do? My father chose the words he did for a reason. That's what translation is—making choices in hopes that you get the right meaning across."

"But your father had to get the right meaning *out* first," Liao observed. "Not to mention, if even the original was based on something older, it was already a translation!"

"There aren't any written languages older than this," Max argued.

Liao shrugged. "Even ideas need decoding sometimes."

Max groaned and dropped his head on the table. "I give up. What do you think it means?"

Liao took the page delicately from under Max's face and read it through again slowly, murmuring to himself as he did. "I think the first part is about how the thing knows what to do," he said, finally. "The second part is about the doing. The third part is about either the why or how of it all." He handed the page back. "That's what I think matters there, but then I just rendered it into Mandarin and back, in addition to your papa's translation, so . . . what's the saying about taking spices?"

"Take it with a grain of salt," Lucy guessed.

"Right. Take it with salt. But I still don't think it's a weapon."

"None of this helps us if we have to break into Jeton's shop," Lucy observed.

"Let's hope it doesn't come to that, then."

"In my experience, it always comes to that. You two can argue over words and what they signify to your hearts' content, but in the end, we're not after meaning, we're after an object, and you get an object by finding it and taking it." She stood, stretched, and headed for the door. "I'll be on deck."

"I wish things were as simple in my life as they appear to be in Lucy's," Max grumbled.

Liao patted his arm. "So does she."

MR. MIDSHIPMAN DEXTER

July 4, 1812

Oliver Dexter (Acting-Midshipman, U.S. Navy!) had been of the opinion that putting to sea at last—and aboard one of the fleet's newest frigates, no less!—was the best present he could possibly have imagined for his twelfth birthday. That, however, was before he had all of his clean shirts stolen right out of his sea-chest by the other midshipmen and then suddenly found himself with his first command, all in the very same twenty-four hours. By the time he was twelve-and-a-month, by which point he had (1) more or less turned traitor to his country, depending upon how one looked at it; (2) had his first encounter with the vessel crewed by silent men in black uniforms; and (3) lost a duel to a girl—and a week after *that* he still wasn't sure which of those things bothered him more—by then he was seriously wondering whether or not he really cared that much for the sea at all.

On the morning of his actual birthday, however, that was all yet to come. On his birthday, the sea was still the sea, alight as it had always been with promises and possibilities. It was his birthright, it was the world he had been born to, it was the only future he had ever wanted. Even though he was going to be the youngest of the young gentlemen aboard the frigate *Amaranthine*, even though he had an acting appointment rather than an actual midshipman's warrant, and even though it would be work, and long watches through the night, with rough weather and possibly even (God be merciful) a touch of seasickness to endure—despite all that, he could not think of anything that could possibly have improved upon his happiness.

Except possibly actually trouncing a British ship or two. Not everyone was in favor of Mr. Madison's war with England, but Oliver was all for it. Of course, one country couldn't go about treating another country as though it were still a colony and expect to get away with it, but mainly he was for war because it meant more ships for the navy, which meant there must be more young gentlemen to serve in those ships. Which meant Oliver, Acting-Midshipman. Which was *grand*.

He had even received his first personal assignment from his new captain, and it was this task that had taken him to the wharves of Fells Point in search of the Bond Street shop of Franklin Jeton, Purveyor of Fine Mechanical Devices. The shop was easily spotted. Instead of a shingle, Mr. Jeton had a brilliantly polished orrery mounted beside the door, a mechanical model showing the planets of the solar system circling a gleaming copper sun.

"Fancy, isn't it, sir," said Mr. Cascon, eyeing the gleaming orrery from under a headful of unruly silver hair. Mr. Cascon was an older sailor, sent along with Oliver to be sure this new young squeaker didn't do anything lubberly like sink the boat he'd borrowed from the *Amaranthine* to run this errand, or fail to return in time for the ship's departure at noon. His tone was not altogether approving, and his accent faintly French. Shipboard gossip had all sorts of theories about him, but since both the frigate and most of her crew were new to the service, nobody seemed to have the real story yet.

"Very philosophical," Oliver agreed now.

Just before they reached the entrance, a tall older boy in a blue velvet coat walked up to the shop. He tried the door, and from his evident surprise and relief when it opened, Oliver could see he'd expected the shop to be locked up tight. The boy hurried in with a strangely forbidding look at Oliver and Mr. Cascon.

"Huh," Oliver said. Odd. Leaving Mr. Cascon outside to smoke on the bench beside the door, he stepped inside, too. It was the sort of place his father would've loved. Like Captain Eager, Oliver's father was fanatical about philosophical devices, and Jeton's shop was packed from floor to rafters with bizarre instruments nautical, astronomical, and mathematical.

The bearded old proprietor was deep in conversation with the boy in the blue coat, so Oliver busied himself looking idly over a case of books while he waited his turn. The old man wasted no time in wrapping up his conversation with the other boy. "I have nothing further to say, young man. I appear to have a customer."

"Mr. Jeton, please," the boy protested. "You understand what is at stake."

"Don't be ridiculous. Of course I do." Jeton lowered his voice. "There's a tavern on Fell Street, the Pawn and Castle. I'll buy you a pint tonight for the sake of your father's memory, and I'll tell you what I can. But it won't be much. Off with you now, Mr. Ault."

The other boy looked like he wanted to carry on arguing, but another black look from the old man sent him walking huffily out the door. "Now, what can I do for you, young fellow?" Jeton asked, coming to stand before Oliver and clasping his hands before him.

Oliver reached into his jacket and produced a letter from his captain. "I've come from Captain Miles Eager of the *Amaranthine*, sir."

"Ah, to collect his torquetum, surely! Yes, it's all seen to. An altogether stunning piece of craftsmanship." Jeton paused and gave Oliver a looking-over. "It's quite large, you know."

"I have the bosun's mate with me." Oliver trotted back outside to where Mr. Cascon sat smoking his pipe on the bench. "Cascon, may I trouble you?" It still felt strange to address an older man by his last name just because he wasn't an officer.

The boy in the velvet coat sat with his head in his hands on another bench on the opposite side of the door, staring down at his shoes in deep thought. He turned his head and caught Oliver looking at him. With an impatient noise he got to his feet and headed up the lane and away from the water.

The bell over the door chimed again as Mr. Cascon returned with a giant wrapped Thing in both arms. "Handsomely, now," Jeton called. "It's quite fragile."

"Thank you, sir," Oliver called back.

And then, all in a moment, the entire world was electrified.

The day, which had been pleasantly crisp and blustery, suddenly fell completely still. It was the sort of stillness that immediately made one stop in his tracks, perfectly motionless as well, as if it were dangerous, somehow, being the only thing to move. As if someone might be watching from somewhere in the ether, waiting for a foolish boy who didn't know better to take just one . . . false . . . step . . .

Overhead, the clouds had thickened and darkened something fierce, and the stillness held all the threat of the storm that was gathering itself to pounce. And then, all across Fells Point, crackling fingers of blue-violet fire flickered to life.

The little electrical lights flared up from the spires of churches, from lightning rods and chimneys and the ends of signposts. A horse tethered beside Jeton's shop stamped in terror as out of the corner of its rolling eyes it spotted the flames that erupted from the tips of its ears. At the quays, dancing blue-violet licks shot up from the tops of masts and from the yards that crossed them. In the storm-darkening sky, these tiny fires stood out in an unearthly fashion, as if some demonic twilight had overtaken Baltimore and the demons themselves had lit candles of hellfire in response.

"Saint Elmo's lights," Mr. Cascon murmured.

"I know," Oliver said defensively. "It's just . . . there's just so much of it."

Mr. Cascon nodded. "Don't know as I've ever heard of so much of it happening at once."

Then, out of nowhere, a ball of lightning collected itself in the middle of the street. Crackling light fizzed up out of nowhere, came together like scraps of iron drawn to a magnet, and began whirling in a ball of glittering, sputtering, blinding brightness not unlike one of the faceted spheres in Jeton's orrery catching the sun. Only this sphere was about the size of a cartwheel, and it didn't only *look* like it was on fire.

The ball of lightning spent five seconds forming itself. Then it began to tumble down Bond Street, gathering speed until it was a thing like a streaking comet, plummeting directly toward them.

Mr. Cascon clamped Captain Eager's device under one arm, grabbed Oliver by the elbow, and yanked him to the ground as the ball plunged past. It shot on down the street toward the only person left in the lane: the fellow in the blue velvet coat.

"Move!" Oliver screamed, disentangling himself from Cascon. "*Move*, you idiot!"

The boy started at the sound of Oliver's voice, as if he'd been so entranced by the thing, he'd failed to notice it was flying directly at him. A look of terror splashed across his face, and at the last possible moment he dove to the ground, flattening himself against the paving stones just as the ball of fire streaked overhead.

When it failed to hit him, the ball burst like a firecracker and was gone. The moment it disappeared, the Saint Elmo's lights across Fells Point went out, all at once. A rumble of thunder echoed across the sky. The heavens opened up, and it began to pour.

The boy rolled over onto his back, breathing heavily as rain began to collect in pools beneath him. Oliver got to his feet and approached warily. "Are you . . . all right?"

"I'm getting soaked," the boy said conversationally. "But I have not been incinerated, which is something to celebrate."

He accepted Oliver's hand and allowed himself to be helped back to standing. "Thank you, Mr.—"

"Dexter," Oliver supplied. Then he realized the other fellow hadn't been waiting for an introduction. He was staring past Oliver with a look of panic.

"I beg your pardon." He turned on his heel and strode away without another word.

Utterly flummoxed, Oliver returned to where Mr. Cascon stood, peeking gingerly under the red ticking-stripe paper in which Captain Eager's torquetum was wrapped. "Just our luck if I broke the thing again," the bosun's mate muttered. "What on earth is a torquetum, anyhow?"

"It's a medieval computing device," Oliver said distractedly. There were two men in black uniforms standing in the intersection where Bond met Fell Street. Both wore dark, smoked-glass spectacles. For no good reason, Oliver felt a vague twinge of unease as he looked at them. Then, as one, the two men turned and disappeared around the corner.

New midshipman though he might have been, the sea ran deep in Oliver's blood, and like most sailors he had a second sense for spotting omens. The question was always how to interpret them. "Cascon, what sort of omen is a Saint Elmo's light? Do you know?"

"Depends, like everything," the bosun's mate said, scratching his head. "Number of lights, whether they're moving up or down . . . and then, of course, we're ashore, which makes a difference. And so much of it . . ." He shifted the package and gave Oliver a hearty smile. "I shouldn't lose sleep over it, sir. Looks to me like if it was a sign of bad fortune, it was a sign meant for that other young gentleman."

Oliver nodded slowly. "Yes, I believe you're right." Still, weeks from that day, he would wonder why he didn't know right then that his first cruise was doomed.

four
EXTRAORDINARY RISKS

Rutting land. It always made Lucy Bluecrowne awkward. At sea, she was constantly on the lookout for enemies, and she knew how to look for them. On land—well, how did anyone keep a weather eye out in a loud, fuggy, crowded tavern?

Or perhaps, she thought as she sprinted over the uneven, rain-slick paving stones of Fell Street under a sky streaked with disintegrating trails of smoky color, *perhaps* it was neither the tavern nor land itself that was to blame tonight. Maybe she had spotted the man in black exactly when he wanted her to. Maybe he really *had* appeared right out of thin air, just the way their uncanny brig always seemed to do at sea. And whoever had tipped the tavern patrons off to the presence of three English citizens in their midst, well—Lucy certainly couldn't be blamed for that. Only by listening in on Max's conversation could someone have worked that out, which made it *Max's* fault. Just like most every other complication in Lucy's life at the moment.

Childish it might've been, but having Max to blame really did help.

Whistles overhead warned of more fireworks coming as she stumbled, hesitating, at the intersection where Fell Street met Ann and Pitt Streets. Max grabbed her elbow to help keep her on her feet and she shrugged off thoughts of eerie ships and sailors right along with his stupid hand. "I'm fine," she hissed, choosing the left just to get them away from the waterfront. "Just run!"

The shouts of the little mob back on Fell were bringing lights alive in the windows, and of course there was no end to the fireworks illuminating them from above. The only really safe place for them was the dock where the *Left-Handed Fate* was being refitted, but they couldn't risk the mob following them and discovering that they were part of an enemy crew rather than just a trio of undesirables. Fells Point had become very much not the place for Englishmen in the weeks since they'd arrived; Baltimore seemed to

have mobilized every ship owner in town to turn privateer and head out to fight. And if there was a worst-possible-day-of-all to be English here, it was on the day the country celebrated signing the Declaration that had set off the last war.

She checked that Max and Kendrick were still with her, then she ducked into an alley between two darkened houses. Hiking up her skirt, she leaped onto a barrel and jumped for the eaves of the roof. A moment later, Kendrick vaulted up after her with Max right on his heels.

The three of them flattened themselves as much as they could to avoid being spotted against the moonlit sky. But it wasn't really the Americans Lucy was worried about just then. It was the man in black.

"Street's clearing," Kendrick whispered from the edge overhanging the lane. "Few minutes, we ought to be able to move on."

"Well," Max said softly, "that was an adventure." He brushed a few leaves from the elbows of his blue coat, then grinned tiredly at Lucy with a look that was probably intended to convey some sort of charm. "Shall I tell you what we learned?"

"We learned something?" Lucy said in mock-disbelief. "Really?"

"We did. You really do think I'm useless, don't you?"

Lucy leaned down onto her elbows so that they were eye to eye. "I look forward to being proved wrong, Max, but . . . well. Here we are. Up on a roof."

He ignored that, and his face got very serious. "Just before all hell broke loose, did I see you talking to a man in a black uniform?"

Lucy's grin disappeared, too. "Aye. Did he look like the ones you saw this morning?"

"I think so. Was he one of *them*?"

"Hard to say. I've only seen *them* through a spyglass." Lucy shook her head. "But I don't think so. Usually there are the lights when they turn up, after all."

"But there were lights, Lucy," Kendrick said, his brows knitting together. "Remember? Just before the panic started, all the candles went out, then flared up again with Saint Elmo's lights."

Lucy gaped at him, aghast. "What?" She thought hard but could manage only the vaguest recollection of this. That alone was unnerving; what else hadn't she noticed when she was meant to be a lookout? Panic rose like bile. The lights that usually announced the strangers' arrivals at sea weren't something you could miss. How could she not have noticed them in a darkened tavern?

Thinking back—still thinking hard, because the memory was oddly difficult to pull forward—Lucy decided the stranger's black-upon-black uniform had certainly seemed the same as the ones they'd seen at sea from their telescopes: raven-black with no ornamentation at all, no shine of epaulets ornamenting a captain's shoulder, no braid or even the brief glitter of buttons. Tonight's stranger had worn a suit like that, one of plain, darkest jet, but also unmistakably a uniform, along with smoked-glass spectacles. The sandy tone of his skin had been not quite the same as the tan burnish all sailors got from the sun. There had been something slightly off, slightly unnatural, about the way he'd moved. And yes, he had spoken to her, because she recalled that he'd spoken with an odd accent, one Lucy had tried desperately—and failed—to place. What had he said?

"Max," Lucy said, stunned, "I can't remember what he said!"

"Just went out of your mind," Kendrick said. "Bit of running, bit of confusion. You'll recall it soon enough."

Max didn't look so sure. "Is it . . . just gone?"

Lucy hesitated, then nodded. "Just gone." A snippet of memory surfaced suddenly, and she licked her lips, feeling faintly sick. "Except—except the last thing he said was, *I shall see you again in time.*" It could've been a promise or a threat.

"Mmm." Max turned his face skyward and promptly disappeared into his head. This was a natural philosopher thing—or maybe just a Max Ault thing—that she simply didn't understand. Slow, wordless, patient thought . . . completely unlike Lucy, who had noticed at a very young age that she did her best thinking when she had to react on the moment amid the hell of cannonfire. Max, on the other hand . . . *Max* had to think *quietly.*

There was the small matter of trying to keep hidden, so Lucy couldn't knock him in the head to remind him that she was still there and waiting for him to speak. "Maxwell. Did you or did you not learn what we went there to learn?"

"Yes, Melusine."

Nobody called Lucy *Melusine* except her father, and then only when she was in trouble. That was two knocks to the head she owed him, when noise wasn't a factor. She counted slowly to four—three wasn't enough. "And?"

"And Mr. Jeton cannot give me the thing he wrote to my father about, because he doesn't have it any longer. The item is aboard the *Honoratus*, which is bound for Norfolk and then on to Nagspeake, where I suspect the piece itself is going. I gather the ship left Fells Point two days ago."

Lucy blanched. "Nagspeake?" Then she registered the rest of what he'd said. "Two days? And *Fate* all the way up here with the whole of the Chesapeake Bay between us and Norfolk?"

"If we left tonight—"

"Can't leave tonight," Kendrick interrupted. "Even if the repairs were anywhere close to finished, the provisioning's not. We got no spare rigging, no spars, no canvas—" And then, because it really didn't look like this was getting through: "We're talking about supplies we simply can't sail without, lad."

"We've been here two weeks already," Max protested. "How does it take that long to buy rope and sails and timber?"

"It takes that long anyway to buy enough for a proper voyage," Lucy said, forcing herself not to correct him for his use of unseamanlike terms like *rope* where he should have said *line* or *cordage*. "It takes quite a bit longer to do it in secret."

"But *if* we left tonight," Max persisted, "is it possible that we might catch the ship before she gets to Norfolk?"

The look that passed between Lucy and Kendrick then carried a full conversation in it: the fact that Max had no idea what he was asking; the slower speeds they would be making without putting right the damage they'd suffered in their last battle; the danger of putting to sea without being able to repair the schooner if she took any damage—which she would, now that the hundreds of ships in the Chesapeake Bay were now officially their adversaries. Baltimore was in the northern part of the bay and Norfolk was at the very south, where the Chesapeake emptied into the Atlantic. There was little chance they could sail the whole length of the bay and not run into anyone else the entire time.

"If this *Honoratus* is slow as drying paint, it might be possible," Lucy admitted at last. It was true, but only pride made her say it. The far smarter—the far safer—thing to do would've been to lie, and from the look Kendrick was giving her, he wished she'd done precisely that. "But only just," Lucy added, "and only if we somehow magically make it there without having to fight our way past any American ships. Or any British ones, either. The first Royal Navy vessel that's undermanned and wants to press sailors from us—"

"Then we run. Like we always do."

"We *can't*," she said with exaggerated patience. "Without the finished repairs we shall be slower than usual, and without supplies we shall be dead in the water if we are damaged."

"But it *could* be done? Could we possibly catch the *Honoratus*?"

Lucy looked across the rooftops of Fells Point to the darkened shipyard where she could just make out the gracefully slanting masts of the *Fate*. That barky could outrun near anything afloat. Except, it seemed, those strange men in black.

For a moment she hesitated, distracted by the missing memory. How could an entire encounter have gone straight out of her head?

I shall see you again in time.

It was near midnight when the three of them made it back to the shipyard where the *Fate* had been hiding in plain sight since their arrival. Over the gate, a wooden sign swung gently, illuminated by the occasional fireworks: MASON WHILFORBER, SHIPWRIGHT AND CARPENTER TO THE MAGOTHY AND BEYOND. The sign was a joke; there was a river off the Chesapeake called the Magothy, but the sign actually referred to a different waterway altogether that happened to share the name. The other Magothy was in the city of Nagspeake.

She gave a little shudder. Nagspeake carried memories for everyone aboard the *Fate*. Lucy's father, for one, was not going to like being asked to go back there. And the reality was, while it was possible that the *Left-Handed Fate* could catch the *Honoratus* before Norfolk, it was extremely unlikely that she *would*. The idea that this mysterious thing of Max's would be shipped aboard a slow vessel coming out of Baltimore, which prided itself on its fleet of fast ships, was preposterous. Which meant they were probably going to wind up making for Nagspeake in the end.

Kendrick gave a long, low whistle that cut through the hushed yard. A moment later there was a second, answering whistle from the schooner's rigging. "Clear," Kendrick mumbled. "But belay what noise you can."

"That means keep quiet," Lucy said to Max. "I know how nautical terms give you trouble." Max scowled.

They threaded their way between piles of oaken timber, feet crunching on curls of wood and kicking up drifts of sawdust. There was a ship being built at the center of the yard, and overhead the graceful ribs that would frame her hull reached up, bone-pale and slender, toward the stars.

"This thing gives me the shudders," Max whispered. "It's like walking under the bleached skeleton of some giant, ancient dead thing."

"It is not." Lucy put out a hand and touched the nearest rib, feeling the good, solid grain of the oak under her fingertips. "It's only just coming to life."

Just a bit farther in, riding gently alongside one of the yard's wharves, was home: the 102-foot length of the *Left-Handed Fate*. The figurehead hadn't been restored to her place at the bow yet. It was too well-known in the Atlantic: a blindfolded woman with furled wings at her back and her left hand raised near her shoulder in a gesture like a benediction. Lucy raised her own hand in a quick salute as she passed the bow anyway, and felt a little pang at the figurehead's absence. There had been times in her life when she had thought of the carved woman as something like a sister, and times when she'd seemed something like a guardian angel. When Lucy had been very, very small, she had been sure her mother, who'd died when she was only a baby, had looked exactly like the beautiful lady at the front of the schooner. All her life the figurehead had been a beloved friend welcoming her home.

"It's not there, you know," Max pointed out.

"I know, you horrible boy. It's . . ." She sighed. "Never mind."

They filed aboard, and Lucy and Kendrick paused to salute the low rise at the back of the ship. It wasn't much of a quarterdeck, but it was more than most schooners had. Mr. Fitch greeted them. "Captain's in his quarters."

Lucy and Max descended the rear ladder and stood before Captain Bluecrowne's closed door in the humid near-dark. Max rapped on the door, a voice on the other side of the door barked, "Enter!" and the two of them filed inside.

The captain's quarters were Lucy's favorite place on the whole schooner. If the figurehead was the friend who welcomed her home, her father's cabin was the heart of that home. It was small and dim, but lantern light made it cozy. It was full of familiar, beloved things—oh, there were the trappings of ship-captaincy, the logbooks and charts and instruments, her father's crates of port and whisky, his favorite yellow silk coat, and the engraved sword that he'd received back before he'd left the Royal Navy—but that wasn't all.

There was the nightcap that Lucy had made for him from scraps when the sailmaker had taught her to sew. There was the lump of wood that had been her first attempt at whittling (the lump was supposed to have been a whale, but it looked like a blob of half-melted cheese). There was the letter opener the armorer had helped her make for her father's last birthday. One whole shelf of his glass-fronted bookcase was dedicated to the journals Lucy had kept for every voyage they'd made since she had learned to write. And there was the workbook she'd used for doing calculations on the two occasions when she'd taken the test to pass for lieutenant.

Those had been unofficial tests, of course, since sailors in a letter-of-marque had no claim to naval officers' ranks (she preferred not to think about the secondary problem of being a girl). Still, Mr. Fitch and Mr. Foster, who were the *Fate*'s first and second mates and who had given the examinations, had once had their own ships in the Royal Navy. They had given the lieutenant's test many, many times, and Captain Bluecrowne had warned them that since they were all stuck with Lucy for the foreseeable future, if they passed her, she'd better have earned it. It had taken her two attempts, but she had done it, and now Captain Bluecrowne kept Lucy's work-book on his desk with his own log. And since there wasn't space on the schooner for anything that wasn't critically important, that meant all of those things, the nightcap, the melted-cheese whale, and most especially the workbook, were precious to him.

Of course, you had to know where to look to spot those things; Captain Bluecrowne generally did not come across as a sentimental man. Especially not when he was about to be asked to do something he would find personally unpleasant, not to mention immensely stupid.

The captain and the shipwright sat with a half-empty bottle of port between them on a sea-chest that served as a coffee table. "Well, Mr. Ault?" Lucy's father asked.

Max swallowed hard. "The piece is gone, sir. It's aboard a ship called *Honoratus*, which evidently left Baltimore two days ago, bound for Norfolk."

Captain Bluecrowne blinked. "I see." Mason Whilforber, the shipwright, said nothing, but he picked up his glass of port and drained it in one long gulp. Lucy's father refilled it. "You said *ship*. What type of ship? Did the fellow specify?"

Mason Whilforber spoke up. "I know the *Honoratus*. She's a ship-sloop. She belongs to a local merchant, name of Moran. Licensed letter-of-marque, as of last week. Sixteen guns, I believe, and she has the bones to carry a couple heavier pieces among 'em."

"Fast, then, but not as fast as our *Fate*, necessarily—though she likely throws a heavier broadside weight of metal."

"That means her guns either can throw more shot at us or throw heavier shot at us, or both," Lucy whispered to Max.

"I know," he whispered back testily.

"Do we imagine this Moran knows what he's carrying?" Captain Bluecrowne asked. "Is he working for the Frenchman?"

The shipwright shrugged. "Moran lost a brother to impressment. One of your ships stopped one of ours last year and took the boy away with some supposed deserters. They were all hanged."

Captain Bluecrowne's face took on the expression of disgust it always did when the subject of impressment came up. The Royal Navy needed sailors to keep up the fight England had been waging against France for decades—far more sailors than signed up voluntarily. Hence the practice of impressment—forcing civilians into service, whether they wanted to go to sea or not. Plenty of people saw it as a necessity and could ignore the fact that pressed sailors' families and businesses might be destroyed in their absence and most of the men would never make it home again. Her father, however, did not fall into that group.

The practice of stopping *American* ships to look for deserters and

British citizens—deserters to be hanged, and citizens to be put to work—was newer. The argument went that defeating Napoleon was so important that America ought to be willing to put up with a bit of inconvenience. The United States disagreed, of course. They also objected to the fact that under British law, anyone born a British citizen was forever a British citizen—even those who now lived in the United States and considered themselves Americans. This was one of the ways in which captains justified pressing men from American ships—by claiming the men weren't American at all, but British, and therefore subject to the needs of the crown.

It was messy, this new war with the Americans. Lucy did believe that defeating Napoleon Bonaparte and France was more important than anything else. But when you heard stories about boys like Moran's brother being taken from their ships and hanged even though they had likely never been aboard a British ship before—well, it made it harder to feel patriotic.

"If Moran is only a merchant, is he any good at fighting?" Max asked.

Mason shrugged. "You heard me say a British captain hanged his brother, didn't you?"

"Anger puts an edge on many a dull blade," Captain Bluecrowne said. "But let me worry about that. And if we were not able to inter-cept the *Honoratus* before Norfolk, Mr. Ault, then what becomes of her?"

Max hesitated. "She sails on to Nagspeake."

Lucy searched her father's face for some hint of what he was feeling, but saw nothing. The captain looked at the shipwright. "Mason?"

Mason Whilforber stood and headed for the door. "I can tell you in an hour."

Captain Bluecrowne gestured at the seat the shipwright had

vacated. Max sat awkwardly. "It is unlikely that we shall be able to sail tonight," the captain said. "And unlikely even if we do that we'll make Norfolk before the sloop does. We may well have to try for Nagspeake."

"But you'll try?" Max glanced at Lucy. "Lucy said—"

She gave him a tight, angry shake of her head. "Lucy said what?" the captain asked, darting a forbidding look her way.

"Nothing," Max finished lamely.

"I presume what Lucy told you is that unless she's not hurrying at all, our quarry is likely arriving in Norfolk as we speak," Captain Bluecrowne said darkly. "But the problem isn't only catching up. If we do catch her, we still have to overpower her, and without fully restocking powder and shot, our gunnery will be a trifle limited." He paused. "But yes, Max, of course we shall try."

Lucy started. Despite what she'd said on the roof about the thing being possible, she'd fully expected her father to be the voice of reason.

Her father looked at her as if she'd spoken her thoughts aloud. "There are times for taking extraordinary risks, my dear, and this may well be one of them." He regarded Max. "If I'm honest, Max, I have never entirely believed in this thing you are chasing, or entirely believed the claims your father made about it. But I am willing to imagine the impossible, if it offers a chance at peace."

Out of the corner of her eye, Lucy saw Max stiffen, but he said nothing.

"The two of you have never known a time without war," the captain continued. "I barely remember myself what peace is like. The war with the colonies, these endless wars with the French, and now here we are at odds with America again as well." He reached for his port glass, but his hand changed direction at the last moment and touched down on a divot in the top of the sea-chest. Lucy remembered the battle that mark had come from. She touched her own forehead, where she herself still wore a needle-thin scar from that day.

"There are not soldiers or sailors enough in the world to fight all these battles," her father said grimly, "and yet we keep on anyway."

Lucy and Max waited out the moment of silence that followed this until at last Captain Bluecrowne spoke again. "If we can end the conflicts, if there is so much as a chance, we must try." He paused to rub his face. "Although Mason will have my hide if he isn't allowed to complete his repairs. After the damage we took last time . . ."

His words trailed off, and Lucy knew he was remembering their last encounter with the men in black-on-black uniforms.

"One of them spoke to me tonight," Lucy blurted. How had that not been the first thing they'd told him? *Because something doesn't want me to remember*, she thought. But that was ridiculous. "I can't remember what he said, Papa," she continued quickly. "It's gone. I didn't forget, it's—it's just gone. Except that he said he would see us again."

"Well." Captain Bluecrowne drank the last of his wine and clapped his hands on his knees. "I suppose that changes things." He corked the bottle of port, stood, and reached for his coat. "Lucy, go tell your uncle Mason he has two hours, but in two and a half we weigh anchor. Then you had better go and collect your brother. My apologies to him, and he will have to blow things up another time."

five
THE BLUE OF THE WORLD

"Good of you to come along," Lucy said as she picked her way along the dock.

Max trailed along in her wake. "He's going to be disappointed. It's my fault."

Two steps ahead, Lucy said nothing, and Max let his mind wander back to the Pawn and Castle.

Franklin Jeton had been waiting in a booth, and Max's mug, when it arrived, held porter. It could've simply been what Jeton himself was drinking, or what he knew to be the only decent beer to be had there, but Max thought he knew better. Porter was what Max's father had always preferred. Perhaps this was a gentle assurance to Max that he and Jeton had common ground between them that was more important than the differences between American and Englishman, even in wartime.

Then, however, the first words out of Jeton's mouth had been, "I beg you to remember, Mr. Ault, that we are on different sides now. Kindly do not put me in the position of having to lie to you." So much for common ground.

"We weren't enemies when your father first came to me for help in finding this thing," Jeton had continued, "but even then, we knew there was unfinished business between America and Britain. I never wanted to be a traitor, so although he alluded to the fact that what he was looking for was part of something bigger, I never asked him what it was. But it wasn't hard to deduce that what he was trying to build—what *you* want to build—is a war engine. A weapon."

"It is meant to *end* the wars," Max corrected. "Not to fight them."

Jeton made a dismissive noise. "In order for a device to end a war, it must either demolish the enemy or threaten convincingly to do so—and even then, for the threat to be credible, the device must still be capable of carrying it out." The old man smiled thinly. "Or have I got it entirely wrong? Does your machine generate peace by electrostatic induction at the flipping of a switch?"

Max shifted, uncomfortable. "Surely the threat is enough."

"That is youth talking. If that were true, no one would challenge Bonaparte's Grand Army. Our age has never seen a greater war machine, and yet Europe continues to fight, even when its attempts at resistance are crushed again and again. No, threats alone are never enough." Jeton's expression, improbably, went even colder than it had been. "But this is neither here nor there. To help you now is to betray my country. The item is gone, Mr. Ault, on a ship called *Honoratus* and with enough of a head start that I don't imagine you'll ever catch it."

Max sagged numbly in his seat while Jeton went on about just how far out of his reach the piece was now. He listened, just in case this information might be useful to Captain Bluecrowne despite Jeton's confidence that the *Honoratus* was beyond catching. But all he could think was, *It's gone? How can it be gone?*

"But when you wrote to my father and told him the thing he was looking for had come to you, didn't you mean for him to come and take it? What did you expect?" Max protested at last. What he wanted to do was to scream, *How could you let it go?* But however good it might feel, howling at an old man in a public house didn't seem like a good idea.

"I had that piece for years," Jeton said. "It was brought to me damaged and the repairs were complicated, but they only took as long as they did because I *made* them take that long. I strung the work out as long as I possibly could, in hopes that your father would answer my letter or turn up. If either he or you had managed to get here before war had been declared, you could have had it, and welcome. I would have lied to the owner, claimed the shop had been robbed—I had the whole story worked out. But you didn't arrive in time."

"My father couldn't come because he was dead," Max retorted. "It made traveling difficult for him, you understand."

Jeton's eyes hardened at the sarcasm. "It was more than a year and a half ago that your father passed, may he rest in peace."

"I came as soon as I could!" Max said wretchedly. "And then we were attacked twice in the Chesapeake. If not for that, we should have been here before—"

"But you *weren't* here, and we *are* at war, and I will not turn traitor. There are those who might do it, but I am not one of them."

Max opened his mouth to protest again, but Jeton waved a knobby hand. "Maxwell, your father was a brilliant man, the kindest, wisest, most honorable fellow I ever had the pleasure to know. I don't want to cast a pall over his final years' work. But if the technology you're trying to re-create has truly existed for thousands of years, have you not asked yourself why the ancients who invented it concluded the experiment by dismantling it and doing everything they could to be certain that it was never rebuilt?"

"They didn't," Max insisted. "They ensured that the device could be rebuilt in a more advanced future. By a more civilized world that would put it to its intended use: to bring an end to war."

Jeton laughed rustily. "My dear boy, that is the most inane thing I have heard you say yet. You know who else thought they were working toward a world without war? The Revolutionaries in France. And out of those wonderful intentions came the Reign of Terror, and then Bonaparte." Shaking his head, the old man stood up with the creaking bones of age and patted Max's head as if he were a child. Max flinched.

"At least tell me what it was, the piece you had," he said. "What did it look like? Who was the owner? Did you keep notes?"

"No," Jeton said distinctly. "Or rather, I did, but I burned them. This evening, right before I left the shop to come here."

"Give me something," Max said wildly, desperately. "Anything! For the sake of my father's memory. Please."

Jeton stopped and turned with painful slowness to pin Max with hateful eyes. "I'll give you this, out of love for your father, and then we are finished: it was the most beautiful device I have ever seen. But now . . . beautiful or not, I wish I had smashed it to pieces."

Then he'd hobbled out of the tavern, leaving Max alone at the booth with prickles of frustration behind his eyes, threatening, of all things, tears. Which was when the lights had gone out, the corposants had appeared, and someone in the tavern figured out that there were English in their midst, all more or less at once.

Now he and Lucy reached the far end of the shipyard, where the retaining wall that marked the divide between dry land and harbor sank gently into a rocky beach. "Do you think it will come to sailing to Nagspeake?" Max asked.

Lucy lifted her shoulders. "I don't know."

"What kind of a place is it?"

She stretched her arms out for balance as she picked her way over the rocks. "It's the kind of place where metal moves of its own will and entire streets sometimes turn up in different places from where they were the day before."

Max studied her, trying to decide exactly how gullible she thought he was. "What on earth are you talking about?"

She turned and raised an eyebrow. "I'm being very literal. Those are the sorts of things that happen in Nagspeake."

"Impossible."

Lucy spread her hands. "Maybe. But true."

"But how?"

"No one knows. It's that kind of place. *No one knows* is the answer to most questions you can ask about it."

Actually, he'd heard of Nagspeake's famous philosophic iron before, but like everyone in the scientific community he assumed it was just a puzzle that hadn't been solved yet, one that would eventually be revealed to have a perfectly logical explanation. The other thing, though . . . "Whole streets moving? That's just ridiculous."

She made an apologetic face. "You'll find Nagspeake a profoundly unsettling place if you insist on having explanations for everything there."

Just then, farther on where the rocks met brambly undergrowth and the harbor became an inlet, Max spotted a small figure crouched over a ball of fire.

For a moment, the ball reminded Max uncomfortably of the incendiary orb that had come hurtling at him near Jeton's shop—but only for a moment. This was no philosophical anomaly; this was chemistry—albeit very impressive chemistry.

The ball plunged skyward as if it had been flung into the heavens by a slingshot and exploded into a fountain of blue sparks over the trees on the opposite bank. A second later, a bang like five thunder-claps shook the night. The little figure on the beach stumbled backward, clapping, his beaming face reflecting azure light.

"Liao!" Lucy hissed. "Didn't Papa tell you we were trying to keep a low profile?"

"He said I could! He said I could set off a rocket! It's their Salut-ing Day here. Lots of people are setting off fireworks." The boy scrambled to his feet and sprinted over the rocky beach toward them. "Did you see?" he demanded, pointing at the smoky trails drifting down from on high. "Lucy, Max, did you *see*?"

It never stopped being a wonder to Max. They looked nothing alike, and yet if you were able to ignore that Lucy was blond and

British and Liao was Chinese and apparently a pyromaniac, they behaved exactly as if they were full brother and sister instead of just half brother and sister. Or maybe Max was just wrong in assuming that having two so very different mothers would matter in that way. It didn't seem to matter to Liao and Lucy in the slightest.

Liao came to a tottering stop in front of them, his black eyes shining. "It was a thumping great blue, wasn't it? I blended it up myself!"

"It was the blue of the world," Lucy agreed seriously. "Blue is quite difficult, you understand, Max."

"It was a tremendous blue," Max said. "I might go so far as to call it cerulean."

Liao beamed. He started back over the rocks to where his bag of explosives sat. "I have a better one. This one's going to whistle."

"Hang on a tick." Lucy caught the boy by his sleeve. "There's been a change of plan."

His face fell. "Papa *said*, Lucy!"

Max's heart sank. Just about the only person he knew who could always be trusted to be perfectly happy from time to time (even if it was because he was blowing things up) was Liao, and thanks to Max, Lucy was just about to smash tonight's bit of joy.

"We've got to sail tonight," Max interrupted. "I'm awfully sorry, Liao, but it's the mission. But the good news is, your papa thinks we just might be able to catch 'em, if we're quick."

The boy folded his arms. Then he nodded. "Well, if it's for the mission."

As Liao trotted back to collect his things, Max felt Lucy's fingers curl into his palm for just a moment. By the time he looked down to see if he was hallucinating, she was running up the beach to help her little brother put away his fireworks.

Two hours and fifteen minutes later, amid whispered commands and lit by ghostly hooded lanterns, the *Left-Handed Fate* slid out of the shipyard dock. Max sat in his tiny cabin under Otto the puffin's watchful eye, with his feet propped on the wooden crate that held the loom-cards. He glowered at his father's (if Liao was to be believed) completely untrustworthy translation of the Egyptian stone. *Give me something,* he begged it silently. *Tell me what I'm looking for.*

We're not after meaning, we're after an object, Lucy had said, *and you get an object by finding it and taking it.*

Max was beginning to tire of Lucy being right all the time.

The creaking wooden world around him shifted subtly, and its collection of attendant noises changed in pitch as the schooner picked up speed and headed for the Chesapeake, where at least three hostile parties would be lying in wait: the French, the Americans, and the men in black. Four hostile parties, if you also counted the ships of the Royal Navy, who would happily press sailors from even a British privateer if they crossed paths.

Yes, there was a veritable swarm of enemies out there, and the damaged and under-provisioned *Left-Handed Fate* was about to sail right into the middle of it.

THE *HONORATUS*

"That's her, sir," the lookout called down. "*Honoratus*, writ right across her backside."

"Unbelievable. She certainly took her time." Lucy's father lowered his own telescope and passed it to Mr. Fitch for a look. Lucy, standing at a respectful distance on the quarterdeck, was itching to ask for a telescope so she could take a look for herself at that faraway puff on the darkening water.

"No way to catch her before she makes Norfolk," Mr. Fitch said after a moment. "Mr. Wooll?"

"Agreed," said Mr. Wooll, the sailing master, who stood beside them peering through his own glass. He sounded a bit self-satisfied nonetheless, and Lucy couldn't blame him. A little less than twenty-four hours had passed since their hasty departure from Baltimore, and impossibly, here they were, about to catch up to a vessel that had had a full two days' head start.

Still, despite all that, the *Honoratus* would reach Norfolk before the *Fate* reached her. This was bad news. The city of Norfolk sat right at the mouth of Hampton Roads, the big natural harbor that emptied into the Chesapeake just before the bay itself emptied into the ocean, and it was chock-full of shipyards, docks, and scores of ships, not to mention a major naval base. If the *Left-Handed Fate* were to be spotted and identified as British—which was possible, even without her figurehead—things could go very, very badly, very, very quickly.

"We shall have to hope our luck holds a bit further," Captain Bluecrowne muttered. "Lucy, pass the word for Mr. Ault."

Lucy turned to Max, who had been pacing rather obnoxiously a few feet away on the main deck. He had certainly heard everything they'd been saying; the schooner was too small for secrets. "The captain's compliments, Mr. Ault, and would you join him on the quarterdeck?"

As the captain, Max, and the rest began to talk about next steps, Lucy borrowed the telescope from Mr. Fitch. She kept an ear cocked toward the discussion, but the rest of her attention was on the *Honoratus*.

Through the glass, the far-off lights of Norfolk outlined the dark shapes of other vessels at anchor in the harbor of Hampton Roads. But here was a strange thing: the *Honoratus* was heading eastward, away from that harbor and toward the open ocean. "Is it possible she's not stopping at all?" Lucy asked.

"What's that?" her father snapped.

"Excuse me, sir, but I don't think she's stopping. She's cutting east."

Just then the lookout called down. "She's headed out, sir!"

"Well, that's odd." The captain took the glass and looked for himself. "Mr. Wooll, keep her in sight, but cut around the harbor traffic and douse the lanterns as soon as it won't look suspicious. I want us right up on her side before she reaches the Atlantic. Mr. Fitch, boats out and ready to launch. We'll take her in the dark, before she makes full sail to head out into the open ocean. Mr. Ault, be ready to go aboard and look for your cargo. Report to Kendrick, red cutter."

The ship burst into motion around them. Max turned to Lucy. "Explain to me what's happening now?"

"We're sneaking up on her," Lucy said patiently. "When the *Fate* engages the *Honoratus*, our boats"—she pointed to the cutter that hung from the stern davits just behind the quarterdeck and then at the one that sat at the center of the deck near the foremast, in case he hadn't noticed them in all this time, which somehow seemed just possible—"are going to row up and take the ship while her crew is looking the other way." *So you can go aboard and get that unknown thing we're after*, she thought but did not say. *Hope it jumps out and bites you so you know it when you find it.*

"Oh," Max said, looking impressed. Then he blanched. "And *I'm* meant to be in one of those boats?"

"Yes, you are. How else do you imagine we're going to get you aboard the *Honoratus* but on a boat?"

"But . . . a *fighting* boat?"

"They're all fighting boats," Lucy said, exasperated. "That's what we *do*." She gave him a little shove toward the boat on the deck. Poor fellow. Max was beginning to look downright terrified. "Everything'll be all right. Remember who we are." Lucy patted his arm. Blast him, why did he always flinch when she was trying to be comforting?

As Max made his way awkwardly toward the cutter, Liao appeared at Lucy's side. "He doesn't look good, Lucy."

She put an arm around her brother. "He likes battles about as well as you do, Liao, and we're sending him into the middle of one. To say nothing of the fact that he still doesn't know what he's looking for."

Liao shook his head. "I don't like him going over there by himself."

"Kendrick'll keep to his side. He won't be on his own."

"But he won't have *us*. No, it won't do, Lucy. I'd better put a bag together for him." And then he was off, disappearing down the aft ladderway. Probably headed for the powder magazine, Lucy thought grimly, though the gunner would tan Liao's hide himself if he got in the way while they were making ready for a fight.

....

MAX SAT HUDDLED IN THE CUTTER, TRYING TO BRING THE SHAKING in his limbs under control. He was the only person in the boat; everyone else was running around the way they did each time the *Fate* made ready to engage another ship, and after all this time, Max still hadn't found any place other than his own cabin where he was really out of the way.

The deck of the *Fate* was a sweep of almost complete darkness now that the lanterns had been extinguished. There wasn't even a moon tonight to glint on any of the metal bits that the sailors polished so obsessively. Stranger still, everything happening on deck was taking place in a state of uncanny hush. Voices carried over the water at night, but the Fates could work well-nigh silently when they wanted to. The lapping of the water against the side was the loudest thing he could hear.

"Ahoy, Max."

Max clapped both hands over his mouth to keep the shriek in, but he jumped hard enough to set the cutter rocking, which earned him a hissed reproof from one of the nearby tars.

Liao perched in the rigging at Max's eye level, holding out a cylindrical canvas ditty bag. "This is for you."

Max took it gingerly. "What is it?"

He couldn't make out much of Liao's face, but he recognized the expression on it nonetheless. The boy's face looked like this every time the *Fate* went to battle.

Liao knew as much as anyone on the ship—maybe anyone afloat, if half of what Max had heard from Lucy and the gunner could be believed—about incendiary things. Some of this proficiency was the natural result of being a sharp and inquisitive boy who'd spent the last few years of his life on a wartime letter-of-marque. But according to Liao, most of his knowledge actually came from before he'd come aboard the *Fate*, from his mother and her family in China. At a mere nine years old, Liao was already something of a genius with fire and what could be done with it.

On the other hand, Liao hated actual ship-to-ship action, when the guns and powders that he loved so much would be put to deadly and destructive work. He hated it so much that Max had several times seen him go round to each gun after an engagement and speak softly to them, as if they needed to be consoled for what they had been made to do.

Now here he was, handing Max a bag that smelled suspiciously of gunpowder. "What is it?" he asked. "A weapon?"

"You know I don't make weapons, Max. These are . . . distractions. Defenses. Cover your face if you set any off."

Max peeked cautiously into the bag, straining his eyes in the dark. Round powder charges nestled inside, maybe half a dozen, padded with straw. "I'll have to find something to light them with."

"I thought of that. Give me your hands." Liao took Max's outstretched left palm and rubbed his little thumb in the center. Then he took Max's right middle finger and did the same thing there. For just a moment, both his palm and his fingertip felt suddenly, brutally cold.

"What did you do?" Max asked, fascinated.

"It's a chemical," Liao said. "If you rub your finger on your palm, you'll get a tiny flame in your hand. Light the fuse from it quick as quick, then close your fist to extinguish it. It won't burn you if you put it out within a few seconds."

"A chemical? What chemical?" He reached for his palm with his finger to test the boy's claim, but Liao grabbed his wrist. "Not now," he whispered. "A sudden flash of light could give us away."

Max eyed him dubiously. "But this'll really work?"

"It'll really work. You can trust me." Then Liao scrambled up the rigging and disappeared, and a moment later a series of whispered orders hissed through the hush. The cutter swung up and over the side, and Max was lowered down to the water.

Even the oars were all but soundless as the boats slid through the oily-dark water toward the *Honoratus*. Max was shaking from nerves. It felt like the kind of uncontrollable shudder brought on by freezing chills.

He watched the dark shape of the *Fate*, surging along on a parallel course to the pair of cutters. The *Honoratus* would spot her soon, and then she would spot the boarding party, and then one well-placed cannon-ball would blast Max and his compatriots out of the water.

When the boats were only a dozen or so yards away from the *Honoratus*, the *Fate* fired her first shot. It was one of Liao's homemade powder charges; once you'd seen one in action, you could never mistake them for anything else. Liao's charges caused the guns to spit bizarrely colored flame, wild greens and violets and gleaming silvers and golds, and they produced equally inexplicable and sometimes terrifying sounds. Mostly they were used for saluting days, because, just as he had said, Liao would not make weapons. He did, however, permit the gunner to use them for warning shots, since warning shots were meant to tell the other side to stand down, and Liao did like the idea of stopping a battle before it began.

This shot erupted in a horizontal shaft of a blinding chartreuse color. The noise it made a heartbeat later could only be described as a scream.

The *Honoratus* leapt into action. From his boat, Max could hear the shouts, the drumming of feet, the rumble of the gun carriages that came from the sloop. But after a year aboard the *Fate*, Max knew what organized fighting sounded like, and the noise from the *Honoratus* was profoundly *dis*organized. The eerie warning shot had thrown the crew into a tizzy. That, of course, had been the point.

The *Fate*'s two boats hove to the far side of the *Honoratus*, and the sailors climbed nimbly up the hull and onto the deck, leaving only a couple of men below with Max. The noise from the deck above changed. The attack had begun.

Max waited in the red cutter as his shipmates fought for control of the *Honoratus*. Then the noise changed again, and a low whistle sounded from the deck. Kendrick elbowed Max. "Follow me. Up and over, fast as you can."

The coxswain braced his feet on the hull and ran up the rope as easily as if he were climbing a ladder. Max followed with Liao's bag slung across his chest, feeling clumsy and slow. But then, far too soon, Kendrick hauled him over the gunwale. The older sailor was smiling in the swirling gunsmoke that wreathed the deck. "It's all right, lad. She's ours."

Just that quickly, it was over. There were very few bodies on the deck, too. It had been a near-bloodless capture, and he couldn't quite remember for certain, but Max thought it was possible that the *Fate* herself hadn't fired anything more than that first sickly green warning shot.

He and Kendrick made their way to a prisoner Max guessed must be the master of the ship. "Our man here has some questions for you," Kendrick said to the master as they approached. "Answer sharp and we'll be out of your way before long."

Max tried to quell his nerves and sound imposing. "You have something aboard that I need, sir. A device. Mechanical, and bound for Nagspeake. Where is it?"

The master's face went utterly blank. "No idea what you mean, sir."

"You want to keep your ship, you'll sing out, mate," Kendrick growled.

"Can't sing out if I don't know the tune. The entire cargo's mechanical, and all of it bound for Nagspeake."

Max's heart sank down into his shoes, but he made his face as expressionless as the master's. "Show me to the cargo. I'll find it myself." God willing and with luck, maybe he had a chance, even if all he had to go on were his father's words and Jeton's meager description: *It was the most beautiful device I have ever seen.*

The master led them down into the hold, where Max's tiny bit of hope flickered and died. The hold was packed with crates, all of them nailed shut, all of them identical.

Well, no time to waste. "Get me a crowbar."

Before the master could reply, another of the Fates came sprinting in. "Can't find the bloody ensigns," the newcomer panted. "Not even the Stars and Stripes."

An American ship, one the Fates didn't want to fight, must've turned up. Kendrick turned to the master. "Where's your colors, mate?"

Now the master smirked. "Overboard. You want to run up false colors, you'll have to provide your own goddamn flags, *mate*."

ENEMY ENGAGEMENTS

Oliver saw the stab of green out on the horizon at exactly the right moment. He'd been just about to fall asleep standing up. It had been a rough couple of days.

The focus for this first stretch of sailing had been speed, the better to get the frigate out of the Chesapeake before any British ships got the idea of blockading the bay. And the *Amaranthine* was a smallish frigate, built for swiftness rather than maximum firepower. As a result, they'd made excellent time, but everyone was exhausted from cracking on like that without pause. To make matters worse, every time Oliver tried to catch a few minutes' sleep, one of the other midshipmen came along and cut his hammock down. With a *knife*. With him *in it*. On *purpose*. To add insult to injury, someone had stolen his entire stock of clean shirts right out of his sea-chest the day before, and since his shirts wouldn't even have come close to fitting anyone else in the midshipman's berth, it was hard not to take it personally.

He could've stopped it, probably; all he had to do was mention his father's name. But he couldn't bring himself to do it. They'd have stopped the hazing, but they would never have forgiven him. Every new sailor had had to go through this sort of thing when he started out. Moreover, it would've immediately become clear that the only reason such a very young squeaker had been put aboard a warship was that his papa had pulled some strings. And yes, that truth was bound to be found out eventually, but Oliver badly wanted to prove himself worthy of the string-pulling before it was. That was the point of the acting appointment rather than a proper warrant any-way—so that he could prove himself and really earn the position before it was made official. Which sounded fine in theory, unless one was a twelve-year-old mid in a berth full of sixteen-, seventeen-, and eighteen-year-olds who already had their warrants.

Now, the green explosion saved Oliver's bacon. A heartbeat after it, the unearthly ghost of a terrible, indescribable scream came wafting over the water.

Every pair of eyes on the *Amaranthine* turned to Mr. Hollis, the second lieutenant, who was on duty on the quarterdeck. There was no hesitation. "Beat to quarters!" he shouted.

The *Amaranthine*, which had entered the Atlantic not long before, turned smartly and headed back toward that peculiar flash of green. As the frigate approached the mouth of the Chesapeake, two ships came flying out of the bay. One was a big sloop, and the other was a dartlike craft with sharply raked masts: a schooner, and a fast one.

They were sailing together, that much was plain, but even at a distance and even in the dark, Oliver could see that the sloop wasn't managing the same elegance in her sailing as her companion. On one hand, compared to that schooner, anything was going to look a little clunky. But this seemed more like perhaps the sloop's crew wasn't quite used to her ways. There were plenty of reasons why that might be the case, but Oliver was aboard a warship, so the first reason that occurred to him was that this was the kind of sailing you got when you put a prize-crew aboard a just-captured vessel.

"Put one across their bows," Mr. Hollis ordered, and one of the forward guns spat out a warning shot.

"Schooner's hoisting the Stars and Stripes," the lookout called.

"And the other?" Mr. Hollis called back.

"Nothing," the lookout said after a moment. "Not a scrap, sir. Not slowing down, neither."

Someone passed Mr. Hollis the speaking trumpet. "The sloop ahoy!" he shouted. "This is the United States frigate *Amaranthine*, Captain Miles Eager. Identify yourself!"

No reply came from the sloop. No flag, either. Instead, both the sloop and the little schooner began to pile on more sail. They were going to make a break for it, to try to shoot past the *Amaranthine* for the open ocean.

Mr. Hollis sighed. "Pass the word for the captain and Mr. Ansby. My respects, and we're about to engage the enemy."

....

ALONE IN THE HOLD OF THE *HONORATUS*, MAX PAUSED IN THE act of leaning into his crowbar. Once again, the quality of noise from the deck overhead had changed.

Feet pounded outside, then Kendrick appeared in the doorway. "Brace up, lad. Enemy ahead." He disappeared again before Max could ask, *Which one?*

He hesitated, decided there was nothing he could contribute in a battle, and put all his weight on the crowbar. The last couple of nails eased reluctantly loose.

The first two crates had held an assortment of navigational tools. This one held painted case-clocks. New-looking, but Max opened each up just to be thorough. The works were ordinary. Beautiful, but only in the way all clockwork was.

He sighed, picked up the crowbar, and moved on to the next box. Three down. Dozens to go.

....

SOME SAILORS LOVED BATTLE; LUCY DIDN'T. SHE LOVED THE strategy of it, and she loved the feeling of being part of a perfectly functioning ship-of-war. And she loved who she became during ship-to-ship action. Everything sharpened: her senses, her thinking, her movements. Sometimes she began to feel . . . not graceful, exactly, because who cared about that, but *efficient*, as if every motion had purpose and accomplished exactly what she wanted. As the world itself faded away, leaving only a few bright and distinct pockets of reality to be seen amid the roiling of smoke and the spray of churning water, Lucy's eyes and mind functioned effortlessly, processing the information that mattered and discarding what did not.

But Lucy was old enough to understand what death was. Death she had seen, and death she didn't love. She feared it for her crew, and she certainly didn't relish the idea of inflicting it on anyone else, even an enemy. It was strange and complex, her relationship with the work her ship did.

She stood beside her father on the low quarterdeck of the *Fate* as the schooner raced through the night on a parallel course with the *Honoratus*. Mr. Fitch was barking orders, and overhead one of the sailors was signaling rapidly with a lantern to the captured ship. Ahead were the lights of the American frigate, which had fired once already and was no doubt ready to fire again.

The *Fate* veered sharply away from the *Honoratus* and across the path of the frigate. The guns fired in succession, throwing six- and twelve-pound balls with devastating precision at the American ship. It was the kind of maneuver only a wickedly agile vessel could pull off, and the kind of gunnery only a truly pitch-perfect crew could manage. Lucy's heart swelled with pride.

Before the Americans could even pick themselves up off the deck, the captured *Honoratus* drew level with the frigate and fired its own broadside. A few of the American guns went off as the *Honoratus* shot past, but it didn't look as if any of them did much damage.

The *Fate* turned so that it, too, could race past the frigate and into the ocean, firing as it went. But the American crew had pulled itself together now, and it fired first. "Down!" someone shrieked. Lucy flung herself to the deck, and the air whined as projectiles shredded the air and tore into the rigging. But the *Fate* was a gazelle, and reloading a gun takes time. Before the Americans could manage another round, the schooner had left them behind.

Now it was all about speed. The Americans would turn and

come after them, but unless something went wildly wrong, they ought to be able to leave the frigate behind in the night.

"Did we lose anyone?" Lucy's father asked once the *Fate* was out of range of fire. "Mr. Fitch, report."

The voice that answered wasn't Mr. Fitch's. "Dead, sir," said Mr. Foster, the second mate. He spoke as if he himself couldn't quite believe what he'd said. "A bullet from one of the frigate's sharpshooters."

Mr. Fitch? *Dead?* Lucy shook her head, bewildered and numb. After all that brilliant seamanship, Mr. Fitch dead—and from a plain old *rifle?*

Someone swore. It was Mr. Bantwell, the third mate, who had a temper Lucy didn't always like. "Other casualties?" the captain said forbiddingly.

"None, sir," Mr. Bantwell retorted. Mr. Fitch had been Bantwell's commanding officer back in the navy. It sounded like he was taking the death personally.

Lucy swallowed her own emotions and faced her father, waiting for the next orders. Captain Bluecrowne's eyes were hard. "Hood the lanterns and catch us up to the *Honoratus.*" He put a hand on Lucy's shoulder.

The American frigate was falling behind. Up ahead, the captured sloop was nothing but a paler bit of night on the water. And then, just when it seemed like things might calm down for a bit again, the *Honoratus* fired into the night.

"What the devil now?" Captain Bluecrowne snarled.

....

IN THE HOLD OF THE SLOOP, MAX FOUGHT FOR BALANCE AS THE ship recoiled from the shots it had just discharged. He looked up at the sound of footfalls, expecting to see Kendrick. Instead, the

Honoratus's master appeared in the doorway, flanked by a pair of American sailors.

"How did you get free?" Max blurted out.

The master ignored him. His eyes darted around the hold until they fell on a corner Max hadn't investigated yet. A brief flash of relief crossed his face. It was there, then, the item Max was looking for. He'd been so close.

"Just so happens I have a couple of your countrymen in my crew, and hidey-holes for 'em to jump into if we run afoul of anything flying the Union Jack what might try and impress 'em." The master took a pistol from his belt. "They hid the moment you fired your warning shot and came to our rescue soon as they could."

Blasted impressment again, Max thought furiously. Overhead, a roar rose: the sounds of hand-to-hand combat. "Everyone's loose?"

"Every soul. Now drop that crowbar, boy."

Max bent slowly and deliberately, set down the crowbar, then shoved his hand into the ditty bag at his feet and grabbed one of Liao's charges. Muttering a silent prayer to whatever saint governed pyromaniacal Chinese boys, he rubbed his finger against his palm. Against all probability, a tiny blue flicker of fire appeared in his hand.

"What is—*drop that!*" the master yelled.

Max touched the short wick to the flame, then curled his fingers and doused the fire in his hand. He lobbed the round ball at the door and dropped to the floor, wrapping his arms around his head as he did.

Even with his face covered, the flash was excruciating. The sound—it was almost like the opposite of sound, actually: a *whoomp*, inaudible but somehow palpable, a thickness in the air, a momentary silence as if all the noise in the world were rushing into a vacuum, and, most bizarre of all, a sensation in Max's mouth as if he were chewing on cotton.

He shook his head clear and opened his eyes cautiously. The master and his men were staggering, blinded and howling in pain. With one reluctant look at those crates—*so close!*—Max grabbed Liao's bag, sprinted through the hold, and shoved his way past the men in the doorway. They were obviously trying to scream, but not a peep came from their mouths.

Sound returned to the world as he dashed toward the nearest ladderway. The din of combat was still audible above, and now and then the ship would lurch as someone managed to fire one of the great guns. Max peeked cautiously up onto the main deck and found himself staring into the wide, dead eyes of a Fate named Abel who only yesterday had offered to fix a torn coat sleeve for him.

A gun belched flame to his left and a ship out in the night returned fire: not the American frigate they'd left behind but a smaller vessel coming in from a different direction.

Max hoisted himself up onto the deck and reached into Liao's bag. "Fates!" he shouted. *"Cover your eyes!"* He struck another little flame on his palm, lit a second charge, and threw it into the air as far as it would go. Max buried his head in his arms again as the deck of the *Honoratus* exploded in blinding white.

....

THE BLAZE THAT ERUPTED FROM THE *HONORATUS* WAS SO BRIGHT that it turned night into broad daylight for a heartbeat and revealed two things to Lucy on the deck of the *Left-Handed Fate.* The first was the ship the *Honoratus* had fired on: a corvette flying France's tricolor flag. Lucy knew her immediately, and so did the lookout. "*Marie Colette* bearing down, sir!" he bellowed from above. Ah yes, they knew that ship. Blast her.

But the sudden brightness revealed something else, too: a mere pinprick far, far to the north at the very limit of the illumination. Lucy blinked and looked again, but before she could even make up her mind about whether she'd actually seen anything at all, the light faded. If there had been anything on the horizon, it was completely invisible now.

The *Fate* raced up firing, but the *Marie Colette* was ready for her, and the French ship's first volley sent everyone on the *Fate* diving for the deck. Chain shot—two half-cannonballs connected by a length of iron links—ripped low through the rigging. *This is bad*, Lucy thought as she got to her feet again. Fighting off the corvette would slow them, and they couldn't afford to lose a minute. They had put some distance between themselves and the American frigate, but it was still coming. Once it reached them, the battle would be over.

The *Fate* fired again, and then again. The French gun crews were slower and their aim left a lot to be desired, but the *Marie Colette* had more crew and more guns, and little by little she began to do some damage.

The *Honoratus* hadn't fired in a while. Mr. Foster packed their last boat, a twelve-foot dinghy, with one last little boarding party and sent it darting across to the sloop. They couldn't really spare the hands, but if they could win the sloop back, the combined guns of the *Honoratus* and the *Fate* just might be enough to defeat the *Marie Colette* before the Americans caught up. Maybe.

....

THE SCHOONER DID MANAGE TO TAKE THE SLOOP BACK, BUT IT wasn't enough.

The *Amaranthine* reached the scene just as the two ships fired together at the newcomer, a French corvette. *"Stand down!"* Mr. Hollis shouted through his trumpet. Instead of obeying, the schooner fired every gun that could be pointed at the *Amaranthine*, and every single shot hit. Oliver barely had time to dive aside as one of those balls came smashing down the entire length of the deck, kicking up splinters the whole way.

"Fire as they bear!" Captain Eager snarled, and the frigate's guns disgorged smoke and flame and iron.

The schooner did not fire again.

Her weather deck was revealed as the fug cleared: it was a slick of scarlet from bow to stern. At some point during the chase, the schooner had lowered its false U.S. flag and run up its own colors. Now the Union Jack descended in surrender. Across the water, the French ship, which had sprinted after the sloop once the *Amaranthine* engaged the schooner, fired one last time into its quarry. The battle was over.

Oliver examined the smaller vessel as the *Amaranthine* closed the distance between them. Her rigging was a shambles of smashed timber, broken bits of rope, and torn sails that hung like rags over her decks. The scene on her deck was chaos. There were a lot of dead men over there, and by now Oliver was close enough to make out the details. His stomach lurched.

"Mr. Dexter!"

He turned to find Mr. Hollis stalking toward him. Oliver straightened and snapped off a salute. "Yes, sir."

"With me, if you please."

Oliver scrambled after Mr. Hollis, trying to match his long-legged pace as he strode to where Captain Eager stood roaring out commands to the rest of his officers.

"S—sir," Oliver stammered, saluting again.

"Mr. Dexter," the captain announced, "you are to go aboard the schooner with a prize-crew of ten men and take her back to Norfolk. Then you are to board the next frigate heading for New York and rejoin us there."

"I—yes, sir." Oliver swallowed his disappointment. His first cruise, over in a day and a half. Still, orders were orders. "To whom shall I report?"

The captain frowned. "In Norfolk?"

"No, sir, on the prize-crew."

The frown deepened into a black scowl. "Mr. Dexter, *you* are to *command* the prize-crew."

Oliver's jaw dropped. "I . . . I beg your pardon, sir?"

"Don't be absurd. You don't have to *do* anything," Captain Eager growled. "Point the boat at the lights and go there. But I cannot spare anyone else so early in the cruise." He fixed Oliver with a horrifyingly dismissive glare. "Do you wish me to understand that you do not feel yourself prepared for this undertaking, sir?"

Disbelief gave way to mortification. Ordinarily, being given the chance to take a prize back to port would've been reckoned an honor. But Captain Eager hadn't chosen Oliver because he'd earned it; the captain was giving him command of the prize-crew because he thought Oliver was the very least useful person aboard the *Amaranthine*.

It shouldn't have hurt as badly as it did. Obviously he was the most worthless member of the crew who was also something like an officer. Still, Oliver's face burned as he forced himself to salute again. Hopefully the captain wouldn't notice that his hands were shaking. "I beg your pardon, sir; no, sir. I mean yes, sir—I can do it, sir."

The captain nodded once and returned to issuing orders. Mr. Hollis drew Oliver away. "See here, Mr. Dexter. All you've got to do is get the rigging functional again—the prize-crew will see to that—and then it's a quick jaunt back to Norfolk. All you've got to do is to look sharp and make a report when you—"

And Mr. Hollis dropped dead at Oliver's feet, caught through the temple with a musket ball.

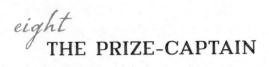

eight
THE PRIZE-CAPTAIN

Oliver staggered away from the body and stared across the narrow space to the captured vessel. The boarding party, which had gone over expecting to take charge of men who had surrendered, was now locked in hand-to-hand combat with the privateers.

"All hands to board!" Captain Eager bellowed.

Oliver's horror at seeing someone fall dead less than a foot from him was almost matched by his shock. The schooner had surrendered! One couldn't just *take it back* after striking one's colors. That went against all the rules of honor and good behavior. It wasn't *fair.*

Then he realized something worse. The two ships lay side by side. Abruptly it occurred to Oliver that if they weren't above a false surrender, the privateers might not be above firing right into the *Amaranthine's* hull, and at this range, the schooner's guns could not miss. Without even having to be pointed they could batter the bigger ship so near to the waterline that the *Amaranthine* would be utterly destroyed.

"Captain!" He fought his way against the tide of sailors rushing from the *Amaranthine* to the captured vessel, searching for Captain Eager's blue coat. Then he stopped short. The schooner was his first command. Time to take initiative.

Oliver skidded to a halt beside a small-arms locker and grabbed a sword and a pistol. "Where is my prize-crew?" he shouted. His voice cracked.

To his relief (and, if he was honest, shock), a handful of voices answered. "Here, sir!"

"To the prize!" Oliver shrieked. "Disable the gun crews!"

He leapt down onto the schooner's weather deck, praying he wouldn't break his leg in the drop or impale himself on his sword, which was heavier and more unwieldy than he'd expected. After that it was all a blur.

There were dead men on the floor and great spills of blood where there weren't bodies. Dodging the clashing blades of the battling crews, Oliver slid, landed on his elbow and forearm, and got to his feet, wiping scarlet onto his trousers. A bullet whined past his cheek. The motion of the air actually stung.

Sure enough, there were crews priming two of the guns on the side facing the *Amaranthine*. A voice cut through the noise. "Slow-match here!"

Oliver followed the voice and spotted the gunner. He sprinted through the battle, launched himself at the gunner's belly, and knocked the fellow to the floor. His prize-crew swarmed the guns. Only one managed to fire.

Oliver picked himself up and leveled his sword at the gunner sprawled at his feet. "Tell your men to stand down," he said with as much dignity as his cracking voice could manage, considering it took rather a lot of effort not to collapse into a heap and scream in terror.

"Stand down, Mr. Harrick," said someone behind him in a voice full of steel. "Everyone, *stand down!*" The voice that gave the order was a girl's.

She was taller than Oliver, brown as toast and with short, sun-streaked hair: the unmistakable coloring of someone who'd grown up at sea. Her eyes glittered with anger. She came forward with a look on her face like the expression Captain Eager had worn when he'd ordered all hands to board. Furious, like some kind of avenging angel.

To a man, the entire privateer crew stood down. Instantly. The man under Oliver's sword spoke from the floor. "Aye aye, miss. Thank you, miss." And he sounded like he really meant that last part.

The French corvette, too far off to have joined the brief fray before then, managed a single shot. But the battle was really and truly over now.

A short while later, Oliver made his way aft to the low quarterdeck, where a surgeon's mate was busy wrapping a bandage around Captain Eager's head and the captain himself was occupied with shooting irritated looks at a white cat that had materialized from somewhere and now sat at his feet, meditatively flicking its tail.

Mr. Ansby, the *Amaranthine*'s first lieutenant, stood nearby, directing the cleanup and the securing of the surviving captives. "Explain," he snapped at the nearest prisoner.

The man shrugged tiredly. "What answer should I make?" He aimed a look of loathing at one of the nearby dead. "We lost, ship and honor both, thanks to that fool."

Mr. Ansby shook his head in disgust. "Take him below."

Captain Eager spoke up from his seat at the edge of the quarterdeck. The bandage around his head was already turning red. "Mr. Dexter," he said, "you did well."

How on earth had the man had time to notice what Oliver had been up to? "I—thank you, sir."

"I dislike leaving you in command of prisoners capable of such dishonorable behavior," he said. "On the other hand, I'm pleased with your leadership. In view of that, in your orders I've named you acting-lieutenant. I recommend you not get used to it," he added coldly. "It is strictly for the duration of your command of this prize, and merely to recognize your valor for the record." Then he muttered something under his breath that sounded unpleasantly like, "I'm going to look like a lunatic for it, too."

It was a handsome compliment to be sure, but what Oliver was really thinking about was that he thought he might vomit, and whether it was more professional to make a run for it to vomit over the side, or try to wait until he was dismissed and risk vomiting directly upon the captain's shoes.

And that's how Oliver Dexter, Acting-Midshipman, U.S. Navy, became Acting-Lieutenant Oliver Dexter, prize-captain of the schooner *Left-Handed Fate*.

....

Lucy Bluecrowne's experience of the battle was somewhat different.

She had been prepared for the possibility of her father's death since she had first gone to sea when she was five years old—or at least, that's what she thought. But when it actually happened, she wasn't ready at all.

It was the last volley of cannonfire from the frigate that had struck the quarterdeck and sent a huge splinter of wood through Richard Bluecrowne's throat.

He crumpled and landed at Lucy's feet, dead as you please. Lucy took one look at her father's body, opened her mouth, and began to scream. Then she fell into the arms of the nearest living human, buried her face in his chest, and allowed herself to be dragged below, still screaming for her father in between sobs. The last thing she saw of the world above was the flag descending: her father's schooner—her schooner now—being surrendered.

"I have to go up there," she howled, trying to push clear of her rescuer's arms. Overhead she heard the sounds of a boarding party. "I have to help Papa! Let me go up there! *They're boarding my ship!*"

The sailor said her name over and over, and he held her tight and close and refused to let her go. At last Lucy collapsed, defeated. Her father was dead, and the rest of them were prisoners—or soon would be.

She shuddered, straightened, wiped her face on her sleeve. Then she looked up at the sailor. It was her father's steward, another man she'd known her entire life.

"Thank you, Garvett," she said, hating the sound of her ravaged voice. "Let me above now to parley with our captors."

Garvett kept hold of her arm. "Don't go up there, miss. Please."

And then, sudden and unmistakable, the sound of hand-to-hand combat. It brought her down to earth as quickly and sharply as a leap into freezing water. "Impossible," Lucy protested. "We surrendered!"

A voice above shouted, "Mr. Harrick! *Mr. Harrick!*"

Harrick was the gunner. They were about to fire on the frigate. *After they had already surrendered.* The only person on the *Fate* within the chain of command who had the capacity to resort to this sort of dishonor was Bantwell, the third mate, which meant that along with her father and Mr. Fitch, Mr. Foster was dead, too.

Instinct took over. Lucy shook Garvett off without another word and scrambled up the ladder just as a little boy streaked past at the head of a handful of American sailors. The boy knocked Harrick, who was not a small man, flat on his arse as if he weighed nothing, then leveled a sword at him.

Lucy strode forward and ordered the crew to stand down. And, bless them, they obeyed.

Now the main deck was all bodies and blood and smoke and smug Americans. Lucy forced herself not to look for her father's yellow coat among the dead as she walked up to the uniformed trio near the quarterdeck. Instead, she looked uneasily toward the sea. The *Marie Colette* was departing, which made no sense. And had she really seen another ship in that one moment of brightness before things had gone so horribly wrong?

The officers looked up as she approached. The injured one was obviously the captain, and the smallest was the boy who had knocked Harrick down. A throbbing started up in her throat. She made believe it was just a bad bite of salt pork or one of the surgeon's horrid pills and forced it down. Her hands were trembling, too, so she put them in the pockets the sailmaker had helped her add to all her dresses and clenched her fingers into fists until the shaking stopped.

"I'm Melusine Charlotte Bluecrowne," she said flatly. "This is my schooner—my father was the owner and captain—and I apologize for the dishonor of attacking after our surrender. I would like to petition for the fair treatment of the remaining crew and to request that while repairs are made, you permit us to bury our dead."

The third American, probably one of the lieutenants, shot a glance in the direction of the quaking hands she was hiding in her pockets. She folded them in front of her with a quick stab of shame. Her father would never have tolerated a sailor standing about with his hands in his pockets, let alone addressing an officer that way.

The American captain spoke. "My condolences, and your apology is accepted. I must ask you for your father's letters of marque and reprisal. Do you know where they are kept?"

"Yes, sir." The letters of marque and reprisal licensed the *Left-Handed Fate* as a private ship of war, and they were what kept privateers from being hanged for pirates if caught. Knowing where to find them had been part of her training about what to do if the *Fate* was ever taken. Not that she had ever believed it was possible.

"As for the treatment of the crew and the burials, you will have to take that up with the prize-captain, Lieutenant Dexter." And he pointed to the boy.

....

CAPTAIN EAGER AND MR. ANSBY TOOK THEMSELVES OFF TO SEE to the state of the *Amaranthine*, leaving Oliver to deal with the girl. He thought he saw Mr. Ansby stifle a tired grin.

"You said this is your schooner," Oliver said stiffly after the girl had gotten over her obvious disbelief. "I beg your pardon, but where is the first lieutenant?"

"The first *mate's* dead," she retorted. "The second mate as well. The third mate's the man who ordered the attack after we struck our colors." The girl turned and actually kicked the hip of the dead man in the wool coat. "All you're left with is me." She looked down at him with a superior look on her face, as if being taller was any sort of accomplishment.

Oliver spoke as patiently as possible. "I am *looking* for the *ranking officer* on board."

"It's a *letter-of-marque*." She was either mimicking his patient tone badly, or she was actually trying to sound like she thought she was speaking to an idiot. "There aren't any *officers* aboard."

"I *know* it's a letter-of-marque! And I think you know what I mean."

"I think you mean you want to speak to the person in charge. Even if any of the mates were still alive, the fact remains that my father owned this vessel." She turned, looked around the deck, and

pointed with a shaking hand to a corpse in a yellow silk coat. "He's dead. As you see. So now it's mine. There are papers with the letters of marque that will prove that. I'll get them now." And with that, she strode to the nearest ladderway. An American standing there made a motion as if to stop her, then dropped his arm abruptly and let her climb down. Oliver decided he was glad he hadn't glimpsed whatever that sailor had seen on her face.

He walked a few paces in the opposite direction. This brought him face-to-face with a slightly older boy in a velvet coat, one of the privateers who'd been brought back from the captured sloop called the *Honoratus*. The boy leaned on the gunwale, pale and unsettled, but when he spotted Oliver he made a show of straightening up and replacing the unease on his face with a lofty expression so inappropriate under the circumstances that before he could stop himself, Oliver said, "I suppose you think you're in charge as well."

The boy shook his head. "You will be much relieved to know that I do not."

He looked nothing like a sailor. Given the perversity of this vessel, he was probably some sort of clergyman in training. Girls, white cats . . . all this ship was missing in terms of bad-luck omens was a reverend. "Who are you, anyway?" Oliver asked.

"I'm a natural philosopher. I study the sciences: mechanics, astronomy, optics, geology, botany, electricity—"

"I know what a natural philosopher is." Something was nagging at Oliver. Recollection dawned: "You're the fellow from Jeton's shop! The one the . . . the lightning took after!"

The boy nodded once, uneasy again. His eyes flicked out into the dark Atlantic, then back. "You are our new commander, I take it?"

"I am." Oliver attempted to stand up straighter. "Oliver Dexter, U.S. Navy. Acting-Lieutenant," he added as an afterthought, mostly just to try it out.

"Maxwell Ault," the boy said. "You will not be able to contend with the crew of this ship without dealing with Miss Bluecrowne, Mr. Dexter. What she says is true—the men will certainly see her as their leader, now that her father is dead. Aboard the *Fate*, she holds a rank equivalent to a lieutenant, in addition to the fact that her father owned the boat." He rubbed his chin thoughtfully. "I have a book that may prove useful to you, now I think of it. It has a section on the managing of females."

"A *lieutenant*? But . . . she's a *girl*!" This was even more unbelievable than his own new position. "What kind of a ship *is* this?"

"It is the *Left-Handed Fate*," Maxwell Ault said, with a significant look on his face that Oliver didn't waste time trying to make sense of. But of course it would be called the Left-Handed something, just to add to its collection of portents of ill fortune.

The sloop they'd rescued wasted no time in getting on its way again. The *Honoratus* returned the schooner's three boats, rushed through basic repairs, then vanished into the night. The French ship that had been so critical in freeing it departed, too, and without much more than a quick shouted exchange with Captain Eager. The *Amaranthine* had twenty-three casualties: eight men dead and fifteen men wounded, out of three hundred and fifty. The *Left-Handed Fate* had fared worse: thirty dead and nearly as many wounded out of only ninety.

The dead—those that hadn't been thrown overboard during the brief battle—were buried at sea by their surviving crewmates. This took some time.

nine

BEFORE THE MORNING WATCH

As the eight bells that announced midnight tolled, Max paced, looking for somewhere to be where he wouldn't step on bodies or get in the way of those who were caring for them. When this didn't seem to be geographically possible, he took a deep breath, tried to subdue the sick feeling that was all at once everywhere in his body, and went in search of Lucy.

It was a ghastly walk across the deck. Every lantern that could be spared had been brought up to give light to the sailors at work. That light glinted on countless needles and lines of thick white thread. The upturned faces of the dead stared up out of the shadows as their shipmates stitched them into shrouds made from hammocks. Max found Lucy where he'd known he would: stitching her father's body into his own canvas pall.

"I offered to do the sewing," Kendrick said somberly as Max approached, glancing at Lucy's hunched figure. "So did about four others. It's no task for her, but of course she's . . . well, she's her father's daughter."

"I thought I might—" He swallowed. "I remember when I lost my father."

Kendrick nodded. "If I could sit there and keep her company, I'd do it, sir, but there's a lot of sewing needs doing, and we're uncommon lucky the Americans are letting us sew up our dead at all. I don't expect you sew, Mr. Ault."

"I—well, no."

"Then perhaps you can take this watch."

Lucy's arm swept out wide, pulling a stitch tight. Her hand was unsteady, and it made the heavy thread vibrate. "I can take this watch," Max agreed.

He walked over and squatted next to her, still trying to figure out what to say. Lucy's stitches were uneven and zig-zagging, but the shroud was nearly finished. Neither the body nor the nine-pound cannonball tucked inside the canvas at its feet was visible.

She knotted off the last stitch, then opened a folding knife and cut the thread. She sat back on her heels and pondered her work. "That's my papa," Lucy said wonderingly. And it did seem unbelievable. Certainly Captain Bluecrowne, like his daughter, had always seemed indestructible.

"My father died a year and a half before I came aboard," Max said, cautiously.

Lucy half-turned and gazed silently into space somewhere near Max's left knee.

"I didn't see it happen, the way you did," he continued, "but I was the one who found him. I remember how it felt. I remember it sometimes, suddenly, when I least expect it." Like right now, for instance. Max blinked, trying to clear his mind and his eyes. This was about Lucy, not about him. Lucy herself waited, still staring at his knee.

"I came to think the world of him. Captain Bluecrowne, I mean." He faltered, swallowed. What on earth was he supposed to say? He had books with charts and tables, he had mathematics and all of natural philosophy, but none of that made this any easier. Death did not permit itself to be measured in books.

"I wish I could say something helpful," he said at last. "If I could sew—"

"It's finished," Lucy interrupted. "It doesn't matter if you can sew or not."

Elsewhere on the ship, someone blew a whistle, and Kendrick appeared beside them. "Are you ready, Miss Bluecrowne?" he asked. Lucy nodded and got to her feet, wiping her eyes. She worked her fingers under the edge of the board her father's body lay upon.

"Let me," Max said quickly.

Lucy looked at him reproachfully. Then she took one step to her left, just enough to make room for him to stand at her side. Max slid his fingers underneath the board, next to hers.

"My soul flee-eth unto the Lord," she whispered, "before the morning watch, I say, before the morning watch." Max didn't know the words of the sailors' burial service, so he simply lowered his head.

On the next whistle, they lifted the board together. Richard Bluecrowne's shrouded body slid into the ocean, along with a score and a half of his men, all of whom had been sewn into their own hammocks and weighted with roundshot to drag them down to the depths. Men who had been Lucy's family, and who had become Max's family as well.

When the water was mostly still again, he put an arm around her. Lucy leaned her head onto his shoulder for a full three seconds. Then she wiped her eyes and went back to work.

....

ON THE QUARTERDECK, OLIVER WATCHED THE BURIAL AND HAD no idea at all what to feel. In the end, he did what Lucy did. He went to work.

Oliver couldn't sew sails or splice rope, but it turned out that he wasn't bad at collecting information, turning that information over in his mind, and making it into decisions that got things done. An hour later, the Amaranthines not assigned to the prize-crew made ready to depart. Mr. Ansby handed Oliver a folded packet. "Your orders and acting commission, Mr. Dexter. I trust we shall see you in New York before long."

The last Amaranthine to leave was the fellow who'd most recently cut down Oliver's hammock. "Your sea-chest's already below," he said awkwardly, then held out a parcel. "Fresh-laundered, sir. A prize-captain needs clean shirts." He followed the others back to the frigate that was supposed to have been Oliver's home, and then Oliver was alone with an all-wrong, barely functional schooner, a girl who thought she was a sailor, a prize-crew of ten men who'd only known him a week, and a bundle of shirts his own peers had stolen from him the last time he'd slept.

Thankfully, Mr. Cascon had been assigned to the prize-crew. "Beg pardon, sir," he said, touching his knuckles to his forehead, "but the young lady seems to want a word."

A red-eyed Lucy Bluecrowne paused as she approached, casting a quick, suspicious glance at Mr. Cascon. The accent, Oliver realized. He had gotten so used to it, Oliver had completely forgotten that Mr. Cascon was French.

"Excuse me, Lieutenant," Lucy said. "Have you . . ." Her voice caught thickly in her throat. "Have you determined on the matter of our parole?"

"Will you give your word that your crew will behave?" It was only a short sail back to Norfolk, anyway, and it seemed that nobody left aboard had approved of the order to attack after surrendering.

"Yes," she said, a bit defensively.

"Fine. You can have your parole. You and any remaining officers." *No officers on a privateer.* "You know what I mean."

"I—oh." She looked a touch taken aback, as if she'd expected to have to argue. "Thank you . . . sir."

She turned self-consciously and walked away. For the first time Oliver realized she couldn't be that much older than he was. Then he remembered that her father had died that day. She herself had stitched him into his shroud. It couldn't have been easy.

The next one to pop up to bother him was the older boy, Max Ault. "I brought this for you, Lieutenant," the older boy said, tossing a meaningful look at Lucy's departing back and holding out a book. "It has excellent bits on managing females. Very scientific."

Oliver took the book and tucked it mechanically under his arm. "Thank you." He gave Max a shrewd look. "What's a natural philosopher doing aboard a privateer?"

"You're wondering if there's some nefarious reason a philosopher might find himself aboard a letter-of-marque?" Max asked tiredly. "Some sort of espionage, perhaps? Some secret mission?"

"Well, yes, I suppose."

"Don't be so dramatic. It's nothing that elaborate, why I'm here."

"Well, what is it, then?"

Max hesitated for a moment. Then he nodded toward the gunwale, where Lucy stood with folded arms. "Her, obviously."

"Her?" Oliver looked from Max to Lucy and back. "What on earth is obvious about *her*?"

"Nothing's obvious about her, that's what makes her so interesting. Not to mention she's quite pretty."

"*Pretty?*"

"Yes, but that's not the important—" Max frowned at him. "Did you even look?"

Oliver bit down a scathing rejoinder. He took a deep breath and looked: still just a girl who for some stupid reason thought she was a sailor, and, annoyingly, was tall enough to look down her nose at him. "She's too tall and her hair's too short." But Max was looking at Lucy Bluecrowne as if she were the only other creature in the world.

"You know," Oliver said after a moment, suddenly too fatigued to care any longer, "the way the wind's blowing, she can probably hear us."

"That's all right," Max said quietly. "She wouldn't believe it, anyhow. And she has other things on her mind."

....

FINALLY, THANKFULLY, THE PRIZE-CAPTAIN TOOK HIMSELF OFF TO do whatever it was prize-captains did. Max took a second book from his pocket, opened it at random, and studied the page as if there was enough light to read by, which there wasn't. The letters swam, and not only because of the dark. Max was as exhausted as he thought he'd ever been in his life.

"Quick thinking," Lucy said, coming to stand at his side. Her eyes were still red, but some of the humor had come back into them. "I shouldn't hold my breath waiting for me to play along, if I was you."

"No need." He watched her for a moment, mentally stringing words together, trying them out, discarding them. "I'm so sorry, Lucy," he said at last. "It's my fault. I feel . . ." Nothing he'd been able to come up with had seemed like a satisfactory end to that sentence.

"It isn't your fault, Max." She spoke dully, eyes on the web of rigging overhead. Probably so that he wouldn't see the lie all over her face.

"It is, though. We ran when we shouldn't have, and now exactly what you warned could happen *did* happen, and the *Honoratus* is out of our reach and your father is . . . and it's all because of me."

"Everything you just said is true," Lucy said, eyes still upturned, "except for one thing. It isn't because of you. It's because of the mission. My father knew the risks." Finally she looked at him. She had that look, that beautiful, fierce, fire-eyed expression on her face again, the one that made her look like a creature out of myth. "Ask me, Max."

In that moment, with her eyes blazing at him, he would've done anything for her. It wasn't the first time he'd had that thought. "Help me finish my mission," Max said. "And forgive me."

She looked at him hard for another moment, then nodded once. Her face, her fierce eyes, turned back up to the rigging, and it was as if night had fallen for a second time. "We'll be back in Norfolk in a matter of hours. As a civilian passenger, you and your personal cargo will be safe. And I imagine they'll let Liao and me go quickly, if only because he's so young and I'm a girl." She said this in a tone of disgust. "But we shall have to find another way to Nagspeake, and pray we don't get there far too late."

Max shook his head, amazed. How had she shifted from sadness to strategy so rapidly? *But of course*, he realized. *This is how she'll make sense of the captain's death.* By finishing his final mission, by hook or by crook, even if it had to be done on land.

A note of real worry entered her voice for the first time. "But I haven't seen Liao since we were taken, Max."

"He isn't among the prisoners below?" He hadn't been among the dead, thank God.

She shook her head. "I'm sure he's hiding somewhere—Max." She squinted into the night, and Max followed her gaze. There were lights on the horizon. Lucy swore. "I knew they wouldn't just leave us in peace."

The *Marie Colette* had come back after all.

....

Someone tapped Oliver on the shoulder. "I'm awake," he blurted, hoping it wasn't obvious that he had dozed off standing upright on the schooner's low quarterdeck.

"Yes, sir," Mr. Cascon said apologetically, holding out a telescope. "But that French ship, sir, the one from earlier—she's signaling. Shall we wait for her?"

Oliver took the telescope and surveyed the lights of the corvette. "All right. We'll see what she wants, then all sail for Norfolk."

"Yes, sir. And if I may, perhaps you might grab a few minutes' sleep. It'll take her a half hour to join us, I imagine. A half hour's nap would set you up nicely for the run back to Hampton Roads."

Oliver began to protest, but Mr. Cascon certainly knew that he was exhausted. Moreover, once they made for Norfolk any chance of sleep was gone, since Oliver would have to spend the coming day making reports to the commanding officer of the Norfolk station. Suddenly he felt very small, and very young. "Yes, all right."

He started forward out of habit; the midshipmen's mess was

forward on the *Amaranthine*. Mr. Cascon cleared his throat. "Sir, I believe the captain's quarters are aft."

The captain's quarters. Oliver shifted uncomfortably. The thought of walking into that man's cabin as if it belonged to him didn't seem right somehow. Still, he was the prize-captain. If he went below and slung a hammock up like a squeaker—well, that would never do. "Thank you, Cascon."

Mr. Cascon saluted. Then: "Sir, if I may."

Oliver stopped, willing himself not to fall to pieces at the idea of staying awake even one moment longer. "Yes?"

Mr. Cascon cracked a small smile that somehow seemed younger than the rest of his lined face. "The way you rallied us back on the *Amaranthine*, sir—well, pardon me for saying so, but it reminded me of some of the stories I've heard about Commodore Underby when he was a lad."

It was a high compliment. Many reckoned Commodore Underby had been the first captain to really prove the young American navy could hold her own against the almighty Royal Navy, but there were also plenty of stories about dashing exploits during his years as a young officer.

"Thank you, Cascon," Oliver said wearily. "I'll tell him so the next time I write."

Mr. Cascon tilted his head. "Sir?"

"Matthew Underby is my father," Oliver mumbled.

"Mr. . . . Dexter?"

Oliver was too tired to do anything but tell the truth. "Our names do not match because my mother is not married to him. My mother keeps a confectionery shop. Wake me when you see fit."

He found his way to Captain Bluecrowne's cabin, where, comfortingly, his sea-chest and shirts were waiting for him. Two minutes later he was fast asleep.

LUCY AND MAX WATCHED, HELPLESS, AS THE *MARIE COLETTE* swept toward them. "We've got to get you off the *Fate*," Lucy said, chewing on a fingernail.

"How? Steal a boat? Swim?"

"And where the blazes is Liao? Maybe if we had one of his flash-bangs. How could you have left them aboard the sloop?"

"I was a prisoner, if you recall," Max retorted. "The Frenchman can't do anything, can he? Not now that we're an American prize."

"He could claim your cards are French property, I suppose. It wouldn't hold up against a proper officer, but this boy . . ."

"But he isn't just any boy, is he? Who did he say his father was?" Max asked. It was a ship too small for secrets, as Lucy often said, and although Max hadn't recognized the name, everyone else in earshot had, and they were still talking about it.

"Underby," Lucy said grimly. "Good point." She sighed. "I just don't know what he'll do, Max. If we can't get you off the ship, we'll just have to see what happens. I don't see any option, other than throw the cards overboard just to keep the Frenchman from taking them."

"Last resort," Max muttered.

They watched the corvette come nearer and nearer. Finally Lucy smacked a hand down on the gunwale. "What the hell. How much worse could it make things?"

"How much worse could what—" But she was already rushing across the deck toward the ladderway. "Lucy!"

DUELS WITH GIRLS

"Lieutenant Dexter?"

Mr. Cascon opened the door and leaned in. Oliver groaned and got groggily to his feet. "Yes?" "Is the corvette here?"

"No, sir. It's the young lady and gentleman. They say they must speak to you before the corvette arrives, sir, and they were quite insistent."

"Fine." Oliver pulled on his uniform coat and rubbed the sleep from his eyes with his knuckles as Cascon stood aside for Lucy Bluecrowne and Max Ault, then stepped out and closed the door.

"Pardon the interruption," Lucy said, "but it's terribly important."

"We need to get off this ship," Max added, sitting without being invited in one of the chairs opposite Captain Bluecrowne's desk.

Oliver stared at him. "I beg your pardon?"

"May we sit, sir?" Lucy asked, shooting a reproachful look at Max.

"Er." Oliver sat behind the desk and waved at the remaining empty chair. "Yes."

Lucy sat. "I understand that what we're about to ask is irregular," she began, "and I understand that your orders are quite specific. But we would like you to allow Max and me to take the red cutter and a few sailors—enough to man the boat, no more—and depart before the *Marie Colette* reaches us."

Oliver laughed shortly. "This is a joke."

"It isn't. When you took us, we weren't involved in any acts against the United States. Yes, the *Left-Handed Fate* is a letter-of-marque, but my father had hired the ship to Mr. Ault here for a voyage to do with his natural philosophy studies."

Oliver jabbed a finger at Max. "You said you were here because you were . . . because of Miss Bluecrowne!"

Max fidgeted. "Surely lying was a forgivable impulse. You'd just captured us."

"Yes, because *you* had just taken an American ship," Oliver protested. "What on earth do you mean you weren't engaged in errands against my country? *You captured a ship.*"

"Oh, that," Lucy said, her voice faltering a little. "That was regrettable . . . but before that, Mr. Dexter. We were already in the Chesapeake when war was declared, and we weren't there for any reason other than that Max had hired us to carry him to Baltimore."

"What for?" Oliver asked. Not that it mattered. Obviously, the only answer he could give to this insane request was *no*.

Despite his confident earlier words, the young natural philosopher looked like he wanted no part of this discussion. "It's scientific," he said unhelpfully. "It's to do with natural philosophy. Very technical."

"I do know something about natural philosophy," Oliver told him. "My father is a bit of a natural philosopher himself. He was a dear friend of Mr. Franklin's, too."

"Mr. . . . *Benjamin* Franklin?" Max asked weakly. "Oh. Well."

"And why are you worried about a French ship when you're

already taken?" Abruptly, Oliver realized something. "You called the French corvette by name."

"We know that ship," Max said after a moment. "She wants something of mine. Something of my father's."

"Any private property of yours that's aboard this vessel is still yours," Oliver said. "That's the law. We're not going to take it from you, and nobody else is going to take it from you while you're in our custody."

"I don't think the master of that ship is going to be overly concerned with the law," Max said carefully. "I am absolutely certain the only reason they're coming this way is to demand you hand my things over—and possibly me, too."

"It doesn't work that way." Oliver turned to Lucy. "Make him understand it doesn't work that way."

She shook her head. "They had the chance to parley with your captain before the *Amaranthine* left, but they didn't. They waited until the frigate got clear, and then they came back. I tell you, we know that corvette. She's after us—after Max—and I promise she's prepared to fight."

"But France and America are allies," Oliver argued. "They can't attack the *Left-Handed Fate* now." But Lucy was right about one thing: the corvette had waited until the *Amaranthine* had gone, and now it had come back to signal the *Fate*. Oliver couldn't think of any legitimate business a French ship had with an American prize. "Why would they want Mr. Ault?"

The other two looked at each other again. "Go on, Max," Lucy said gently.

Max stared at the floor. "Back at the end of the last century," he began, "my father discovered something—a piece of an engine. Or a piece of the *plan* for an engine, maybe. He died before he could find the rest of it. I'm trying to complete his work. We came here because . . . You recall the first time we met, back in Fells Point? I thought Mr. Jeton might have some insight into my father's notes, being a mechanical gentleman."

A privateer in wartime hiring itself out to a private citizen for a scientific voyage? That made no sense. Even if Max had hired the *Left-Handed Fate* before the States had declared war, Britain had already been at war with France, and no private voyage could have paid as well as raiding French shipping.

A memory drifted forward: Max Ault beseeching Mr. Jeton for something in Fells Point. *You understand what is at stake.* And Jeton had said something like, *For the sake of your father's memory, I'll tell you what I can, but it won't be much.*

"But Jeton wouldn't help you," Oliver said. "Why? What kind of engine is it?"

"I'm not certain yet," Max said hesitantly. "I need the rest of the pieces, one of which is on its way to Nagspeake now."

"Nagspeake?" Oliver repeated. He frowned. "The sloop you took, the one we freed—she was bound for Nagspeake, wasn't she?"

Lucy stiffened. Max said nothing.

Oliver shook his head, disgusted. "I thought you just had bad timing. But it was perfect timing, wasn't it? You were in Baltimore just long enough for you to take the ship that had what you wanted and it would be a legal prize."

"It was important," was all Max could come up with.

"Oh, I'm sure it was," Oliver countered. "It *must've* been important for someone aboard the *Left-Handed Fate* to order an attack after you'd surrendered."

"Mr. Bantwell had a distorted sense of personal honor. His giving that order had nothing to do with the mission," Lucy said coldly. "You must let us go, Mr. Dexter. It is that simple."

Oliver gaped at her. "It certainly is not that simple. Captives asking to be released, just like that? With a boat? And crew?" He had orders written out by Captain Eager himself, and those orders were perfectly clear: to conduct this ship safely to Norfolk. Moreover, the *Left-Handed Fate* was a licensed letter-of-marque, and she and her crew were agents of the enemy. Never mind letting them loose with a boat; to so much as give comfort to them was an act of treason punishable by death.

Oliver met Lucy's eyes. Her expression had hardened, as if somehow she knew exactly what revolutions his mind had been going through and exactly where he'd wound up.

"You said it was simple," he began, steeling his nerves. "As far as I can see, the only simple thing about this is that it would be treason to let you go, and I should be court-martialed and probably hanged if I did what you ask." Well, that wasn't so hard! Oliver folded his hands before him, a thing he had seen his father do when he had made up his mind. "And so I cannot."

To his surprise, Lucy nodded. "Just Max, then. He's a private citizen. Let him take his things and go."

"No," Oliver said. "The authorities in Norfolk can sort out Mr. Ault's status, and if you're both telling the truth about his purposes, he'll be let go in no time."

"It's not the authorities in Norfolk I'm worried about," Lucy said evenly. "We're not going to *make* it to Norfolk if we're still aboard this ship when the French arrive. Please let Max go."

Oliver held her gaze, but barely. "I promise I won't hand Mr. Ault or his belongings over to the French, and I promise you they won't commit an act of war against an American prize."

Max looked stricken. Lucy, on the other hand, looked like she might breathe fire, and if Oliver hadn't already been working so hard to keep his composure, that expression might've made him duck under the table.

"You cannot," she seethed. "You mean you *will* not. You certainly *could*, if you weren't afraid to question your precious *orders*. Damned navy swabs! Cowards, even the bravest of you, when it comes time to think for yourselves."

Oliver, who had never heard anyone of the female persuasion say the word *damned* before, felt his eyes nearly pop out of his head. "What?"

"You heard me." Lucy leaned across the desk. "I called you a coward."

"What?" Oliver had been so stunned by her use of profanity that he'd completely missed the rest of what she'd said.

Max dropped his head into his hands. "No, no, no. We don't have time for insults." He looked up, agonized. "Suppose I just go and put my cargo and notes overboard?"

"No."

"Damned swabs!"

"Lucy, settle down before you talk yourself into a duel!" Max hissed.

Oliver laughed. "I would never duel a girl, even if she does call me a coward."

Max slumped lower. "No, no, no. . . ."

Lucy's eyes narrowed dangerously. "No, of course not. I suppose you wouldn't want to damage a delicate creature like myself. Certainly it wouldn't be because you were a *coward* and a *scrub* and a *ba*—"

Max clapped a hand over her mouth before she got the word out, but there was no mistaking what it was going to be.

Before he could stop himself, Oliver had shoved his chair back from the desk and was fumbling for the sword he'd taken from the *Amaranthine* the day before. Then the hilt was in his hands and he flung off the scabbard and leveled the blade at Lucy.

She shoved off Max's hand and smirked. "So much for never dueling a girl."

Furious with himself, Oliver tossed the sword aside. "This is ridiculous."

Now Lucy came shooting to her feet. "Don't you dare disregard me, Dexter." She plucked a saber from a rack on the wall by the door and pointed it at Oliver.

Max begged her to be reasonable and not to do anything rash. Oliver looked in disbelief at the weapon, some sort of ornamental presentation sword with blue satin braid and gold plate on the hilt, and realized he had no idea what to do. Even if he had known anything at all about dueling—or even about using swords for anything other than pointing them menacingly—she was still a girl. He couldn't possibly—

And then she gave a shout and lunged at him, and without another thought Oliver flung himself to the floor. The gleaming point of the saber jabbed into the wood inches from his head.

"Lucy!" Max shrieked. "Don't kill him. He's just a child!"

Lucy snorted. "Don't be an idiot. I'm not going to kill him."

Blood rose to Oliver's face, and with a bellow he launched himself up at Lucy's middle. She went flying with a loud *oof.* Unfortunately, she didn't let go of the saber, and the force of Oliver's blow helped her yank it free of the floorboards. Then they were both on their feet again, and once more Lucy had a weapon pointed at him and Oliver had none.

"I'm not a scrub," Oliver snarled. "And I'm *not* a coward."

She stared down the length of her blade. The edge shook ever so slightly.

His eyes prickled. He glanced at the weapon he'd cast aside. "Give me my sword."

"Lucy," Max said softly.

"That isn't how a duel works," she said evenly.

"This isn't a duel!"

Lucy's heavy sword shook a little more. "Because I said I wouldn't kill you? Because I'm a girl?"

He forced his anger and humiliation down and came up with the right answer. "No, because you're a prisoner." Then, hoping he wasn't making a terrible mistake, he stepped back and dropped his hands. "And unless this is some sort of coup, you'll lower your weapon, Miss Bluecrowne."

A voice he didn't recognize erupted from somewhere to his left. "Stop, stop! Everyone just stop!"

Out of the corner of his eye—he didn't dare look away, even for a heartbeat, from the sword in Lucy's hand—he saw a chest against the wall fly open. A boy scrambled out of it and leapt between them. "Lucy, you mustn't!"

The boy was a few years younger than Oliver, and Chinese. *This ship*, Oliver thought. A hysterical giggle tried to fight its way up out of his throat. *This ship just keeps on throwing surprises at a fellow.*

A wave of relief swept over Lucy's face, and she let the sword fall. Max sprang forward and swept it from her hands. She reached out and pulled the Chinese boy into her arms. "Thank God. Liao, I was so worried!"

There was a quick knock and Mr. Cascon stuck his head inside. Max hid the sword unconvincingly behind his back. "Everything shipshape, sir?" Mr. Cascon asked, his eyes darting from Max to Oliver's weapon, which lay naked on the floor at Lucy's feet. Then he gave a little start at the sight of the strange boy in her arms. "Where on earth did *he* come from?"

Oliver willed his voice even. "The captain's sea-chest."

The boy had gone from hugging Lucy to crying in her arms.

"Mr. Dexter," she said in a wavering voice, "this is my brother, Liao."

"Your brother?" Oliver repeated.

"Yes." Her features softened. "Liao, our ship has been taken and Mr. Dexter is in charge now. You understand?"

The look that passed between them then actually made Oliver avert his eyes. "Has he—have you been in there the whole time?" he demanded gruffly.

The boy nodded miserably. "Ever since the battle started. I breathed through the keyhole."

Mr. Cascon cleared his throat. "Compliments, sir, and the corvette is signaling again. She would like to send someone aboard."

"Thank you." Oliver rubbed his face. He returned to his chair and sat stiffly. "I believe that is all, Miss Bluecrowne. And . . . Liao, was it? You'll have to find other quarters, understand?"

"Think about it, won't you, Mr. Dexter?" Max asked, herding Lucy and Liao toward the door. "There's still time to change your mind."

"Never mind 'think about it,'" Lucy shot back. "We're asking you to put a civilian ashore. There's a right answer. Find a way to it before we have to resort to dramatic solutions."

Mr. Cascon stiffened. "No, no, no," Max whined again. "Lucy, for the love of—"

Oliver glared at the girl. "I beg your pardon, Miss Bluecrowne, but did I just hear you make a threat?"

A red flush swept up her tanned face. She clamped her mouth shut tight.

"She didn't mean—" Max began.

"Obviously she did," Oliver interrupted. "If she's going to demand"—he glanced at Mr. Cascon, unwilling to utter the word *treason* in anyone else's presence—"this sort of thing from me, she'd certainly be willing to undertake something similar herself." Max wilted. "Cascon, Miss Bluecrowne's parole is revoked. Please confine her to her quarters."

Lucy's hands curled into fists at her sides. Liao looked up at her, worried. "What does he mean, Lucy?" Nobody answered him.

Mr. Cascon tapped his knuckles to his forehead. "And the gentleman, sir?"

In for a penny, in for a pound. "Yes, I suppose you'd better. And confine everyone else to the forepeak." Max knocked his head against the door frame.

"And the boy?"

Lucy's belligerent expression vanished in a twinkling. "No, sir, please. He's nine years old. He's no danger to you."

"Fine, but he's to keep out of the way."

Mr. Cascon leaned out and shouted across the deck. A former Amaranthine appeared and took Lucy and Max each by an arm to escort them below. "Think on it, Mr. Dexter, please," Max said as he allowed himself to be pulled from the cabin. "If you have any other questions, I shall be glad to answer anything."

"Except for what the engine is," Oliver retorted.

"I told you, we don't know," Max insisted. "Not exactly."

It was obviously at least partly a lie, but it didn't matter. The only way all the bizarre threads of this conversation as well as the unthinkable post-surrender attack made sense was if the mysterious engine was some kind of weapon.

When Max, Lucy, and the boy called Liao had gone, Oliver turned to Mr. Cascon. "Tell the French they may send their emissary. But . . ." He hesitated. "See that our men keep a sharp weather-eye out. I don't like that that ship didn't take up whatever business she has with Captain Eager when she had the chance."

"Yes, sir."

"And see if someone will rouse out some coffee, will you, please?"

Oliver gave in to his nerves and allowed himself to pace until the coffee came in, hot and strong. He had just finished his first cup when Mr. Cascon knocked again. "A Mr. Cloutier to see you, sir."

"Send him in. And, Cascon, I think I should prefer that you stay while this Mr. Cloutier and I have our conversation."

"Aye aye, sir."

The Frenchman called Cloutier burst enthusiastically past him and into the cabin. "My dear Captain—" He looked around, confused, then lowered his chin until his eyes came to rest on Oliver, making it look like the boy's head was approximately a foot lower than he'd expected. "But it's a child," he exclaimed, turning to Mr. Cascon. "A joke, perhaps? Where have you hidden the captain?"

"*That* is the prize-captain, sir," Mr. Cascon growled.

On hearing Mr. Cascon's accent, the man brightened and began speaking rapidly to him in French. Mr. Cascon shook his head. "Lieutenant Dexter is the commanding officer. You may address him directly."

The stranger narrowed his eyes for a moment, then turned back to Oliver. He made an elaborately apologetic face, but there was no surprise or embarrassment in his eyes. "Please forgive me . . . Lieutenant. My very great apologies." Just as Max Ault had, he dropped into one of the chairs without waiting for an invitation. This time, however, Oliver was certain the insult was intentional.

Oliver scowled, but decided not to comment upon it. "What business do you have with me that you couldn't take up with Captain Eager?" And then, because Cloutier's repeated affronts seemed to call for some sort of tit for tat, Oliver poured himself another coffee and added milk and sugar slowly and deliberately. He didn't

offer Cloutier a cup. From his post beside the cabin door, out of view of their guest, Mr. Cascon gave a single approving nod.

The Frenchman made a soft but disdainful noise. Then he reached into his embroidered waistcoat, took out a folded dispatch, and held it out. *"S'il vous plait."*

Oliver took the paper. "I don't read French." But by then he had the thing open, and he was almost disappointed to find it was written in English—very official English, too.

From His Honor, Louis Barbe Charles Sérurier,
Consul General to the United States of America from the
government of His Excellency Napoleon the First, Emperor
of France, King of Italy, and Protector of the Confederation
of the Rhine, to the captain in the loyal service of our great
friend, the United States of America:

Greetings.
    As it is clear that our great friendship is critical to both
of our nations in this time of international crisis, please be so
good as to assist the bearer of this document, Michel Albert
Cloutier, Lord etc., in the commission of the consular
mission to which he is assigned and by which he is engaged
upon business critical to the success of endeavors near and dear
to both our interests. Mssr. Cloutier will be pleased
to provide you with all necessary remuneration for your
difficulties as well as official documents of thanks, should they
be necessary to present to your superiors.
    With thanks and confidence in your duty to both your
country and her allies, I remain

                    Yours sincerely,

Below that was Minister Sérurier's scrawled signature. It was a lot of fancy titles and fancy language, but the gist was unmistakable: *Dear whoever-you-are, please help our fellow out with whatever he's up to, even if it gets you into trouble. Signed, France.*

"I trust you comprehend it all?" Cloutier inquired.

"I can read *English*," Oliver growled. "It's a request for cooperation. But cooperation with what?"

Cloutier crossed one ankle over his knee. "This ship is carrying French property, and I want it back."

Oliver's pulse leapt, but he kept his face neutral. "Well, then you may follow us to Norfolk and take it up with the authorities."

"That is not acceptable."

"Well, in that case, I can't help you. I have my orders." He picked up his cup and took a sip.

Cloutier gestured at the diplomatic letter. "You also have this. Lieutenant."

"But I've never heard of a foreign diplomat's request overruling an officer's direct orders!"

Cloutier spread his hands. "Well, you are young, Lieutenant. Certainly there must be many things you have never yet heard of."

"Begging your pardon, sir," Mr. Cascon said in a clipped, cold tone, "but you aren't the only one who's never heard of it."

Cloutier shot a dark look at Mr. Cascon. "During war we are called upon to do extraordinary things. But as you see," he added, turning back to Oliver, "my embassy is confident that you will know your duty. And it is a very small matter, in the end."

"What is it?" Oliver asked. "The property in question."

"Merely a set of cards belonging to a French citizen. And the thief who took them, of course." *Max Ault.* Oliver's blood was beginning to run a few degrees colder. If Lucy and Max had been right about what he wanted, what about their warning that he would be willing to fight if Oliver refused him?

Thank goodness for orders; he could worry about the rest after. "We should arrive in Norfolk quite quickly, where I'm certain this can all be straightened out for you in no time at all. I'm sorry I can't be more helpful." Oliver nodded pointedly at the door. "The sooner you are returned to your vessel, the sooner we can all get under sail."

Cloutier got slowly to his feet. Then he made a short, condescending bow and marched out of the cabin.

Mr. Cascon paused before following. "You did well, sir. And if I may say so, I do believe you made the right decision."

Oliver smiled weakly. "Thank you." But he had the creeping, uncomfortable feeling that matters with the master of the *Marie Colette* weren't settled yet. Not quite.

eleven
ACTS OF WAR

Lucy pressed her ear to the bulkhead that separated her tiny cabin from her father's quarters, even though she knew from experience that the bookcase bolted to the wall on the captain's side perfectly insulated it against eavesdropping. Whatever discussions Dexter was having over there, she couldn't hear a word. So she climbed into her hammock and began to sob.

The very idea of crying horrified Lucy. It did happen to her now and again, but she preferred to think of it that way: as something that happened to her, like catching a cold or being shat upon by a gull, not something she *did*.

But today was different. If Max's mission failed now, it would mean Captain Bluecrowne had died for nothing. And now she had ruined their last, best chance. So she gave in to the tears and let herself cry, not because it made her feel better but because it made her feel worse. It was penance of a sort.

Then a gentle scratching at her door brought Lucy to attention. She wiped her eyes, hopped out of her hammock, and crouched to peek through the keyhole. A familiar eye appeared out of the gloom on the other side. "Liao?"

"It's me!" The door opened and her brother slipped triumphantly inside.

Lucy glanced past him as she closed the door. "Isn't there a guard?"

"They're busy putting everyone in the forepeak now," Liao said, climbing into her hammock. "Everyone but Cook, I think." He held up a little folding tool with a handful of attachments. "And your lock isn't difficult."

"Well done, you." Lucy ruffled his hair. "But keep your voice down. They'll set a guard eventually, and he shall be suspicious if he hears two voices in here."

"We're really taken, then?" Liao asked.

"Yes, I'm afraid so."

He shifted the folding tool from hand to hand. "And . . . Papa?"

Lucy shook her head slowly.

Liao reached for the end of his braided pigtail, and he worried it between thumb and forefinger for a moment. "Did you . . . see it? Was it very terrible?"

"I wish I hadn't." Lucy tried to think of a comforting lie with which to answer his second question, but when she spoke, the truth came out anyway. "It was like walking through fire."

"Now we haven't any parents left at all," Liao said in a vaguely confused voice. "Either of us."

"Well, we haven't any *parents*," Lucy replied haltingly, "but we have you and me. And we have the crew, which is a kind of family. We aren't alone."

Liao nodded, sniffling. He fumbled in his pockets and came up with something wrapped in one of Captain Bluecrowne's best linen napkins. "This is from Cook. He made me a bunk in the galley, since I can't sleep in Papa's cabin any longer." Lucy unwrapped the napkin. Toasted cheese and two fried eggs, sandwiched between two slices of hard bread to soak up the juices. She discovered she was ravenous.

"Mustn't we break you out, Lucy, before they set a guard here?" Liao asked, lowering his voice again. "You can slip out with me, and then I can open Max's door for him."

"Not yet," she said between mouthfuls. "Not until we have a plan for after we're out. The Americans will just put us right back in."

Liao nodded very seriously. "Well, couldn't we just go and let out all our friends once they start us sailing again? They'll need all hands to work the ship, won't they? Or you and Max can create a distraction, and I can go and let everyone out. Then we could have the ship back."

"No, that won't do." But as she spoke, she thought back to what Oliver Dexter had said in her father's cabin. *If she's going to demand this sort of thing from me, she'd certainly be willing to undertake something similar herself.* It was a bit troubling, the thought that perhaps she shouldn't have asked Dexter to do something she wasn't actually willing to do herself. If she was so sure he ought to be willing to sacrifice *his* honor, did that mean she ought to be willing to sacrifice hers, too?

Then Liao said something that sent a wholly different chill up her spine. "There's a French person aboard, you know. Six of them, actually. Cook told me."

Six Frenchmen had come aboard from the *Marie Colette*? "What sort of French people?"

Liao scratched his head. "I didn't see them. Cook said . . . just a minute, I shall remember exactly." Lucy made herself wait, counting slowly and silently while Liao tried to recall what he'd been told. She was very near shaking him when he finally spoke up. "He said, 'Spruce coats, not as who should say uniforms, but bleeding close to. Very spruce coves.' That's what he said, just exactly. Do you suppose they're some of Max's Frenchmen? Oh, and then he said, 'Six'd make for a sad'n, but she'll remember when we've sent fewer with a prize when it was that or let'n burn.' What's that mean?"

Her smile at Liao's efforts to reproduce the cook's accent along with his words faded. "He means there are enough Frenchmen aboard for a prize-crew, if somehow they were to take charge of the *Fate*." Now her brain launched into a series of calculations of how likely that was. But the unknown variable was the American crew, and she just didn't know enough about it—or its young acting-lieutenant—to come to any conclusions.

"All right, Liao," she said at last. "We've got to find out exactly who these French coves are and what the prize-captain intends to do about them. Then we shall know what we're up against, and what we must plan for."

"Huzzay!" Liao beamed the smile of a boy who's just been told a great adventure is afoot. The next bit, however, he wasn't going to like.

"Liao," she began apologetically, "I may need your help with some sort of infernal device, if it comes to that or the French taking our ship."

Her brother's smile fell away. He looked down at his fingers, which even at their cleanest had begun to take on the gray tone of a gunner's hands, permanently stained with powder. "A device . . . to hurt someone?"

"Well, you know I don't like asking . . ." But even as she spoke, she began to feel sick. *It won't come to that, to asking Liao to build a weapon*, she decided. *I won't let it.* "Never mind, Liao. Forget I asked, would you?"

"Forget?" he asked in the tiniest of voices.

"Forget." Lucy squeezed his hand. "Truly. But I need to know everything I can about the Frenchmen. And find out who else from our crew is still at liberty, other than Cook. Can you do that for me?"

Liao brightened. "Of course I can." He hopped out of the hammock and landed silently. "Shall I lock the door again?"

"I suppose." Lucy crouched to look through the keyhole again. There was still no guard to be seen. Liao gave her a quick hug, opened the door just enough to slip through, and disappeared.

If it came to it, Lucy decided as she listened to the sounds of her brother locking her in, sacrificing her honor would be infinitely easier than asking Liao to build a weapon. If that turned out to be the choice, well, then it would be a choice she could make without a single pang of conscience.

....

MR. CASCON ESCORTED CLOUTIER OUT OF THE CABIN AND UP TO the main deck. Not wanting to feel like a child following the adults, Oliver drank the rest of his coffee and counted to twenty before going up, too. The sky was beginning to lighten at last, and the *Marie Colette* drifted darkly against the grayness. But this was odd—she had sailed past the *Left-Handed Fate*, so that now she lay between the schooner and the mouth of the Chesapeake. The corvette was keeping a respectful distance, but Oliver's nerves were still tingling ominously as he joined his lieutenant and the Frenchman at the gunwale.

"Ah, Lieutenant. I am glad you have joined us," Cloutier said.

There was something wrong with his tone. Oliver's nerves jangled even faster. "Thank you for your visit," he said, holding out his hand. "It's a calm sea. You shouldn't have any trouble departing." He might have put a little more emphasis on the word *departing* than strictly necessary, but it was better than saying what he was really thinking, which was, *Just get off my ship already.*

Cloutier shook his hand uninterestedly, then made an unconvincingly apologetic face. "In fact, it is you who will depart, Lieutenant. You must stand down your crew—such as it is—and you may take one of the cutters to Norfolk."

Oliver goggled at him. "I beg your pardon?"

"This is a joke," Mr. Cascon said.

Cloutier shook his head. "Unless I give the *Marie Colette* the signal that you will relinquish the ship without fuss, she will engage, and she will certainly take you. And you see that you cannot get past her if she does not choose to let you pass." He shrugged gracefully. "I don't like this solution, but what this ship carries is too dangerous to leave in your hands, however briefly. My office will make all necessary explanations to your government and your superiors. I will send a letter."

"You'll *send a letter*?" Oliver repeated incredulously. Then he realized what else Cloutier had said. *What this ship carries is too dangerous* . . . The bottom of his stomach dropped out. This wasn't about French property. Oliver had been right: it was about a weapon. "You know," he said before he could stop himself.

"*You* know?" Cloutier demanded. "Well, then, my dear sir, then certainly you understand the situation." Then he beamed. "What a great relief. I should not have liked to point out that from the looks of things, the *Marie Colette* throws nearly twice the broadside weight of metal you do. Not that you have enough men to fire a broadside in any case."

The French ship was just out of range. The *Fate* could run, and she might well turn out to be the faster ship, but—blast it—Cloutier was right. With the *Marie Colette* blocking the way to Norfolk, the *Fate* would have to run farther out into the Atlantic. And even then, the *Marie Colette*, with a full crew to work her sails, would catch the undermanned *Fate* in no time flat.

And yet, Oliver discovered rather to his surprise that he wasn't going to yield. *I'm not surrendering the ship.* It wasn't a conscious choice so much as a realization, the awareness of a decision already made, and it flooded him with surprise and relief. *I'm not surrendering my ship.*

"So let me just clarify our position." He faced Cloutier with his back ramrod-straight and his palms clasped behind his back. *My hands aren't even shaking*, he thought with wonder. *This is amazing.* "If I do not surrender my ship to you, you will commit an act of war against a lawful prize of the United States Navy? An act of war, sir, against the United States of America?"

"I should not look at it like that," Cloutier said with an indulgent smile. "You are young, and no doubt you—"

"There is no other way to look at it, sir," Oliver snapped. "You are a French official. This is an American ship. If you fire upon us, you are firing upon the United States. Are you, in fact, threatening to fire upon us?"

"I should not like to—"

"Yes, yes, enough." Oliver grabbed the pistol that hung from his belt. It was the one he'd taken from the *Amaranthine*'s small-arms locker during the battle, and he wasn't quite sure he knew how to fire it, but he leveled it at Cloutier anyway. Well, *leveled* wasn't quite the word, as he had to point it up in order to aim it at the Frenchman's chest. "Clap the Frenchmen in irons," he shouted.

"Take 'em!" Mr. Cascon bellowed, diving for Cloutier even as the startled diplomat reached for his own weapon.

It was a peculiar thing about life aboard a ship; with so many people confined to such a small space, it took a certain amount of skill *not* to overhear conversations one wasn't part of. The rest of the prize-crew had been listening, and although not a man would've taken action without an order, they'd been waiting for one.

The five men in Cloutier's entourage clearly hadn't expected any resistance. There was a single gunshot from Cloutier himself before Mr. Cascon wrestled the pistol from him, but it did nothing more than whiz away overhead and out of sight, and then he and his men were prisoners.

"Don't be a fool," Cloutier snarled. He launched into a tirade in French aimed at Mr. Cascon, whose sole response was to spit derisively over the gunwale.

Oliver turned his attention toward the *Marie Colette*. She was on the move now. Another ten minutes, maybe, and then shots would be fired.

"Prisoners taken below, sir." Mr. Cascon's voice was thick with relief and worry in equal measure. "Could be he was just bluffing. What you said is true: if she fired on us, it'd be an act of war."

"I suppose," Oliver said. But if Max Ault's theoretical engine *was* some sort of weapon, then Cloutier likely wasn't bluffing in the slightest.

Mr. Cascon was eyeing him closely. "Sir, he said something about what this ship is carrying. It's not my place to ask, but—"

Oliver kept his eyes on the oncoming ship. "He thinks the ship is carrying part of a weapon. I think they won't sink us, but they'll do everything in their power to take us." Mr. Cascon swore under his breath, which Oliver took to mean he agreed with the assessment.

They were running out of time. Oliver thought hard. "Where is Lucy Bluecrowne confined?"

Mr. Cascon put on another of those wary looks. "Sir—"

"There's no time. Where is she?"

....

JUST AS THE *FATE* WAS TOO SMALL FOR CLOUTIER'S THREATS above to go unheard by the prize-crew, the ship was also too small for six protesting Frenchmen to be confined in the cabins across the aft platform without Lucy and Max hearing the commotion.

Max rapped on their shared wall. "Lucy! Can you make out what's going on?"

"It seems they've taken charge of the Frenchmen." Another knock sounded, this time against the door. "Come in," Lucy called, surprised.

The door swung open, and the prize-captain stepped inside. "The corvette is bearing down on us," Oliver Dexter said without preamble. "She will fire on us when she's in range."

"*I told you!*"

He raised his voice over hers and kept on talking. "I was offered the chance to surrender the *Fate* and her cargo peacefully—"

"No, you can't, you *mustn't*—" Lucy's voice was almost drowned out by Max's frantic banging on the wall.

"—*and I refused!*" Dexter shouted over the commotion.

She slumped. "Oh, thank heaven. Max, *shut up!*"

"So I—" Dexter glared at her, insulted. "Why does everyone think I'll give up the confounded ship, just because someone tells me to?"

"I beg your pardon, sir."

He shook his head. "A prize-crew can't take on a fully manned corvette. I need your help."

Aha. Just when she'd thought the game was up, the blasted French had given her another bargaining piece. Hope leapt in her chest. Hope, and calculation.

He must've seen the cunning plain on her face. "This is not a negotiation. And even if I were willing to negotiate, there isn't time. Ten minutes, she'll be in range."

"What would you have me do?"

The boy took a deep breath. "I will put the *Left-Handed Fate* into your hands, and you and your crew will fight off the corvette.

We will give whatever support you require. After that, you will have your parole again, and we'll discuss what happens next."

"You mean—"

"I mean we'll discuss it," he said curtly. "I make no promises, except that you'll have your parole. But you'll promise right this minute to give me back the ship afterward. Otherwise I have no choice but to surrender to the French right now."

"Done," Lucy said, the grin already working its way over her face. "You have yourself a crew, Mr. Dexter. Shall we see about trouncing a corvette?"

"If you please." Dexter took her outstretched hand and shook it.

Still not quite believing her luck, Lucy darted out of her cabin, up the ladderway, across the weather deck, and down again to the fore platform, where, at the very front of the ship, the rest of the Fates were being held in the forepeak. When she arrived, the guard, who must've been forewarned about Dexter's proposition, unlocked the door and stepped aside. Lucy stood in the open doorway staring at her father's crew. *My crew,* she corrected herself. *My family.*

"Fates," she said, her voice cracking a little with the sudden weight of emotion in it, "our old friend *Marie Colette*'s in the offing." The grimy faces before her broke into an assortment of wide smiles. "We are still prisoners, but we may keep from being totally lost. And we can wipe *Marie Colette*'s eye, which I suspect would take a bit of the sting out of this situation."

A rumble of laughter now, a scattering of *aye, miss*es and, even more encouragingly, *aye aye, miss*es. *Aye aye,* the affirmative reserved for replying to superior officers.

"I am not my father," Lucy said, "and you did not come aboard to fight and die at *my* side. But if you can trust me as I trust you, we may win the day yet, prisoners or no." She took a deep breath, trying to raise the ghost of her father near enough to channel some of his authority, some of their love for him, some of the strength she felt certain she must have inherited, without giving in to the weight of the ache of his loss and without thinking of him dead on the deck or sewn into a sail with roundshot at his feet.

Captains do not cry.

She raised her voice to a shout. "What say you, Fates? Shall we be Furies this day?"

The roar of their reply was deafening, although it was hard to believe anything could top the pounding of Lucy's own heart. Relief surged over her, but only for a second. There was no time for sentiment now.

"Mr. Prim, Mr. Harrick, Mr. Wooll," she shouted. The bosun, the gunner, the sailing master, and their mates were already pushing their way through the rest to report. "Ship cleared for battle and company ready to fight in five minutes." She turned to the master, whose task it was to oversee the navigation and sailing of the ship. "With me, Mr. Wooll."

He touched his knuckles to his forehead. "Aye aye, miss."

"And if there's a few hands to be spared, I want the figurehead back on the prow before the first shot's fired."

Mr. Wooll's lined face broke into a grin. "Aye *aye*, miss!"

Lucy broke onto the weather deck just ahead of the Fates, shading her eyes from the rising sun as she and Mr. Wooll sprinted aft to join Dexter on the quarterdeck. "So?" he demanded.

Lucy gulped air to calm her breathing and nodded at the deck. "Watch."

The Fates came pouring up the forward ladderway. Dozens of sailors swarmed up the ratlines to man the sails with Mr. Wooll's mates barking at them from below. The gun crews rushed to their pieces as Mr. Harrick and his mates passed through to find out which crews had lost men in the engagement with the *Amaranthine*. The main hatch was opened, and up through the center of the deck came the tools of gunnery: tubs of smoldering slow-match, butts of water, fresh powder charges.

And then a familiar shape rose up from the hold. Emotion heaved, tidal, through every inch of Lucy's body. "There she is."

"There what—" Dexter followed her gaze. "What is—is that a figurehead?"

Lucy nodded. "If this is the last time we fight as masters of this ship, we're taking her into battle whole." She glanced briefly at Dexter, who was staring after the carved woman with a curious expression. Did he recognize it?

But there was no time to waste in wondering. Lucy looked to the master. "Take charge of giving the orders, Mr. Wooll, if you please; you and Mr. Harrick. Batter the will out of the *Marie Colette* and . . ."

She hesitated. The French ship stood between the *Fate* and Norfolk. It would be so easy, especially now with the crew already out and in command of the ship, to just take her out into the Atlantic, and then south toward Nagspeake.

So easy.

Lucy sighed. "Batter the will out of the *Marie Colette*, and take us to Norfolk."

twelve
THE *SINISTER FURY*

The noise of the Fates emerging from the forepeak and surging through the ship was like a herd of elephants thundering up and down a wooden staircase. The clatter was not a normal sound aboard the *Left-Handed Fate*, but the roaring that accompanied it was. That was the sound of battle coming on.

The discussion between Lucy and Oliver Dexter had been audible through the thin wall, of course. But long minutes after all that noise had dissipated, nobody came to let Max out. He sighed. It was probably for the best. He would only have been in the way.

He heard the first shot from the corvette. Then he felt the ship turn, and hard. Max looked instinctively around for anything breakable that might not be tied down, then grabbed his hammock for balance. Then came the unimaginable wave of noise, painful noise, head-crushing noise, as the *Fate*'s broadside erupted, the sound amplified as it ricocheted and resonated through the wooden hull. The schooner lurched, and Max bounced off his hammock and sprawled to the floor.

Up above, smoke would be wreathing the firing side of the ship, and the crews would be readying their guns for the next broadside. He started counting seconds as he got back to his feet. When he got to fifty, instinct went against his better judgment and he let go of the hammock to clap his hands over his ears. The broadside exploded again, throwing Max back to the floor.

In the relative hush that followed, a scrabbling noise sounded at his door. After all the clash and clamor, the softness of this new sound was oddly shocking in its own way.

And then, out of nowhere, a violet-blue flame crackled to life on the latch that served as a door handle. It was precisely the same sort of light as the ones that had flickered into being on the street in Fells Point.

Max stared at the flame, horrified. *May no new thing arise*, Captain Bluecrowne had liked to say. This certainly counted as new. They'd seen corposants aboard the *Fate* before, but only just before the ship crewed by the men in black appeared—and then only up above, at the tops of the masts. Never below.

Meanwhile, the scrabbling stopped and the latch lifted. "Why are you lying down?" Liao demanded. "Get up, Max! Hurry!"

"Oh, thank God," Max breathed, scrambling to his feet with Liao plucking at his shirt as if somehow that would hurry the process along. "How is it up above?"

Liao gave him an injured look. "You know I never go up there when they're fighting. Come on!" Then he turned toward the door and saw the dancing violet flame. "Here, too?"

"What do you mean, *here, too?*"

"They're everywhere. It's why I came to get you." Liao grabbed his sleeve again and tugged toward the door. Up above, the commands of the gun captains were muffled shouts broken by the thunder of the guns being hauled against their ports. Both Liao and Max grabbed for handholds just in time for the next explosion, which was a ripple of smaller bursts rather than a single massive concussion. Soon the crews would be firing at will, just as fast as they could reload and aim.

The lower deck ordinarily smelled fuggy, dank, and mildewed. But not now. Now the air was dry, almost prickling-dry, and it felt alive, as if with an electrical charge. Max staggered out of the cabin after Liao, then stopped cold. "What do you think it is?" Liao whispered. "It's beautiful."

Unnerving was the word Max would've chosen. He and Liao were alone on the platform, which was bizarre to begin with. Privacy didn't exist aboard the schooner; there were too many people and there was too little space. The solitude alone gave Max a creeping feeling of the uncanny. And then there were the corposants.

The below-decks gloom was gently lit by tiny violet-blue lights that flitted along the handles of the doors of the cabins that lined both sides of the passage. Liao nodded forward, and Max turned toward the well that separated the fore and aft platforms. "Oh my God," he murmured.

It was as if an indigo twilight were shining up out of the hold. Max walked slowly toward the railing at the end of the aft platform and looked down.

Hundreds, maybe thousands of corposants lit the hold nearly as bright as day. They danced at the corners of crates. They twitched ominously at the ends of old spars. Several slid along the edges of stacked barrels like tiny satellites traversing wooden orbits.

"I tried to put one out." Liao pointed to a nearby flame. "I tried smothering it, dousing it with water—I tried everything I could think of, and nothing would do. But look." He passed a hand through it, batting Max away as he instinctively moved to keep the boy from reaching into the flame. "It's not hot. It doesn't burn at all." Liao waved his undamaged fingers. "*Nothing's* burning. I checked. The first

thing I did was to go down and make sure the powder magazine wasn't on fire and about to blow us all out of the water."

"Good thing." Max walked cautiously into the eerie light. So much fire, so much wood, and so much gunpowder—and yet Liao was right. Where the little corposants burned, there was no char, not even a burning scent to mark the spot. The ones that moved seemed to flow across surfaces as easily as skimmer bugs on a river, leaving nothing to show where they had been. "Liao, you know something about things like this, don't you?"

"Yes, but there are so many kinds of fire." The boy's expression was a mix of wariness and excitement. "I've seen fire that doesn't seem to harm the thing it sits upon, but if you held it too long, it would burn you eventually. Like the fire I gave you before. But these really aren't burning *anything*. It's not the same at all."

"We'd best let someone know, I suppose," Max said helplessly.

"Had I better stay and keep an eye on them?" Liao asked, his eyes still glittering with reflected violet fire.

"I think so, yes. But suppose you keep an eye on the one in my cabin? Since that's where . . ." He hesitated. "You know." *Since that's where the cards are.*

Liao nodded. "Yes, of course."

When he finally emerged onto the weather deck, Max found himself stumbling into a whirlwind of hellfire and activity. Voices shouted orders from both aloft and alow, and the air was thick with smoke and the smell of hot gunmetal. Overhead, the gray dawn was turning into an equally gray overcast morning, promising what the sailors called dirty weather.

Max hurried aft, remembering to pick his way through the center of the ship, where he was least likely to be run over by a recoiling gun carriage. The four people on the quarterdeck—Lucy,

Dexter, the sailing master, and the silver-haired French-American sailor, Mr. Cascon—gave him the briefest of looks and then went back to whatever they had been doing. Then came a noise from across the water, and someone dragged him to the floor. Lucy's eyes bored into his as chain shot whipped through the rigging overhead, splitting rope and sails with an assortment of taut, almost musical zinging sounds.

She grinned. "That's the best they've managed so far, and it's hardly what you'd call crack shooting." She got to her feet and helped Max to his. "You look like you've seen a ghost."

"Lucy," Max said, "I think we're about to—"

"Sail ahoy!" The lookout's cry cut right through the noise on the deck. Max's stomach churned. It had to be, it could *only* be, the ship of the men in black. The hundreds of corposants below couldn't be there by coincidence.

....

"WHERE AWAY?" LUCY GRABBED OLIVER'S TELESCOPE AND surveyed the horizon. "Apologies, sir." Then she swore. "It's them."

"It's who?" Oliver demanded, snatching his telescope back. There was a brig out there, far off to the east where no ship had been, as suddenly and inexplicably as if it had risen straight out of the water. At least, Oliver *thought* no ship had been there. He had been watching the Fates work their ship like a fine instrument of war, maneuvering so quickly and efficiently that even though the *Marie Colette* had the wind on her side, the *Fate* was always in the better position to fire. And the privateers' gunnery was just remarkable. It was miraculous to behold, especially since, in the absence of a captain, the person in charge was Lucy. But while Oliver might have been distracted, if the lookout was as good as everyone else aboard this ship, it didn't make sense that *he* hadn't spotted the brig before now.

"Impossible," Mr. Wooll muttered. The sailing master was visibly shaken.

Max Ault cleared his throat. "There are corposants below. Hundreds of them. Mr. Dexter, do you remember the Saint Elmo's lights in Fells Point?"

Oliver nodded and looked up to see if similar flames had popped into existence among the yards without his noticing them.

"Well, that's what it looks like belowdecks right now. A thousand little flames. More, even. Everywhere."

"The schooner is *on fire*?" Lucy demanded, lowering her voice to a horrified whisper.

"No, no—nothing is burning," Max said quickly. "But when I saw the lights below, I was afraid that it meant *they* might turn up again."

"You know that brig, then?" Oliver asked.

Lucy nodded. "One of our pursuers. She's been following us for half a year."

"Is she French?"

"We don't know. We've never seen her run up a flag, and she's always come upon us quite alone."

A long and rending crack sounded overhead: thunder breaking through the heavens over the Atlantic. The sky was darkening, too, as if an early dusk were falling in the wake of that rolling thunder.

"Dirty weather coming, on top of all," Mr. Cascon muttered. "Not bad for us, if this wind holds." He reached over to scratch a nearby line in the rigging for luck, but the wind chose that moment to die away to a charged hush. Everyone on the quarterdeck swore, and all but Max shot Mr. Cascon wrathful looks for mentioning the need for a favorable wind out loud, thereby guaranteeing the opposite.

But the sudden stillness that becalmed both the *Marie Colette* and the *Left-Handed Fate* did not seem to affect the brig. She was still flying at them with all the appearance of a crisp breeze in her sails.

"Where is she finding that wind?" Oliver grumbled.

"She's never without a wind," Lucy said grimly. "And we've seen her top sixteen knots before."

"Sixteen knots?" Oliver said, aghast. It was a near-impossible speed, sixteen nautical miles per hour. A fast schooner like the *Fate* might just manage it for a heartbeat under the exactly right conditions, but a brig? Not likely.

The French corvette fired again, but now that the wind had died, the ships were drifting too far apart. Oliver watched the shot skip harmlessly across the water as the first drops of rain began to fall. He looked at the becalmed *Marie Colette*, which still stood between the *Fate* and the Chesapeake. Then he looked at the brig, still rushing toward them on a course to cut them off. It was as if the universe itself were driving Oliver deeper into the Atlantic, farther and farther from where he needed to go.

"We shall have to go south," he said helplessly. "There is no other choice."

A forked bolt of lightning cut across the forbidding sky, followed by another tearing crack of thunder. The rain began to pour as if floodgates had been torn open overhead, and the wind that had been carrying the brig hit the *Fate* hard, flinging her right over on her side.

Then the schooner was off, flying southward, with Mr. Wooll shouting orders and the seamen in the rigging furling sails in response faster than Oliver would've thought possible. The *Marie Colette* found the wind, too, and she came plunging down after them, nowhere near as fast but firing all the while. And in the midst of this, the brig chased both ships, faster than the corvette, and possibly—impossibly—making nearly the speed of the *Fate*. Then, as she took up a parallel course to the schooner, the brig fired.

She was still just out of range, and her roundshot came skipping across the water to thud harmlessly against the *Fate*'s hull. But the guns had been double-shotted—the brig's gun crews had loaded two balls to each cannon for extra destructive power, and they had plainly aimed for the hull.

"Well," Lucy said briskly, "that's new. She's always gone for the rigging before, like the corvette."

"What's different now?" Oliver asked.

"The corvette, of course," Max said after a moment. "This is the first time the brig's engaged us with another ship present."

"So they'll sink us if the alternative is someone else taking the *Fate*." Oliver eyed the brig rushing along at its improbable speed. "Who are they? Other than the French, who else knows about this miraculous thing you're after?" But he was beginning to have the first inkling of an idea.

"Down!" somebody shrieked. Everyone dove for the deck as shots from the French ship whistled just over their heads.

"Her aim's improving," Lucy grumbled.

Oliver banged a hand on the deck and got to his feet. "I know how we can slow up the *Marie Colette*. Can your men hoist out the dinghy while we're running like this?"

"They will if they have to. Why?"

"Let's put the Frenchmen over the side. The *Marie Colette* will have to stop and pick them up. We had better do it before the brig comes in range, though."

"I love it," Lucy said with relish. "All but the part where we give them a boat, but I suppose that's only the humane thing to do."

Cloutier and his prize-crew were brought up swearing. "This is madness," Cloutier snarled as the Fates shoved him toward the little boat. "It will overturn! We'll drown! You will have murdered a consular—"

"If the boat capsizes, just hold on until your ship comes for you." Oliver shrugged. "But if you can't swim, that's your own problem."

He watched without emotion as the Frenchmen were forced into the dinghy in the choppy water. The boat, somewhat miraculously, did not capsize as it shot along in the *Fate*'s wake. The corvette passed it, then began rapidly to shift its sails to go back and rescue the frantic, gesticulating occupants.

"That leaves us the brig," Lucy said, chewing her thumbnail. "And I don't see much to do but keep on running like smoke and oakum and hope the weather helps us survive until nightfall, when we might lose her in the dark."

"I suspect I know who she is," Oliver said. Among seagoing folk, certain ships, certain captains, and certain battles became legend quickly. There was Oliver's idol Stephen Decatur, for example, who had been a hero before Oliver was born and was still a hero today— and whom he might have met in person, had the *Amaranthine* managed to join the squadron in New York without incident. There was his own father, Commodore Underby. There were any number of famous British captains and vessels. And there was the ship known as the *Sinister Fury*.

The only thing anyone knew for certain was that the *Sinister Fury* was a privateer. By some reports she was British, by some reports she was Dutch, and some said she was a true mercenary and would serve anyone who paid enough. But no one who had ever run into her had been able to catch her. She fired first, she fired devastatingly, she made her captures, and then she disappeared.

Lucy Bluecrowne was staring at him. "You *know* that brig?"

Oliver nodded somberly. "There is a ship I've heard of—only I thought she was just a myth." He swallowed. "The *Sinister Fury.*"

There was a moment of silence. Then Lucy burst into laughter. "I beg your pardon, sir," she sighed at last, wiping her eyes.

"Why is that funny?" Oliver demanded.

She grinned. "You've forgotten your mythology. And possibly you've also let your Latin go, Mr. Dexter." And she wiggled her right hand in the air.

Oliver looked at her blankly.

"It's Latin." Lucy waved her right hand harder. *"Dexter."* She waved her left. *"Sinister.* Right: dexter. Left: sinister. I suppose technically a *fate* is not the same as a *fury,* mythologically speaking; but then, we're sailors here, not scholars."

Realization dawned. "No." Oliver felt his face go red. *The figurehead.* "Oh, no. But you said—"

Lucy nodded, still grinning. "I said you were aboard the *Left-Handed Fate.* Yes, Mr. Dexter. You are the acting-commander of the *Sinister Fury,* although obviously *we* don't call her that. It's a name for enemies to use." Her smile disappeared and she pointed at the brig. "And that is the only ship that has ever really challenged us. Pray we escape her again this time."

thirteen
WHAT IS BEAUTIFUL
AND WHAT IS NOT

The *Left-Handed Fate* spent that whole strange, awful day flee-ing from her two pursuers. Somewhere along the way, the murky morning became midday, and then afternoon. Sometime after dark, when at last they seemed to have lost the brig, Oliver Dexter summoned Lucy and Max to his cabin.

Dexter's French crewman, Mr. Cascon, opened the door for them. "Please have a drink and something to eat," the prize-captain said. "But quickly. I want to get back on deck."

"Thank you." Lucy's entire being ached as she reached for the coffeepot and a biscuit.

"I want to be sure there isn't going to be any unpleasantness when this chase is over," Dexter continued, inconveniently waiting until both her mouth and Max's were full. "And I want to know exactly what we're carrying."

Max swallowed and glanced uncomfortably at Mr. Cascon, who stood impassively at the door like a sentinel. "Have you reconsidered what we discussed, at all?"

"Why would I have reconsidered?" Dexter asked forbiddingly.

"Well," Max said, and fell silent.

"It's a weapon, isn't it?" the younger boy asked.

Lucy stopped breathing for a moment. "No, it isn't," Max said unconvincingly.

Dexter rolled his eyes. "It's the only answer that makes sense. You said you'd answer more questions if I had them. So, what are we carrying?"

Max coughed and nodded his head pointedly back at Mr. Cascon.

"If I wanted Cascon out of the room, I'd have asked him to leave," Dexter said, exasperated. "Quit wasting time."

"Max, tell him," Lucy said shortly. If ever there was a time to speak the truth, this was that time. They were running in the right direction at last, and the Fates couldn't be sent back to confinement now, not while Dexter needed every hand to keep up this speed. If they had to—she felt ill even thinking it, but if they absolutely *had to*—her crew could take the ship back in a heartbeat.

"Fine. Well, you're right," Max said. "My father believed that the engine his discovery described was an incredibly potent weapon, one that could bring the wars to a permanent end. He believed the threat of it alone would be sufficient to discourage armed conflict . . . well, forever."

"What sort of weapon?" Dexter asked, puzzled. "What on earth sort of weapon could do *that*?"

"I don't know," Max admitted. "The description my father found is quite arcane and terribly vague—I gather the rest of the details are encoded somehow in the three scattered pieces the text alluded to."

"But certainly it would have to be . . ." Dexter hesitated. "A thing like a rocket or a Fulton torpedo, do you mean? Some sort of infernal device?"

Max shook his head. "You're thinking too small. You're thinking of weapons that could destroy a single vessel. Think instead of a weapon that could destroy an entire navy at once. An entire army. An entire *nation*, even."

The boy was silent for a moment. "I can't," he admitted at last.

"I know," Max said, nodding. "I don't believe it would be like anything anyone has right now. Perhaps not like anything we have a way to *imagine* right now."

Lucy sat silently during this exchange, watching Oliver Dexter go through probably the same mental acrobatics she'd gone through when her father had first explained this mission to her. It was a hard concept to wrap one's head around. But her patience had its limits. "You see what they're willing to do to win this war," she said at last. "The French, I mean—present company excepted, I suppose," she said with a grudging glance at Mr. Cascon. "They were willing to take your ship, even without a declaration of war between you. Please, *please* consider what we're fighting against."

"You're fighting against *us*," Dexter protested. "You're at war with *us*, largely because *you* were willing to take our ships and kidnap our sailors without a declaration of war."

Impressment again. Lucy groaned.

"But we weren't actually *fighting* against you until you declared war on us," Max said cautiously. "The main thing we're fighting is France, and Napoleon Bonaparte. His intelligencers are after this machine, too. We must have it first."

"But they aren't at war with the United States," Dexter persisted. "Despite what happened today."

"Even after France tries to take your ship against all international law, you're still sticking up for them," Lucy grumbled. "Unbelievable."

"May I say something else?" Max asked. "The goal here is not just to use the machine to defeat France. It's just as important to

141

keep France from having that machine. Napoleon Bonaparte is on a mission to conquer the world. Europe is only the beginning. If he succeeds in Europe, how long do you think it will be before he turns his attention to the Americas? He's already tried once. And even if you cannot imagine the weapon itself, can you imagine that much power in the hands of someone with that much ambition?"

"Britain has plenty of ambition, too," Dexter grumbled. "I'm pretty sure you lot would colonize the world if you could."

"And America wouldn't?" Lucy retorted. "Didn't you just buy half of the the North American continent from the French? And it's not as if you were the first ones to live on that bit of land, either."

Max actually swatted her on the arm to shut her up. "Would you give an all-powerful weapon to Napoleon Bonaparte, Mr. Dexter? Yes or no."

Dexter glowered at him for an aggravatingly long time without saying a word. Lucy counted silently to six, and when she couldn't take the silence a moment longer, said, "Bonaparte is the greater evil, Dexter. If you don't believe me, ask your man there." And she turned and pointed to Mr. Cascon.

....

OLIVER WAS SURPRISED, BUT FOR HIS PART, THE BOSUN'S MATE looked as though he had been expecting this for some time. And yes, Oliver, too, had been half-expecting some kind of confrontation between Lucy and Mr. Cascon, because after someone—even a girl—has yanked a sword from the wall and pointed it at you, you have to consider the possibility that she might just be capable of anything. And Lucy certainly hated France. But Lucy calling on a French expatriate in support of England?

"Tell him," Lucy said. "Tell him why you left the French navy."

Mr. Cascon looked at her evenly. "I wasn't in the navy. But if you must know, I left because of the Vendée."

A momentary silence fell. "What is the Vendée?" Oliver asked.

Mr. Cascon turned to him. "Permission to speak freely, sir?"

"Of . . . of course."

Mr. Cascon was quiet for a moment. When he spoke again, his first words were directed at Max. "Pay attention: In the beginning, a politician called Robespierre stood up in Paris and said, *France is for peace.* And then France went to war, with itself and with everyone else, to bring that peace to the world. The Revolution in France, the civil war in the Vendée, the Terror and the reign of Madame Guillotine, Bonaparte's rise and twenty years of battle—all of it began with the idea of renouncing war."

Max was now looking distinctly uncomfortable. Oliver couldn't blame him.

Mr. Cascon rubbed a hand over the lower half of his face. "There is a place on the coast of France called the Vendée. It is true that there were rebels and royalists there, and it is true that at first, when armies went in to subdue the region, both sides were terrible. We—" He paused, shook his head. "It does not do to dwell on what we did to each other there. The armies of the Republic subjugated the rebels, but what it took . . ." He stopped speaking again. He did not shudder, or tremble; he merely aimed eyes as glassy and blank as those of a just-killed fish at the opposite wall of the cabin.

"Best not to think about that," he continued at last. "The Republican army defeated the rebels of the Vendée . . . but they never stopped fighting them."

Max cleared his throat. "I've read some of what was written in those days. The sentiment must've lived on for a long time after."

"I don't mean they never stopped fighting *figuratively*," Mr. Cascon said shortly. "I mean real combat. It was as if the fact of life remaining in the Vendée meant the rebellion lived on, too. As if geography alone defined every man, woman, and child there as an enemy of the state, whether they were truly rebels or not."

He leaned back against the wall, aiming his dead-fish eyes on the ceiling. "The Republican Revolutionaries had another constant problem: they could never be sure who was loyal and who was just pretending in order to keep from being executed. There were some who would call for the death of a general if he wasn't victorious enough, or violent enough. They called this sin *moderation*, and it was a very grave sin indeed. Therefore, many generals attempted to prove their loyalty with blood. Some of these generals found themselves fighting in the Vendée."

He paused, opened his mouth, closed it again, and shook his head once before continuing. "I will not tell you what they did, the ones who issued the most vile orders. I will not tell you what their soldiers did, the ones who obeyed. But if you passed a house still standing on the road, it was best not to look in. Or into the ditches along the sides of the roads. Or anywhere, really, other than at the back of the man marching in front of you."

"You couldn't look . . ." Oliver began, confused. Then he got it. "Oh."

Mr. Cascon nodded. "You have it, sir."

Oliver began to feel sick.

"In two months, more Vendeans were killed than would go to the guillotine in the entire year of the Terror. And this *after* the true rebels in the Vendée had been defeated. And still that wasn't the worst of it."

"So these weren't rebels who were . . . making it so you couldn't look anywhere?" Oliver asked in a small voice. "The other army was killing men who *weren't even fighting*?"

Mr. Cascon shrugged. "I suppose there might've been a handful of true rebels still scattered about, but no more. And it wasn't only men the armies were killing. It was said the women and children over twelve were the cruelest rebels of all, so they were considered combatants, too. Some generals didn't specify that anyone at all of any age was to be spared."

Now Oliver really felt sick, but Mr. Cascon wasn't done. "Then came General Turreau, who gave these orders: *All will be put to the sword.* But his men took too many prisoners for that, or for the guillotine, which is slow since it can kill but one at a time, and firing squads wasted too many bullets. So they piled captives by the thousands into barges, and just sank them in the river." Mr. Cascon rubbed his jaw. Were his fingers shaking? "Then, of course, came the Terror."

Oliver held his breath, afraid of what was coming next. Even he had heard stories about the final chapter of the French Revolution, the part called the Reign of Terror. But when Mr. Cascon spoke again, he sounded almost dismissive. "I've heard the guillotine took forty thousand lives during that year, but after the *hundreds* of thousands that died in the Vendée, the Terror seemed . . . small, somehow. Insignificant."

The room was still for a moment. What would it take to make forty thousand dead seem insignificant? Oliver tore his eyes away from Mr. Cascon to glance at Lucy. She and Max both looked as horrified as he felt.

"A few years after that, the young general Napoleon Bonaparte rose up and took power, and after all that bloodshed to become a republic, France became an empire instead. And here we are." Mr. Cascon studied Lucy. "Have I answered your question?"

"You were there?" Lucy asked softly. "I'm very sorry. Did your family survive?"

Mr. Cascon uttered a short, pained laugh. "I was not in the *rebel* army, Miss Bluecrowne."

Lucy and Max went pale as milk. Oliver wondered if it was vertigo he was feeling, or if the whole world had really turned upside-down.

Mr. Cascon shared a rueful smile out among the three of them. "It is very easy to be convinced that war requires terrible choices, that sometimes one must burn a village to save it." He looked at Lucy. "You asked why I left. I once saw a very young, very fearful soldier hesitate in following an order. My general was not *moderate*. He had no patience for squeamishness. He ran the boy through with his sword, and then he turned to the soldier beside him and said, '*Il est beau de périr.*' It's from a poem. It means, 'It is beautiful to die.' The soldier he said it to was fourteen years old. The one he killed couldn't have been much older." His expression darkened. "It is *not* beautiful to die, but that boy's hesitation was beautiful. He'd been given a monstrous order. In that one moment of misgiving, he was braver than I. And so I left.

"I would have liked to believe France could be changed from within. But our leaders worked hard to destroy the distinction between citizens and soldiers. *All French citizens are the army*, they said. A truly military people. And the generals whipped their soldiers into a fervor until they gathered their patriotism about them like cloaks and went off to conquer and kill and die."

"But not everyone believed all that," Oliver protested. "Did they?"

"No, that is true," Mr. Cascon agreed. "Many disagreed, and certainly not *all* of them were executed."

"But what about now?" Oliver asked, desperate to find some hint of why so many people in the United States seemed to be so eager to side with France. "I'm sure Bonaparte is nothing like the Republican generals, is he? They're all gone now, aren't they?"

Mr. Cascon gave a small sound, halfway between a snort and a sigh. "But Bonaparte *was* a Republican general. Not one of the worst, perhaps, but one of them. And yes, many of the worst revolutionary generals were later tried for their crimes. But many were acquitted. The one who ordered the murder of every soul in the Vendée, for example?" Mr. Cascon gave Oliver a half-smile. "He was Bonaparte's ambassador to the United States when Mr. Jefferson purchased the Louisiana Territory from France."

"But—" How on earth had his own country decided a man like that made an acceptable ambassador?

"If you really wanted to fight to change things in France, you should've come to England, not here," Lucy said. "They love Bonaparte here."

"It was said when I was a boy that young French republicans must suck hatred of the name of *Englishman* with their mothers' milk," Mr. Cascon said evenly. "I do not pretend I am without bias." He hesitated. "*France* is not bloodthirsty. *France* is not evil. *France* is not the problem—bloodthirsty and evil men and women *in* France are the problem." He gave Lucy a sharp glare. "Someday I'll fight for my country again."

"How old were you?" Max asked. "When you left?"

"*Escaped* is perhaps the better word," Mr. Cascon replied. "And I was fourteen. I fled the night after the general told me it was beautiful to die."

"That was *you*?" Oliver wasn't sure which was more shocking: the idea that Mr. Cascon had fought for Robespierre's side in the nightmarish civil war he'd described, or that he'd been barely older than Oliver at the time. That would make Mr. Cascon . . . he did rapid math. Thirty-two? Oliver had been sure he was *ancient*. Fifty, at least. He took in Mr. Cascon's colorless hair and deep-lined face. Perhaps the lines could be explained by years at sea—sun and wind and salt water did that to everyone, eventually—but the hair?

He hadn't realized he was staring until Mr. Cascon ran a hand through the silver that lay on his forehead. "I'm not the only one who went white from the things I saw." He turned to Lucy again. "How did you know I'd served in France?"

Lucy shook her head, still pale. "It was only a guess." She shuddered, then faced Oliver again. "So the question remains: would you give Max's weapon to France as she is now? To Bonaparte?"

"No, I should not like Bonaparte to have this great mythical device of war, if it really exists." Oliver licked his lips. "You said you have one piece here already," he said at last. "Show it to me."

"All right." Max got to his feet, and Mr. Cascon opened the door for them. As she passed Mr. Cascon, Lucy paused and put one hand on his arm for a moment, then hurried out without another word.

Oliver paused in the doorway, too. "Thank you," he said. Mr. Cascon nodded, but it looked like he might want a few minutes alone. "Please wait here for me. There's some coffee left."

"Yes, sir. Thank you."

....

THE AFT PLATFORM WAS STILL LIT BY THE GHOSTLY ILLUMINATION of the Saint Elmo's lights. Passing sailors moved around the corposants fearfully, crossing themselves and spitting for luck each time they had to approach one or touch anything also touched by the little lights. Lucy, still shaken from Mr. Cascon's account, found it impossible to focus on anything but the tiny flames as Max led Oliver Dexter to his cabin, speaking all the while.

"At the end of the last century," he began, "Napoleon set out for Africa to conquer Egypt. He took soldiers, philosophers, historians, men of languages, artists . . . It was evidently a very strange and wonderful and terrible time, and many treasures were found. A great number of the antiquities were handed over to England after what remained of Napoleon's army left Egypt. My father was brought in by the British Museum to examine them, and one tablet in particular caught his attention."

Liao stood at Max's door like a guard. At a nod from Max, he opened the cabin door, and they all wedged themselves inside. Dexter took in without comment the sight of the scores of violet lights that now illuminated Max's cabin, too, but behind his enviable calm, his eyes were frightened.

Max continued as if they weren't all standing awkwardly close to one another waiting for him to get to the point. "In those days, Egyptian writing was such a mystery that my father was certain he was the only one to have managed a translation. But the tablet had caught a French scholar's attention as well, and it was never supposed to have been surrendered to Britain. Someone had made a mistake, and I feel quite sorry for that fellow, whoever he was. I don't imagine they let him live."

"So this device is Egyptian?" Dexter's eyes kept darting around at the spectacle of the corposants, which were thicker in Max's cabin than they were out in the passage. His calm was deteriorating, and now he looked like he wanted to swat at them like flies. Lucy couldn't blame him.

"It could be, but my father thought the Egyptian engraver was writing of something out of the past, the way we write of the Egyptians today."

"And you have the engraving here?"

"No. I have my father's notes, and these." Max opened the crate and lifted the first long, flat rectangle from the stack of cards. Violet light glinted through its pattern of rectangular holes.

Dexter leaned close for a better look. "What are they?"

"Loom-cards. Weavers use them to make elaborate images in fabric. The punches contain the instructions that direct the loom."

The boy scratched his head. "How did we get from an Egyptian stone to weavers?"

"The engraving described three elements of the device: three pieces that had been scattered ages before. The French scholar had already begun the search for them. He convinced Bonaparte that he could build a weapon no army could withstand, and Bonaparte gave him every resource he asked for." Max nodded into the crate. "He found these in Venice. Then he told Bonaparte they needed a machine to read them. They found a weaver who had been an officer during the Revolution, a brilliant inventor named Jacquard. Jacquard went on to invent a loom that just happens to read its patterns from a chain of punched cards."

"And did he manage to read these cards?"

Max shook his head. "Jacquard was still working on that when . . . well."

Dexter rolled his eyes. "When you stole them?"

"All right, yes. Or rather, my father did. The cards had been put aboard a French ship, and my father hired the *Left-Handed Fate* to find it."

"All right." Dexter gave the card one last curious look, then Max tucked it neatly back into its bed of straw. "It's going to be a long night. I'll have an answer for you by morning." And he returned to the captain's cabin without another word.

Liao opted to stay with Max, so Lucy stomped into her cabin alone, closed the door, and kicked it hard. Then she slid down the door and crouched with her head in her hands. She had very nearly given in to the tears that were threatening when someone banged on the door. Lucy scrambled to her feet and stepped back. "Come in."

It was Kendrick. "I gather the council didn't go the way you wanted, miss?"

"We did what we could." Then she kicked the door again, even more viciously. This time she yelped in pain and dropped onto her sea-chest, cupping her aching foot in both hands. "The damned swab," she managed, hiccupping. "The damned swab!"

Kendrick rifled his pockets for a handkerchief. "The young man's waiting out there, if you'll talk to him."

"The prize-captain?"

"No, miss. Mr. Ault."

"Oh." She scrubbed at her face with the handkerchief. It smelled like sawdust and oil soap, and for a moment a pang of homesickness clutched at her heart. *This is still my home. It's my home until they turn me ashore. And then it'll* still *be my home, even if it takes me years and years to take it back.*

She stood up, and Max came in. "It's not hopeless yet."

"I suppose all we can do now is hope he believes us, the d—"

"Lucy, it isn't a matter of whether he believes us." Max sat on the sea-chest she had just vacated and rubbed his head. "In fact, I think he does, don't ask me why. But we're asking him to commit treason."

Lucy shook her head. "But after everything that Cascon fellow said—"

"It was all very moving, but the problem for Mr. Dexter—the only problem that matters, Lucy—is the problem of treason, and nothing's going to make it *not* treason if he gives you back the *Fate*, or even lets me go free with my cards. And he's right about what they'd do to him. They'd hang him. He's a *boy*."

"The sea is no place for someone who's that frightened of death." But there was no conviction in her voice. In a dark corner of her mind, she heard Mr. Cascon's emotionless voice intoning, *It is not beautiful to die.* True enough.

Max watched her closely. "It isn't death. It's that it would be a dishonorable death. And I think you can understand that. Wasn't it honor that made you give up the ship when one broadside would've sunk the *Amaranthine* and we'd have gotten away free and clear?"

"She could've have dragged us down with her."

"Not the point."

Lucy cursed silently against her palms. Another knock came. "Come in," she called, raising her eyes to look out from between her clawed fingers.

Dexter stood in the doorway. "I've made a decision." Whatever the decision was, he didn't look happy about it. Lucy felt a stirring of hope.

"That was quick," Max said warily.

Dexter shrugged. "Here's what I propose: Since I can't go back to Norfolk with both the *Marie Colette* and the brig in the way, I'll take you to Nagspeake. We'll put you ashore there with your weaving cards, as they're Mr. Ault's personal possessions. But then you're on your own."

Lucy's heart lurched. The mission might go on—*but my ship*, she thought wildly. *That means he'll keep my ship.*

"How will you explain that?" Max asked.

"I'll tell the truth," Dexter said. "We needed your crew to defend the *Fate* against two attacking vessels." He looked at Lucy. "There's no way I can negotiate on the matter of our keeping the schooner. Hired or not, she's a licensed ship-of-war, and the navy needs ships. If I'm going to keep from being hanged, I shall have to have something to show for this string of misadventures." He looked from Lucy to Max and back. "What do you say?"

There was, of course, nothing to do but agree. Lucy nodded, numb. "We accept, of course."

Max held out his hand and clasped Dexter's. "With gratitude, Mr. Dexter."

Lucy slumped onto her sea-chest the moment the boy had gone. "My ship," she whispered. "My ship."

The mission might just be salvaged, which meant Captain Bluecrowne wouldn't have died for nothing. But if they lost the *Left-Handed Fate*, Lucy and Liao not only lost their home, they lost what was left of their family. The surviving crewmembers would go their separate ways and sign on aboard other vessels. It was the way of the sea: sailors needed ships.

"Lucy," Max said in an achingly gentle voice, "I'm so sorry."

Sailors needed ships. Then what was she? How would *she* survive without the *Fate*?

My ship.

— *Part Two* —
NAGSPEAKE

fourteen
MAX IN THE CROSSTREES

"The lieutenant's compliments, sir, and would you care for a cup of tea?"

"Mmmmff."

"Begging your pardon, Mr. Ault, sir," the voice said apologetically, "but if you will just open your eyes, it really does help with the queasiness."

"Impossible. With my eyes shut, I can at least imagine that there are not several hundred feet between myself and the deck."

"Well, if you will look at the *horizon*—"

"Which serves only to remind me that there are several hundred and *twenty* feet between myself and the *water*, which is not at all comforting."

The sailor—Whippett, Max thought, although he wasn't planning on opening his eyes just to confirm it—gave up. "Shall I bring you up a cup of tea? Or chocolate? A nice mug of chocolate would settle your stomach almost as nicely as looking at the horizon."

Max raised his head and looked blearily at the sailor—Whippett it was—then, against his better judgment, looked down at the incomprehensible network of rope and sail that hung between the two of them and the deck far, far, farther than seemed reasonable, below. "How on earth would you get a cup of chocolate up here?"

Whippett gave him an affectionate, pitying look. "Much the same way we got you up here, Mr. Ault. Only begging your pardon, a cup of chocolate weighs rather less, and I shan't have to worry about it putting its feet wrong on the climb up."

Max tried to look indignant, but a wicked rumble in his stomach interrupted his efforts before he felt he'd really gotten his point across. "I suppose I will try to take a bit of chocolate. Could you manage some ship's biscuit as well?"

"I'll try, sir," Whippett said. "I imagine if I can manage porting chocolate up here, I can manage ship's biscuit, as it not only weighs less than a natural philosopher, but will fit into a pocket."

"While we're on the subject of me being up," Max added, "perhaps you could pass my respects to Lieutenant Dexter and inquire whether I might come down?"

Whippett scrambled back down the rigging with the same sense of *this-is-no-different-from-walking-down-the-street* that all sailors seemed to have and that Max still found utterly baffling. One foot in the wrong place, one hand missing its grip, and down to certain death it was.

On the other hand, he reflected, the fellow had been right: against all logic, having his eyes open did make the seasickness a little better. And the view was fantastic.

The Atlantic was a blue dish, unbroken all the way to the thin violet line of the horizon; the sky was a robin's-egg-colored bowl, unmarred except for the pale thumbprint of an early summer moon. All around him the rigging sighed as the wind played on the ropes like fingers on guitar strings.

They had left the Chesapeake two days before. Since then, there had been nothing but sailing and waiting, and Max was going rapidly out of his mind. In the end, Lucy had suggested that he run up to the crosstrees, the place where a little group of horizontal timbers crossed the foremast and held up a collection of ropes that he probably ought to have known the name of. There, Lucy said, he would have the same view the lookouts had. Max, of course, could not simply "run up" to anything higher than the quarterdeck, particularly when the *Fate* was flying along at the remarkable speeds she'd been making. So he'd had help, in the form of the sailor who'd all but carried him up.

Then—and Max was certain this was Lucy's doing—each time he had expressed a wish to return to civilization, whichever tar he asked had apologetically explained that he could not bring Max back down just then.

Whippett reappeared, held out a steaming cup with a lid, then reached into his pocket and produced two biscuits. "Still nice and fresh; barely a fortnight old. Should go down nicely with the chocolate."

Only a sailor could call biscuit baked almost two weeks ago *fresh*. "Thank you." Max worked one hand loose from the rope it had been clutching with a death-grip and arranged his little meal in his lap. "I don't suppose when I am finished—"

"The thing of it is," Whippett began, scratching under his cap, "we ought to be raising Nagspeake this hour—spotting it on the horizon, that is—and Miss Bluecrowne says you oughtn't miss that. Which it's amazing philosophical, and ever so much nicer to see from up here."

"Never mind what Miss Bluecrowne says," Max argued. "What does the *prize-captain* say?"

The sailor made an uncomfortable face. "Well, sir, Mr. Dexter says the only person he can spare just now to help you down is Miss Bluecrowne. What with us likely to raise Nagspeake soon, he fears the French or the brig might turn up and make one last try at us before we get there."

"But there's no one out here," Max protested, nodding his head to indicate the surrounding waters since he couldn't spare a hand.

"That's how it looks, Mr. Ault," Whippett agreed. "But that brig does come up out of nowhere, sir."

"Fine. Then when I'm finished with the chocolate, I shall come down on my own."

Whippett gave him a dubious look. "I shouldn't recommend it, Mr. Ault." And then he was gone, leaving Max alone in his exile.

"This is a conspiracy," he grumbled at the biscuit.

He'd just about finished his sad little tea when Lucy's face popped into view. She scrambled up next to him as if gravity had no hold on her. "And how are *we*, Maxwell?"

"Oh, thank God," Max sighed. "Get me out of this aerial hell, Lucy, I beg you."

"Not yet," she said breezily, swinging her legs in the air like a child on a swing. When she took to the rigging, Lucy had a bizarre system of tying up her skirts to keep them out of the way so that now she looked like she was wearing a short, puffy bit of skirt over a pair of the same heavy cotton trousers the crew wore. Max could never quite decide whether he found this scandalous or hilarious. At the moment, however, when all he wanted was to get down, the sight of those carelessly swinging ankles was merely infuriating.

"I understand that I am being punished for something," he said with as much fortitude as he could manage, "and I will do my best not to make the same mistakes again, whatever they were. *Any* mistakes. *Ever* again. I promise. Just get me down."

Lucy patted his knee. "Yes, you were being punished for being annoying. But not now. Now I don't want you to miss Nagspeake." She pointed off the starboard bow. "Keep your eye just there."

There was an odd tone in her voice. Max thought about the strange things he'd heard about the city but had never really believed, and how in Fells Point Lucy had suggested it really was rife with the unexplained. *Something about this city*, he thought. *What a place it must be.*

"It will be a thickening of the horizon first, the way land always appears," Lucy continued. "It'll take shape; a bit of a peak that will become the high point as the Atlantic coastline becomes visible again. That'll be Whilforber Hill."

"Whilforber, like the shipwright in Baltimore?"

"Exactly like. He hails from Nagspeake himself. Now, when you spot the hill, keep your eye upon it, for there are lights that shine there, beacons called bonelights that can be seen from great distances. Some say they're the torches of wraiths from the cemeteries of the monastery on the hill, made from thighbones wrapped in old shrouds. Some say it's Yankee peddlers sending coded messages to smugglers and privateers in the city below, and that in their lanterns the peddlers burn charcoal made of different types of bone in order to get flames of different colors." She gave him a half-smile. "You're thinking there must be a scientific explanation. Anyhow, I wanted you to see them."

"Well, then I am glad you came up before I came down."

Lucy laughed. "You would've climbed down on your own? What a liar."

"I would've tried," Max said with wounded dignity. "At least say you believe I would've tried, and that you came up to stop me putting myself at such unnecessary risk."

"All right, Max." She sat silently for a moment at his side, watching the horizon. "The truth is, I didn't want to be alone when we raised Nagspeake." She looked at him a little defiantly. "Laugh at me, if you like."

"I would never," Max said, surprised. "Why should I?" She didn't answer, only turned to look out at the ocean again. "What is it, Lucy, about Nagspeake?"

"It's a very strange place, Max. It isn't like anywhere else at all. Certainly nothing like the rest of North America. You'll see when we get there."

"That isn't what I mean. What is it about the city for *you*?"

Lucy looked down at the deck below. Liao was sitting on one of the stern-chaser guns at the back of the schooner. As they watched, something in his palms flared to life, fizzing with bright red sparks. He threw his head back, laughing delightedly, then flung the fizzing thing from him. It sailed over the cutter being towed along in the *Fate*'s wake and burst just before hitting the water in a gleaming puff of red and gold light radiant enough to be seen even in the bright afternoon sun.

"Something to do with Liao?" Max guessed.

She nodded. "We lost his mother in Nagspeake."

"Oh." The ship swayed; Max grabbed for a tighter handhold and tried not to vomit. "Do you think he'll want company?" he managed. "Perhaps he won't want to be alone, either, when we raise the city."

Lucy shook her head. "I asked him. He said he had a salute planned and there was no time to waste being sad. So I don't want to waste time being sad, either."

"And you believe him?"

Lucy made an uncertain face. "I think so. I don't believe Liao lies about his feelings. Still, I keep watching for him to worry at that queue of his like he does. Usually that's when I know he's trying to soothe a big feeling he isn't talking about. He's worn it ever since he was a tot in China—it was the law there, did you know? The head shaved to here, and the rest in a pigtail."

Max shook his head. "I didn't."

"Well, when they came aboard the *Fate*, Liao and his mama, she asked if he wanted to cut it and wear his hair in some other way. But apart from the fact that having the braid in his fingers was a source of comfort—he was five then, I think, or six?—by then he'd noticed how many of the Fates wore long pigtails, too, and how ridiculously vain they are about them. So of course he wasn't doing away with his. Stopped shaving the top, though. Made it his own." She smiled down at the little figure cavorting below. Max did, too, as he tried to picture a six-year-old Liao having opinions about how he'd like to wear his hair now that he was a privateering child and had a say in the matter.

But Lucy's smile faded. "Then we lost Madame Xiaoming." Her voice went chilly. "After that, the queue was a reminder of his time with her, and his time in China, that he could carry with him always and that couldn't be lost or washed overboard in dirty weather. It still comforts him in ways I can't." She took a deep breath. "Anyway, I've been watching him, and until I see him messing with that pigtail, I'll believe him when he says he has better things to do than be sad."

Max nodded, wondering if he ought to pat her shoulder or something. But in the end, he only said, "All right," and followed Lucy's gaze toward the invisible coastline somewhere just over the horizon.

....

REALLY, SINCE ALL OLIVER HAD WAS AN ACTING COMMISSION, THE navy could just kick him out. There was no earthly reason for a court-martial—not unless he had fouled things up so badly that the navy wanted to make an example of him, or of Captain Eager for giving him charge of the schooner. And surely he hadn't done that poor a job of it. Had he?

To settle himself on this point, Oliver had spent a good part of the voyage south in his cabin poring over the copies of the *Naval Regulations* and the *Marine Rules and Regulations* that his father had contributed to his sea-chest, searching for guidance and consolation. But the guides were not comforting. Things were looking so bleak, in fact, that the sound of the lookout's cry of *Land, ho!* came as a blessed relief.

He barreled out of his cabin and sprinted to the quarterdeck. "Where away?"

"Pilot says that ought to be Whilforber Hill," Mr. Cascon replied, pointing, "which means the harbor's just there."

"And no sign of our pursuers?"

"Nothing, sir, but . . ." Mr. Cascon hesitated, then shook his head. "No, sir."

Oliver nodded, fairly sure he knew what Mr. Cascon had decided not to say. *But if that brig comes out of nowhere again . . .*

Mr. Wooll came up the stairs and touched his knuckles to his forehead. "My respects, Mr. Dexter, and there is a district called Flotilla that's less visible than the main harbor. The *Fate* has friends there. With your permission, the pilot will take us in through a different waterway."

"My thanks, and he may take the tiller whenever he chooses." Oliver turned his eyes up to where Lucy Bluecrowne and Max Ault sat in the crosstrees. For a moment every worry he'd been having—whether this was the right choice to have made, whether it would turn out to get him hanged, whether *that* was even worth worrying about because to be hanged he'd have to eventually get back to the States, which would be an accomplishment at this point—dissolved in a deep gulf of loneliness.

Lucy and Max had plenty to worry about, too, but they also had each other. And Lucy might've been the de facto leader of the privateers, but she had no orders, no superiors to take her to task if she failed, no navy expecting her to be the all-knowing and all-seeing master of everything between the wind and the waves.

Oliver glanced at Mr. Cascon. If there had been any sort of justice in the world, the bosun's mate would have been made prize-captain himself and been allowed the glory of bringing the prize home. *Who knows*, Oliver thought crabbily, *he might even actually have done it.*

But Mr. Cascon hadn't been put in charge, and the unthinkable had happened over and over, and now here was Oliver: a lonely boy who ought to have been skylarking in the rigging and making a mess of his trigonometry lessons but who was instead ridiculously in charge of a schooner full of prisoners, under pursuit by not one but *two* unfriendly vessels, and about to put in at a dubious international port hundreds of miles from where he was supposed to be. An acting-lieutenant, against all logic, who hadn't a chance in the world of even being confirmed a midshipman when all this was over and done—not unless his famous father got involved again. *And look how well that had turned out last time*, he thought glumly.

"Maybe they sank each other," he said aloud.

"Could be, but we haven't been that lucky so far," Mr. Cascon muttered. "Begging your pardon, sir."

"No need," Oliver said glumly. "Will you take charge of hiring the crew we need to replace the Fates? I imagine we'll need at least twenty men or so. Does that sound right?"

Mr. Cascon nodded. "I should've said about that number, sir, yes."

It wasn't very commanderlike, but Oliver felt a little bit of happiness at the approval, and a touch more confidence than he'd felt before. "Since it will take a bit of time to find those men, I will let Miss Bluecrowne and her crew stay aboard until we have our full complement, to save the Fates the trouble of finding lodgings."

"Very civil of you, sir. I think I should feel fine about trusting the Fates for a few more days, seeing as we've trusted them this far. So long as they leave the ship when the time comes. Of course," he added, scratching his chin, "we haven't got much of a choice now they're loose. Won't be as easy to put them back again."

Oliver cringed before he could stop himself. It didn't escape Mr. Cascon. "Permission to speak freely, sir? You saved the ship by handing it over to the Fates, even if they fail to honor the agreement later. And should it come to a . . . to an inquiry of any kind, sir, I shall be glad to say so."

Red-faced, Oliver nodded. "Thank you, Mr. Cascon."

A sudden and shocking blast erupted behind them. Oliver whirled, searching the horizon for enemy sails. Instead, over the ship's wake, a bright green blaze of light was fading away into smoke and vapors. *What a shocking shade of green*, he thought despite himself. *What a wild puff of fizzing sparks!* No mere cracker, that—a proper firework!

Then he remembered that he was the commander of the ship and forced his expression into something more forbidding. "Belay those explosives!" he snarled. Startled, Liao tumbled sideways off the stern chaser and only scarcely missed knocking himself unconscious or falling overboard.

Despite Oliver's attempt at ferocity, the boy came trotting up with delight on his face. "Did you see? It was *such* a thumping good green!"

Liao had been playing at the stern for a bit now, and his games had started innocently enough. There had been small fizzing noises and little pops and odd not-quite-gunpowder smells, but nothing overly obnoxious or troubling. This last noise, however, had sounded almost like a gun going off, to say nothing of the fact that the sort of firework Liao was so delightedly celebrating must certainly have required proper gunpowder, which meant the boy had been in the powder magazine, of all places. A prisoner—and a nine-year-old prisoner at that—had gotten into the gunpowder storage! Unthinkable.

"Have you been in the powder magazine?" Oliver demanded.

"Did you see the green?" Liao demanded back.

Oliver glared. *"Have you been in the powder magazine?"*

Liao glared back, tapping one foot. *"Did you see my green?"*

Behind Oliver, Mr. Cascon made a snorting noise that sounded troublingly like a stifled laugh.

"I saw the green, yes," Oliver said finally. "It was very . . . green."

"Emerald, even? Would you say emerald?" the boy asked hopefully.

"But you—yes, emerald, I suppose. But you can't go running in and out of the powder magazine!"

"But I'm allowed! I have my own barrels."

"You have your own barrels?"

"Yes, I made them myself. Not the barrels—Cooper made the barrels—but I made the powder in them. I don't use Mr. Harrick's powder. I know that's not mine to take," he added a little defensively.

"It's not Mr. Harrick's any—" Oliver began, exasperated. Then he stopped and examined Liao skeptically. "You made your own gunpowder."

Liao shrugged as if this were nothing more remarkable than having patched his own trousers. "It isn't hard. All you need is brimstone, charcoal, and saltpeter. Of course I know how to make fancier powders, too. And I can make rockets and igniter balls and other things that use powders. And I can make them so that they have colors, if I add other things like ivory or potash or chlorate of potash or black oxide of—should you like to see some, sir? You could tell me what color you like best and I could mix it up right there before your eyes!"

This was ridiculous. "Never mind that. Just look, now: the powder magazine's off-limits from here on out."

Liao's face drooped. "But what about my barrels? And my rockets? There are rockets in there that I made, and those are mine, too!"

Oliver debated explaining what it meant for a ship to be taken by an enemy power—that the ship and all its weaponry, including every barrel of powder aboard, now belonged to the United States, represented at the moment by Oliver—but he decided against it. Probably Liao would just understand him to be saying, *it isn't yours, it's mine,* which wasn't the sort of thing you said to a small child under any circumstances if you wanted to have a remotely rational conversation.

"I won't *take* them," Oliver said at last with exaggerated patience, "but you can't just go running about playing with incendiaries. Not on a wooden ship."

"Why? I always do. I'm allowed!"

"Not anymore."

"Why?"

"Because . . . because it won't do, don't you see?"

"But *why?*"

"Because . . . because . . . because I'm the prize-captain and that's what I say!"

Liao broke into an incomprehensible storm of what Oliver assumed was Chinese. Oliver put his palms over his ears until Liao stopped ranting. The boy waited till Oliver lowered his hands, then demanded again, louder, *"Why?"*

Mr. Cascon seemed to be struggling too much with his muffled laughter to be of much help. "Pass the word for Miss Bluecrowne!" Oliver yelled.

Lucy's voice trailed immediately down from the rigging. "Coming, coming." She scrambled down and hurried to the quarterdeck. "Yes, sir?"

Before Oliver could do more than sweep an arm toward Liao and open his mouth, the boy was already speaking. "Lucy! Did you see my green?"

"Ah." Lucy looked with a bit of embarrassment at Oliver, then back at Liao. "It sounded a bit louder than your usual crackers."

"It *was* louder, and it *wasn't* a cracker. And it was *green*. But *he*"—Liao pointed a waving finger at Oliver—"says I mayn't have my powder, Lucy! Or my rockets or *anything* in the powder magazine!"

Oliver was about to cut in, but Lucy was faster. "Did you set off a rocket just now?" she demanded. "One of the ones you know you're not to set off aboard ship?"

Liao shrank a little. "Well—"

"Yes or no, Liao? *Shi* or *bu*?"

He wilted, then straightened and nodded contritely. "*Shi*, it was a rocket."

"And you wonder why the prize-captain took your privileges away? Papa did the same thing the last time you tried to set off a rocket aboard ship."

"But that was Papa!"

She pointed to Oliver. "Lieutenant Dexter is the captain of the ship now, and he certainly may revoke any privileges he chooses to aboard the *Left-Handed Fate*. And you gave him a good reason to do so, don't you think?"

A moment's pause, then, "Yes," Liao said with downcast eyes.

"Perhaps you ought to apologize," Lucy suggested. "Properly, and seamanlike."

Liao faced Oliver contritely. He took a deep breath. "My best respects, Lieutenant, and I should like to apologize. Even if it was a thumping good emerald rocket and went all fizzy, too," he added in a breathless, slightly guilty rush.

"A very handsome apology," Mr. Cascon said.

"That's all right," Oliver grumbled.

The boy's face went bright with hope. "Then I may have my powder back?"

Lucy cleared her throat. "Might I suggest when we go ashore, perhaps, Mr. Dexter?"

"Why not?" Oliver said, spreading his hands helplessly. "Why on earth not?"

Liao beamed. "Thank you. When we go ashore, I shall show you a very good blue I know." He pointed up into the heavens. "Very like the color the sky is right now." Then he squinted. "Lucy, Max is waving his arms about alarmingly. Perhaps he wants to come down. Shall I go up and get him? He can't climb down by himself."

Lucy glanced at Oliver. "With your permission, sir."

"As if anyone around here cares about my permission," Oliver muttered sourly.

fifteen
FLOTILLA

At nightfall, Max, rescued at last from the masthead, leaned on the gunwale with a cup of tea and watched the lights of Nagspeake come to life. Lucy handed him her telescope, reached for his cup, and took a sip. "There they are."

Max raised the glass and swept it across the hill on the far side of Magothy Bay until he found one of the will-o'-wisps called bone-lights. "Fascinating," he murmured. "I count one, two . . . six? How is it they remain unexplained?"

"Nagspeake is full of things like that. I told you. It's a tough town for a philosopher. Or an unfriendly ship." The bay and the city on the far side of it were sheltered by two crescent arms of land, both of which were fortified with fortresslike walls, batteries of guns, and a small fleet of gunboats.

"It looks to be about the size of Baltimore," Max observed.

"It's bigger. There are whole inland districts hidden away from view. Like Flotilla, where we're going."

The *Left-Handed Fate* sailed on past the mouth of the bay until all that could be seen was a stretch of crumbling yellow cliffs topped by knotty trees. The pilot turned the ship hard toward the shore. Suddenly, just as it looked as though the *Fate* was going to fetch up against a wall of rock and root, a narrow inlet opened up before it.

The schooner's remaining boats glided forth, each carrying a small kedge anchor. The first boat surged forward and dropped its kedge. Then the *Fate* hauled in the cable, so that instead of the anchor coming to the ship, the ship slid through the water to the anchor. The second boat dropped its anchor farther on, and the process started again. Length by length, the *Fate* crept up the twisting inlet. And then the quality of the night changed and the yellow glow of lantern light seeped across the surface of the water like oil. The inlet widened, and a strange cluster of buildings came into view.

It was and was not a town, just as it was and was not a mass of boats. At its nearest edge lay a harbor with assorted craft riding at anchor or tied up to tumbledown quays: most were smaller, single-masted vessels, but some had masses of metal cylinders and pipes amidships, which Max suspected meant they were driven by steam rather than wind or oar. Fascinating.

Beyond the harbor, buildings clustered above a bulkhead made of alternating sections of thick wooden posts and curved plank walls like the hulls of ships. The houses and shop fronts stood at different heights, piled as close to one another as in the most crowded streets of London. At the higher levels, networks of rope and rigging made walkways above the streets. Here and there, pennants snapped in the breeze, half-lit by clusters of lampposts that might have done service in past lives as spars.

The air here had an odd quality to it. There was the mossy damp-canvas-and-wet-wood scent that he had come to associate with coming into port; there was a hint of wax and a faint whiff of beer; there was a mineral-and-mud river scent; and overlaying that, the odor of old paint and oxidized metal. But there was another

flavor in the air, a bizarre combination that reminded him at once of night-blooming things and the smell of a gun when the metal has grown hot enough to need to cool down.

The schooner slowed, and the sailors extinguished every light on deck. A lantern at the top of the mainmast flared to life, then proceeded to flash on and off in some sort of code. Max joined Lucy and Dexter on the quarterdeck. "Where—"

"That is the quarter called Flotilla," Lucy said. "We have just sent a private signal to the Quartermaster—which means something different here than aboard a ship." She paused and correctly guessed that Max hadn't a clue what *quartermaster* meant on a ship or anyplace else. "He's in charge. We have let him know we are here and have made our request."

"What is our request?"

"We need a place to hide, of course. We can't just anchor in plain view out in the bay." A green light began flashing above the rooftops. "And here is his reply."

The *Fate*'s cutters towed her along the wharves to the west. Here the local boats were more decrepit and the maritime smells were thicker, as if something had recently stirred up still waters. A deep whine cut through the night: the ache of old mechanisms cranked to life. Lucy pointed at the bulkhead. "Look there."

A wide sweep of pilings shuddered and swung out, radiating deep ripples that rocked the nearby boats as it revealed a dark space: a channel into the main bulk of Flotilla.

Dexter leaned on the gunwale next to Max and regarded the void. "What on earth . . . ?"

"A lot of Flotilla has solid ground under its keel," Lucy explained. "More or less solid, anyhow; most of the stationary bits are just hulls held up by pilings. But Flotilla also has a number of channels and hidden berths, like this one. We'll be safe here, for a while."

"And they just . . . just *let* ships . . ." Dexter waved a hand at the moving bulwark.

"No, they do not just *let* ships do *anything*, here or anywhere else in Nagspeake. That's why there's a huge bloody battery defending the bay," Lucy retorted. "Mr. Wooll told you, didn't he, that the *Fate* is not unknown in these waters?"

The schooner eased into the dark channel and came to rest in a space that might have been measured and built specifically for her. When the bulkhead swung closed again, the *Left-Handed Fate* had been incorporated into the fabric of Flotilla as snugly as if she had been part of the quarter forever. Lucy, Dexter, and Max looked up at the shambling district overhung by rigging and brass lanterns.

"Welcome to Nagspeake," Lucy murmured.

sixteen
THE HONORABLE
JONQUIL LEVINFLASH

All around the quarter, eight bells struck at midnight, just as if Flotilla were a ship. Oliver wanted nothing more than to tumble into his bed and find out whether tonight, at last, he might have a decent night's sleep—insofar as any such thing existed in the navy. Instead, he watched Garvett set out a late snack of toasted cheese and fruit-studded biscuits, along with pots of coffee and chocolate and a bottle of sherry. The members of the little council that had collected in the captain's cabin helped themselves to a bit of food and something to sip.

Oliver spoke up first. "I should like us to be under way within a week. Mr. Cascon?"

"Impossible to gauge, now we're not technically on United States soil any longer. With your permission, I'll go ashore tomorrow. I shall be able to answer better by evening."

"Very good." Oliver turned to Lucy and Kendrick. "What will the Fates do?"

"They're eager to pretty up the barky before we leave her," Kendrick said. "If you have no objection, sir, we'll send 'em ashore when they're off-watch to find work, but they won't have any trouble there. They're prime seamen, every last one."

"If they may be allowed to have use of their berths in the meantime, perhaps even until you have found enough men to depart, I would be grateful." Lucy's face was stonily neutral. "We will, of course, make no trouble for you."

"You are still paroled prisoners," Mr. Cascon warned. "You would be honor-bound not to undertake any acts against the United States while aboard."

Lucy nodded sharply. Max looked uncomfortable for a moment, but he, too, nodded his agreement.

Garvett knocked and poked his head inside. "Begging your pardon, sirs, but there's a person here wishes to speak to you, come from the Quartermaster."

Lucy straightened and looked at Oliver with an expression of naked pleading.

Oliver swept crumbs from the front of his jacket. "Thanks, Garvett, and show him in."

A moment later, a tall black-haired lady of twenty years or so entered. Lucy shoved her plate and glass at Max and was on her feet in a moment. "Nellie! I mean . . . my compliments, madam—"

The woman gave a short, hoarse laugh and wrapped Lucy in a tight hug. "Oh, Lucy, Lucy." Sadness and regret were plain on her face. In the time it had taken to cross the ship to this cabin, this woman had clearly formed some understanding of what had befallen Lucy and her ship. "We shall have more to talk about in a bit, you and I. Introduce me, will you, love?"

Lucy stepped away and straightened. "Lieutenant Oliver Dexter, Prize-Captain, United States Navy, and formerly of the frigate *Amaranthine*," she said formally, "may I present the Honorable Miss Jonquil Levinflash, First of the Office of the Quartermaster of Flotilla,

Sovereign City of Nagspeake." She hesitated. "And my cousin, in a manner of speaking. Honorarily, you might say."

Oliver stuck out a hand. The Honorable Jonquil Levinflash clasped it with a grim smile. "Mr. Dexter."

"Miss—Mrs.—Your Honor?"

"Miss is accurate, and will do fine. We do not stand on ceremony here the way you naval fellows do."

"Er, all right. Would you care to join us? We were just taking a bit of a snack."

"If those are Roddy Garvett's currant biscuits, then I should be delighted to." Kendrick stood to offer her his chair. She sat and smiled a little forlornly. "In the interests of full disclosure, Mr. Dexter, I should tell you I was once a master's mate aboard this schooner."

"A . . . a master's mate, Miss Levinflash?" Oliver repeated, trying and failing to keep the disbelief from his voice.

"And a first-rate navigator she was, too," Kendrick said from beside the door. "Begging your pardon, sir."

Miss Levinflash grinned at Oliver's surprise. "I wasn't much older than Lucy then, I think." Her smile vanished. "Very strange it is for me to be addressing opposing sides in the same cabin, but here you are. Mr. Dexter, I fear you will find the questions I'm about to ask rather awkward, particularly due to the connection between the Bluecrownes and myself, but I assure you the Quartermaster's Office finds them necessary." Reaching into an inside pocket of her jacket, she produced a little leather wallet and passed it to Oliver. "My credentials."

Oliver opened the wallet and skimmed the elaborately inked and stamped document it contained. It was full of a good deal of official language confirming that the Honorable Jonquil Levinflash was et cetera et cetera Office of the Quartermaster et cetera. He nodded and handed it back. "Thank you."

"Very welcome. Now, was this ship taken prize by legitimate and lawful naval action?"

"Yes. By the frigate *Amaranthine*, Captain Miles Eager. You may know that war has been declared between England and the United States."

"We do. Did you acquire the private signal made by your ship this evening as part of the capture?"

"No. We have arranged a sort of temporary truce with the Fates, and it was judged by Lucy Bluecrowne that it was safer for everyone aboard for the *Fate* to put into Flotilla rather than the main harbor, if possible. She arranged for the signal."

"Please explain this *sort of temporary truce*. Are the Fates not reckoned prisoners of war?" There was the slightest edge of skepticism in her voice. Oliver didn't like it.

"They are, but we were attacked by a French corvette and our prize-crew was too small to fight her off. And then a brig hostile to the *Left-Handed Fate* turned up." As quickly as possible, Oliver explained the action and the agreement he and Lucy had made. He didn't mention Lucy's and Max's mission. That, fortunately, was no longer his problem.

Nell Levinflash turned her gaze on Lucy, who had been sitting mutely during this exchange. "Oh, Lucy. Brave girl." She sighed. "Well, that explains that. You can imagine we were confused to hear that the *Fate* had come in crewed by a party of Americans but still making our signal."

Oliver nodded. "It's a confusing state of affairs, miss."

"I can't say I'm pleased to find my former ship taken, but I thank you for treating her crew so handsomely." She paused to dip a corner of biscuit into her glass and take a bite. "Nagspeake will almost certainly remain neutral in this war, so I cannot offer any official assistance in the raising of crew. Unofficially, however, I can tell you that there is a public house in Shantytown called Smith's Tot whose clientele is mostly American expatriates. You might do well to try there for volunteers. And if you choose to give the Fates their parole in the city, you may say that Nell Levinflash vouches personally for Mr. Dexter and his conduct. It may do you some little bit of good."

From the looks on Lucy's and Kendrick's faces, Oliver guessed that this was likely to do plenty. "That's very handsome of you, miss. Thank you."

"I should also let you know that it is standard procedure, when we bring a foreign ship into our midst, to post a sentry with her. Our man will not venture aboard except at your express invitation; you might think of him as a local lookout. But should you have any difficulty, he can get a message to the Quartermaster's office quickly."

"Of course. Thank you again."

"Welcome, and I thank you for the hospitality." Miss Levinflash set aside her plate and glass and rose to her feet. "I won't keep you any longer. Any of the Fates can show you the way to my offices at the Masthead, should you require."

They bowed all around, and with a moment's pause to squeeze Lucy's hand, the Honorable Jonquil Levinflash swept from the cabin. Just before the door shut, Oliver saw Garvett rush to her with a parcel wrapped in a napkin. More of the famous currant biscuits for the former master's mate, no doubt.

Lucy was sitting with her hands tightly clasped. "If you'd like to say good night . . ." Oliver began.

"Thank you, sir." She sprang for the door.

....

UP ON THE WEATHER DECK, NELL WAS WAITING. SHE HELD OUT her arms as Lucy levered herself up the ladderway and rushed to her. "Poor love," Nell whispered, hugging her tightly. "I'm so sorry. So very, very sorry."

Lucy wasn't sure how long she stood there clinging to Nell. She could feel tears on her cheeks but couldn't bear to let go even long enough to wipe them away. "It was a splinter," she said in a whisper. "One splinter."

"That's all it takes, love. You know that." Nell touched Lucy's forehead with one finger, tracing the hairline scar. "I told the captain once that your heart was the size of an eagle. Look what you've managed, even as a captive. It's remarkable, Lucy. He would be so proud."

"But I shall still lose the ship," Lucy said miserably. "It's like losing Papa all over again."

"Like, perhaps, but not the same at all. A ship can be replaced, and you and I both know that when Mason Whilforber learns of this, he'll knock another schooner up for you in a heartbeat, try to call it a birthday present, and refuse to be paid for it. What of Liao?"

"He's capital. I thought he might be troubled, coming back here, but sadness runs off of him like rain off tarpaulin." Lucy lowered her voice again. "Perhaps if we had found ourselves in the district where it happened . . . or if we went to the house itself . . ." She sighed. "He must be asleep at last or he would be here now, telling you all about the superb green he managed in a rocket this afternoon." She paused. "Nell, how much do you know about what Papa was . . . what we've been doing, these last months?"

"Not much. I know he'd been hired by a natural philosopher of some sort. Wasn't that just before you came to Nagspeake the last time?"

Lucy nodded. "Recently that fellow's son hired us for a voyage, and we were taken while chasing a ship called the *Honoratus* that was due to call here. Have you heard of her?"

"Not off the top of my head. I'm sure no such ship has put into

Flotilla, but I can't speak for Bayside or Shantytown or the Quayside Harbors. I can write you a letter of introduction to the Port Admiral in the morning, if you like." She studied Lucy closely. "What else?"

Lucy hesitated again. "Have you ever heard of a brig whose crew wears black-upon-black uniforms?"

"I've heard of captains fitting out their crews in all sorts of outlandish shore-going rigs. Scarlet jackets if the ship's called the *Rose Red*, that sort of thing?"

"No. Every man on deck in a proper uniform, only coal-black without so much as a button in any other color. This brig's an uncommon fast sailer, too. We've had to squeeze fourteen or fifteen knots out of the *Fate*, running from her. And when she turns up, we find Saint Elmo's lights aboard ship. And not just a couple at the tops of the masts, either. Hundreds of them, Nell." Now Nell was staring. Lucy gave an awkward laugh. "It sounds like something out of a fairy tale."

"It does, rather. But not a fairy tale I've ever heard, and I've heard more than my share in this city." Nell squeezed her hand. "Come see me tomorrow. And Lucy, when the Americans leave, you and Liao shall stay with me. For as long as you choose. Perhaps until Uncle Mason writes that your new barky is ready for launching, and then we shall all go up to Baltimore and see you off on your first voyage. Or we can go hunting for your next command here, together, just as you and Liao did the last time. What did you call that little cutter your papa bought you?"

"The *Driven Star*." A thick knot of pain stitched itself together between Lucy's collarbones. But this was no time to dwell on the past. There were pressing matters to consider in the present. Like seeing her father's last mission through. *Focus on that*, she told herself, and pictured Max's crateful of loom-cards instead of the cutter that had been her salvation last time she'd been in Nagspeake.

"Nell, where would you go if you wanted to find the best weaver to be had in the city?"

"The best *weaver*?" Nell repeated, incredulous. "With a *loom*? What on earth for?" She laughed. "Have you turned into a proper girl since the last time we saw each other? Weavers indeed."

Lucy smiled sheepishly. "Please, Nell?"

"Well, I know nothing about weaving, but in the Printer's Quarter there's a Warpandye Street, and merchants make a big to-do about Warpandye cloth, so perhaps that's a thing that means something."

With one last hug Nell took her leave, accompanied by the thin piping of a bosun's whistle played by a young mariner waiting on the quay with a lantern. Perhaps she'd been too distracted before to notice, or perhaps her defenses had simply given out at last, but as Lucy watched Nell and her attendant disappear into Flotilla, memories flooded into her heart: sore memories and lovely ones, mixing like the fresh and salt water out there in the Magothy.

She shook her head to clear it, then descended the ladder again and returned to the cabin. "Thank you, sir," she mumbled, suddenly exhausted and without a clue as to how she could possibly face another minute of discussing how the Americans would complete the process of taking away her home.

"Why don't we call it a night?" Dexter suggested. "We all have busy days ahead. As long as you and your crew do nothing to jeopardize our work and make no attempt to take the ship or any of her provisions, you may come and go as you like. Though you're not to work on your miraculous engine while you're aboard," he added pointedly. "Building a weapon would certainly qualify as an act of war."

"Understood, sir. With your permission, I think I will turn in." Max got to his feet and held out a hand to Lucy. "You look tired."

Lucy allowed him to pull her to her feet. "Good night, Lieutenant."

Max threaded Lucy's arm through the crook of his elbow as they left the cabin and emerged into the dark, musty air of the aft platform. "All right?"

"I suppose."

They came to stand before the doors of their cramped little cabins. "Tomorrow . . ." Max began reluctantly.

She sighed. "Tomorrow, you and I will go to the Masthead. You shall take the introduction to the Port Admiral and make inquiries after the *Honoratus* and whether she's arrived yet." She lowered her voice. "And if you choose, I will take your cards and see if I can trouble out what they're for. Nell has given me a place to start—a sort of weavers' street."

Max followed her into her cabin. "I take it you're choosing to interpret Mr. Dexter's words the way I am?"

"I'm interpreting them literally. We shan't work on your engine while we're aboard."

"In that case, wouldn't it make more sense for you to track down the ship? You'll know better what sorts of questions to ask."

"They're simple questions, Max. Has the *Honoratus* come in, and which one is she?"

"I meant—"

"I know what you meant, and, yes, it would make more sense, but despite the evidence of Cousin Nell, it will seem less notable if it's a boy asking after a ship and a girl asking after looms. And despite how it might offend my pride, I can't see the point of drawing more attention to ourselves than we absolutely must."

Max nodded. "Very well, then." He stood for another moment, long fingers twitching at his sides.

"What?"

"After. What then?"

"Well, even if you find the *Honoratus* now and somehow manage to acquire what she carries, you're still short the last piece of your puzzle, so I imagine you'll have to hire another ship, Max. As you see, I haven't any others stowed in my sea-chest."

He made a frustrated noise. "I mean for *you*. Obviously I can hire another ship."

Just once, Lucy wished someone would ask her an easy question. "The crew will have no trouble finding work. Nagspeake is a seaman's town if there ever was one, and the Fates are the best seamen there are. As for Liao and me, our father had a man of business here, so we are not without funds. And Nell will put us up for as long as we wish, I believe."

"But . . . will you be happy without a ship?"

Well, that one was easy enough. "No." It was strangely comforting to be able to answer something so simply. "But I cannot afford another, not right away."

Max reached across the space between them and took one of her hands, which was shaking from fatigue and the effort of keeping her composure in the face of everything. He kissed her knuckles. "Sleep well."

Lucy smiled weakly. "You, too." As soon as the door had shut behind him, she buried her face in her hands and cried for the third time.

seventeen
THE QUARTERMASTER

When Max climbed up to the weather deck early the following morning with the loom-cards in a bag slung across his chest, he found the Fates as busy as he thought he'd ever seen them, with Kendrick overseeing what looked like some kind of exaggerated make-and-mend day.

"Watch where you're walking, sir," yelped a sailor, bustling Max to one side just as he was about to tread upon a length of sailcloth. "Begging your pardon, sir."

Lucy waited with an expression of disapproval on the prow of the cutter in the waist of the schooner. "Don't let me rush you, Maxwell."

Liao popped up out of the cutter, causing Max to stumble over a bit of coiled rope and nearly sprawl flat on his backside. "Morning, Max!"

"Morning, Liao. And sorry to keep you waiting, Lucy." He rubbed his eyes. "Is there any chance of coffee before we go?"

"Don't be ridiculous. We'll stop at a coffeehouse along the way."

Liao clambered out of the boat. "Lucy says I may come along with you if you say it's all right, and perhaps even set off one or two of these." He leaned back into the boat, feet kicking in midair, and came up triumphantly with a satchel Max assumed was full of things that made tremendously interesting noises as they burst into thumping great blues and greens.

"It's best you have someone with you when we go our separate ways," Lucy said. "And Liao can show you a bit of the philosophic iron, too."

"Miss Bluecrowne, there! Mr. Ault!" Lucy and Max turned and found Oliver Dexter hurrying across the deck, dressed in his full uniform with a bicorne hat perched on his head. "Would you be heading in the direction of the Quartermaster's place of business?"

"We are. Should you like to join us?"

"If you don't mind."

"By all means," Lucy replied. "Who else is coming along with you?"

Dexter hesitated. "Who else?"

"Someone ought to, if only so you don't get lost or set upon out in Flotilla. Kendrick would be best, but he'll be too busy." Lucy whistled. "Whippett! Whippett, there!"

Whippett looked up from his splicing. "Aye aye, miss?"

"Whippett, Lieutenant Dexter is paying a visit to the Masthead and ought to have a good solid hand who knows the district at his side. You might bring him back by the Petrel Walk so he can have a look at the harbor."

Whippett's lean face slid into a wide grin punctuated by two gold teeth. "Aye aye. With the prize-captain to the Masthead, then home by the Petrel Walk it is, miss. I'll just put up my work."

"Last time we were here he had a sweetheart in Flotilla," Lucy explained to Dexter. "You might have a sherbet on the Petrel Walk and let him go say hello. It won't be time wasted. You'll have a good view of the harbor and the battery."

When Whippett returned, the five of them descended the gangway to the boardwalk. Then, with a terrible jerk, Max stepped onto solid land. It was always like this at first, coming ashore: the rolling gait that came so easily to seamen but that took Max an eternity to manage at sea suddenly didn't work any longer, and the rigid, unyielding ground made him feel as if his clumsy feet were made of lead.

The quay around the *Fate* was packed with peddlers hawking everything from grilled sausages to fresh fruit and vegetables to knickknacks, fabric, and tinware. At one nearby booth the seller was loudly touting what appeared to be empty embroidered bags and lengths of knotted rope, shouting, "Winds here! Drafts and gusts and wafts at market prices! All sorts of breezes and winds here!"

"Is it a festival day?" Max asked.

"No, this is what always happens when a ship comes in here." Lucy's eyes roved through the crowd of vendors. "Just a minute." She caught Whippett's eye and the two of them darted away, disappearing between a knife grinder's millstone and a bookseller's wagon.

"What was that about?" Max asked when they returned.

"Nothing," Lucy said, tucking a small rectangle bound with green ribbon into her skirt pocket. "This way."

They emerged from the thicket of peddlers and followed the boardwalk. As it left the quay, it became a sort of road through the cramped passages that passed for streets in Flotilla. Sometimes it was solid underfoot and behaved as a path ought to behave; at other times it became a little bridge where two hulls were lashed not quite side by side; and in places it had a very specific give that told Max they were crossing a floating surface, even if it looked like a small open square planted with red-flowering shrubbery.

Crossing one softly heaving square, Whippett gave a short whistle. "Hang on," Lucy said. She and Whippett hurried to a tall building on the opposite side of the square. "Half a minute," she called back. "Just wait there."

"What's all this?" Dexter asked.

Max shook his head. "Not a clue." The building had a steeplelike mast atop its peaked roof, and above the doors, a great stained-glass window depicted a ship beneath three golden balls. "Is that a church?"

"Chapel of Saint Nicholas," a passing man replied. "Just come ashore, have you? Which one are you looking for?"

"Which what?" Dexter asked.

"Chapel," the stranger said. "You looking for a particular saint?"

Before either of them could answer, the church's door opened again and Lucy and Whippett sprinted across the square. "Right," Lucy said. "Off we go."

"What was that about?" Dexter demanded.

"Nothing. This way."

They followed Lucy through the twisting passages, and Max began to dread when they opened out. His body couldn't quite determine whether it needed sea legs or land legs at any given time, and more than once either Lucy or Whippett had to save him from dropping into the water below through the gaps that occasionally appeared underfoot.

"Remember how we always tell you 'one hand for you and one for the ship' to remind you to clap on to something at all times to keep from falling?" Whippett said after one of these incidents. "Well, in Flotilla it's one hand for you, one hand for the *town*."

"Thank you, Whippett, that's very helpful. Lucy, you'll sing out if you see any of the philosophic iron, won't you?"

"There's none in Flotilla. Only on the mainland, where there's proper earth underfoot. Of course, there's no way to tell when it'll actually do anything."

"Philosophic iron?" Dexter asked. "What does it do?"

"It's said that it moves," Max told him. "All on its own."

"That's ridiculous. Don't play tricks on me."

Max shook his head. "Having been the butt of many of those tricks since putting to sea, I would never attempt to play one myself."

"It's true," Liao put in. "I've seen lots of it. I'll show you some when we get to Bayside, Max."

"Hang on a tick." Lucy and Whippett sprinted away again and

disappeared through the arched door of another chapel, leaving Max, Dexter, and Liao standing alone in the overhanging shadow of what had certainly been the prow of a vessel at one point but which now supported a tall, slender house. Max and Dexter exchanged an impatient glance and waited with matching folded arms until the other two emerged again. "Masthead's this way," Lucy said with a wave.

They turned another corner and found themselves staring at an edifice that was a bit like a lighthouse, a bell tower, and a topmast with a crow's nest all rolled into one soaring structure of weathered gray teak and pine-green planks. A short flight of stairs led to a stoop and a rounded green door. As they ascended these stairs, bells began to ring across Nagspeake to announce the half hour. When the Quartermaster's bell sounded, it

rang out with five deep bongs. Half past six in the morning: *five bells in the morning watch*, Max thought, pleased with himself for coming up with the right phrase.

Lucy tugged the bellpull. The front door opened and a man in a white cotton uniform with a seaman's long braid leaned out. "Our best respects," Lucy said, "and Melusine and Liao Bluecrowne and Maxwell Ault for Miss Levinflash, and Lieutenant Oliver Dexter to wait upon the Quartermaster, if convenient."

The man at the door nodded. "Miss and Master Bluecrowne, Master Ault, and Lieutenant Dexter it is. Come right in."

Whippett took a seat in the entryway, and the rest of them followed the doorman into a parlor. "Wait here." The seaman disappeared through a paneled door at the back of the room and returned a moment later with a tray in one hand. "Mr. Dexter, the Quartermaster will be glad to see you, if you do not mind waiting ten minutes. Miss Levinflash ain't in, Miss Bluecrowne, but she left these for you." He held out the tray. Two letters sat upon it, one sealed, the other not. Max read over Lucy's shoulder as she unfolded the unsealed page. *The compliments of the Office of the Quartermaster, and the Honorable Jonquil Levinflash wishes to introduce*—and then a long space—*to the Honorable Alistair Yeowarder, Port Admiral of the Sovereign City of Nagspeake.*

"Which it's blank for you to write in a name," the doorman explained. "I've got ink and the seal in my pocket. The other one has your name already in it, miss."

"Capital!" Lucy smoothed the letter out and wrote *Maxwell Ault* in the space. The footman produced blotting paper, sand, and sealing-wax, then closed the letter up neatly. "Pass our thanks to Miss Levinflash and our compliments to the Quartermaster," Lucy said as she tucked her own introduction into her ditty bag and handed Max's to him. "And here's for your trouble." She handed the doorman a shilling. "Good morning, Mr. Dexter."

"What good is a shilling here?" Max asked as they returned to the street.

"They're good luck. Or sometimes sailors use them for offerings," Liao explained.

"Offerings?" Max asked, thinking of the two churches Lucy and Whippett had scurried into.

"Offerings," Lucy said breezily. "Come on, step lively, will you? And try to watch your step. The ferry dock's still a good long pull away."

....

OLIVER KNEW IT WAS GOOD MANNERS TO CALL UPON THE FELLOW in charge when one brought a ship into port. It seemed especially important now, since the *Fate* had been treated so well by the district of Flotilla even after it was discovered that she wasn't in the hands of the Bluecrownes any longer. But beyond saying thank you, he wasn't sure what he was supposed to do when he was shown in to see the Quartermaster. He still wasn't entirely clear on who this Quartermaster fellow was. Aboard ship, a quartermaster was a petty officer responsible for things like navigation and signaling and steering, but here it seemed to mean exactly what the name implied: the master of the quarter of Flotilla. Perhaps he was something like a port admiral, or a mayor.

I ought to have just asked Lucy, he thought glumly. But it hadn't gotten any easier to admit when he didn't know something. It wasn't so bad admitting a gap in his knowledge to Mr. Cascon behind closed doors, but the idea of admitting ignorance to Lucy or Max or any of the Fates was still very, very distasteful.

The sailor in the white uniform opened the paneled door again. "The Quartermaster will see you now, Mr. Dexter."

Oliver followed him down a hallway, up a twisting stair, and into a round chamber with sweeping concave windows. Outside, the rooftops of Flotilla lay scattered about. People hurried this way and that in the rigging like sailors readying for a complex maneuver.

"Quite a view, no?"

Oliver started, mortified that he'd let the room distract him from the dark-haired figure sitting behind the desk at its center. Nell Levinflash laughed. "Not to worry, Mr. Dexter. I've seen admirals do the same."

"Miss Levinflash?" He turned, glancing around the room. Then he had a sudden and horrifying recollection of Monsieur Cloutier doing precisely the same thing when he had been shown into the captain's cabin on the *Left-Handed Fate*. "Oh, lord."

"Yes, it's just you and me, Mr. Dexter," she said dryly. "Come and sit. I have coffee and toasted soft tack and there's a pot of preserves here, a kind that folks in Bayside get into fisticuffs over."

Oliver made an awkward bow and sat. "That's very kind of you, miss."

"I shouldn't say it was *very* kind. I ate all the bacon before I invited you up." She poured coffee and passed it across the desk, along with a plate of toast and dark red jam. Oliver took a bite. The preserves were tremendously good, with a flavor like port and half-melted candy.

Miss Levinflash grinned. "Top-notch, no?"

"Mmff," was all Oliver could manage.

"From Mirabelle Béchamel's shop, not that I imagine that means anything to you." The Quartermaster took a bite of her own toast, which allowed Oliver to finish chewing and take a sip of coffee to wash the bite down. The coffee was so strong he could feel it running through his nerves all the way to the ends of his hair.

"It was good of you to come by last night," he said at last. "I regret any trouble the present situation causes."

She waved one hand. "There is no trouble with the present situation. Flotilla was built by seamen, for seamen. Despite my personal connection with the Bluecrowne family, I am bound by the laws of the sea, and of maritime war. And Nagspeake's neutrality is very important." She folded her hands and regarded him with an unreadable expression. "I imagine you're wondering why I didn't see Lucy just now, and why I didn't mention my promotion last night."

That was a curiosity. Oliver had just taken another bite, so he could only nod.

"The arrival in Nagspeake of the *Left-Handed Fate* under these conditions, at the start of this war—it's troubling, Mr. Dexter. I have obligations to the city to be sure the situation is handled correctly. But I love Lucy and Liao and the *Fate*, and I wanted to greet them as a friend and former shipmate first, before I put on my Quartermaster hat, as it were. Do you understand?"

"I think so. Excuse me, but what's left to be handled now that you've put on your Quartermaster hat? I thought there was no trouble."

"I did say that, didn't I? But there is something I confess I am quite curious about."

"Yes, miss?" Oliver took another bite of his toast. Even his own mother, he thought guiltily, didn't make preserves as good as these.

"You came into Flotilla in command of a prize-ship in which the entire former crew was not only at liberty, but was actively engaged in working the ship on your behalf. I have *never* heard of an entire crew of prisoners working willingly for its captors. And you were put in charge of the *Fate* in the Chesapeake, yet you turn up all the way here, in Nagspeake? This makes no sense."

"Mmff—well—"

"No, no, keep eating. But it seems to me there must be more to the story. And while it isn't my job to get involved in the affairs of either the United States or Britain, it *is* my job to make inquiries when a ship arrives in my quarter and something's so obviously a-hoo."

Oliver hesitated. Then, in what he hoped was a not-too-obvious ploy to buy more time to think, he shoved the rest of his toast in his mouth. The Quartermaster leaned back in her chair and waited.

It wasn't for him to peach on Lucy and Max's mission. On the other hand, the Quartermaster was practically part of Lucy's family. In any case, if Oliver was going to find enough able seamen to get the *Fate* back to Baltimore, he needed her goodwill.

"Well, I tell you what it is, miss," he began, scratching his head. Immediately he regretted it. His hair stuck to his fingers, and he cursed himself for not checking to be sure he hadn't gotten any of the preserves on his hand. The *red* preserves, which would certainly show up in his blond hair. The Quartermaster waited with one eyebrow hitched up, entirely unconcerned with twelve-year-old boys and their problems with eating jam properly. "I tell you what it is," Oliver repeated weakly, fumbling for his handkerchief and rubbing at his fingers.

"Do," the Quartermaster said. "Or perhaps it will help you if I tell you what *I* think it is."

"Well—oh." Oliver's hands stilled in his lap. "All right, miss."

Nell Levinflash poured herself another cup of coffee and stirred a lump of sugar into it. "There have been rumors circulating in Nagspeake for several months," she began, "about shipments of weaponry being sold here to outside nations. Now, this is not unheard of; smuggling has always been part of the city's economy. But with war declared between the United States and Britain, it becomes problematic for our precious neutrality."

Oliver frowned, trying to figure out how the Quartermaster thought this might explain the *Fate* and its peculiar situation.

"It becomes even more problematic when the whispers begin talking about a particularly fearsome weapon," the young woman said deliberately. "A war engine like no other. Something unlike anything the world has seen before."

She *knew*.

The Quartermaster smiled a very thin smile. "I see these rumors are not confined to Nagspeake."

"No, miss, I'm just trying to imagine what sort of thing you mean," Oliver stammered. "Some sort of infernal device?"

"Rumors do not tend to come with specifics," she said evenly.

"I take it you wish me to believe you have no knowledge of such an engine."

Oliver dropped all pretense of looking like a naval officer and tried as hard as he could to look like nothing more than a boy with jam in his hair. "Perhaps if you could explain the engine a bit better. So I can visualize it, like."

The woman across the desk was unimpressed. "Two ships have been named in connection with this thing, Mr. Dexter. The *Left-Handed Fate* is one of them. Now, I can conceive of exactly one explanation for your particular situation. The *Fate* has enough of this device aboard that her crew was able to force your assistance in getting here; and you agreed rather than calling their bluff in the hopes that, once here, you might be able to steal the thing for yourself. True or false?"

"False! It happened just as we told you last night, Miss Levinflash. That's the truth."

"Ridiculous. You're enemy combatants. It's as simple as that."

"And the French are supposed to be my allies, but they still tried to take my ship," Oliver countered. "It wasn't simple at all."

"Yes, and why was it, again, that they tried to take an American prize?"

Oliver hesitated. Dangerous ground, this. "It was a matter of a diplomat thinking his title and my youth gave him some sort of all-powerful weather-gauge. Your Honor."

They regarded each other across the remains of toast, preserves, and coffee for a long moment. "Neutrality is another thing that seems it ought to be straightforward, but turns out not to be," the Quartermaster said thoughtfully. "In principle, it ought to be as uncomplicated as saying to the world, *You will have to figure this one out on your own and leave us out of it.* But of course, many hundreds of little details and negotiations come into it."

"The United States wanted to be neutral, too. Britain forced us into this conflict," Oliver said. The Quartermaster was coming it a touch high, going on and on about Nagspeake's famous neutrality as if it meant the city was above such tawdry things as wars. *Also,* he added mentally, *it helps to be so small that no one cares whether or not you join the fight.*

"That is my point precisely." The Quartermaster's voice had gone very cold. "Countries may be forced into wars they would otherwise not wish to enter. Pray be certain that your actions here are as you've represented them. Were it to be discovered that this weapon is real and that you were involved with it and didn't cooperate with the city, you might do more damage than you realize. Do not, *do not* force Nagspeake to compromise its neutrality. We are small"— could she read his mind?—"but if this weapon crosses our borders, we will be forced to act, and with such a thing in our possession . . . well. Neighbors we might be, but our interests do not always line up with those of the United States."

"That doesn't sound particularly neutral at all," Oliver observed. "It sounds an awful lot like a threat."

"Neutrality is complicated, as I said." The young woman smiled a vague, whimsical smile. "At its simplest, it's rather like holding a pie that can be knocked out of your hands and trod upon at any time by someone else. And then the pie is utterly destroyed, and all that's left is to do your best to kill the person who took it from you." Her gaze sharpened again, and the smile became less whimsical. "More toast, Mr. Dexter?"

Oliver swallowed. "No, thank you, miss."

eighteen
BAYSIDE

The quarter that stretched along the harbor frontage of Magothy Bay was called, appropriately enough, Bayside. It was here, on a set of mossy steps leading up to a stone quay, that the ferry-gig deposited Max, Lucy, and Liao after their trip across the crowded harbor. Max had cherished a dream that finding the *Honoratus* would be as easy as passing her on their way across, or discovering that the ferryman had spotted a ship by that name on one of his crossings. They didn't, and the ferryman had not.

"Wouldn't have mattered," Lucy said when he expressed his disappointment. "If she's here, it won't be as easy as it would at sea. It's a neutral port, so we can't touch her. We'll need to know if she's unloaded cargo—and when, and where, and to whom—and how long she's expected to stay."

"Anything else I should ask that you didn't mention before?" Max grumbled.

"Nothing springs to mind, Maxwell, but should common sense suggest anything to you in the moment, why, don't you hesitate."

Small warehouses and wholesalers and shipping offices lined the harbor, interspersed with shops and chophouses that sent mouth-watering aromas out to mingle with the rest of the harbor smells. Max's stomach groaned.

"That's the Port Admiral's office, there." Lucy pointed to a brick building not far from where they stood, where a crowd milled restlessly around the scrubby lawn. "Looks like you might have a bit of a wait."

"In that case I'm going to get a proper meal first. Come along?"

Lucy shook her head and reached for Max's bag of cards. "No, I think I'd better get on my way. I know my way around Nagspeake a little, but not the quarter where this weaving street is. Can you find your way back to the *Fate*?"

"Don't worry, Lucy," Liao said. "I'll make sure we get back to the ship."

"Do you have one of the special rockets in your bag, in case you need me?" Lucy asked.

"Of course. I have one every time I leave the ship, just like we agreed. But I don't think Max can get into that much trouble. After all, there's no rigging here for him to fall out of."

"Look, the both of you," Max interrupted. "The thing about being a landsman is that you tend not to be quite as useless when actually *on land*."

"But you keep on almost falling in," Liao protested.

"Oh, please, that was in Flotilla, which hardly counts as dry land!"

"If you say so." Lucy gave Liao a broad wink. "Good luck, then."

"Good luck to you," Max replied. Lucy disappeared inland, and he turned to Liao. "Let's see about breakfast."

"I already had breakfast," Liao said righteously. "I was up at three bells."

"Well, then, you can set off a firework or two while I eat," Max suggested, eyeing the passing sailors. Some crews embroidered the names of their ships on the ribbons of their straw shore-going hats. Now, as he and Liao hiked along the quay, they passed tars whose hats proclaimed them to be Whimsies, Blackthorns, Celestines, and Holyroods. He saw no Honoratuses.

Liao stopped and tugged on Max's hand. "That's the philosophic iron, Max."

Max followed the boy's pointing finger to an iron fence that ran around the periphery of a shop yard. Other than the fact that it was exceptionally finely wrought, it looked perfectly ordinary. He crouched for a closer look. "How can you tell?"

"Because it's . . ." Liao scratched his head. "Because it's wrong."

"Wrong?"

"Can't you see? It doesn't look right."

Max leaned back on his heels and examined the whorls of metal. The fence was definitely warped a bit out of true here and there, as if it had bent under some sort of impact. It also had a rusty reddish-gray tone to it in places. When Max reached out to touch one of those spots, however, it was smooth as porcelain, without any of rust's grain. And the metal was warm to the touch, warmer than it ought to be so early on such a mild morning. Max prodded it. "And it can really move on its own power?"

Liao crouched beside him. "It's probably sleeping. Evenings are better for watching it."

Max watched it for another minute, willing it to do something. The iron steadfastly refused to oblige. "I suppose this isn't really why we're here anyhow." Conveniently enough, the shop with the iron fence also had a shingle with a bright red beefsteak hanging over its open door. The smells of frying meat and frying dough drifted out. "All right. If anyone bothers you—"

The boy lowered his eyelids and reached into his bag. He made a throwing motion, a sort of hocus-pocus gesture, and the ground at his feet exploded.

Max picked himself up off the street, as did several others who had been a bit too close for their own good. "If anyone bothers me," Liao said calmly as wisps of dissipating smoke curled around his ankles, "I think they will decide not to bother me for long."

"I think you're right," Max agreed.

Inside the chophouse he had to push through the crowd that had rushed to the windows to see what had exploded before he found someone in an apron to show him to a table. He ordered a pot of coffee, a skewer of sausages, and a plate of the local pancakes called planekooch, then glanced out the window to make sure Liao wasn't getting carted away for disturbing the peace. Instead, it seemed he'd gathered himself an audience, and was now giving an impromptu lecture.

The coffee arrived with a pitcher of hot milk sweetened with brown sugar. Then the food came: four red sausages with crisp, crinkly skin and the planekooch layered with roasted cherries and drizzled with lemon syrup and more brown sugar.

"I suppose you see most of the ships that come in," Max said to the serving man.

"Aye, most of 'em."

"I'm trying to track down a ship that—that my brother was coming into town on," Max said lamely, wishing he'd thought to plan his story in advance. "*Honoratus* is her name."

"*Honoratus?* It don't ring a bell."

"She'd have come in from the United States. From Baltimore."

"There was a ship came in a couple days back that had put in at

Baltimore. Supposedly had to shoot her way past a British ambush leaving the Chesapeake, we heard. Couldn't say whether she's still about, though."

Max nodded his thanks and ate rapidly. Then he settled up the bill and headed back out to collect Liao.

A few moments later, in the next high-backed booth over from Max's, a man in a dark blue coat stood. He left the chophouse and strolled casually along in the wake of the two boys making their way toward the Port Admiral's office.

....

OLIVER SAT UNDER AN APRICOT-COLORED AWNING AT A CAFÉ that pitched and rolled slightly under his feet. When Lucy had suggested a sherbet, Oliver had pictured something like a frozen sorbet, but it had turned out to be a red juice tasting of hibiscus and lemon, which went down very well after his interview with the Quartermaster.

There wasn't much steerage room in a conversation after one party began tossing out threats disguised as unbelievable overreactions to lost pie. In the panic that set in after he'd realized that yes, the Quartermaster had, in fact, suggested that Nagspeake would find any compromise of its neutrality to be legitimate grounds for having a twelve-year-old boy killed, Oliver had nearly gotten right to his feet and bolted out the door. Only the fact that he had no idea where he could possibly bolt *to* had kept him in his seat.

There must be someone who can clear things up, he thought desperately. *Someone who can do it without my dragging Lucy and Max into things.* Some sort of consul or ambassador—certainly the United States had to have one here.

He hadn't wanted to ask Nell Levinflash herself where the United States' diplomatic representative kept his offices, if he existed at all. But it was exhausting, this constant pretending he didn't have any questions. "I beg your pardon, but perhaps the best thing for me to do would be to go to my government's representative in Nagspeake. Where may I find him?"

The Quartermaster had regarded him with narrowed eyes. "Are you not at some risk from your government, having so completely disobeyed your orders?"

"I don't see it that way, miss, no." He did, of course, but he hadn't been about to admit it.

"Hmm." She'd picked up a pen and scrawled a few lines on a slip of paper. "The United States' Minister Plenipotentiary keeps an office in west Bayside. A fellow by the name of Otterick, I believe."

Now, across the harbor, a little trail of smoke lifted over the scattered sails and erupted with a delayed pop into a spray of fizzing red. Somewhere over there Liao, at least, was having a good time. Oliver finished his drink slowly, and just as he swallowed the last sugary sip, Whippett appeared around the corner. "Ahoy, Whippett!" he called. "I am thinking of making another stop. I have the address here. Do you know the city well enough to find it?"

"Aye, sir, I reckon so. Straight there, rather than to the ship, is it?"

"If you please."

"Aye aye, sir." Whippett touched his knuckle to his forelock. "This way, sir."

nineteen
WARPANDYE STREET

Nagspeake, Lucy well remembered, was a ridiculous city to navigate. Streets went halfway to the road they ought logically to intersect with and then curved back in sharp doglegs, depositing one nearly where one had started out. Or they led to bridges that arched up, hit a stone wall, and stopped there without connecting to anything. There were lengths of rowhouses that went on for miles without breaks in between. Woe to the walker who by some bit of bad luck found herself on the wrong side of one of those stretches.

Lucy had left Bayside behind for the inland artisan district called the Printer's Quarter. She found her way to the quarter without difficulty, then stopped for directions at a café where the proprietor gave Lucy a set of convoluted instructions that seemed to have too many left turns to do anything but bring her right back to the same place. On the other hand, she reflected, given the way Nagspeake streets behaved, Warpandye could be a stone's throw from where she was and still only be accessible by some roundabout route involving nothing but left-hand turns.

Here the iron that Max called *philosophic* and Nagspeakers simply called *old* was much more common than in Bayside. It climbed the sides of houses and twined alongside stairs like ivy, always looking suddenly frozen, as though it might have been moving only a moment before and might move again if one stopped looking at it directly. An old iron railing climbed alongside a flight of stairs on Lucy's route, and when she touched it a faint thrum pulsed through her fingers that was not unlike the vibration she felt at the tiller of the *Fate*.

At the top of the stairs, there was nothing but a fingerpost with a single hand-shaped sign pointing down the other side of the ridge she'd just climbed. Lucy swore. There was no path to be seen, just a steep, rocky, and weedy slope that angled down into a gorge. Still, the one word on the sign was *Warpandye*, so Lucy grumbled, "This city . . ." and began looking for places to put her feet.

Following the pointing finger exactly, she found a flat piece of iron set right into the slope. From there, the next foothold was just visible under a knot of briar. So it went, with each step revealing itself only when Lucy stood on the one just above. It was such tricky going that Warpandye Street came upon her abruptly: without warning the next flat surface was not another iron foothold but a cobbled street overhung with hawthorns. Across the lane, the slope continued down to the stony bottom Lucy had seen from above. The street itself, with its white-flowered trees and row of cottages set against the back of the hill, had been completely hidden from view.

Lucy wandered up the street, past the workshop cottages of a dozen weavers, spinners, dyers, knotters, and embroiderers. She squinted at the signs over each little house, looking for anything to suggest which might be the most likely place to start—logically, the fewer people she showed the cards to, the better. But nothing gave her any hint, so she just kept on walking.

At a bend overlooking the bottom of the gorge she came to a house covered in twisting lilac and looping ironwork. A creeping plant with lacy silver-gray leaves dripped languidly from the eaves of the roof. She was about to pass it as she'd passed the others when Lucy realized the graceful, lacy creeper had been knotted from cloud-gray thread and thin silver wire. The shingle beside this door bore a carved spider at the center of an elaborate web. Woven into the threads above the spider was the name *Tilly Gallfreet*; woven below, the words *Matelassé, Brocade, Damask.*

Lucy rang the bell and stepped inside. Bolts of fabric were piled behind two long wooden counters, and where there weren't counters there were glass-fronted cabinets stuffed with cone-shaped spindles of thread in every shade imaginable. From the back of the house, through a door cracked just enough to let the sound through, came a rhythmic noise: *clack-thump-shush, clack-thump-shush.*

"Hello?" Lucy said.

A woman with graying red hair bustled through with a tray of tea and cups, which she set on one of the counters. "Hello, there."

"I'm Lucy Bluecrowne," Lucy said. "Are you Tilly Gallfreet?"

The woman shook her head. "I'm Mrs. Henrietta Allis, from down the street. Tilly's just finishing something up. She'll be out shortly, won't you, Tilly?" she added, raising her voice. "The tea'll get cold."

"Is it a customer?" came a woman's voice from beyond the open door. *Clack-thump-shush, clack-thump-shush.*

"Could be," the red-haired lady replied. "You a customer, girl?"

"I'm not sure," Lucy said. "I have some loom-cards, and I was hoping someone could tell me what pattern they might show."

The red-headed woman unearthed a pair of spectacles from her hair and perched them on her nose. "Let's see, then. Bring 'em this way."

"Thank you." Lucy took the stack of cards from the bag and set them on the counter.

Mrs. Allis whistled as Lucy began to unfold them. "You've come to the right place. This is a puzzle for Tilly. Only the Spinster knows more about this sort of thing. She's a proper Arachne, is Tilly, if she ever deigns to show herself."

"All right, all right." The sound in the back room died and Tilly herself emerged, pushing her own spectacles up onto her freckled forehead. Lucy's eyes slid past her to the apparatus just visible through the open door to the back room. It looked like the sort of thing one might draw if asked to imagine a loom, a gallows, a camel, and a waterfall of paper at the same time.

"Miss Lucy Bluecrowne, Miss Tilly Gallfreet," Mrs. Allis said. "Miss Bluecrowne has some very interesting loom-cards, Tilly. They look like jacker-cards, only . . . well. You'll see."

"Jacker-cards?" Lucy repeated.

"*Jacquard* cards," Tilly corrected absently. Jacquard—that had been the name of Bonaparte's weaver, the one they'd taken these from. Lucy stiffened immediately, but neither of the weavers noticed. They were both too busy staring down at the big, oblong stack and the cards Mrs. Allis had unfolded from it.

"Oh, these are old," Tilly murmured. "The ribbon's old, too, but not nearly so old as the cards. They must've been relaced." She lifted the first panel so that light filtered through the pattern of punch-holes. "Usually they're made of paper or pasteboard, but these are . . ." She flicked the edge. "Whalebone, perhaps? And how can they possibly be this old?" Tilly shook her head. "It's impossible, yet here they are, and they look to be antique several times over. Where did they come from?"

"From a passenger on my father's ship. But why is it strange that they're old? Everything gets old, if it survives that long."

"Well, yes, but these are cards for Jacquard's weaving process, or something very like it, and Mr. Jacquard only invented his process a decade or so ago." Tilly shook her head. "Even if they were somehow his own pieces from early on, they would only be twenty or thirty years old. But look." She ran her finger along part of the network of fine, time-stained cracks along the surface of the top card. "Only age does this. And the insides of the holes are the same. It's not only old bone, the pattern upon it's old, too."

Then Tilly lifted the card up, which in turn lifted the next in the chain. "And then there are these lacings," she continued. "There's something off here as well." Holding the top card by one of its short edges, she turned it back toward the pack. It flipped over easily in its fastenings, and so did the next card, and the one after that. They cascaded in succession like a falling-block toy, a Jacob's ladder, so that now the pattern was reversed.

"Is that normal?" Lucy asked. Max would be horrified if he knew his precious cards could be reordered that easily.

"No indeed," Tilly replied. "It makes no sense. These patterns aren't symmetrical. Reversing them changes the pattern. But it looks as if someone *meant* for the cards to be able to do that—otherwise why connect them this way? Most Jacquard loom-cards are fastened in ways that hold them quite firmly in place. These, though—what on earth is the point of making them so that they *can* do this if you don't *want* them to do this? Any other fastening at all would be preferable." She unfolded the stack across the counter, and the packet became a long chain of slim slats interlaced with the thin, fraying blue silk ribbon. The chain ran the entire length of the countertop and spilled off onto the floor.

Lucy had never seen them laid out all the way. Her eyes wanted to find a pattern in the punch-holes, and they roved over and over the length, seeking some point from which to build the image she thought must be there, if only she could find the right way of looking.

"Frustrating, isn't it?" Tilly asked as Lucy tilted her head at a painful angle for a different perspective. "Don't give yourself a headache. We don't even know if these cards are in the right places. You saw how easily they turned, and look." She reached down and pulled one right out of its ribbon.

Lucy yelped. "What are you doing?"

Tilly slid the piece back into place. "I don't think I'd give myself a headache over that, either, miss. Who knows how many times throughout the years these pieces might have been switched around?"

Mrs. Allis spoke up. "So you can't make heads nor tails of it neither, Tilly? Won't they work on your loom? Takes a particular sort of loom to weave Jacker-fabric," she added to Lucy. "One with a Jacker-head on it."

"*Jacquard.*" Tilly ran her fingers over a row of punched rectangles. "Oh, I could get the chain on the loom somehow, I imagine. But I'm certain they're out of order, Miss Bluecrowne. As old as they are, I can't believe they've never been scrambled when they seem *made* to be scrambled. No, you need more than a loom. You need someone who can put the pattern back together again, and that's past my knowing-how."

"But Mrs. Allis said there's no one to surpass you," Lucy protested.

"Oh, but there is," Tilly said. "You must go and see my mother. There's nothing she can't do with warp and weft."

Mrs. Allis stiffened. "Don't be ridiculous. The girl can't go there."

"It's not ridiculous. Not if she really wants to know what's on these cards," Tilly said sharply. "Anyhow, it's only scared, superstitious folk that make that place into more than it is."

"What place?" Lucy asked impatiently.

"Mama lives on the hill, up at the top."

"*Lives on the hill*," Mrs. Allis muttered in a tone that made it clear that there was something very wrong with how Tilly had phrased this.

"All right. And how do I get there?"

"Oh, easy. Just follow the signs to the madhouse," Mrs. Allis said. "Knock on the door and ask for the Mad Spinster."

"I wish you wouldn't call her that," Tilly said curtly. "She's no danger to anyone else," she said, turning to Lucy, "though it's true that she isn't what you'd call *all there*. But she's a painter with thread, is my mama. She taught me everything I know, and even now she teaches me something new every time I go to her. Which isn't as often as I ought," she admitted. "It's not what you'd call a nice place to visit; that far I'll agree with Mrs. Allis."

The older woman harrumphed. "That is putting it mildly."

Tilly ignored her. "Will you go?"

Lucy began refolding the cards. "If she'll have the answer, I will. I'm not superstitious, and I'm not scared." Of course, that was a lie on both counts. Like most sailors, she was *extremely* superstitious, and she couldn't really imagine anyone not being a bit afraid of going into a madhouse to seek out one of its denizens. "Will she be able to weave what's on them for me, then?"

"Oh, certainly, if she can work out how. And if you have the time."

"I have some time, I suppose. How long will it take?"

"Assuming she can figure out what she needs to know to reconstruct the proper order?" Tilly rubbed the bridge of her nose. "Well, even my mother can only weave a foot or so a day, and she's about as fast as any alive. But if this pattern is as complicated as it looks at first blush . . . well. I wouldn't expect it to be that quick."

"I don't suppose I have any other options," Lucy said, trying to hide her disappointment as she put the cards away.

"All right, then. Wait here. I'll give you something to take, so she'll know I sent you." Tilly disappeared through the door at the back of the room.

"You'll really go to Saint Whit's?" Mrs. Allis asked in an undertone. "I wouldn't."

"Is this lady the one you mentioned before?" Lucy asked. "When you said Tilly was a proper Arachne and only the Spinster knew more?"

"Sure she is, but I didn't mean you should go to *her*. I meant to say Tilly's the best there is who isn't bleeding insane." Mrs. Allis stopped talking abruptly as Tilly came back with a jar of preserves in one hand and a beautiful piece of fabric in the other. From the size, it was probably meant to be a napkin, but it looked like a miniature tapestry. Tilly wrapped the jar in it and tied the ends together.

"Tell her I said I thought you had a fair fascinating puzzle." She handed over the parcel. "Tell her this is the last jar of Mirabelle Béchamel's preserves and I saved it for her. And tell her the rain crows are back in the cherry laurel behind the house. Say that I'll come soon myself and bring her red feathers if I find any."

"Are you certain it's all right to bother her?"

"A puzzle like this, she would never forgive me for keeping from her. There isn't much that gives her pleasure these days."

"Well, thank you." Lucy slung the bag back over her shoulder. "How do I get to this place?"

....

BACK IN BAYSIDE, MAX WAS VERY NEAR TO BANGING HIS HEAD ON the desk of the Port Admiral's clerk. Only the suspicion that the clerk was waiting for him to do it kept him from caving to the frustration.

"Have you any further questions I might answer, Mr. Ault?" the clerk asked, after answering precisely none of the questions Max had put to him so far. "If not, I really ought to move on to the next fellow in the queue."

"Isn't it public information, which ships have come in and which have left?" Max had already asked this three times.

"It is, but of course as you can see, my colleague has the register and is at present using it. If you wish to wait until he is finished with *his* queue—"

"And I suppose it would be entirely out of the question simply to ask him for the register." The ledger in question was sitting unused and ignored on the corner of the other clerk's desk.

"It would not do to interrupt."

"Of course not." Never mind that the desks were only two feet apart and that the other clerk could certainly hear the conversation taking place over here.

"So perhaps you might . . ." The smiling clerk made a sweeping motion with his hands, as if to suggest that Max find a likely breeze and waft himself away upon it.

It was a universal truth that life among humans meant occasionally dealing with jackasses. "Oh, by all means," Max replied, matching the clerk's smile. He reached one long leg out and kicked the other clerk's desk, hard. The register teetered and slid to the floor, along with an inkwell, a full cup of tea with saucer and spoon, and a globe that immediately bounced free of its stand and went rolling along the uneven floorboards, past the fellows waiting in the entry, and out into the street.

"Allow me." Max plucked the register from the pool of tea and ink and handed it to his clerk. "*Honoratus*, sir, is the name of the ship, in case you have forgotten it in the quarter hour that has passed since I sat down."

The clerk half-rose from his chair, red rising on his face. "My dear sir—"

Max opened the book. "Make haste, sir. The ink is coming toward your chair."

Two minutes later, Max emerged, whistling, with everything the Port Admiral's office knew about the *Honoratus* scribbled on a bit of paper in his pocket. She *had* come in. She *had* unloaded cargo. The register even had the name of the agent who'd handled the storage of that cargo until it had been taken away. That agent would certainly know who had taken it, possibly even where it had been taken to.

He headed toward the quay where Liao was still happily setting off crackers, and he was waiting for a carriage to pass in the street when the globe from the office rolled suddenly into his path. He stumbled, more out of surprise than anything else. And just then, a pair of strong hands grabbed Max by the collar and jerked him backward into an alley.

The globe rolled on, bounced past Liao, and dropped with a *plunk* into the harbor. The boy looked up from the fuse he was about to light and saw a flash of blue. Liao extinguished his match between thumb and forefinger. The blue flash—Max's coat—disappeared into a coach. And since he knew perfectly well that Max would never go and leave him behind without a word, Liao decided his helpless friend had somehow managed to get himself snatched.

The boy rolled his eyes, muttering to himself, and took off on foot after the carriage.

twenty
KIDNAPPED, MONSIEUR

"Explain yourself," Max demanded, yanking himself free of the men who'd shoved him into the carriage that was now scraping its way through the confining alley.

"It ought to be clear enough," laughed the first in accented English. Max's heart sank. "You have been kidnapped, monsieur. Abducted."

"I am a—how dare—I demand—" But Max didn't finish any of his protests. If the fellow had said, *You are being summoned*, or *Your presence is required elsewhere*, indignance might have done some good. But when your captors happily admitted they were kidnapping you . . . "Hell," he grumbled, folding his arms and flopping back against the back of his seat.

"Nowhere so dramatic," said the second stranger.

"I don't suppose you'll tell me anything along the lines of what on earth this is all about?"

"You know precisely what this is about, monsieur." The first man regarded Max with unfriendly eyes. "The *Honoratus*."

Max's stomach twisted.

After a bit, the noise of the carriage scraping against too-close walls ceased. Not long after that, the sound of the city outside diminished and the road pitched upward. At last the carriage rolled to a stop. The man who'd spoken first opened the door and waved a hand. "After you."

Well, that meant there was going to be nowhere to go if he ran. Max slid past his captor and stepped down into a sunlit courtyard surrounded by a high brick wall. The two men herded him up a gravel walk and through the front door of a large house. Inside, they conducted him to a parlor that was empty except for a tall case-clock, a horsehair sofa, and a desk with a small letter box on it, a sort of portable secretary meant both to hold correspondence and to provide a writing surface. "Wait here, please," said the first man.

"Sit," ordered the second, who was rather larger and very nearly filled the single doorway after his colleague had gone.

Max sat and thought. Had these two been among the Frenchmen who had tried to take the *Left-Handed Fate* in the Chesapeake? Had the *Marie Colette* made port in Nagspeake that quickly? Were they from the *Honoratus* herself, or even from a contingent that had been in Nagspeake all along?

He heard the kidnapper trot up a flight of stairs and knock on a door. Voices spoke, then footsteps drummed: ghostly, disembodied sounds that echoed strangely in the mostly empty house and blended with words in lilting French.

Max spoke French as well as was to be expected from an English boy brought up by a scientific father, which is to say he had enough to scrape along with, and usually enough Latin to make sense of any words he didn't immediately know. This snippet, therefore, was well within his capability: *We shall have to make other plans, then. Arrange to claim it at the bazaar.*

More footsteps descended the stairs, and a moment later Max's guard stepped aside and the newcomer entered the parlor.

He was an older man than either of the others, perhaps some-where in his fifties, and he wore his black-and-gray hair swept back from his forehead and a little long over his collar. His coat had prob-ably once been very splendid: a midnight blue affair with beautiful tailoring but without much shine left to the velvet. There was a slightly bald patch above the watch pocket that brought to mind a memory of Max's father reaching for his spectacles in a motion that had worn away the very same patch. Max was immediately certain he was looking at some sort of philosopher.

He had half-constructed a story about someone he knew stow-ing away on the *Honoratus*, which he thought would perhaps ex-plain both his interest and his reluctance to talk about it. He was just about to launch into this fiction when the man stopped beside the desk, looked down at Max, and froze him completely with a single sentence.

"You don't look anything like your father."

....

THE OFFICE OF THE MINISTER PLENIPOTENTIARY OF THE UNITED States to the Sovereign City of Nagspeake was tucked at the end of a tiny street at the very edge of the district, so far inland that Whip-pett grumbled that this was hardly Bayside at all.

The house itself was a bit overgrown and the plaque bearing the Minister's name and title was so tarnished that the verdigris all but disappeared into the ivy. Oliver shoved the gate open with some difficulty and rang the bell. A young man in a clerk's black coat opened the door. "Yes, sir?"

"Acting-Lieutenant Oliver Dexter, U.S. Navy, prize-captain of captured British letter-of-marque the *Left-Handed Fate*," Oliver re-cited, saluting. "My duty to the Minister, and may I see him please, if it is convenient?"

"Oh." The young man scratched his scalp under his curled wig.

"Well." He hesitated, then mustered a wide smile. "That is to say, please do come in, Lieutenant. Right this way."

The young man led Oliver into an office overlooking the street and indicated two chairs beside the window. "My name is Hoveller, incidentally."

Just at that moment there was a bizarre squeal of metal on metal from somewhere above their heads. Oliver leapt halfway out of his seat.

"Ralph Hoveller," the young man continued. He took a book and pen from the desk and sat beside Oliver. "I'm His Excellency's clerk."

"Very good to meet you," Oliver looked warily up at the ceiling and then back at Hoveller, who was pretending very hard not to have noticed anything untoward.

"Could I trouble you for the particulars of the reason for your visit to Nagspeake in general, and to His Excellency in particular?" Hoveller asked. Again the shredding metal noise ripped through the house, and again he ignored it, staring politely but fixedly at Oliver with his pen poised over the page of his journal.

"The frigate *Amaranthine* took the *Left-Handed Fate* just out of Norfolk," Oliver said when his heart had stopped hammering. "It being so early in the cruise and Captain Eager not wishing to lose"—he forced himself to be honest—"any of the more critical hands, he put me in charge. I was to take the vessel back to Norfolk, but fate intervened—" He paused as Hoveller broke into a fit of chuckles.

"I beg your pardon. Ha! Fate intervened—the prize was named the *Left-Handed Fate*—" He whipped a handkerchief from his pocket and wiped his eyes. "I beg your pardon. Carry on, sir." Another overhead screech of metal erupted. "Carry on, sir," Hoveller said again, politely.

"Well . . . due to interference from a French ship—a French ship with diplomatic connections, I should mention—and a second, unidentified opponent, I was obliged to make a bargain in order to have enough hands to fight, so here we are. The ship remains an American possession, and I plan to make sail for Norfolk as soon as I have built my crew up again. And I was hoping to make some sort of report, since I imagine there is no official American naval presence in the city."

Hoveller nodded. "Quite sensible. And His Excellency's office will be glad to send a report on your behalf."

Oliver hesitated. "There is one other matter, but I'd prefer to discuss that privately with the—"

This time the ripping shriek was louder than any of the earlier incidences. The thud that followed knocked a bit of plaster loose from the ceiling. The clump fell with unlikely precision exactly between the two chairs. Hoveller looked down at the clump; Oliver looked at Hoveller.

"Begging your pardon, Mr. Hoveller," Oliver said casually, "but what's the commotion?"

Hoveller picked up the chunk of plaster. "I suppose I should admit that His Excellency isn't likely to be able to see you," he said, turning it over in his fingers. Another squeal overhead, and for the first time Hoveller looked up. "He's gone quite out of his mind, you see. He hasn't been downstairs for over a year."

Oliver's jaw dropped. "Over a *year*? But then—how—who's running things?"

"By 'things,' you mean what, precisely?"

"Well, United States interests, I suppose." Oliver winced as another bout of noise and thumping jarred loose another clod of ceiling, exposing a wooden beam. "I don't know. Whatever it is diplomats do! We're at war, for goodness' sake!"

"Well, to the extent that there's any work for this office to do at all, *I* do it," Hoveller said, sounding a little wounded. "There isn't much. It's not Paris, you know, or London. It's Nagspeake, and half the world doesn't even know it exists. So long as there's someone here to get the dispatches, that's most of the job." At exactly that moment, a particularly earsplitting *screech–thump* sent a lump of plaster straight down on the clerk's head.

Hoveller forced a smile through the chalky dust as he took a handkerchief from his pocket. "I'm as much of an ambassador as you have, sir. But if I can help you, I swear I'll do it. It's been what I should call a rather difficult year, and I would relish the chance to do something useful."

Oliver considered the clerk, from the ivory bits that sat like thick-caked powder on his wig to the nervous hand brushing plaster crumbs from his nose. Just another fellow with an acting commission who wanted to do the right thing while the office was his.

"All right, then," Oliver said, mentally adding *insane ambassador* to the list of injustices the world kept piling up at his feet. "I suppose I'm a bit worried that I might be about to cause some sort of international incident."

"Really?" Hoveller brightened. "How exciting!"

twenty-one
THE MAD SPINSTER

"Saint Whit Gammerbund's Home for the Mentally Chaotic," Lucy read, staring at the wrought-iron lettering over the massive gates. "I suppose this is the place."

The carriage driver called from the rutted track that passed for a road. "Shall I wait, miss?"

"Yes, if you please." She had a feeling when it was time to leave, she'd want out fast.

There didn't seem to be anyone in the gatehouse, but there was a plaque that read RING BELL AND ENTER between the big gate and a smaller entrance to one side. Lucy found a hanging cord and gave it a pull, then entered by the smaller door. Inside, on the far side of a few yards of scruffy landscape, stood a red stone wall with another door in it. An orderly in a suit of pale cotton emerged. "Yes, miss?"

"I've come to see Mrs. Gallfreet."

The orderly looked at her blankly. "No one knows all their names."

"I've also heard her called the Mad Spinster," Lucy said reluctantly.

"Oh, certainly, that one's here." He shuddered. He ushered her inside, went to his desk, and rummaged in a drawer. "You'll need this if you want to enter the Liberty."

"The Liberty?" Lucy studied the old folded page he thrust into her hand. *The bearer of this passport has requested passage through the Liberty of Gammerbund and is traveling under the guarantee of the guards of the Office of His Honor the Warder. Kindly render all necessary assistance.* "What's this?"

"Passport," the orderly retorted. "Can't you read? Bring it back when you're done."

Lucy tucked the page into her ditty bag and followed him through an office and onto the grounds inside the red stone wall. A sign standing waist-high in the weeds beside the path proclaimed that if she went any farther, Lucy would be entering the Liberty of Gammerbund.

Here the buildings looked far older: rambling low structures that met at odd angles and had unlikely and mismatched second and third stories piled on top. Uneven roofs of warped planks and slate overlaid everything. It was as if the madhouse—*the Liberty*, Lucy corrected herself—were less a single asylum than a small, walled town. Of course, fortified towns usually meant to keep people *out*, rather than *in*. Then she remembered the passport that she had tucked into her bag, and wondered if there was something going on here that she wasn't understanding properly.

The orderly stopped at the sign. "This is as far as I go. You'll want to report straight to the Warder, through that red door."

"And what am I to say to this person?"

"Whatever you like, but it's up to the Warder whether or not you'll be allowed to speak to any of the residents. Only you'd better say *citizen*. They like *citizen* better."

"Can't I just go straight to the Spinster?"

"I shouldn't skip the formalities if I was you," the orderly warned. "They can get violent if they think they're being invaded. You ought to see the red tape we have to contend with when it's time for someone's pills. Import duties, everything inspected, forms in triplicate. My mate Byron filed an outdated Dosage Order Request Form last week and tried to bluff and bully his way in anyway, and he got his nose near bit off with a set of wooden teeth for his trouble. Bit off," he repeated darkly, in case Lucy's attention had wandered.

Lucy gaped. "But they're your patients! How can you let them run wild like that?"

"You try and tell 'em they're patients," the orderly countered. "But if you do, you'd better already be running."

She swallowed. "Anything else I ought to know?"

The orderly rooted in one pocket and came up with a whistle. "You can take this if you like. Blow nice and loud if you get into trouble."

Lucy took the whistle. "And you'll come for me?"

"Well, yes," he said, "but remember I'll have to file a Request to Remove Visitor Form first. That's a ten-page document, and then there's the time it takes to have it notarized. If you're trouble-prone, you could give me your name, and I'll start on one just in case."

"Lucy Bluecrowne," Lucy managed, aghast. "Yes, please."

"Right, then." The orderly shook her hand. "Good luck."

She pocketed the whistle and started down the path to the red door. "This is ridiculous," she muttered, not certain whether *ridiculous* was the word she wanted, or *terrifying*. She lifted the brass knocker and let it fall.

The door swung open immediately. A youngish woman peered at her from behind a giant pair of tortoise-shell spectacles with improbably thick lenses. "Passport?" the girl chirped pleasantly.

"Oh, certainly." Lucy fumbled in her bag for the passport.

The girl brought the paper right up to her nose, frowned, pushed the spectacles up onto her forehead, and moved the paper away to arm's length. "This looks all in order." She waved Lucy inside. "Won't take a moment. Tea? Or there's arrack punch, unless you find it's too early for arrack punch."

"Thanks very much, but I'd better not. I have to see the Warder, I believe."

The girl laughed. "I'm the Warder, silly. Punch, then?"

"Oh. Well." Lucy had been raised among sailors, and though she herself wasn't a drinker except for when the available water was likely to make her sick, she had no particular idea that it was ever too early for anything. "I wouldn't say no if you poured me just a sip."

The girl brightened and led Lucy into an office. It was dusty but well lit; the ceiling was hung with a massive collection of twinkling cut-glass chandeliers. Sliding behind a desk, the Warder picked up a decanter and poured punch into two tiny faceted glasses. She passed one to Lucy and they clinked rims solemnly. Then Lucy waited while she began rifling through a drawer. She chose a form at last, dipped a pen into a pot of ink, pulled her glasses back down onto her nose, and looked up at Lucy. "Name?"

"Lucy Bluecrowne."

The Warder pushed her glasses up onto her forehead and scratched Lucy's name onto the form. Then she pulled the glasses down onto her nose and looked at Lucy again. "Reason for visiting the Liberty?"

"To visit the . . ." Lucy hesitated. Surely this was the wrong place to use the word *mad*. "Wishing to visit a famous weaver I believe is a . . . a citizen here."

The Warder pushed her glasses out of the way and scribbled Lucy's answer. Down came the glasses again, and: "Reason for visiting the Mad Spinster?"

Lucy hesitated, taken aback. "Er . . ."

The girl looked at her kindly. "You must know she's barking mad, Miss Bluecrowne."

"Oh. Well, yes, I suppose I did, I just didn't want to offend—"

The Warder laughed. "How on earth would calling a *madwoman* mad offend me? It's not like you implied *I'm* insane." She chuckled again. "Reason?"

Lucy forced a laugh of her own. "No, of course not. Well, I have a present from her daughter, and I want her advice about a fancy sort of weaving."

"Consultation and present-visit." She made a final note, signed the form with a flourish, opened a drawer, deposited the page in it, and put the spectacles back on her nose. "Very good. Will you be needing directions?"

Lucy got to her feet. "Yes, please, and thank you."

"The shortest way to the Mad Spinster is to take the first set of stairs heading upward and keep on taking every upward stair in view after that until you reach the top."

"The top of what?"

"Of the Liberty. You can't miss it." The Warder gave a little shudder. "Spiders like high places, and good thing, too. Nobody likes when they come down where the people live, spiders."

Lucy forced a smile, thanked her again, and stepped out into the Liberty of Gammerbund.

It was a still and hushed place, far more peaceful than she had imagined a madhouse could be. On the other hand, the silence itself was a bit unnerving. The denizens of Gammerbund kept mostly out of sight as Lucy made her ascent, climbing a series of staircases and occasionally ladders that seemed to have no end. Now and then, however, a curtain would twitch aside or a door would crack open and a curious face would peep out at her, then disappear again.

She came at last to the highest point in the Liberty: a square tower with a red tile roof. There was a creaky, rattling clatter within, an uneasy mechanical noise that would've set Lucy's teeth on edge if she hadn't heard similar sounds coming from the back room of Tilly Gallfreet's shop. Trying not to think about the fact that even the Warder, who was obviously a nutter in her own right, had said the Spinster was out of her mind, Lucy screwed up her courage and rapped at the warped green door.

The sound stopped. Slow, rasping steps came close, then Lucy heard a soft scraping, like hands bracing against the other side of the door. "Who calls?" The voice was even, quiet, curious.

"Lucy Bluecrowne, madam. I'm a friend of your daughter's."

"A friend of Tilly's?" The voice sounded dubious.

"I have some unusual weaving cards. Tilly thought you would find them a capital puzzle. She sent you a gift as well, and said to say the rain crows have come back to the cherry laurels and that she's looking out for red feathers for you."

"Show me."

"The gift? It's here, if you'll open the door."

"One of the loom-cards. Slide it underneath."

Lucy took the top card from its laces and slid one edge under the door. It was jerked abruptly from her grasp and vanished. There was a silence, then a sigh.

"A capital puzzle indeed." A bolt shot open on the other side. "Come in, girl."

Lucy opened the door and stepped hesitantly inside. A strange and wild chaos filled the room around her—wood, brass, an explosion of colored thread—but her eyes could not, would not tear themselves away from the woman before her.

The Mad Spinster was gaunt and bent, and Lucy could well understand why the Warder had likened her to a spider. She was also the wrong color. Or rather, she was many colors, and all of them were unnatural.

The faded blond hair she wore twisted up in a knot of braids was streaked with rust and russet and eggplant and watchet blue. Indigo fingers held the card Lucy had passed under the door, dark at the fingertips and knuckles and fading to a paler blue in between. Irregular stripes of blue ran up her arms at odd angles: Egyptian blue and lapis lazuli and a darker shade like that of a naval officer's jacket; underneath those were the ghosts of other stains, like fading bruises. Sapphire spatters like tears littered her sharp, triangular face. Her huge eyes were yellow-brown where they should've been white, and threaded through with rufous bloodshot streaks.

The Spinster looked up from the card and caught Lucy staring. Her lips curled. These were stained a purple-red wine color. "Silk might grow on trees, girl, but blue silk doesn't. What did Tilly send?"

Lucy handed over Tilly's parcel mutely and took a look around the room while the old woman unwrapped it. In one corner, wide

loops of azure thread hung to dry over a huge copper pot. Bolts of fabric stood against one wall, and on another, shelves held bobbins full of dyed thread. And around and over and through it all, surrounding the room like a set of inner walls, was the kind of thing a child might dream of building for a fortress: a massive wood-and-brass structure with waterfalls of thread descending from it in several places.

The indigo-stained woman

slouched deeper into the room and into the loom-structure. "Mind the webs," she called.

"Webs? Oh." Lucy slipped past the nearest group of parallel threads and followed, squeezing past the mechanism and into a small interior room where she found the Spinster tucking Tilly's jar into a cabinet. Then the old woman smoothed the napkin out on a work-table and examined the very detailed rendering of Warpandye Street woven into it.

"She's coming along," the Spinster said with a note of pride. "All right, girl. Bring me those cards, and tell me how you came by them."

Lucy worked the cards out of the bag as she repeated the half-truth she'd told Tilly and Mrs. Allis. "A ship-girl, are you?" the Spinster asked, eyeing the stack. "And some everyday passenger had these? Absurd. Still, I suppose the only reason to lie is that you won't tell the truth, so there's not much point in arguing."

"But I—"

The old woman waved a blue-fingered hand. "It's information I want, not lies to pick through. Pity, though. There's a story I heard once about something like these—but then, I suppose if you knew what they were, you wouldn't be here. You want to know what these cards are for, is that it?"

"Yes, ma'am, please," Lucy answered sheepishly.

"Pity," the Spinster said again, shooting Lucy a grim look made even worse by her discolored eyes. "All right. Let us see what there is to see." She began stripping the cards from the lacings and tossing them onto the floor. Lucy sucked in a breath at the sight of the thin whalebone rectangles clattering into a heap. "Stop fussing," the Spinster snapped. "The array won't work in this order. We have to find the *right* order, and the first thing to do is find the root. If the cards alone don't tell us what they mean, then their places in the tree will."

"What tree? They were already in a chain," Lucy protested.

"So now you know about looms, do you, ship-girl?" The Spinster's discolored lips pulled back over equally stained teeth. "The chain *itself* does not have meaning; the meaning has to be *retrieved* from it. And this chain is misleading." She turned one of her ochre-and-red eyes on Lucy. "You see?" The expression was probably intended to convey nothing more than inquiry, but it still looked like the old woman might be about to try to eat her. Out of nowhere, Lucy heard Liao's voice in her memory: *They're only clues, signs that point you on toward what they're trying to say. You have to pull the meaning out of them by how they all work together.*

The Spinster buried her blue fingers in the pile of whalebone cards and began sifting. From among the cards that now lay heaped on the floor, she chose a few at a time to examine against the light. Every now and then she tossed one aside. "What are those?" Lucy asked as the pile of discarded rectangles grew.

"They don't belong."

"How can you tell?"

"I can tell."

Lucy picked up one from the discard pile and another from the regular pile and held them side by side. "They look the same."

"No, they don't." She snatched the card from Lucy's left hand, squinted at it. "Well, those two probably do. This one doesn't go, either." She slapped Lucy's fingers as she reached for the pile again. "The punch-holes are wrong for a loom, ship-girl, and the guide-marks on these cards are on the short ends, not the long. They don't belong to the same array. They're for something else." Then, with a motion like a snake darting after a mouse, the Spinster plucked another card from the heap. "There you are." Light shone through the punch-holes and illuminated the shape of a plant with branching roots. "The root card. And look." The Spinster tapped a spot on one long edge.

Lucy squatted beside her for a closer look. "A stain?" The Spinster gave her a sharp thwack on the forehead with the card. "Ouch! It just looks like another of those little cracks!"

"Here," the Spinster said, "and here." Her chipped fingernail tapped another stain on the same edge. "They aren't stains. They aren't cracks. They're the places to start."

She set the root card down at the top edge of her worktable, then began going through the rest and lining them up under it. Instead of a chain, however, what the Spinster was building looked like a tree branching downward. She had found a card to line up with each of the markings on the root card, and another two off of each of those.

Lucy examined these first seven pieces. Now that she knew what to look for, she could see a little smudge of extra-dark cracking on the lower edge of each card below the one the Spinster had called the root. And now that she was *really* looking, Lucy saw that part of each card's staining exactly matched that of the one above. "Is that how you can tell which one goes where?"

"Yes. Each one carries a bit of the one that came before."

"But they can't possibly work like this, can they?" Before, the cards had been laced end to end. Now Lucy couldn't even begin to picture how they could be connected and fed through the loom.

"Stop asking questions." The Spinster waved at the pile of whalebone cards on the floor. "And don't stand there like a spectator." She handed Lucy one of the cards. "Find everything that bears this string of marks. Those will be the child-cards of this one."

twenty-two
VOCLAIN

Back in the parlor in the house behind the brick wall, Max Ault stared at the man in the faded blue coat. "What did you say?"

The Frenchman smiled thinly. "I said, you do not look like your father. Or at least, I see no resemblance. Would you like tea?"

"How do you know what my father looked like?"

The Frenchman gave him a disappointed look. "My name is Théodore Voclain, Mr. Ault. Is it familiar?" Max's stomach plunged down toward the vicinity of his knees. "I see that it is, which means I need not ask how much you know of your father's work on the great engine."

Max willed his nerves to behave. "I don't know what you're talking about."

Voclain made a dismissive face. "If you did not, there would be no reason for you to have ever heard my name, young man. We get nowhere, you and I, if we dance around fencing rather than speaking as men do. As fellow philosophers, we may treat each other as colleagues. In any other sense, we are enemies."

"Colleagues?" Max repeated, affronted. "You *abducted* me!"

"I take it you would not care for tea. I will ask your pardon while I have mine." Voclain nodded to the guard in the doorway, who turned and spoke to someone out of sight in the passage beyond. "You have been inquiring about a ship called *Honoratus*," Voclain continued, "and not very subtly, I might add. You may well turn out to be a philosopher of note, but as a spy, I am afraid you are likely to wind up getting yourself killed." He paused as his tea arrived and poured himself a cup. "Are you certain you will have none?"

"I should very much like to leave, sir."

Voclain took an unhurried sip. "Where are my loom-cards, Mr. Ault?"

"I know nothing about any loom-cards." Thank goodness Lucy had insisted on this division of labor.

"You do, because your father had them stolen from me by the same ship you hired earlier this year. Why do people bother to lie when the truth is perfectly obvious?"

"Why do you pretend that offering me tea somehow makes this *not a kidnapping*? We're not colleagues. You and my father weren't colleagues. If I know your name, it's because my father knew he was racing against you, and he knew his life was at risk because of that."

Behind his spectacles, the Frenchman was watching Max through hooded, vaguely reptilian eyes. "If your father had been so very concerned about his life, he would not have undertaken such a deadly project. You cannot expect sympathy from me that he died as he did."

Max screwed up his courage and actually went as far as opening his mouth, but in the end, he didn't dare actually ask the question on his tongue. *Did you have my father killed, monsieur?*

"I beg your pardon," Voclain said in a polite tone that was

completely at odds with his expression. "Was there something you wanted to say?"

Max wanted to say plenty, but he held his tongue. The Frenchman looked down to dip a biscuit into his tea, and just then a small face popped into view outside the window behind him. Liao.

....

IT WAS CLOSE TO NOON, OR NEARLY DINNERTIME BY NAVAL standards, by the time Lucy and the Spinster had finished sorting the cards. The arrangement that the old woman called the *array* had quickly outgrown the table and spread across the floor, with some branches forking again and again and others stopping altogether, dead ends. Piled nearby were the cards that the old woman had determined did not belong.

The two of them appraised their handiwork. "There's the proper chain," the Spinster said with satisfaction, pointing at the very bottom row. "That's where the meaning is."

Lucy looked at all the cards between those and the root card at the top. "All those other cards—they're just meaning*less*?"

"They don't contain the meaning you want, but they did plenty of work, didn't they? Hid your chain, for one, and then showed us the way to it when it was time. Now we string these together, the ones the array led us to, and we weave."

"And how long until . . . I understand the actual weaving could take ages, but can you at least tell me what's on the cards?"

The old woman smiled. Had it been biting through dyed thread that had colored her teeth that way? "Come back tomorrow; I can tell you then. Take the rest of the cards with you."

Lucy hesitated. Max wouldn't much like the idea of her leaving anything behind in this place. These cards were still the only piece of the puzzle they actually possessed, and if the Spinster's theory was to be believed, the very cards Lucy was being asked to leave were the only ones that mattered. "I don't know if I should."

The Spinster raised her bony shoulders. "Choose your risk, girl. Risk leaving them to learn something, or take them and risk never finding out what they say."

Lucy chewed her thumbnail for a moment, then nodded once. Calculating risk, that she could do. If the Spinster was the only one who could solve the puzzle in the cards, then the Spinster would have to do it. And if it was going to take time, well, there was no way Lucy was sitting here all day and night just to keep an eye on a bunch of whalebone. So she collected the cards of the array while the old woman gathered the discards and bundled them separately. Then Lucy packed both sets in her bag. "Until tomorrow, then?"

The Spinster said nothing as she began to line up the remaining cards, the all-important third set from the bottom row. Lucy let herself back out into the Liberty of Gammerbund.

The disgruntled carriage driver had very nearly given up on her, but to her tremendous relief he was still there when she emerged from the gates. They were halfway down to the city when a stream of lavender smoke shot up from among the trees below with a wild whistle like the shriek of a bird of prey. A mixture of gold and orchid-pink light erupted in the air over the lower slope of the hill, miraculously visible even against the midday sky. Liao's signal, followed a second later by a head-splitting bang.

Lucy leaned out the window of the carriage. "Did you see where that came from?"

"What am I, blind?" the driver called back as the ashes of the firework sifted down over the city.

"Take me there, then, please, as fast as ever the horses will go." The colors Liao had sent up told Lucy to come right away, but that her brother was not in danger himself. On the other hand, Liao never seemed to think he was in trouble, so it was hard to know where he might draw the line.

At last the driver brought the carriage to a stop before a wooden gate in a brick wall. "Can't go farther, miss, but I'm dead certain the flare came from somewhere on this estate. You can see part of this same wall from up on the hill."

Lucy climbed out of the carriage, leaving the big sack full of cards but taking her ditty bag. "That flare was a signal from my younger brother. If he's in trouble, we'll need to make a quick exit."

The driver slumped. "You want me to wait again. After I sat for hours outside that madhouse."

"I can pay," Lucy said, taking from her bag a handful of coins. "Please?"

"Fine." He reached down and took the money. "But if I find out I'm waiting out here to be a getaway for some unsavory—"

"You're not!" Lucy slung the ditty bag around her neck and faced the gate. It was three times her height, but it was also striped with thick creepers. She tied up her skirts, found handholds in the ivy, and scrambled up as easily as if she'd been running up the *Fate*'s rigging.

She crouched at the top of the wall and surveyed the grounds. A carriage stood in the drive near the house, but there was no driver or footman with it, nor any people anywhere to be seen. Then a single small foot in a black shoe dropped out of a tree beside one of the chimneys on the side of the house.

Lucy scurried along the wall to the tree. "Liao!"

A quick flurry of motion in the branches, and her brother peeked out from between the leaves. "Lucy, they've got Max in there!"

"Who?"

"French coves!"

She cursed. "How many?"

"Four. They're all inside now, and the leader has Max in the parlor." He pointed at a window below.

"Have you any explosives left?"

"Yes. Two more rockets and four smaller ones that will make a good bang. I would have tried rescuing him myself, but I didn't think I could drive the carriage."

"I have one outside the gate." Lucy leaned under the branch for a look at the window. "Think you can get into the kitchens, or whatever's at the back of the house?"

Liao gave her a hurt look. "Lucy."

"All right, all right. This ought to be simple enough, then."

....

"I ENJOY YOUR COMPANY, MR. AULT," THÉODORE VOCLAIN SAID AS he cleaned the lenses of his spectacles with an embroidered handkerchief. "But I have too much to do to spend much more time convincing you to answer my questions."

"Does this mean we're moving on to threats?" Max asked. "If I did have these things you want, why on earth would I admit to it? If the situation were reversed, what would you do in my place?"

"If the situation were reversed, I should not have been caught," Voclain snapped. "That is what comes of being a child and meddling in things you are not equipped to handle."

Max huffed. "I can't take you seriously, talking about what children are and are not equipped to handle."

"Young man," the Frenchman said in the most patronizing tone imaginable, "I'm not sure what you're talking about, but I will kill you if I have to. Do you understand that?"

Max loaded his voice up with the same condescension. "I understood that the day I found my father dead on the library floor.

Moreover, I've heard your generals find children about my age to be the fiercest fighters there are. Why *wouldn't* you be willing to kill me?"

Voclain shook his head. "I cannot take credit for—" He stopped talking abruptly. "You are talking about the Vendée."

"That, and my father!"

"Your father is one thing. The Vendée is another." He looked at Max for a long moment. "It is best that children are not made to fight. When there is peace, that will be a thing of the past, a nightmare we remember but mercifully have woken from and need never return to again." The condescension was gone, and for just a moment, the philosopher's reptilian air dropped away, too. Suddenly Voclain looked painfully sincere. "This I promise you, Maxwell."

Max was saved from having to figure out how to reply to this sudden and strange sincerity by the sound of an explosion from behind the house.

Max allowed himself a glance out the window. No sign of Liao. "Is it a holiday I'm not aware of?"

Voclain and the man in the doorway looked at each other. "Another one?" the guard asked doubtfully. He shouted an order to one of his compatriots just as yet another blast came—an eruption of complete pandemonium, and this time from within the house itself. From the sound of it, every pot and pan in the kitchen had been pressed into service.

The guard sprinted away in the direction of the noise. A heartbeat later, a brick sailed through the parlor window and hit Voclain square in the knee.

Max flung himself toward the broken window, then dropped to the floor instead. Outside, Liao was setting a match to a wick attached to a rocket that was pointed straight into the parlor. Voclain took one hobbling step after Max, then stumbled backward in horror and took cover behind the sofa as the rocket blasted through the room on a river of smoke and vapor.

The next few seconds were a jumble of noise and shock. The rocket hit the wall and detonated violently. Max levered to his feet and, driven by a sudden instinct, grabbed the portable secretary on the desk. Then he dove over the windowsill out onto the lawn, where Lucy hauled him to his feet alongside a clapping, delighted Liao.

Lucy shoved him toward the ivy-covered wall. "Climb up and stay on top. There's nothing but a cliff on the other side."

Liao scrambled up first and reached down for the letter box. Max dragged himself onto the wall with Lucy on his heels, and the three of them dashed toward the gate as quickly as they dared. Miraculously—perhaps because here there was no moving water under him—Max managed the flight without putting a single foot wrong.

Voclain's men sprinted around the house after them. When they saw how much of a lead the three fugitives had, they made for the coach, only to discover that the two horses were now loose and grazing at opposite ends of the lawn.

Max and Lucy and Liao reached the gate, dropped over one by one, and sprang into the carriage that was waiting there. With a shout and a whipcrack from the driver, the carriage bolted into motion.

Lucy watched out the window for a few minutes, then dropped back onto the bench. "I believe we've done it." She ruffled Liao's hair. "Well done, you."

"Liao, how on earth did you find me?" Max asked.

"I didn't. I caught up with the coach before it got away and rode on the back."

"And Lucy followed your flare?" Max shook his head. "I am amazed."

"Well, properly speaking, the carriage driver followed it," Lucy admitted. "The man has earned his fee today. What's that, then, Max?" She nodded to the secretary on the seat beside him.

"No idea. Perhaps nothing. Taking it seemed a good idea in the moment." Max gave the lid a tug. "Locked."

"Pass it here," Liao said, taking his folding knife from his pocket. He extracted a slender, notched blade from the handle, and he was just about to insert this into the keyhole when a tiny, lavender light popped to life at the very tip of the knife. He raised his eyes warily to Max's. Max inhaled sharply, but neither he nor Lucy dared move. Very carefully, Liao folded the blade closed again, extinguishing the flame.

Immediately, tiny blue-violet lights burst into existence around the carriage. Six popped up at the corners and angles of the slanted lid of the letter box. They flared up from the knotted opening of the bag in which Lucy had carried the cards into town, and at the corners of the frame around each carriage door. Two fluttered to light at the tips of Liao's ears, and an odd shivery feeling told Max there might be a matching pair of corposants on his own.

"No!" he blurted, swatting at them.

"What do we do?" Liao whispered. "Can we get out and run?"

Lucy spoke from the window. "If they're watching, they'll see."

Max beat his fists against his knees. *"How could they possibly be watching?"*

"Worry about that later." She leaned farther out the window for a shouted conversation with the driver.

"Max," Liao said, "this is a little scary."

"Blood and eyes," Lucy swore as she sat back down. "Well, it's the devil to pay and no pitch hot, that's for certain. The driver thinks if he cuts through a marketplace nearby, we can perhaps slip out in the crowd unnoticed, and I haven't got a better plan."

The horses slowed, and a sharp knock rattled the woodwork behind Lucy's head. "We must be getting close to the market." She fished in her ditty bag for money and turned to her brother. "Liao, I suspect they're following Max, so he and I had better not go back to the ship yet. Go and let them know what's happened so they can be prepared if I'm wrong and the men in black uniforms turn up there. You can make it back to the ship, can't you? This will cover any extra cost."

"Well, yes, of course, but . . ." Liao looked worried. "I don't know if I ought to leave you alone. Do you want my last fireworks?"

"No, love. You had better keep those. We'll make our way back before long."

"Let me see if I can at least get this open first." Liao unfolded his knife again. He ignored the little flame that reappeared and tucked the tiny blade into the keyhole. A few quick flicks of his wrist, then *snick*. He lifted the lid just enough to be sure it was unlocked, then passed it to Max.

The driver knocked again and the horses slowed still further. "That's our signal." Lucy gathered up the big sack on the floor. "Send a flare up when you get back to the *Fate* to let us know you're safe, will you, Liao?"

The boy nodded and kissed Lucy's cheek, then bounced across the carriage to hug Max. Then Lucy opened the door and the two of them slipped out into a crowded market square full of noise and odor and jostling bodies, both human and animal. Max felt for her hand and they wove through the bustle until they reached a tavern hung with flags. By the time he turned to look, the carriage had disappeared into the throng.

"Well, we may have done it," Lucy said. "The fires on your ears are gone."

Max was about to reply when a shape out in the square caught his eye. It was a carriage, a large, old-fashioned Berline coach of the sort that might have been quite the thing when Max's grandfather had been a boy. The body of the coach sat high above its wheels, with a driver in front and a footman perched on a little seat in the back. All of them—driver, footman, horses, and coach—were rendered in black upon black upon black. It might've been a shadow given substance, the rig that was now cutting its way through the crowds.

"I shall see you again in time," Lucy whispered.

Max held his breath. *Please let Liao have gotten away.*

Neither of them moved until the black Berline had passed from view. Then they turned and fled into the tavern.

twenty-three

THE PHILOSOPHIC IRON

First things first: Lucy hired a private room and ordered a meal. "We shall have to learn something about this bazaar where the *Honoratus* thing is going to be, and before tomorrow," she said when they had eaten and caught each other up on their respective adventures. "And this fellow, Voclain—you knew him?"

"I knew *of* him. He was the one, you see. The scholar who'd studied the Egyptian text first, and the one who'd tracked down the cards in Venice." Max stared down into his coffee as he stirred it. "He and my father were racing against each other the whole time, until—"

Lucy nodded. "Until your father died."

"I always assumed Voclain had him killed. It was supposed to have been apoplexy, but there are poisons that would've given the same result."

"And you're not certain now?"

"He said he wasn't behind Papa's death." Or, at least, Max was fairly certain Voclain had been about to deny any involvement before he'd gotten sidetracked by Max's reference to the Vendée.

Lucy made a scoffing noise. "When do murderers ever tell the truth about what they've done?"

Max shrugged. "He was trying to convince me that my life depended upon giving up what I knew. Why not just say, *Max, you'd better sing out or I'll kill you like I killed your papa*? It would've made his threats a bit punchier. No, I think he might've been telling the truth, which makes me wonder how my father *did* die."

"You're thinking about the men in black uniforms. Did you ever see them when your father was alive?"

"I don't think so. I'd remember, wouldn't I?"

Lucy shook her head. "I *spoke* to one of them, and most of that memory's utterly gone. What if they took your memories of them, too?"

"No one can take a memory from someone else, Lucy."

She leaned back in her chair. "There's a splendid line in a play about what philosophers think and what's really out there in the world. Perhaps you know the bit I mean. It comes from the one about Hamlet."

Max grinned. "Melusine Bluecrowne reads *Shakespeare*?"

She scowled and reached for the coffeepot. "Belay that look, you. I have read a book or two beyond navigation and trigonometry." She nodded toward the portable secretary. "What about that? Shall we have a look?"

"I suppose this is as safe a place as any." Max opened the lid and they surveyed the contents: pages upon pages, written in French. He lifted out the stack of paper, set it on the table between them, and began to leaf through. "Have you any French?"

"Some. You never know whether a few words shouted in another tongue at the master of an enemy ship might buy you a few minutes that matter."

"See what you can make of these, then." He passed a handful to her, then kept leafing through.

Diplomatic credentials, letters of credit at banking houses in Nagspeake, Washington, Venice, and Malta, something that looked to Max like a recipe for some sort of punch . . . He did find what appeared to be Voclain's half of the correspondence arranging for the *Honoratus* to deliver cargo described as "philosophical and mathematical devices" to Nagspeake, but there was nothing that gave any clue as to what the all-important piece of that cargo was. The information Max needed simply wasn't there—either that, or even aided by his Latin, his French simply wasn't up to the task. He sat back in frustration. "We need someone who reads French properly."

"Amen to that." Lucy tossed her pages back into the pile. "There are a couple Fates who I suspect could do better, but I wonder, dare we go back to the *Fate* at all?" She chewed on her thumbnail. "If only the house weren't so far away."

"What house?"

"My house," she said, looking down at the thumb she'd just bitten red.

"You have a house here?" Max asked, surprised. "Why on earth haven't you mentioned it?"

"When everything's sorted out, I suppose that's where Liao and I will go, but for now it's too far. To get there it's a trip upriver or half a day's drive on a bad road, and if we ran into any trouble, we'd be well and truly alone." Her words made it sound like she regretted the distance, but there was relief in her tone. She clearly wasn't eager to return until she had to.

"Where do we go, then? And for how long? And how do we let Liao and the rest know what we're up to?"

"Those are the questions." Lucy took two rolls and the last of the ham and turned it all into a pair of sandwiches. She handed one to Max and tucked the other into her pocket. "Let's head toward the harbor and look for a boardinghouse. Then we can figure out how to get a message back. One problem at a time."

"All right." Max returned the papers to the secretary and tucked it under one arm, then waved Lucy away as she reached for the canvas bag of cards. "I'll take that. You've done a lot of running about today. All I had to do was sit and listen to a Frenchman make ineffectual threats."

"I don't know, Max; that sounds exhausting to me." But she allowed him to take the bag, and together they headed down the stairs. Then she stopped at the door. "Just a moment."

She trotted to the girl behind the bar and exchanged a few words—was that a giggle? The girl called someone else over, and he called someone else, and the four of them held a whispered conference while Max waited, feeling suddenly awkward, near the entrance.

At last Lucy came back, grinning. "What on earth was that?" Max asked as they descended the stairs to the market square. "Were you *giggling*?"

"I told them you were my beau. That's what girls do when they talk about their beaux, isn't it? Giggle?"

"Your *beau*?" That burning was definitely his face getting red. "Who are you? What have you done with Lucy Bluecrowne?"

"Take that look off your face, Maxwell. What a fellow you are! It was a *ruse de guerre*. I said I wanted a present for you, and where ought someone go tomorrow to buy something quite philosophical? They all agreed there was one place I should certainly find what I was looking for."

"A bazaar?"

"The Hackers' Bazaar, in fact."

"That, sir, is quite a tale." Ralph Hoveller set down his pen and regarded Oliver over his plaster-dusted journal. "How dreadful to find yourself in the middle of all this. I only wish I could offer more than my own counsel."

"I'll be very grateful for that much, sir." It was a huge relief, having everything off his chest. "I wish I knew how the Quartermaster came to know about the device."

"Oh, it's terribly difficult to keep secrets in a place like Nagspeake," Hoveller said. "All boundaries are, shall we say, porous. Things slip through, and what's true of a smuggler's cutter is doubly true of information."

"So what is your advice?"

"Well," said Hoveller carefully, "I shall put it this way: if I were in charge of a city like Nagspeake, it would have occurred to me straightaway that if *I* possessed such an object as the one you've described, no other country should ever be able to drag me into any sort of conflict."

Oliver collapsed into his chair. "You think the Quartermaster might actually *want* the thing? That she might try to take it?" He thought for a moment, then shook his head. "No. She's practically kin to Lucy Bluecrowne."

Hoveller shrugged. "If I were in charge, I might see it as my duty, even if it brought me into conflict with my own heart or conscience. But perhaps I can give you some more cheerful advice as well." He went to his desk, picked up a map, and shook it clean of debris. "I know of a public house where you might look for hands."

"Smith's Tot?" Oliver asked, recalling Nell Levinflash's suggestion that morning.

Hoveller beamed. "That's the one. Try there, and then for the love of God, get out of town as fast as you can." Hoveller tapped his finger on a spot on the map up the river from Flotilla. "This is Shantytown. Smith's Tot is here, on Morbid Street." He made an X on the map and handed it to Oliver. "I hope it proves to be helpful. I should so adore to be helpful."

Oliver folded the map and tucked it into his waistcoat. "I'm sure it will be." He shook Hoveller's hand, then wondered how to brush the plaster from his palm without the clerk's noticing. Another colossal din sounded from upstairs. "And I do hope *that* sorts itself out. Is it possible that the fellow might recover?"

"In this city, anything at all is possible," Hoveller said philosophically.

In the entryway Whippett sat with his legs sprawled out before him and his chair canted back against the wall. Oliver gave him a gentle push, and the sailor snorted and jerked awake. "I believe we may head back to the *Fate*, Whippett."

"Back to the barky it is, sir."

They had just turned onto the main thoroughfare when Whippett pointed across the street. "Begging your pardon, sir, but that's our Miss Bluecrowne and Mr. Ault."

Oliver put his fingers to his mouth and whistled. "Miss Bluecrowne, there!"

Lucy and Max looked about furtively before they crossed the lane to join them. "We're trying to keep a low profile," Lucy explained. Speaking in undertones, the two of them gave Oliver an account of Max's capture and rescue.

"You were *taken by Frenchmen*?"

"And then very nearly found by the men in black uniforms," Lucy said grimly. "But we were afraid of leading them—or this French cove—back to the ship, so I think we might do best to find a place to stay ashore tonight."

"That might not be a bad idea." Oliver debated telling her about

Hoveller's warnings and decided against it. Surely, if Lucy trusted Nell Levinflash, then the Quartermaster could be trusted, even if she had done her level best to scare Oliver senseless.

"Begging your pardon," Whippett said, "but there's a boarding-house on the street where the lieutenant and me was. Which I noticed it particular, because there weren't much else to look at from that parlor chair and because there was some broken gingerbread-work around the porch." He added this last bit in a tone that made it plain that he didn't want to be taken for *recommending* a house with damaged woodwork, but he felt it his duty to point out that the place was there.

"The Minister's clerk suggested the same place Miss Levinflash did for finding hands. A place in Shantytown." Oliver hesitated. "And it seems your mission may not be as secret as you hoped. The Quartermaster mentioned that there were rumors in Nagspeake about some sort of mysterious war engine."

Lucy's face hardened. "I had better talk to Nell about it."

Oliver nodded fervently. "I think so. The sooner the better."

"Perhaps we shall see each other in Shantytown tomorrow," Max said. "I heard of a philosophical marketplace there and I thought I'd have a look round."

"Perhaps," Oliver said, wishing he had time to wander around a philosophical marketplace. They parted ways, with Lucy first asking him to make sure Liao sent up a rocket to let her know when he made it back to the ship. Then Oliver and Whippett headed toward the harbor.

....

THE BOARDINGHOUSE WAS CALLED CRICKET LANE HOUSE, although the street upon which it stood was not called Cricket Lane. Despite the irregular gingerbread that had so bothered Whippett, the place was cozy and the landlady was pleasant, and she didn't question Lucy at all when she explained that she and her companion were siblings from out of town waiting for their father's ship to come in.

Dusk found them in the little parlor that connected their two tiny bedrooms, Lucy sprawled on the sofa, half-snoozing under a page she was meant to be reading, and Max at a writing table piled with neat stacks: the correspondence from the letter box, sorted according to his notions about what the letters contained, and the ink-spattered beginnings of his attempts at translations.

"Are you making any headway with the notes about the loom-cards, Lucy?"

Lucy sighed and roused herself. "No, Maxwell, I am not. As far as I can make any sense of them, Voclain and Jacquard hadn't got anywhere near so far with them as the Spinster did. They don't seem to have had any notion that there was a second set hidden within the first. Certainly not a third." No answer came. Lucy sat up. "Max?"

"It *has* to be in here somewhere," he said, head in his hands. "There has to be *something*, some hint of what he's meant to be claiming tomorrow."

"You'd better hope there's not." She pointed at the piles on the desk. "The Frenchman knows you have these. If a description's in here somewhere, won't he make different arrangements? He said what he did about the bazaar practically right in front of you."

Max groaned. "I'm never going to find it."

"I think you will. Though don't ask me why, after everything that's happened so far."

Max gave a half-choked laugh, and the sound was so miserable that Lucy crossed the room and put an awkward arm around him. For once, he didn't flinch. "There, there," she said. For some reason this made Max chuckle again, although this time it was almost a real laugh. Then, to Lucy's surprise, he leaned into her so that his head rested against her side.

The moment stretched, Max saying nothing and Lucy wondering if she ought to say something else, something more than "there, there." It felt uncomfortably like it might suddenly be an altogether different sort of situation.

From her angle, Max's face was hidden under the hair that fell forward over his brow. It had been brown once, but the sun and salt water had taken its toll over the past year and now it was lighter. He did usually try to keep a hat on, but being Max, he had a habit of losing them in preposterous ways. Once, an albatross had swooped down out of nowhere and plucked one right off his head, an occurrence the likes of which no one aboard the *Fate* had ever seen before and which everyone took to be good luck. Except for Max, of course, who'd been furious.

"What are you smiling at?"

He was looking up at her now, and his eyes were very serious—it was the sort of look he generally reserved for interesting bugs or taxidermied puffins or other philosophical things.

"I was thinking about the albatross that stole your hat." The bug look wasn't unpleasant, and it was curiously difficult to look away from.

"I think I made it twelve hats lost at last count, but I might not have included that one."

"How on earth could you forget the albatross?"

"I didn't forget it; I was counting the hats I'd lost that were actually my fault," he said defensively. "Surely no one could think having a bird come and snatch a hat from my head, entirely unprovoked, was my fault."

All this time aboard the *Fate,* and he still had no notion of bluewater logic. "We *all* thought that, Maxwell, if only because we were mortally certain it could only ever have happened to you."

Max picked up her free hand, the one that wasn't on his shoulder, and turned it palm-up to examine the calluses she had from years of climbing the rigging and hauling on cordage. He had none, of course. Max's hands were lean and unmarked, except for a few nicks here and there that she imagined were from experiments he'd done with his father.

"I'm not much of a seaman, even after a year, am I?" he asked.

"Everyone loses hats."

"Twelve of them?" He turned his gaze from her hand—which had somehow come to be fully entwined with his—up to Lucy's face, and there was the bug look again.

It's always on land that things get confusing, Lucy thought. Her heart was speeding up like it did in the moments before a battle at sea, when every instinct began to shift into a different state of awareness.

She smiled what she hoped was a jaunty smile. "It's thirteen, Maxwell. The albatross counts. I make no doubt if you'd come aboard as a proper sailor—" But that idea was too ridiculous to continue. Just that quickly, the strange moment came to a sharp end as the two of them burst into laughter.

Max let go of her hand and rubbed his forehead—which had gone very red. "It's late," he said. He corked the ink and got to his feet, and for a moment the two of them were standing very close.

"What's that look for?" he asked gently, and Lucy realized she'd been giving him an interesting bug look of her own.

Enough. "What look?" she asked, turning on her heel. At that moment, an unearthly whistle pierced the quiet, followed by a deep, resonant *bang*. Lucy went to the room's single window and watched the fountain of light that was Liao's signal drift down over the rooftops. "He certainly took his time," she muttered. Then she spotted something else. "Max, come here."

He joined her there and together they looked through the thick green-tinged glass. On the other side, a vine was reaching for the last warm scarlet light of day, the tendril at its very end swishing elegantly in the breeze. Except it wasn't a vine, and there was no breeze. The trees across the street were perfectly still, without even the faintest rustle of leaves. And not even the tinted glass could make the vine look green—it was gray-brown, except where it was patched with red.

"What is it?" Max asked, leaning close to the glass. "Is it—that's the philosophic iron, isn't it?"

"In Nagspeake they call it old iron. But yes, that's it."

Together they leaned on the windowsill and watched the metal frond twist and rotate. "There was a balcony below this room, I think," Lucy remembered. "This is likely metal from that."

Outside, the tendril stretched, then separated suddenly into three

strands, like a braid coming undone. "What's it doing, do you think?" Max asked.

Lucy shrugged. "I don't know much about old iron, really. Last time I was here, I was too concerned with convincing Papa not to leave me ashore to care much about it."

"What do Nagspeakers say?" Max asked as the iron began to weave itself into a rectangular shape right outside the window.

"I don't actually think they understand how odd it is. Oh, I see!" Lucy laughed as curls of metal sprouted from the rectangle like shoots breaking from soil. "It's a flower box. Look."

"Unbelievable." Max rushed to the writing table and dragged the chair back to the window with paper and a pencil in his other hand.

Poor fellow might just sit up all night watching the ironwork, Lucy realized. Might as well leave him to it. "Good night, Max."

"'Night," he murmured, eyes glued to the iron.

"Don't stay up too late. We have places to be in the morning." Something made Lucy pause in the doorway to her little bedroom and add, "I like shipping with you, Max, sailor or no."

He turned at last, but she only gave him a small wave and closed the door between them. Then, with her heart still going a bit faster than it ever did by land, she crawled into bed. Fortunately, some old habits take more than a passing strange moment to unseat, and Lucy was asleep nearly as soon as her head hit the pillow.

twenty-four
SHANTYTOWN

"**M**r. Dexter!"

Oliver leapt half out of his skin as Liao sprang at him before he had even made it all the way out of his cabin. "Yes?"

"Is it true you're going to Shantytown and Max and Lucy will be there?"

"I don't know about Miss Bluecrowne," Oliver said when his heart had slowed back to its normal pace. "Mr. Ault mentioned that he was going to visit a philosophical market."

"May I come along?" Liao asked, hopping up and down with his satchel flapping against his side. "I want to see the philosophical market with Max!"

"Well, I—" Oliver glanced to where Mr. Cascon and Whippett waited at the gunwale. "I suppose. Whippett can look after you once he's gotten us where we need to go."

"I don't need looking after," Liao sniffed. Then he brightened. "What color do you like best, sir? Once we're off Flotilla I shall send a rocket up just for you."

Oliver began to retort that he had no time to waste on fireworks. Then he changed his mind. "Thank you, Liao. Red is my favorite, if you've got red."

Liao scoffed. "Of course I've got red. Red is easy."

"And will we really be able to see it? It's broad daylight, after all."

"Oh, certainly. I have daylight fireworks."

"Daylight fireworks?" Oliver asked as they filed down the gangplank and into Flotilla.

"Yes, sir! They're not easy at all, you know. I'll send it up when we get to Shantytown, and then Max can find us instead of me having to look for him."

The quarter called Shantytown looked exactly like what its name implied. First the warehouses that lay thickly along the southern edge of the Bayside Harbor became a bit more decrepit and neglected in appearance; then Oliver realized he wasn't actually seeing warehouses any longer, but tenements that overlooked everything with a vaguely disapproving air. In between these were smaller houses, one and two and three stories tall, that managed to be a bit more cheerful.

Whippett paused to take his bearings, and Liao took the opportunity to fish a rocket and a little folding stand from his bag. "Watch, Mr. Dexter!" The explosive whistled skyward and an eruption of bright, gleaming red sprouted against the blue sky, followed by a resonant boom.

"That's splendid!" And it really was. The red was not merely visible in the sunlight, it stood out against the blue as if a deep crimson sunset were peeking through gaps in the heavens.

As the scarlet dissolved into smoke, Lucy Bluecrowne's voice called from down the street. "Ahoy!"

"Ahoy, Lucy!" Liao shouted. "Ahoy, Max!"

"Well, this is convenient," Oliver said as Lucy and Max joined them. "Liao was hoping to go along with Mr. Ault to the market-place."

"I'm sure that'll be fine," Lucy said. "Oh! Be right back." She and Whippett sprinted away toward yet another church, leaving Oliver, Max, and Mr. Cascon staring after them. Liao, unfazed, sat on a curb to wait.

"What on earth is she doing?" Max asked. "That's the third one this morning."

"How many altogether?" Liao asked.

"Two yesterday in Flotilla, three today . . ." Oliver said.

"And there were two yesterday after Flotilla and before we met you," Max added.

"So seven?" Liao thought for a moment. "Well, that only leaves fourteen."

"Fourteen what?" Oliver inquired.

"Saints, of course."

Lucy and Whippett rushed back. "All right," Oliver demanded, "what is it with you and churches? I mean, really." He pointed at the green ribbon trailing from Lucy's pocket. "What have you got there?"

She hesitated, then sheepishly took a little rectangle from her pocket. "It's a prayer deck, special for seamen. Just the holies that look out for mariners and folk who make their living on the sea."

Oliver took the short stack of cards and flipped through them. On each was a picture of a saint, with his or her name and the address of a specific chapel emblazoned below.

"Which it's a sort of tradition in Nagspeake to go round and say a prayer to each one," Whippett explained.

"I never would've guessed you for a Catholic, Lucy," Max said.

"I'm not a Catholic," she retorted, "but there's popery and there's plain good luck, and it's silly not to take advantage of good luck when you can."

"I never would've guessed you for superstitious," Oliver said, handing the deck back.

Her jaw actually dropped. Whippett wore an identical expression of shock. "Have you *seen* my schooner?" Lucy demanded. "Are you utterly blind?"

"Which it's *called* the *Left-Handed Fate*," Whippett put in. "Left-handedness is awful bad luck, and apart from the figurehead, Mr. Santat the purser's left-handed, too; plus Mr. Harrick the gunner's got a cat, and is it a good, lucky black cat? No, sir, it is not. And one of his mates *will* carry a white-handled knife, no matter how many times we've put it to him tactful-like that a white-handled knife is worse luck than a white cat—"

"Aren't black cats the unlucky ones?" Max asked Oliver in an undertone. "Some nonsense about witches or devils?"

"Not at sea," Oliver whispered back. "At sea, black is about the only acceptable color for a cat."

"Not to mention we had to leave Fells Point on a Friday," Lucy continued, "and it's dreadful luck to sail on a Friday—"

"It was a Saturday," Whippett corrected her. "It only felt like a Friday. And then there's the other gunner's mate," he continued, "whose *actual name is Jonah*, God help us. And of course we don't like to mention"—he broke off speaking, winced with great embarrassment, and aimed his thumb at Lucy from behind the palm of his other hand—"sailing with a *girl*."

"No, we don't like to mention that," Lucy said a bit defensively. "And we could go on. Suffice to say that most of us feel that while we don't have time to worry about such things aboard ship—"

"Which it's always been a lucky ship, despite—"

"... It isn't a bad idea to store up as much good luck as we can manage when we're ashore."

"Likely every fellow who goes ashore is making the same rounds," Whippett said. "We call it the Pilgrimage."

"Almost wish I'd known earlier," Mr. Cascon muttered. "I might've joined in."

"Lucy, did you forget to save me the card for Mazu?" Liao asked from the curb.

"Never." She passed one of the cards to Liao.

"Thank you." He slipped the card into his bag and shrugged at Max and Oliver, who were both scowling at him. "What? You didn't ask me yesterday, and I didn't like to interrupt. You're both so *serious* all the time."

Max rolled his eyes. "Can we get on our way?" He started walking, mumbling something under his breath, the only word of which Oliver caught was *preposterous*.

"I suppose you think it's preposterous, too," Lucy said to Oliver with exaggerated dignity as she rewrapped the deck in its green ribbon.

"Actually, it's a bit of a relief." The number of bad-luck omens aboard the *Fate* had never quite stopped giving Oliver the crawling creeps, and it had occurred to him more than once to wonder how it was that the crew managed not to go crazy surrounded by them all the time. This, at least, explained that.

After a few more blocks, Lucy halted at a broad intersection. "That's Morbid Street, which is where your tavern is, Mr. Dexter. And the marketplace is meant to be somewhere—" She consulted a scrap of paper from her pocket. "Somewhere on Misericorde. The girl at the tavern said to follow it uphill, away from the water, and you can't miss it."

Oliver wondered if they were all thinking the same thing: that if anyone could miss it, it was Max. Liao spoke up. "I'll make sure he finds it."

Max threw up his hands. "I did survive perfectly well ashore for rather a long time before shipping with you lot, you know."

"And because none of us can quite work out how that happened," Lucy said, patting his cheek, "we're inclined to take no chances. We'll rendezvous at Cricket Lane House, you and I, beginning at six bells in the afternoon watch."

"That's three o'clock," Liao whispered to Max.

"I *know*," Max said peevishly.

Lucy gave Liao a hug and whistled for a carriage; the rest headed down Morbid Street. About a block in, the lane passed under a stone arch with three chipped words carved into the lintel at the top: MORBID STREET CHURCHYARD. After that, Morbid Street began rapidly to live up to its name. Gravestones sprouted all over: stone crosses and stone trees, towering marble angels, and huge, elaborate tombs. Where there weren't memorials, there were thin, tall buildings. They sat at odd angles and at strange distances from the road, surrounded by death-markers and mausoleums so closely that Oliver was sure the buildings had been thrown up wherever they could go without having to actually move the dead.

"Well, this is cheery," Mr. Cascon said grimly. "Begging your pardon, but something occurred to me. I hope you'll take it without offense, sir."

That sounded ominous. "Certainly, Cascon."

"Well, sir, might it be best if I do some poking about this Smith's Tot place myself? As we don't know that they won't form some all-wrong notion of a ship with such a youthful commander. Whippett can show me to the pub, and this evening you could look over the recruits for final approval."

"I can tell you what notion they might form," Whippett said, casting a dark look over his shoulder. "Begging your pardon, sir."

"No need," Oliver said, well and truly embarrassed now.

"It would be an all-wrong notion," Mr. Cascon said, scowling at Whippett.

"Oh, certain it would. We all think gold dust of the lieutenant, always considering we're prisoners, of course."

"Of course," Oliver agreed, wishing he could make his face stop burning.

"And if we *wasn't* prisoners, we'd think proper gold dust of you, Mr. Dexter. But that's as we've come to know you, sir, and as we really didn't have a choice in the matter anyhow. But *volunteers*—"

"That'll do, Whippett," Mr. Cascon growled.

"I take your point," Oliver admitted. It made sense; plenty of sailors might reasonably refuse a perfectly good voyage if they knew they were nominally commanded by a twelve-year-old. But it was still one more reminder that he was just a boy playing at being an officer.

Max cleared his throat. "This appears to be our turning, Liao."

"Very good." Oliver saluted to the still-apologetic Mr. Cascon. "Mr. Ault, I suppose I'll come along for a look at this philosophical market of yours."

"Huzzay!" Liao cheered.

Max Ault, on the other hand, looked a little discomfited. But he recovered quickly. "Certainly."

At the top of the hill, Misericorde Street dumped Oliver, Max, and Liao unceremoniously at the mouth of an alley between two warehouses overlooking the graveyard on one side and the river on the other. "I suppose we just keep following it," Max said dubiously.

The warehouses were too tall and too close together to admit much sun this early in the day, so the alley was as dark as twilight.

"I don't see how there's room for any sort of market here," Oliver protested.

Max paused. "I don't either, but I can hear it. Can't you?"

Tilting his head to listen, Oliver realized he could hear something echoing through the alley walls. The sound swelled, and as they walked on, it became a chaos of voices punctuated by an assortment of bangs, clangs, and whistles. Then the three of them turned a corner and there it was: a huge square tucked into the shells of four warehouses. The inner walls had been knocked down so that the space inside was open to the air, leaving the standing outer facades to shield the market from the world.

"Wow," Liao said, clapping his hands in giddy delight. *"Wow!"*

twenty-five
THE HACKERS' BAZAAR

It was as if Mr. Jeton's shop had exploded in color and noise and excitement. Oliver felt like clapping, too; but clapping wasn't captainlike, so he tucked his hands in his pockets as they filed into a riotous and dazzling array of carts and pavilions and stalls roofed with tin or copper or painted sailcloth. These were surrounded by bales and crates spilling straw, cabinets stuffed with sheaves of paper, rows of blown-glass instruments and wooden boxes labeled with yellowing cards. Stray pieces of machinery hunkered like animals, some gleaming and smelling of wood polish and brick dust, others touched with verdigris and smelling of rancid oil.

At ground level the floors above cut off most of the sunlight, so glowing strings of lanterns, tin and glass and bright paper, overhung everything. Ramshackle staircases stood strangely aloof where the walls they had been attached to had been cut away, which made the dodgy assortment of ladders scattered about look like the safer way to get to the upper floors. Now and then the voices of hawkers rose, barking and arguing and laughing, but mostly they only

looked up from their books or mechanisms to answer questions with brief replies, then returned to what they'd been doing before.

Max Ault looked like a starving man at a banquet table. "I don't know whether to despair at my chances of finding the thing here, or despair at all the things I'm not going to have time to look at."

"What thing?" Oliver asked.

"A spherical chalkboard," Max said hastily. "I lost mine back in the Chesapeake."

Liao sniffed the air. "I smell powder. Max, Mr. Dexter, may I go?"

"I suppose," Max said. "Check back here in an hour, then every half hour afterward. Have you got a watch?"

"I'll ask someone. An hour it is, and every half after that. Mr. Dexter, should you like to come with me?"

"That's a splendid idea," Max said, too quickly and too enthusiastically.

"How did you lose a spherical chalkboard in the Chesapeake?" Oliver asked, suddenly suspicious.

"Oh, you know." Max waved his hand. "Over the side. As one does."

Oliver turned to Liao. "Is that true?"

"Oh, Max loses things over the side all the time," Liao said carelessly. "We can't keep track of them all. Are you coming with me, Mr. Dexter?"

"No."

"Back in an hour, then!" Liao bounded off and disappeared into the jumble, leaving Max and Oliver looking at each other.

"A spherical chalkboard," Oliver said dubiously. "Over the side."

"Sometimes I feel moved to do mathematics under the stars," Max replied. He very nearly kept a straight face, too.

"You know," Oliver pointed out, "if a fellow wanted to hide

something wondrous and mechanical, this would be the place to do it."

Max made a show of mulling this over. "That's a fascinating thought."

"Oh, stop it," Oliver grumbled. "Don't embarrass us both."

They wound their way deeper into the market. Here a crowd surrounded a man machining bits of brass into gears; there another fellow was grinding lenses; yonder a man with black freckles and long fingers watched the crowd from under a mane of dark red hair as he bound pages into books with thick black thread. But mostly it was stand after stand of philosophical instruments, and pieces of instruments, and books about instruments.

Abruptly Max halted, and Oliver ran smack into him. "Oof! I beg your pardon." The older boy didn't answer. He was staring at something on the other side of the stall before them. "What is it?" Oliver asked.

Max nodded at a pair of browsing men. "I think—if he would turn, I could tell you for certain, but I *think* that's the man from whom I was obliged to be rescued."

The man in question was tall and gray-haired, with spectacles on his nose and muttonchop whiskers on his cheeks. He pivoted toward them, and Max ducked. "That's him! That's Voclain!"

"Wait here." Oliver left Max and edged toward where the Frenchman and his companion stood looking at clusters of copper and steel wire twisted into birds' nests.

The man with the whiskers leaned in to speak to the vendor. "Pardon, monsieur, but where would one go in this place to find the Yankee Peddlers?" The vendor answered in a mumble without looking up from the length of wire he was snipping. "I beg your pardon?" the Frenchman said, and the vendor—was the fellow just being perverse?—answered in an even lower mumble. But Oliver heard the answer: the vendor had said the Yankee Peddlers could be found up at the top.

Oliver returned to Max's hiding place. "He's asking for something called a Yankee Peddler."

"What does that mean?"

"I don't know, but I know where to find them." Oliver headed for a woven rope ladder that appeared to be the closest upward route. He scrambled up and through a freestanding window frame to reach the second floor.

Max followed less gracefully, managing to kick the ladder straight into the stall beside it and send a tower of metal boxes crashing to the ground. "Which way now?" he asked when he'd hauled himself up, too. "Up another level?"

The answer was yes, and there was another aged rope ladder to the next floor right there. But Oliver hesitated. Clearly it wasn't coincidence that had brought Max and his Frenchman to this place at the same time, and Max's kidnapping certainly had something to do with the mysterious weapon. But for just a moment, Oliver had forgotten that he and Max weren't in this escapade together.

I could try to find the missing piece myself, he thought suddenly. *If I did, neither England nor France would be able to build the thing.*

He and Max eyed each other, and Oliver was sure the other boy knew exactly what he was thinking.

"Move." A heavyset man shoved past and grabbed the ladder as if it weren't obviously a death trap. Momentarily distracted, Oliver and Max watched, transfixed, as he climbed up, apparently completely unaware of the creaking protests of the ropes involved. In four separate places, broken strands popped out right in front of Oliver's eyes. *Not a chance I'm climbing that.* Oliver dashed for the nearest stairs. Then he heard the sound of a collision, followed by Max's voice, swearing.

The stairs weren't much better than the rope ladder. They'd

been bolstered from underneath—badly—with a collection of wooden boards and pilings and little hammocks that held up individual stairs. "Any decent carpenter would have this fixed in a day," Oliver snarled under his breath as he sprinted upward, ignoring the shaking underfoot.

The maze of vendors on the third floor was mostly made up of booksellers. He darted through to a wooden ladder propped against the far wall and hauled himself up and through a hole in the floor to arrive on the top level. Here, in addition to a smattering of stalls, there were long tables surrounded by clusters of people, some eating and drinking, some playing games with cards and dice. Somewhere bacon was frying.

Oliver trotted to a booth whose counter was piled with astrolabes. The vendor, a young woman, sat with her feet up and her nose in a book. Oliver put on his friendliest smile. "Pardon me, miss. Where on this floor might I find the Yankee Peddlers?"

"Nowhere," she said from behind her book.

Oliver frowned. "I beg your pardon?"

"Nowhere, I said." She turned a page without looking up.

"You must be mistaken—"

"I'm not."

The seller downstairs hadn't been terribly helpful when Voclain had asked directions, either. Oliver glanced over the nautical instruments piled on the girl's shelves. "Oh, a torquetum! Captain Eager had one of these; quite a big antique one, too, though I never did get a good look at it."

The girl set her book down immediately. "You like antique mechanisms?"

"Oh, yes. Navigational devices especially."

"I always liked that particular torquetum, even though it's got a nasty chip. I daresay you noticed it. Makes measuring the elliptic troublesome." She smiled. "If you really want to see some splendid devices, you ought to go up to the roof. There's a fellow there by the name of Lung, Alphonsus Lung, who has a really amazing assortment. One of the Yankee Peddlers."

Oliver blinked. The girl had the good grace to look embarrassed. "You asked where *on this floor*, you see, so when I said *nowhere*, it was technically true."

Somewhere behind him, Max swore again, and several other voices began to yell. "I do see," Oliver said quickly. "Thank you. I'll go up right now."

"There aren't any inside ladders to the roof, but you'll find one outside on the southeast wall." With that, she disappeared behind her book again. Max, meanwhile, was busy trying to calm a pair of game players gesturing furiously at an overturned table and a mess of scattered cards. Of the Frenchmen there was still no sign.

Getting to the southeast wall required crossing a swinging bridge between two of the four buildings that made up the shell of the market. The handrails, such as they were, had been strung from more of that frayed stuff that Oliver couldn't bring himself to actually call *rope*. He took a deep breath, dashed across and to a window casement in the wall, and found the ladder—metal, thank the heavens—bolted to the bricks outside it. A moment later he arrived on the roof.

"Well," Oliver said aloud, "this is not what I was expecting."

Three of the four rooftops were taken up with chimneys blowing smoke, vents pouring steam, and rickety pigeon-cotes dredged in feathers and dung. The entire southeast rooftop, however, was covered in a park. It was as if he had climbed all this way to be somehow miraculously transported back to ground level and a sweet little sunlit square complete with a gurgling marble fountain.

A score or so of wagons were parked around the square. Unlike the ones below, these were neatly painted and perfectly kept. As he began hurrying through the wagons, Oliver spotted another difference: where the vendors on the lower floors had seemed rather like they thought customers were an annoyance to be borne, the peddlers up here were hawk-eyed and aware. Their jackets were of a better cut and dyed in deeper and brighter colors. As he passed among them, each peddler caught his eye and nodded, as if to say, *You will let me know if you have questions, but I hope you understand it is not for me to chase after you.*

Most of the stands had a sign announcing the purveyor and his or her wares: WHITSUN, HOLLOW-WARES; PELLICLE, LOOKING GLASSES AND REFLECTIVE GOODS; CALCINE AND FULGOR, INCENDIARIES AND RADIANTS. Here Oliver found Liao deep in conversation with either Mr. Calcine or Mr. Fulgor. "Mr. Dexter, ahoy! Wait until you see all the treasures I've found. And Mr. Fulgor is showing me how to make up a firework called a furilona!"

"Ahoy, Liao," he said, hoping the boy wouldn't ask where Max was. "And Mr. Fulgor. I don't suppose you could direct me to a Mr. Alphonsus Lung's shop, sir?"

"By all means," Fulgor said, extending a powder-stained finger. "You'll find him there, in the red wagon."

"Thank you." Oliver hesitated. Whether he found the device before Max or not, there was still the Frenchman to consider. "Liao, I should wrap things up if I were you. There may be need for a quick exit."

The front door of the red wagon stood open. Above it, a brass shingle cut with teeth like a gear's read ALPHONSUS LUNG, CLOCK-MAKER. Oliver stepped inside. Yellow lantern-glow reflected off curves and angles of brass, bronze, glass, and polished wood. Clocks of all kinds lined the walls: pendulum clocks, astronomical clocks, pocket chronometers, even water clocks and a row of candles marked to burn down at specific intervals. It ought to have been a noisy place, but it wasn't. Oliver couldn't hear a single sound from anywhere until a voice spoke from a doorway at the end of the room.

"Please let me know if I may assist you, young man." Alphonsus Lung sat behind a desk piled with clockwork and peered at Oliver through a large brass loupe that magnified one pallid green eye to a monstrous degree. "If there is anything specific you are looking for."

Had the man placed an odd emphasis on the word *specific*? "Actually, I am," Oliver said. "Or at least, I'm interested in mechanical devices, and someone suggested I might see something particularly interesting if I came to you."

Mr. Lung removed the loupe and appraised Oliver with his pale eyes. "Is it only clocks you're interested in?"

"Oh, no, sir. All sorts of things." On impulse, he added, "I recently saw a splendid astrolabe at a shop in Fells Point."

"Fells Point? Would that be Mr. Franklin Jeton's shop?"

Heart beating fast, Oliver nodded. "Yes, sir."

"I am acquainted with that establishment." The peddler got to his feet and opened the door behind him. "Pardon the state of this room. It is where I keep what I'm not yet ready to put out for sale. Have a look around. Excuse me for not joining you. I am in the midst of a tricky little repair."

It was *here*. It *had* to be. The thing Max and Lucy had been chasing was right here, right under Oliver's nose.

The back room was lined with shelves, and both they and the big worktable at the end were piled with instruments and pieces of mechanical this-or-that. He glanced back through the door, but Mr. Lung was hunched over his tricky little repair with his back to Oliver, ignoring him completely.

Oliver circled the room, peeking into boxes, poking under

wrappings, lifting particularly interesting bits and bobs and occa-sionally examining one in the light of the single small window. The only thing he really had to go on was the idea that whatever he was looking for, it had to be very, very old.

Then, as he blew the dust from an ancient-looking thing rimed with the grunge of the ages, he happened to glance outside just in time to see the Frenchman, Voclain, drop over the retaining wall and into the square.

"Oh, no." Oliver looked desperately around the room. Then he stopped. It was on the table *right there.*

It was oblong, about the size and shape of a large loaf of bread, and wrapped in faded ticking-stripe paper. And Oliver had no idea what it actually *was*—but he knew that paper. Heart thudding under

his ribs, Oliver reached for a tag tied to the string that held the wrapping closed. It was embossed with the initials *FJ*. Captain Eager's torquetum had been wrapped in the same paper, and it, too, had worn a little tag like this when Oliver had retrieved it from Jeton's shop.

He looked out the window again and saw Voclain reach down to help his companion over the wall. No time for hesitation. Oliver picked up the parcel and hurried back to the main room. "Mr. Lung? I wonder if this is for sale."

The peddler looked up as Oliver set the wrapped item on the desk, and once again Oliver thought he sensed something in the eye that inspected him through the loupe. "It does not seem that you have opened it."

No time for lies. "I didn't."

"Then how do you know this is what you want?"

The conversation was beginning to feel like a test. Since he hadn't a clue how else to answer, Oliver told the truth again. "It came from Jeton's shop. I don't need to know what's inside to know it's what I want."

"Mmm." Mr. Lung tapped a thin metal tool on the desktop. Then he took the lens carefully from his eye. "Since you have answered honestly, I will do you the same courtesy. This item is meant for a specific buyer I have been told to expect today, and whom I will know by certain signs. Answer me one further question, and I will have done my due diligence."

Oliver nodded. He was about ten seconds from collapsing in a fit of panic.

"Tell me the other name associated with this parcel."

"The . . . oh." The only name Oliver knew was Voclain's, but that couldn't be right since Mr. Lung had claimed he didn't know who his intended buyer was. The consular officer from the *Marie Colette*, maybe? Cloutier? But he'd been occupied with the *Fate* and Max's piece, not this one.

The peddler nodded. "I see." And he curled one long-fingered hand over the parcel.

"*Honoratus*," Oliver blurted. "The other name is *Honoratus*."

Mr. Lung cascaded his fingers, *ta-ta-ta-tap*, on the top of the parcel. Then, with a faint smile, he pushed it across the desk. "In the future, try not to forget your passwords, young man. I thank you for stopping by."

Oliver clutched the precious thing to his chest. "How much—"

"As I'm sure you know perfectly well but have also forgotten," Mr. Lung said as he fitted the loupe back into his eyesocket, "the item has already been paid for."

"Of—of course," Oliver stammered. "Thank you, sir." He tucked the package into his waistcoat and hurried out of the wagon. A moment later, Voclain and his companion appeared on the path directly before him. Oliver tensed, about to break into a run, and then remembered that these men had never seen him before. It was Max Ault they would be looking for.

He forced himself to stroll past them without speeding up, then rushed around the back of the wagon, where he ran smack into Max.

"You've got nerve!" Max snapped as they picked themselves up off the ground. "What's the idea, leaving me behind like that?"

"*I've* got nerve?" Oliver countered. "*You've* got nerve! You're on parole!"

Max pointed at the lump in Oliver's waistcoat. "What is that?"

Oliver curled an arm across his middle. "None of your sealing-wax."

"You've got it, haven't you? Give it here!"

Oliver shook his head. "No. And don't argue. Voclain just went into the peddler's wagon, and he'll know in a minute that it's gone."

Max's face drained of color. "Let's go."

They found Liao waiting at Calcine and Fulgor's stall. He leapt to his feet. "Quick escape?"

Oliver nodded. "The quickest."

"Then why are you going that way?" Liao asked as Oliver and Max headed for the ladder. "The moving floor is faster than anything." He led them to the opposite side of the peddlers' square, where a deep channel ran between this rooftop and the next. "Hello again, Mr. Kharon," Liao called, waving to a man sitting with his legs dangling into the abyss. I'm ready to go back down now, and my friends are in a hurry."

The man nodded at Liao's bulging satchel. "I'm guessing you've spent your pocket money. Does one of your friends have the fare?"

"Max has money," Liao said. "Max, give Mr. Kharon a coin for each of us. The big silver ones."

Max fished money out of his pocket and handed a clinking mess of money to the man named Kharon. "A little extra, if it will help move us faster."

"It might." Mr. Kharon pocketed his payment and got to his feet. "Stay where you are. Or sit, if you prefer." He strode to a cluster of machinery on the wall and threw a huge lever. With a squeal of metal on metal, the ground lurched beneath them, and the square of rooftop upon which they stood began to descend, just as two angry voices began to shout nearby in a blend of French and English. Voclain and the other Frenchman appeared at the edge of the roof above them. The second man crouched and swung his legs over the brink.

"He's going to jump!" Max shouted.

Liao fished in his bag. "Cover your eyes."

Oliver obeyed, but even so he sensed the flare of blinding light that erupted over their heads. When he opened his eyes again, no one was visible above anymore, and the square of rooftop had dropped too far for anyone to jump down onto it.

At last they came to rest with a creak and a heave on the ground floor, and Oliver, Max, and Liao sprinted away from the market and back toward Morbid Street.

twenty-six
WHAT DOES NOT BELONG

Lucy had barely raised her hand to knock on the green door at the top of the Liberty of Gammerbund when it swung open and the Spinster gazed triumphantly out at her with those wild, discolored eyes. She glanced at the stairs behind Lucy, as if some stranger might have crept up behind her unnoticed, then pulled her inside by her sleeve and swung the door shut with a bang.

"I said there was a story I heard once," she said, locking the door. *Clunk, thud, clank*: three separate bolts all in a line, one above the other. Had she done that yesterday? "Even as we were sorting the array, I wondered. With these cards so old, how could I not?" She pointed an accusing finger at Lucy. Today it was stained the color of blackberries. "You knew, didn't you, ship-girl, that something was very wrong about them being so old? I could see there was a lie in you when you told me how you came by them."

"I didn't know until yesterday. Your daughter told me about how the loom inventor only made his machine ten or so years back."

The Spinster grinned, baring her discolored teeth. "Did you

know these cards are the *reason* Joseph-Marie Jacquard invented his loom?"

"How did *you* know that?" Lucy asked before she could stop herself.

"Aha!" The Spinster spun in a delighted, surprisingly graceful circle. "I knew it!"

"But how?"

"Because while Jacquard was trying to adapt his loom to read the cards, who was he writing to for advice? Who would that have been, ship-girl? Where did he turn when the loom worked but the cards didn't?" She sighed joyfully. "What a tremendous puzzle that was."

"Napoleon's weaver wrote to *you*?"

She bowed. "He did."

"But—then why couldn't he make them work? Why didn't you tell him to do what we did yesterday?"

"Because I never saw the cards themselves, only drawings of them. I didn't work out how to find the right way to sort them until you showed them to me. Joseph certainly didn't mention the markers in his letters—if he noticed them at all, which I doubt."

Lucy nodded, but panic began to churn in her stomach. The Spinster had corresponded with Napoleon's weaver. She had tried to help him then, and she had just called him by his first name.

The Spinster smiled thinly. "I see your mathematics, girl."

"My country is at war with Jacquard's," Lucy said. "Did you know that?"

She nodded. "That sort of news travels fast in Nagspeake. Even as far as the Liberty of Gammerbund."

"Well, then did you know what was supposed to have been encoded on those cards?"

"No, because Joseph himself didn't know, although I think we both understood that with Napoleon Bonaparte personally involved in the project, it probably wasn't really about a faster way to weave a brocade."

Lucy sucked in a breath. "And now?"

"And now I have an even better idea." She waved a purple-clawed hand, gesturing toward the inside of the room-within-a-room that was her gigantic weaving apparatus. "Come."

Warily, Lucy followed. "But . . . why are you helping me?"

"For the same reason I was willing to help Jacquard," the Spinster said. "I am not political. These cards make a wonderful puzzle, and there are so few truly wonderful puzzles to be had these days."

Could things really be that simple for anyone in a time of war? Perhaps for a madwoman . . .

The newly laced cards were sitting in a neat pile at the center of the table. Lucy slumped. The Spinster hadn't even started weaving.

"Why the glum face? I told you I should be able to tell you what the cards have to say. Although I think you know," the old woman added with a curious smile.

"I don't."

"Liar," the Spinster said softly.

Lucy hesitated. "I know it has something to do with a very old device, but beyond that, I'm entirely in the dark. I had hoped that even a little weaving would show something, give some hint about it."

"Oh, that's what you're upset about?" The Spinster snickered. "Well, calm yourself, ship-girl. I started the weaving."

"But—but don't the cards have to be on the loom, somehow?"

"Telling me about my craft again, are you? Yes, the cards have to be on the loom; or at least they *did*, until I *finished*." She lifted a roll of silk from the top of the cabinet behind the chair and held it out to Lucy as if it were a sword being surrendered.

"I don't understand," Lucy said as the Spinster lowered the soft weight of fabric into her arms. "Your daughter said you couldn't weave more than a foot or two a day. She said no one could."

"It's a funny thing about children," the Spinster said. "As they grow up and become miraculous in their own ways, they stop thinking their parents are miraculous any longer." She snorted. "But sometimes they're wrong."

Lucy's fingers ached to unroll the silk. "May I look?"

"Not here. I'll wrap it for you, then take it and your cards and be on your way. The sooner the better." But then the Spinster did an odd thing. She sat down in one of the armchairs, and motioned for Lucy to do the same. "There's a story they tell out there."

Lucy glanced toward the window as she perched reluctantly in the other chair with the roll across her knees. "Out there in the Liberty?" She wasn't all that sure she wanted to hear any stories from out there, and she was quite certain she wanted to get under way so she could have a look at this fabric they'd gone to all this trouble to have.

"Out there in *Nagspeake*," the Spinster said sourly. "And there is a reason I think you should hear this tale, if you'll shut up for it."

"I beg your pardon." Lucy sat as primly as she could manage.

"It's a matter of metal and dreams," the old woman began. "You know about the life of old iron?"

"I know it moves. I've seen it. I think it's beautiful, actually."

"Good girl. And it is beautiful. But iron isn't the only metal in Nagspeake with life in it. Of course, all elements have life, in the sense that if you combine them just right, life comes out of the mix— but that isn't what I mean." She stretched her long, thin legs out in front of her. "It's said that long ago, in the centuries before so many people roamed the lands and seas, the elements of Nagspeake rose up bodily and walked the shores of the Magothy as if they were human as you and I. Or not quite *human*, I suppose.

"Iron walked as a woman, red as rust and gray as flint. Copper was a girl the color of sunset with a head like a fox." The Spinster ticked these off on long, stained fingers as she spoke. "Nickel and Tin might have been brothers, but for Nickel's golden tinge and Tin's wings, which were made of a thousand folds of paper-thin metal. Mercury was a creature like something from the margins of a map of some terra incognita—a serpent when I first heard the tale, an otter when I was told it a second time by someone else. And I suppose there might have been more elements than just the five, but those are the only ones mentioned in the yarn."

Lucy was torn between impatience and curiosity. "This is a fairy tale?"

The Spinster gave her an unimpressed look that made Lucy shrink a little. "When you call things 'fairy tales,' you mean stories for children, in which fantastic things stand in for real ones and some sort of truth hides behind a wondrous fiction, yes?" The Spinster smiled her cerulean smile. "This is a Tale of Nagspeake. That's all I can tell you, except that in these parts, there are strange wonders enough that we aren't quite so quick to invent new ones."

"You're saying this is true, then?"

"I'm saying *there's a thing I'd like to tell you*, and *you keep interrupting.*"

Lucy sighed and leaned back into her chair. "Go on, then."

"Thank you. The metals of Nagspeake walked abroad, and although they sometimes fought with one another, they were united in their love of the world around them. They loved the bay and the pines and birches of the forests," she said, her sharp voice taking on an almost singsong quality that surprised Lucy with its gentleness. "They loved the sunrises and sunsets and the mists that rose and fell, sliding off the water and creeping up the slopes of the hill. They loved the star-spattered skies, the winds that curled through the land in the summer and the snows that dusted it in the winter. Most of all, they *felt* things—deep aches brought on by the beauty of the world through which they walked. And, as I mentioned, they butted heads sometimes, too—that's a whole other handful of stories, but what they agreed on was that the deep feelings the world stirred in them made them want . . . *something*."

She paused, drumming blackberry fingers on the arms of her chair and looking at Lucy expectantly. Lucy swallowed her impatience and forced herself to wait the old lady out until at last the Spinster gave the slightest quirk of a smile and continued her tale.

"For a long time they tried to work out what it was they wanted. Eventually they realized they wanted to contribute to the world they loved so much. To *make something*. And although each privately doubted it would be as beautiful as what already existed, they decided to try. So they put aside their petty quarrels and worked together to come up with anything that might stand alongside the wonders that gave them so much inspiration."

It was so hard for Lucy not to fidget or glance at the clock on the Spinster's mantel. A story about creating some kind of natural wonder or even a piece of art couldn't have any bearing on a quest to build a weapon. What was the point?

"They thought, they discussed, they debated . . . but in the end, the metals simply didn't have any ideas that seemed worthy of the need they all felt. Or, when one had an idea that seemed perfect to that particular individual, it didn't work for the others. Nickel's heart soared when the bay turned pink and gold at sunrise; Copper was mesmerized by the dance of trees in the windsong; winged Tin dreamed of painted skies; the imagination of Iron conjured cities like living sculptures; and the creature Mercury watched the arcs of the stars in the night skies and envisioned wheels-within-wheels, driving all of creation and spinning new worlds minute by minute. But when any one of them tried to captivate the rest, it turned out that no individual element's inspiration carried the same . . . the same *punch* for the rest. They all agreed upon the ache but, being five different beings, could not agree on what might soothe it. Are you paying attention, girl?"

"Yes, yes, for the love of—"

"Just making sure. 'Is it possible that none of us are dreamers?' Tin worried. 'Perhaps the problem is that we are *all* dreamers,' was Iron's opinion, 'and so we are all dreaming different things.' 'We have been searching for a grand dream,' Copper said, 'one that will capture us all—but perhaps that's the wrong way to go about it. Perhaps that each of us has a different idea in mind is a good thing.' Nickel spoke up and admitted, 'I don't think I can create my masterpiece alone.' The rest reluctantly agreed that the things they conceived of were too big and too grand for any one of them to accomplish on his or her own. It was Mercury who finally came up with the answer.

" 'In that case,' she said, 'I believe I know what we should do.'

"The five elements put their individual dreams aside for a time, and together they designed and built a device capable of—well, not so much of *creating* great things, but *assisting* in the creation of great things. It could not dream on its own, but it could fill in the missing pieces that dreams always seem to have. And when it was finished, the five elements sat back and looked at their handiwork and saw that the grand desires of each had found their ways into this creation after all. And for a while, each felt the ache subside."

"Only for a while?" Lucy asked.

The Spinster made an amused noise and looked around her workspace. "A mind meant for making things never finds peace for long.

The ache always comes back. But that's nothing to worry about. The worry is that one day it will go for good."

"Is that . . . the end?" Lucy asked after a moment. "Of the story, I mean."

"Well," the Spinster said, drumming her fingers on the arms of her chair, "I've heard versions where there's another line or two about the elements taking turns with their invention to bring the things they'd imagined into the world, but nobody ever says what they really did with it, and that's not the point anyway."

"Then what *is* the point?"

"For the love of all that's holy, girl, what did I just tell that story for if you weren't listening?"

"I was listening!" Lucy protested. "Shall I tell it back to you?"

The Spinster reached out and smacked the top of her head. "Listening, perhaps, but did you actually *hear it*?" She shook her head. "Never mind. I'm done. Take your prize and go. Perhaps it will make sense when you see." Lucy peered into one exposed end of the fabric and the Spinster whacked her on the crown again. "Not. *Here.*"

Exasperated and grumbling under her breath, Lucy waited for the Spinster to wrap the roll, then she put it over her shoulder and followed the old woman out.

When they emerged from the loom, the Spinster cracked the door open and peeked out again. "You're cagey today," Lucy commented.

"We're all a bit cagey in Gammerbund," the Spinster said, closing the door again. "You might have noticed it. Or did everyone else come out and say hello?"

"This is different. Who are you looking for?"

"No one I had to worry about until I saw those cards. Answer this one truthfully, my little lying ship-girl. Do you really not know who else might be out there?"

"Other than the French?"

"Other than the French."

"There are men who wear black-upon-black uniforms." Lucy reached out instinctively for the nearest wooden surface to scratch for luck against bad omens. The Spinster nodded slowly. "Have you seen them?" Lucy asked incredulously.

"No, but Joseph did. They spoke to him twice. The first time it was just one man, and Joseph could only remember afterward that he had promised to return."

I shall see you again in time.

"But after the second visit," the Spinster continued, "Joseph remembered more. The man appeared in his workshop with another who looked very like him. They examined the loom without a word. Then the first said to his companion, 'We have nothing to fear from this man. He does not have the mind for the riddle, and the war in his heart has faded.' I reread Joseph's letter to me about it yesterday, after you left." She rubbed a spot of carmine on her wrist. "Hearing someone declare that he lacked the mind for the task spurred him on, of course. But the men in black frightened him, too, so he moved his shop from Lyon to a more secret location. And of course you know what happened next."

Lucy nodded slowly. "The more secret location was a ship, a floating workshop. It was captured by a British letter-of-marque." *My letter-of-marque.*

"That's right," the Spinster said evenly. "That's exactly right."

"We're at war." Lucy shifted the roll in her arms. "I don't know what else to say."

"You don't have to say anything. You asked who I was looking for and I'm telling you I was looking for those creatures in black coats. And if I were you, I'd be looking for them, too."

"I will. I am."

"I thought as much." The Spinster gave Lucy an awkward pat on the head. "Get out of here before you bring them to me. I don't need anyone telling me I don't have the mind for any riddle that might still cross my path. Though I do thank you for bringing me this one." She touched the roll. "I had to make some guesses about colors, but I think it came out nicely."

It was before one o'clock when Lucy arrived at the turning that led to the Cricket Lane House, but early or not, there were Liao, Max, and Oliver Dexter hiking up the road at exactly the same time. Why on earth was the prize-captain with them? Liao looked troubled; Max and Dexter looked angry.

Dexter's figured out that we kept working on the engine, she realized with a sinking heart. Well, of course he had. They hadn't been trying particularly hard to look like they *weren't* working on it.

She reached the little group and regarded them warily over her armful of silk. "Well?"

"Well, we have retrieved a thing," Dexter said, curling his arm over an oblong lump in his waistcoat. "It remains to be seen what it is. And what's to be done about the matter of you two breaking your parole."

"We've done no such thing," Lucy protested. "You said we shouldn't undertake any acts of war *while aboard*."

"You knew perfectly well what I meant!" Dexter shouted.

"You dictated the terms," she shouted back, shoving the fabric at Max to better jab a finger at Dexter's nose. "We took you at your word!"

"Lucy," Max said warningly.

Dexter shoved her pointing hand aside. "I revoke your parole!"

She snorted. "What brig will you throw us in, Mr. Dexter, when you've overpowered the three of us with that brute strength of yours?"

Liao plucked at her sleeve. "Lucy, don't."

"Well, don't dare come back to the *Fate*!" Dexter sputtered. "And perhaps I can't throw *you* in the brig, but when I get back, I'll lock up every privateer left aboard!"

That took the wind right out of her sails. "Don't do that," Lucy said quickly. "It was only Max and I who broke parole. And we thought certainly you must have known."

"Well, I didn't. I thought we had an understanding."

There was no good way to answer that. Lucy nodded at the lump in his waistcoat. "You didn't come all the way out here with that thing just to try to clap me in irons, did you?"

Dexter glowered at her. "Mr. Ault and I have come to an agreement. You show me how far along your weapon is, and I'll show you what's in the parcel. But whatever's in it, I'm taking it with me."

She turned to Max in disbelief. "You agreed to this?"

He nodded, looking very uncomfortable. "Short of knocking Mr. Dexter down and prying it from his hands, I don't see what choice I have. This way at least I get a look at the thing."

Reluctantly, Lucy considered. "Three of us and one of him. . . . We could just take it."

"And I suppose you'd do that, too," Dexter fumed.

"We would never!" Liao protested, aghast. "Lucy, tell him we would *never* do such a thing!"

She sighed. "Of course not."

They trooped into the Cricket Lane House and up to the little parlor. Dexter produced a parcel covered in paper, which Max peeled away to reveal a tall, polished wooden box inlaid with a pattern of concentric circles and woven filigree.

"What is it?"

"It is," Max announced, "a *box*, Melusine." Lucy whacked him gently on the back of the head. "Ouch." He undid a little clasp at the front and eased the box open. A few notes, faint and hesitant but incredibly pure, spilled out and died away.

Inside, a gleaming tree wrought from a dozen different metals stood upon a cluster of gears and discs studded with tiny pins. More mechanical bits poked through where branches etched with a wood-grain pattern parted from the bole. The leaves had been hammered from copper, and although someone had recently cleaned and polished the tree itself, the leaves had been allowed to keep their green patina. A complex network of roots twined and tangled with the components of the mechanism below.

"Jeton did say it was the most beautiful mechanism he'd ever seen," Max said reverently.

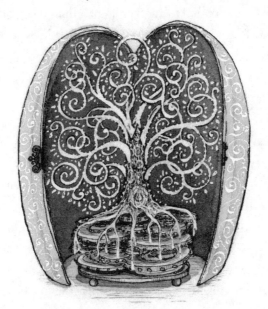

"A tree." Lucy thought immediately of the array the Spinster had laid out back in her roost in the Liberty of Gammerbund, and how it had branched, treelike. She reached for the canvas bag and fumbled inside until she found the root card that had begun the Spinster's array. "Max, look." She laid the card on the table beside the tree and pointed to the stained root structure at its edge.

Max studied it closely. "The cracks?"

"Not cracks. *Roots.*"

"Oh. Oh!" He held the card up alongside the metal tree. "They do seem to match! Amazing."

"But what is it?" Dexter asked.

"A music box, I think." Max pointed to one of the studded discs among the roots. "See how some of the root-ends lie against these pins?" He flicked one of the ends with a fingernail. *Plink.*

Liao leaned in closer. "How does it wind up? Oh, I see." He pointed at a root at the bottom just as Max pointed to a branch near the top and Lucy pointed to another branch that poked off the main trunk. They looked at one another, befuddled. Max took the root between cautious fingers. He tested it, then rotated it. The structure in the roots twitched into motion, and a delicate musical phrase drifted out. "I was right!" Liao said, charmed.

"But none of the higher gears are moving." Max gave the branch he'd pointed to the same gentle test, then a few turns. Through a hole in the engraved bark they saw a second set of gears go to work, and from higher up in the tree a slightly different tune began to play. When he turned Lucy's branch, yet another tune plinked to life, layering itself perfectly over the other. Shaking his head in wonderment, Max began testing and turning other branches, and a dozen separate phrases came together in a strange but lovely fugue, each perfectly complementary to the rest. As the tree became a symphony, its paper-thin copper leaves rustled and shivered as if in a breeze.

"Outstanding," Max breathed.

Liao broke into delighted laughter and began flapping his elbows like a duck. "I told you! I told you, back when we were reading Max's papa's papers! *Movement* meant movement!"

For her part, Lucy watched the tree with an odd sense of déjà vu. *"Copper was mesmerized by the dance of trees in the windsong,"* she murmured to herself as one by one each system came to a stop and the music dwindled to silence again. At last only the bit in the roots kept on playing, and then it, too, wound to a halt.

"All right, it's lovely," she acknowledged when it had fallen still. "But how does it fit into your mechanism?"

Max began carefully winding it again, and the mechanical symphony began anew. But when the music died the second time, he still wore a confounded expression on his face. "I don't know."

"Well, while you're mulling that over, does anyone wish to see what I've brought to the party?" Lucy took the roll from where Max had laid it on the sofa, untied the wrapping, and unfurled it carefully. A picture revealed itself inch by gleaming inch until the whole extraordinary thing, a rectangle roughly two feet wide and four feet long, lay open on the floor.

The background was a deep and lustrous indigo, the same color the Spinster's fingers had been stained yesterday. Laid across that background was . . . Lucy searched her vocabulary and couldn't come up with anything that precisely fit. If one had passed the thing hanging on a wall as a bit of artwork, the eye might only have seen a sort of fanciful decorative thing, all loops and filigree, wheels-within-wheels twined through with elegantly twisted vines that wove in and out, snaking and splicing and branching again. A rosebush that had been allowed to overtake some sort of philosophical garden ornament, perhaps. There was even an object like a flask in the foreground with one slim frond dipping into it.

But the Spinster had not woven the vines in green. Instead, she'd chosen grays and dusty oranges and brassy yellows: colors that evoked metals, not flora. Those colors caused Lucy's eyes to seek and find more details that appeared to be mechanical. The framework supporting the vine structure was built of concentric circles that formed a sort of sphere, like an armillary or a spherical astrolabe, which in turn sat on a horizontal wheel much like the capstan that wound the anchor cable aboard the *Fate*. Below that were four more sets of wheels-within-wheels. Other round, blossomlike things were scattered here and there; they might have been roses or spoked gears. At the margins the Spinster had woven the shapes of words, although they did not seem to be written with letters Lucy could identify.

And the creature Mercury watched the arcs of the stars in the night skies and envisioned wheels-within-wheels, driving all of creation and spinning new worlds minute by minute. . . .

It was a plan. A diagram, the organizational scheme of a very beautiful machine fashioned of wheels-within-wheels.

The five elements put their individual dreams aside for a time, the Spinster had said, *and together they designed and built a device. . . .* The voice in her memory shifted and became Max's, reading from his father's translation . . . *That takes the name and creates the work and draws creation and destruction from its hidden places, from the spokes of the wheel and from between the teeth of the gears, that turns and drives and moves the world by its movement and makes of the world a new thing. . . .*

So *that* was why the Spinster had told that story. She put a hand over her mouth.

"There it is," Max murmured. "That's the engine."

"It looks . . . feral," Dexter said. "Wild, if you take my meaning."

"I think I do." Max looked from the tapestry to the metal window box outside, with its iron shoots and flowers. "These tendrils remind me of the philosophic iron."

Lucy was only half-listening to them as she tried to recall the details of the Spinster's tale. *Long ago, in the centuries before so many people roamed the lands and seas, the elements of Nagspeake rose up bodily and walked the shores.* Had the old woman actually believed this thing she had woven showed the device in her tale? How on earth could there really be a connection between a piece of batty Nagspeake lore and this machine, the search for which had led from Egypt to Venice to France to Baltimore to . . . to *Nagspeake* . . . Her mind raced, torn. Fairy tales were fairy tales, but her superstitious mind, always on the lookout for connections between occurrences and what they really meant, couldn't quite accept the idea of coincidences. No, the repetition of these images—and the old weaver hadn't even *seen* the musical tree—told Lucy there was meaning in that story. But, in the Spinster's words (*Get out of my head, old woman!*), the meaning would have to be retrieved from it.

Liao, meanwhile, sat beside the tapestry with his arms wrapped round his shins. "It looks sad to me."

Lucy shook off her musings and squatted beside him. "How do you mean, sad?"

He pointed at a sort of articulated arm tucked across the device's front. "It looks like it's clutching its heart. As if its heart had been broken."

"I don't think it looks sad." It was a war engine; of course Liao thought it looked unhappy. This was the boy who claimed that ship-to-ship engagements made the guns melancholic.

"Lucy." Max pointed to one of the rings of the main sphere. There, each set perpendicular to the inside surface, was a series of rectangles pocked with little specks. "Those are the same cards!"

"I bet they're the ones the Spinster said didn't go with the rest, the ones that weren't part of the final chain or the array we used to find it." That stack was still beside the sofa where she'd left it the day before. Lucy reached for the top whalebone rectangle and found a tiny stained mark on one short end: a guide mark. "I bet I can even tell you in what order they go."

Max reached over, took her face in both hands, and kissed her forehead. "But the music box, then? I suppose the bit we want could be a particular piece of it. The discs and drums are where all the information is."

Something nagged at Lucy as she scanned the image. Something about the whalebone cards. About how so many of them had existed only to hide—and then to reveal—the correct chain. About how others had been entirely unrelated to either the array or the chain, but hidden in plain view, just waiting until their part in the device was revealed. "*The chain* itself *does not have meaning; the meaning has to be* retrieved *from it*," she said slowly. *But then really, old woman, get out of my head.*

Max looked sharply at her. "Say that again."

"It's something the Spinster said yesterday. Reminded me of what Liao said back in Baltimore about translations, actually." She pictured the Spinster tossing aside card after card. "Max, wasn't there something in the inscription about things that aren't like the others?"

"Yes. The word my father used was *singularities*," Max said. "*From the singularities is built the great engine.*"

Lucy nodded. "I thought so. Look for something that doesn't go with the rest."

Max rushed to the tree and began winding it again. Phrase by phrase, tune by tune, the delicate fugue built and gained complexity. "Can't quite reach this winder. . . ." He looked around. "Liao, have you got your folding tool?"

Liao fished in his pocket and handed the gadget over. Max fiddled in the base of the music box for a moment, then lowered his hands and watched the shivering tree. "There." He pointed to a disc in the root structure. Everything around it turned, spun, or plinked, but that one piece sat motionless. "Look quickly, all of you. Have I missed anything?"

Four pairs of eyes roved over the tree as the various mechanisms began to slow. Every branch, every root, everything that looked as though it could be wound, had been wound. Everything that could move was moving. Everything but that one disc.

"That's it, then," Max said. "That's what we want. Somewhere in the mechanism in the tapestry, there should be a spiked disc."

Liao, who had returned to look solemnly down at the tapestry, spoke up: "I see a disc fitted into the base."

Dexter muttered something that sounded like, "Sweets?"

"What?" Lucy asked, distracted.

He was looking down at the pages scattered across the desktop. "These are the papers you took from the Frenchman?"

"Yes, not that we learned anything from them. Why?"

"No reason." Dexter returned to the tapestry. Lucy glanced at the page he had touched. It was the sheet that contained what Max had guessed was some sort of recipe, the name of which seemed to be *manus Christi*.

If the key to locating the pieces of Max's engine was finding the bits that didn't go with the rest, the bits that were *singular*, a recipe among intelligence documents certainly fit that pattern neatly. There was no reason Dexter needed to know that, though. He'd already seen enough for Max to have fulfilled his part of their agreement.

Then Liao spoke up again. His voice was both miserable and reluctant. "I thought that last part of Max's translation had to do with the why or the how of the device. Maybe it's the *how*. People and creatures aren't the only things that eat."

Lucy glanced at Dexter meaningfully. "Maybe we've worked on this enough for today."

Max didn't take the hint. "*The sustenance that feeds the hunger that drives and grows* . . . Liao! Brilliant! Ships eat wind and turn it into motion. Guns eat powder cartridges and turn them into explosions. The music box needs to be wound before it can turn anything into music. *Energy.*"

Liao nodded, not looking at all pleased with himself, and pointed to the flask on the tapestry. "This machine is eating, too."

"Enough." Dexter darted back to the desk and plucked the disc from the tree roughly enough to send the whole thing toppling. Lucy and Max lunged for it, cracked their heads together, and fumbled the tree between them to keep it from smashing on the floor.

"How could you?" Max set it carefully on the desk and adjusted a few bent leaves. Then he whirled back to the prize-captain. "Wait! Please, let's discuss this!"

But Dexter had already shoved the disc in his pocket and was heading for the door. "We did. I've done my part, which is more than I should have. Now I'm going back to the ship, unless you plan to overpower me. I daresay you could."

Liao looked at Lucy, obviously heartsick. She felt Max's eyes on her, too. Dexter was right: certainly they could stop him. *She* could stop him. But she couldn't bring herself to do it, and if *she* couldn't do it, she had no business asking Max and Liao to.

"No," she said at last. "We aren't pirates."

"I won't revoke your crew's parole, then, but you're to report to the *Fate* immediately and clear out your things. I want everyone off the schooner by the end of the first watch." Dexter slammed the door behind him and was gone.

"Lucy," Liao fretted, tugging on his queue, "he doesn't mean it, does he?"

"I imagine he does," she said, rubbing a hand over her face. "Impossible bargains. All we have are impossible bargains."

"But . . . but the ship is home!"

A sick hollowness bloomed in Lucy's middle. "It was going to happen eventually, Liao," she said mechanically. "You know that. A ship is a fighting machine. It's only home so long as you hold it. And Dexter holds the *Fate* now." Little by little, the hollowness gave way to numbness. Good. Numb, she could still work. "Max, if you can make sense of this schema, I suspect that the *Fate*'s armorer, carpenter, and sailmaker can run up everything you need to build the thing."

"But . . . all of those people are aboard the schooner, Lucy."

"Which is fortunate, because otherwise you'd have to go all over the city to find people to do the work. And with the Fates already busy with the shipboard repairs, the prize-crew isn't likely to notice a few more bits and bobs on the worktables. Not to mention that the *Fate* is also where your disc is going to be, Max."

"Well, as to that . . ." Max turned to the tree, took a second disc carefully from inside the base, and held it up triumphantly. This one was smaller than the first, and loaded with even more tiny spikes. "I wedged a splinter into the teeth of the disc in front of this one so it wouldn't move," he said, looking slightly embarrassed at the subterfuge. "It was just big enough to hide the fact that this one wasn't moving, either."

Lucy grinned. "So Dexter has the wrong piece?"

"He does."

She shook her head in admiration. "I would never have believed it of you, but I'm dashed grateful to be wrong. All right. Then we have a plan."

"About that. If we're meant to be vacating the schooner by . . . by when, exactly, was it?"

"By midnight. So pack slowly. Pack very, *very* slowly. Clumsily. Lose things, hunt for them, find them at the bottom of the chest you packed. Then you'll have to repack the whole thing again. You two can manage that, can't you?"

Max and Liao looked uncertainly at each other, then nodded. "What will you do, Lucy?" Liao asked.

"I'm going to see about the last piece of this puzzle, this stuff called *manus Christi*." Max thought it was a punch recipe; Dexter had called it a sweet. What they needed to sort it out was a confectioner. Fortunately, thanks to Tilly Gallfreet, Lucy knew at least one good confectioner in Nagspeake. She went to the desk and reached for the *manus Christi* recipe.

It wasn't there. "No," she muttered. All her good, useful numbness dissolved into panic.

"What is it?" Max asked, as she flung notes and letters aside in a frenzy.

Lucy stepped back and covered her mouth with one hand. "He took it," she said in disbelief. "Dexter stole the recipe."

twenty-seven

MANUS CHRISTI

He could simply have torn the page up. He could have weighted a bag with roundshot and sent it and the disc to the bottom of the bay. Instead, Oliver ran through the streets of Bayside, following the masts that peeked above the rooftops until he reached the waterfront. He stopped for directions, then followed those past the warehouses, shops, and chophouses to a stretch where the piers thinned out, the bulkhead sank away, and waves of sandy dunes rose in their place. Reeds and tall waving grasses sprouted alongside the road.

I should just burn it, Oliver thought as he walked. *I know enough about the device to make a report to the Minister's office.* Twice he nearly stopped and shredded the recipe. Twice a single thought kept him walking.

Two pieces might not be enough to build Max's device, if in fact the device wasn't just the fever dream of an obsessed old man and his son. But they might be enough to redeem Oliver, if this adventure ever came to an end. Yes, he had failed to follow his orders. Yes, he had entered into a truce with the enemy on no one's authority but his own. But he had thwarted the building of a great weapon, and brought evidence of it home. That would have to count for something. Wouldn't it?

A quick flush of guilt swept over him at the idea of betraying Lucy, Max, and Liao, but Oliver kicked a rock and willed those feelings to sail away with it. *It isn't a betrayal. We aren't friends; we are enemies at war. I must never forget that again.*

As he reached the shop called Magothy Treats, a harassed-looking woman in a patchwork apron came out on the porch and took a long sip from a mug. "Shop's closed," she called as he started up the stairs. "Also, I'm out of preserves, so if that's why you've come, you're out of luck."

"I didn't come for preserves," Oliver said. "I came to ask your advice."

"I can manage advice, I suppose. Anyhow, it usually goes away after a few minutes." She dropped into a chair and gestured at a matching bench. "And after some good strong Plymouth gin."

"What goes away?" Oliver asked as he sat.

"The haunt." She eyed him grimly, as if he might be a haunt as well. "And you are . . . ?"

"Oliver Dexter, U.S. Navy," Oliver answered, rising just enough to bow.

"Mirabelle Béchamel," the woman said. "What sort of advice are you after?"

He took the recipe from his pocket. "I wonder if you can make up a batch of this."

"That's not advice. That's work." Mirabelle Béchamel put on a pair of spectacles that hung from a cord around her neck and reached for the page. "A batch of what?"

"I think it's called *manus Christi.*"

Mirabelle's reaching hand froze. "I beg your pardon?"

"Perhaps I've got it wrong. My mother's a confectioner and I've never heard of it."

"No, I don't think you've got it wrong, young man." Mirabelle collected herself and took the page. "Impossible, perhaps, but not wrong." The paper quivered as she read, although there was no breeze stirring the sea grasses surrounding the porch. "There's something wrong with this, though," she said at last.

"It's in French," Oliver said helpfully.

"Thank you. While that certainly counts as annoying, the fact of having been written in French does not generally keep a recipe from working."

"Unless you don't read French," said an angry voice. Oliver turned to find Lucy Bluecrowne hiking up the path to the house.

Oliver got to his feet. "Now, wait."

"She's a bundle of smarts, isn't she?" Mirabelle said. "Friend of yours, Mr. U.S. Navy? Never mind, I don't care." She gave the page a little flutter. "I can read French just fine. This is gibberish. The instructions don't make sense with the ingredients, and I don't see how you can follow both."

Oliver turned to Mirabelle and reached for the recipe. "Never mind, then. I'll just—"

With irritating ease and apparently without even pausing in her reading, Mirabelle lifted the page out of his reach. "It's as if I were looking at the ingredients for a pie and the instructions for a petit four," she said as Oliver threw his dignity to the waves and actually jumped for the paper, "and yet I'm supposed to wind up with a spun-sugar castle when all's said and done."

"I understand. I'll just take it back," he said, jumping again as Lucy stomped up the porch stairs.

She strode past him and addressed Mirabelle. "So . . . you can't make heads or tails out of it?"

"I didn't say that," the confectioner said defensively. "Well . . . I can't, that's true enough; but then again, if this is actually related to *manus Christi* . . . well, then perhaps it's not so strange. Stop that," she added as Oliver snatched at the page again. She took one last look at it, then, to Oliver's surprise, handed it back. Lucy grabbed for it, but Oliver was quicker. He shoved the entire paper into his mouth, chewed, and swallowed.

Lucy's face went white. Mirabelle patted her shoulder. "Never mind. I don't forget a recipe after I've read it once." She began rattling off ingredients in French. Oliver groaned. Lucy grinned. Mirabelle paused in her recitation. "Utter nonsense. Still, *manus Christi* . . ."

Oliver gave up. "What is *manus Christi*?"

Mirabelle smiled. "Why, young man, it's *myth*. It's a vitamin, it's a cordial, it's manna, it's the elixir of life—unless it's just sugar candy made with pearls, or marchpane in the shape of the Sacred Heart. It's a *legend*." Her expression sharpened. "No haunt's keeping me out of my kitchen with this to look forward to."

She burst through the door and back into the shop. "Haunt?" Lucy repeated.

"Haunt," Oliver confirmed. He looked at the mug of gin Mirabelle had abandoned on the porch. "Is she drunk, do you think?"

"Not by naval standards," Lucy said grumpily. "Bundle of smarts indeed. I'd like to see her work out a sail plan." But there was a quick flicker of something else on her face. A look of recognition: something Mirabelle had said had caught Lucy's attention. What was it?

Mirabelle reappeared at the door. "Have a bite to eat while I work. I put some things out."

Oliver and Lucy regarded each other for a moment. "You have the disc and I have the plan," Lucy said. "And even if she succeeds, you'll still have the disc and I'll still have the plan. We'll be at the same stalemate."

"So it's a truce under this roof, then?"

Lucy nodded. Oliver walked inside without another word.

Inside, the shop resembled nothing so much as an apothecary's—except for the aroma, a mouthwatering blend of baking crust and burned sugar and butter and juniper and oranges. The long counters were packed with jars and bottles and mismatched dome-covered dishes. Most of what he could see Oliver recognized right away: sugar-dusted cubes of jewel-toned Turkish delight, marzipan in the shapes of fruits and vegetables and glittering beetles, spun-sugar birds' nests with blue confit-almonds standing in for eggs, tiny pink rum-soaked cakes and sugar-loaves tinted in unlikely colors.

But then here and there were stranger things: bottles of pearlescent liquor, standing cookies cut into the shapes of unrecognizable beasts, a tree hung with glimmering, glassy icicles, a raised pie with its top crust peeled back, apparently broken open by the candy-floss birds suspended above it.

"Table at the end," Mirabelle called from the kitchen. She had set out a pitcher of cold sherbet and a plate of cakes, and for a few minutes Oliver and Lucy ate in silence, listening to the confectioner at work in the kitchen and watching the ships in the harbor.

"Mr. Cascon seems very efficient," Lucy said at last. "I make no doubt he shall have your complement rounded out by tomorrow."

"If there are that many willing to ship aboard an American vessel in wartime," Oliver said grimly. "Seems unlikely when these Nagspeakers love their famous neutrality so much." Lucy's fingers clenched in the tablecloth, and too late Oliver realized he'd referred to the *Left-Handed Fate* as an American vessel. *But it* is *an American vessel*, he reminded himself stubbornly.

"You must promise me to take care of her, Lieutenant," Lucy said after a moment. "She is my sister, my mother, my home and country.

She carries the blood of my father in her seams." She gazed southward. Somewhere that way lay Flotilla, and the *Fate*. "I wish I knew that they would let you keep her."

"Me?" Oliver started, surprised. "Are you mad? A ship like the *Fate* would go to a master commandant at least—I don't think they'd ever give her to a lieutenant, not even a real one. If I'm lucky, I'll wind up right back in the midshipmen's berth, having my hammock cut down and my shirts stolen. If I'm not . . ." He forced the word *court-martial* from his mind.

"Is there no chance of your promotion being confirmed? There wouldn't be in *my* navy, not if you hadn't already served your six years and passed the lieutenant's examination. But it's different for your navy, isn't it?"

"My father said I should expect to spend three years or so before thinking of promotion," Oliver said automatically. "Yes, there are officers who've been promoted faster, for whatever reason. Doubtless they earned it."

"Doubtless," Lucy said in a tone that sounded as though she actually meant the opposite. "But why don't you think you've earned a promotion?"

Oliver glowered. "Are you poking fun at me?"

"No, why?" She both looked and sounded serious.

"Because I'm *useless!*" He slammed his glass down on the table, sending fuchsia liquid sloshing all over the white linen. "Because every time you call me *Lieutenant* it's like a kick in the knee. I'm *not* a lieutenant. I'm not any sort of proper commander. If I were, I wouldn't be here, having cake and sherbet while someone else rounds up hands." He glared at her. "And I would have known better than to trust you."

She ignored that last bit. "Generally captains don't actually round up hands themselves. They delegate things like that."

"Maybe so, but not because most sailors would refuse to volunteer aboard a ship if they knew that a child was commanding it."

"Most sailors think whistling calls the wind." Lucy shrugged. "And most wouldn't ship with a girl, either."

"A proper commander wouldn't be in Nagspeake at all. A *proper* commander would—"

"Somehow magically have located enough hands in the middle of the Chesapeake to fight off the *Marie Colette* without releasing his prisoners?"

"Would have come up with some other solution, yes," Oliver finished irritably.

"The pitcher stands by you, Mr. Dexter." She pushed her glass toward him, and Oliver reluctantly unfolded his arms and refilled it. "You have it wrong, you know," Lucy said as he poured. "I don't know how you can possibly have a clue how you're doing at it when you don't understand what a captain really does."

"I know what a captain does," Oliver protested.

"You're hung up on titles and the idea of being in charge," she said patiently. "A captain *leads*, which I don't think is how you're looking at it at all."

"Well, I don't see how it's different."

"It's different because being in charge—commanding people—doesn't have to mean any more than telling them what to do. *Leading* people means . . ." She paused and scratched her head. "Well, I think it means a lot of things, but it definitely means more than just giving orders."

"Like what things?"

"Well, like making decisions, for one thing. Coming up with strategy. Like making the right choice when time is short and there *are* no good choices, which is exactly what you did when the *Marie Colette* was bearing down and you and I made that first bargain."

"But most of what happens on a ship isn't about strategy and sudden decisions," Oliver protested. "Most of it's just everyday shipboard work. The crewmen know their jobs better than I do. I don't know what they need me for."

"Exactly! That's the goal—when everything's running smoothly, they *don't* need you, which is important because if you're wasting your time wondering if you could tie a knot better than any random foremast jack, you're not thinking about the bigger things, or about what's coming over the horizon. Yes, it's good for a captain to know how to hand, reef, and steer; one day he might need to lend a hand in a storm when he's closest to a rope that needs hauling on. But mainly he's just got to make sure he has the right crew in place, the best people he can find, and he's got to make sure they have everything they need to do their jobs as well as they possibly can." Lucy took a triumphant bite of cake. "He's got to keep the whole ship in his head, and the whole ocean it's sailing in, too. You're thinking about knots when you should be thinking about hemispheres."

"I suppose," Oliver said warily. He wasn't totally sure he agreed, but there was a certain poetry to Lucy's view of running things that made him ache for the romantic view of sailing that he'd had on his birthday, back in Fells Point. It seemed so long ago now.

"Have you never thought about what it takes to be a captain like your father?" Lucy asked curiously.

"I'm still working out how to be a midshipman," Oliver said glumly. "That's the sort of thing my father and I talk about, when we get the chance."

"Well, from your observations, then."

Oliver shrugged against a surge of jealousy. "I've never served under my father."

"Oh." Lucy looked like she wanted to add, *I'm sorry.* "Well, if you want my advice—which really only amounts to what I think it would take for me to be a captain like *my* father—here is what I should do, if I were you."

She paused and put a hand over her mouth, and Oliver realized to his horror that she looked like she might be about to cry. But just that quickly the moment passed and Lucy recovered her poise.

"What I should do if I were you," she said, "is work on keeping the whole ship in your head. From the water in the well to the name of the fellow in the maintop whose eyes are your eyes on the horizon to every soul and every scrap in between. Know it all, all the time, until the tone of the rigging tells you when you've hit upon the best plan for the sails. Until when you put your hand on the tiller you can feel the rudder speaking to you and you know immediately what it's trying to say."

It was as if she were hearing and feeling all these things at that very moment, as if the ship itself were speaking through her to him. Oliver had a sudden memory of the day they'd sighted Nagspeake, when he'd been on deck and she'd been up in the crosstrees skylarking. But maybe it hadn't been skylarking at all—maybe that's where she'd have been even if she'd been in command herself: feeling the heave of the ship below, but looking seaward, ever seaward.

"Of course," Lucy added, "that kind of knowledge takes time. So in the meantime—if I were you—I would think about how to do best by the crew, because I think that's how to get them to do their best by the ship and by their fellows. And perhaps even by me, if I earn it." She smiled. "Nell and I used to talk about this, when I was younger."

Oliver hesitated. "About Miss Levinflash—" he began. At the same time, Lucy said, "About our breaking parole—"

Just then, something exploded in the kitchen, and a thin curl of smoke reeking of scorched sugar rolled out across the floor. A moment later Mirabelle stumbled out with a bigger cloud on her heels. "It doesn't work," the confectioner announced.

"Perhaps it's the haunt," Lucy suggested.

"Yes, perhaps," Mirabelle said acidly. "Because despite the evidence of all of this"—she waved an arm to encompass the elaborate and varied collection of sweets in the shop—"I can't actually tell when I'm being haunted or just misreading the instructions." She pulled up a chair and poured herself a glass from the pitcher. "No, it's not my ghost, nor my stove, nor even the humidity. It's the recipe."

She took a paper from the pocket of her apron and scanned the rewritten recipe. "Three or four fewer ingredients, certain of the instructions struck out—it's plain to see places where if I just removed

a few lines, I could make any number of things. But they would be everyday things. They would be pies, or petits-fours, perhaps even spun-sugar castles—special, perhaps, but they would not be marvels." She studied the page for a moment. "And it feels like it should be marvelous. Reading a recipe is a bit like reading a poem, and there's a poem in this one for certain. There must be a way."

Lucy's Spinster had woven the tapestry out of cards that did not belong. Max's music box had contributed a disc that did not belong. "Take them out," Oliver said abruptly. "Whatever doesn't belong—ingredients, instructions, whatever doesn't go with the rest, take it out and then see what you can do with what you've removed."

Mirabelle's eyes sharpened. She turned her attention back to the page in her hand. Then she shoved back her chair and darted for the smoky kitchen.

twenty-eight
THE DEVICE

Aboard the *Left-Handed Fate*, the silk tapestry lay across the little desk in Max's cabin, which was crowded with the specialists Liao had quietly summoned. The *Fate*'s purser sat in Max's chair busily sketching up a clearer schematic of the engine; lovely though it was, the tapestry wasn't easy to read. It was only after much discussion and debate in hushed voices that Max, the carpenter, the armorer, and the sailmaker had worked out most of the details.

"I still say this coily bit above the little flat part here must be a spool of paper tape, but as no one agrees, I've had to be a bit vague." The purser held up the drawing. "Have I got it, do you think?"

"All except for these'uns." The armorer tapped a section of the curlicues that looked so like vines. Nobody had any good ideas about what they were. The sailmaker had thought it looked like cordage, except all knotted up like that he couldn't see the function of it. They reminded the armorer of Nagspeake's philosophic iron. Then the *Fate*'s surgeon had poked his head in, and after they'd all collapsed in relief that it was one of their own and not a member of the prize-crew, Dr. Domanova had said that those vine things looked like veins, and did Max have a set of Napier's bones he could borrow to work out some mathematical figures, since his own set was already packed?

"I suppose we have enough here to be starting with, anyhow," Max said at last. "Can you all manage your parts without drawing suspicion?"

The specialists gave him a collection of wounded looks. Then the carpenter glanced around the tiny cabin. "We're going to need more space to assemble it. I suggest the forepeak. Not quite as visible as the hold, nor quite as suspicious as here in the cabins."

The committee dispersed, and Max carried his box of Napier's bones up the ladderway, across the weather deck, and down again to the surgeon's cabin on the fore platform. Dr. Domanova took the box and looked Max over. "Why don't you rest now for a bit? You look exhausted."

"Couldn't possibly," Max said, glancing longingly at the surgeon's chair. "Or perhaps just for a minute." He sank into the chair and closed his eyes to the sound of Dr. Domanova rattling the calculating rods from their box.

....

It was awkward, the return to the *Fate*. Lucy and Dexter tried to pretend for a bit that they weren't going back to the same place, or at least that they weren't traveling back together. But as each was slowed by having to carry a huge green-glass bottle of the golden liquor that had been the result of Mirabelle Béchamel's efforts to interpret the recipe, neither could walk fast enough to put any distance between them. In the end, they gave up and shared a ferry back to Flotilla.

"When we get back . . ." Dexter began.

"Yes, yes." Lucy glared at him over the top of her bottle. "I shall pack and go ashore." She gestured at the matching bottle sitting beside him on the bench. "What do you think you're going to do with that, anyway?"

"I'm going to find someone in charge when I get back to Norfolk," he said stonily, "and I'm going to tell him, 'This is what I have to show for my failures.'"

"That and the fastest schooner on the Atlantic," Lucy muttered. "And the disc," she added as an afterthought. "Will your government try to build the device?"

"I don't see how they can build it with only two pieces any more than you can." He looked at her warily. He'd given her that same look at least four times on the walk to the ferry dock. "Why didn't you just take it back? Why don't you just take it back now?"

Why *hadn't* she tried to overpower him back in the boarding-house, before she'd known Max had tricked him? "I don't know," Lucy admitted. "Maybe because up until you actually put us off the ship and leave, there's still a chance for—"

"For what? For fate to intervene? For me to change my mind?" He shook his head. "Every compromise I've made up until this point I can justify. But letting you build a weapon under my nose—"

The weapon Max and the officers were building under the noses of the entire prize-crew right at that very moment. "Of course you can't do that," she agreed with a twinge of guilt. "But I suppose I don't see any point in trying to force you to do anything when we haven't exhausted every option. I can keep on trying to find a way to keep my ship right up until you sail her out of town."

The outer boundary of Flotilla slid closer, and Lucy wrapped her arms around the big glass bottle on her lap. Suddenly the backward-slanting masts were visible against the tangle of masts and cordage and walkways over the district. *Home*, she thought. Home, but for the last time.

....

It felt as though only a moment had passed when Max opened his eyes to discover that he was alone in the surgeon's quarters, slumped in the chair with his chin on his chest. He fumbled in his pocket and consulted his watch: nearly five o'clock. More than two hours had passed since he had left his compartment. "Why didn't anyone wake me?" he mumbled to the empty room.

It had taken years, but now, at last, a weapon that not even Bonaparte would be fool enough to challenge must be nearing completion. Peace, true peace, would come for the first time in Max's life, and forever after.

"There might even be a Royal Society fellowship in it for someone," Max said to himself as he got to his feet and smoothed his wrinkled clothes. "Perhaps even a Copley Medal." For a blissful, guilty moment he let himself dream. Benjamin Franklin had won the Royal Society's Copley Medal, along with Captain James Cook, William Herschel, Alessandro Volta, Sir Humphry Davy . . .

Max stepped out of the cabin, tripped, and sprawled headlong into the dimness of the fore platform. "Ouch," said a small voice.

"Excuse me!" Max located the crouched shape of Liao tucked into the corner. "What a fellow you are, Liao. What on earth are you doing here? You're missing all the excitement," he added in a whisper.

"Yes, I know. Everyone has been sneaking pieces into the forepeak. And Lucy and Mr. Dexter came back to the ship, too. Each of them had a big bottle of something that smelled of honey and miracles." His voice was unpleasantly flat.

"They're back? Why didn't anyone wake me?" Max paused. "Dexter has some of the stuff as well?"

"Yes." Liao lowered his voice. "I don't like this sneaking about, Max. We're meant to be packing right now. Mr. Dexter wants us off the ship, and if he finds out about the . . . the thing in the forepeak, he'll be ever so angry."

"Never mind Dexter, but speaking of the thing in the forepeak, why aren't you in there, too?" Max asked. "After all we've done, it's nearly finished at last! And you helped an awful lot."

"Yes," Liao said, his voice sounding even flatter than before. "I know I have."

Max crouched next to him. "What is it?"

Liao sighed. "I just don't like thinking about machines that hurt people."

"It's not going to hurt anyone," Max said quickly, glancing around to be sure they were still alone. "It's going to stop people from hurting each other."

"That's what you say now. But you can't know that. And that thing in the picture—it's so beautiful, Max. No one will believe it *can* hurt anyone unless they see it work at least once. It will be like pointing a carronade at someone who's never seen one before and who thinks it's just an interesting piece of metal. Threats don't work unless everyone knows what they really mean."

"I see." Max leaned back against the hull. "But think about how you feel about gunnery."

"I hate it," Liao said vehemently.

"You hate it when we're aiming *at* anyone. But you love firing your own charges over an empty sea. At those times, gunnery is beautiful, isn't it? It doesn't always have to be sad."

"Yes, it does. It's always sad, even when we win. And if not for the times when we aim them at enemies, the guns wouldn't be here to fire for any happier reason. I have to be sad for the guns and the powder charges, just like I have to keep making them into fireworks when the battles are over, so they can be beautiful and joyful some-times to make up for the other things they do. Because we don't give them a choice, Max. We make them do what we want them to do, and it's almost always hurtful."

Max considered refuting the idea that cannons and gunpowder and fireworks had feelings, but somehow this didn't seem like the time to try to convince a child that the things he loved most were nothing more than chemical reactions. Primarily because he sus-pected Liao might be sharp enough to counter that people were nothing but chemical reactions, either.

"All right," Max said at last, "perhaps they don't have a choice, but you do. Twice since we've been here, you've used fireworks to save me without hurting anyone. Someone else who didn't care so much might've killed people instead of just making a lot of noise."

Liao tucked his chin on his knees. "So you think you can find a way to use the device to do what you want but without hurting anyone?"

"I—well, I expect it'll be the government who'll work that out. But they don't want to hurt anyone unnecessarily, either. They want to keep their family safe, too, only their family is a whole country." Max got to his feet. "Shall I—is there anything I can do for you?" Liao shook his head, and Max reluctantly left the boy sitting there alone, mourning the feelings of naval munitions and half-built war engines.

Just then an urgent voice from inside the forepeak hissed, "Pass the word for Mr. Ault!" And then Lucy's voice, louder, rising to a proper yell: *"Max!"*

He dashed across and ran smack into her as she opened the door. Her face was fish-belly pale. "It—nobody saw it happen, Max," she whispered. "It just . . . it just *happened*."

She yanked him inside, and at first Max could see nothing but the backs of the specialists. "What is it?" he asked. Then he stopped in his tracks. "Oh my God."

The framework of gears, bellows, and wheels-within-wheels stood about four feet tall. The whalebone cards and the spiked disc from the music box had not been added yet; the cards lay to one side, where someone—presumably Lucy—had begun to line them up in order. And on the floor before the thing was the big glass bottle Liao had mentioned, full of flecked liquid. A length of hose lay unused beside it; instead, the bottle was connected to the device by a cable of thin, quicksilver-colored filaments.

The cable reached up into the framework, where it branched and twisted and twined throughout the entire structure. Nobody had paid much attention to the surgeon's words earlier, but it did look a lot like a system of veins and arteries. Or nerves, perhaps.

"It happened without any of us seeing it," the sailmaker insisted. "You'll ask how six people could miss such a thing, and I can't tell you. But one minute there was nothing but what we'd built, and the next . . ." He gestured uneasily.

Max walked around the thing, watching the silver webwork glitter in the candlelight. "It's beautiful." And yet a slow, seeping dread had begun to creep through his bones. *Focus.* "Well, it's exactly what the tapestry shows, so—impossible though it seems—this must be what's supposed to happen. What's left to be done?"

Lucy nodded at the cards. "I've nearly worked out the chain. I only stopped because . . . well." She eyed the filaments.

"Begging your pardon," the sailmaker interrupted, "but that was full when you came in, and now it's half-drunk!"

The silver threads of the cable had unspun themselves inside the bottle and spread along the inside surface of the glass like roots to reach the liquid as the level dropped. Max put a hand to his heart, not sure if he was fascinated or horrified. Before he could make up his mind, one of the machine's internal bellows gave a sickly wheeze, and the articulated arm in front began to move.

It swung outward toward the assembled group, making every one of them flinch, and came to a stop above a small flat surface to one side of the main body. A slender appendage with a sharp point shot out from the arm and began to move across the surface, trailing silvery liquid in its wake.

"I told you!" the purser bellowed. "It wanted a spool of paper!"

Max hurried back to the surgeon's cabin for paper, then tore a thin strip and slid that under the still-moving arm. A silver shape took form under the point of the writing mechanism: something round and pocked with little dots.

The writing arm came to a halt, and the arm flicked the slip off the platform. Max caught it and studied the drawing. "It wants the disc!"

The filaments that had woven themselves throughout had left an open space just big enough for him to reach in and add the disc at the center of the main sphere. It fit neatly into a slot in one of the concentric rings so that the disc's outer edge meshed with a gear below. Instantly, there was movement. Max withdrew his hand in a hurry as the filaments swarmed in. They moved like dozens of tiny serpents, winding themselves into holes in the gear and stringing themselves up in a network of silver wires crossing each other at various angles alongside the disc.

The gear began to move; driven by that motion, the disc began to turn. The tiny spikes on the disc twanged against the filaments. The sound resonated throughout the device as those filaments vibrated against others, and in a moment, the entire thing was humming: part music box, part violin.

"It sounds almost like music," Lucy said. "The way the rigging sounds like music sometimes."

"It must be somehow taking in whatever information's on the disc," Max said, unable to look away from the motion inside the device.

"It's doing something in front again!" the sailmaker announced.

Max rushed around and watched, transfixed, as the arm began moving, this time drawing a neat series of rectangles on the paper tape the purser had now rigged to flow beneath the pen. "It wants the cards."

One by one, Lucy passed them to Max, who placed the cards into slits cut into the ring perpendicular to the one holding the disc. As he positioned the last card, the filaments went into motion again. Then the ring itself began to move, weaving the silver threads through the holes in the cards and into a patterned ribbon. Minute sparks flickered to life along its length. Then the filaments that covered the outside of the device reached across the opening and knit themselves together, hiding the inside from view. The internal thrumming took on a new and deeper pitch.

"Mr. Ault, it's writing words now," the armorer said. "Will you look at that?"

twenty-nine
OUCH

Lucy leaned in for a better look at the new shapes on the paper tape. "Is that Latin?"

"Certainly not," Max scoffed. "The thing is far too old for it to have any but the most ancient languages. Egyptian, or something even older, if such a thing exists."

"But I've seen some of those old languages, and they look like pegs and squiggles and pictures. These look like *letters.*"

The arm stopped moving, briskly shoved the tape forward, and cut it neatly from the rest of the spooled paper as it did. Max caught the scrap. Then he clapped a hand over his mouth. The string of silvery words soaking into the page was not only perfectly legible, it was in English.

Standard library assimilated. Program assimilated. Beginning algorismic calculations. Language chosen based on ambient noise. Please confirm language preference.

Max stared down at the paper in disbelief. "That's a bunch of babble," Lucy commented, unfazed by the impossibility they were witnessing. "And how does it expect you to—"

The arm flicked a small length of paper forward and tilted the writing appendage sharply outward. The motion was exactly as if it was offering a pen. With a shaking hand, Max took it. It remained connected to the device by a thin braid of filaments, and it vibrated faintly in his fingers as if some sort of current ran through it.

"What shall I say?" And how could the thing possibly have English as a choice at all, considering when it was first created? *Language confirmed*, he wrote at last, and he tucked the pen back into place. The arm drew the paper back toward itself, touched the pen to the page, and neatly retraced what Max had written. As it did, the words on the paper disappeared.

"I need to sit," Max said faintly. The arm swept into motion again and flung another scrap at him.

"What does it say?" Lucy demanded.

Max read the message in his hand. He licked his lips. "It says, *Needed to complete algorism: What am I?*"

"Is it a test, like?" the armorer asked. "A password, or a private signal?"

"I don't think so. An algorism is a set of rules governing how something functions, what operation it performs in the first place. Perhaps it needs that question answered before it can work out what's expected of it."

"I never thought of machines as having to work out how to work," Lucy commented. "I always figured them for a collection of moving pieces. As long as the pieces come together correctly, the thing does what it's meant to do."

"This one seems to be something more than the sum of its parts," Max said warily.

Overhead the bells of Flotilla began to toll the watch, and abruptly the specialists made a break for the door, muttering explanations of how far behind on their various obligations they were, and how if they lingered much longer, they were bound to draw suspicion, and that certainly Mr. Ault would let them know if anything else needed doing. Then Max and Lucy were alone.

She curled a hand around his wrist, and Max realized he was shaking. "What's wrong?" Lucy asked.

Suddenly *everything* was wrong, though he didn't know how to explain why. The words still gleamed dully on the scrap of paper in his hand. *What am I?*

Lucy followed his eyes. "Odd it says *I*, isn't it? Is that what's got you out of sorts?"

"Yes. And no." He fought through the unease that was rapidly becoming a truly sick, frightened feeling and made himself focus. "This doesn't look like any sort of science I know. It's not behaving like a machine. I can't wrap my mind around it to begin with, and then it asks that? How on earth do I answer it?"

"You could wait now, couldn't you? It was always going to be turned over to the government in the end. Couldn't you let them figure out the right answer?"

"But we've still got to get home first. We still have to figure out how to get it off the *ship*, Lucy. What if someone takes it from us?"

Lucy nodded soberly. "That's the trouble with a weapon, isn't it? Be it the fastest ship or the strongest battery, there's always someone faster and stronger who can take it from you."

"Exactly. I don't think we can wait for anyone else to answer the question. Clearly the thing won't work until someone does, and until it works, just as you say, anyone could take it."

She shook her head. "No, Max, what *I'm* saying is that weapons are *never* safe from being taken."

"This one will be. How could it not? It will be more powerful than anything anyone's ever imagined."

"If power was all that mattered, a smaller ship would never take a larger."

"You're still thinking about it as something like an army or a ship or a battery." Max nodded at the beautiful, bizarre, strangely terrifying configuration of wheels and filaments and gears. "Look at it. It's unlike anything else in the world."

"If it's a weapon at all, then it's exactly like an army, a ship, or a battery, if only because, like all those things, *it's a weapon*. It's a thing for an enemy to get past, or to take. Some are harder to overcome than others, but there's always a way. Max, I know what I'm talking about here."

"What would you have me do, then?" Perhaps somehow she'd miraculously have an answer.

"Not a clue," Lucy said apologetically. "I'm only pointing out that you have a wrong idea in your head that you'd best correct, and quickly."

Max studied the thing. What if it was as simple as telling the machine what he wanted it to do? That would be simple enough: *End the wars. Defend England, destroy the French, ensure peace forever, preferably with minimal bloodshed.*

But what if the machine asked for parameters? Max was no strategist, so if it needed more than basic instructions, they had a problem. Or perhaps the simple answer was all the machine required. After all, it had taken in a lot of information from the cards and the disc. Maybe those things would give it what it needed to determine on its own how best to follow its directives.

That was comforting, until suddenly it wasn't comforting at all. What if the machine *didn't* ask exactly what it meant to 'destroy the French,' and decided to obey by wiping out an entire nation?

I could tell it to destroy the French army and navy, not just the French.

No, defeat *the French army and navy*. Defeating them would be sufficient, certainly—although the British government might not agree with that, he realized with mounting confusion. A line he'd read somewhere came back to him: *Only the dead do not come back to fight again*. Who had said that? One of the French Radicals, he thought. But of course his own government would see things differently.

Or would they? After more than twenty years of wars, perhaps London would prefer France's fighting forces wiped clean off the earth. And Napoleon had recruited nearly every man within a stone's throw of fighting age, even boys as young as Max himself, if the French-American sailor was to be believed. What if London decided that to *destroy France's fighting forces* meant *destroy every man in the country*? Or worse? No, that was impossible, surely. And yet . . .

And what if Lucy was right and the device was no safer in Max's helpless hands than the *Left-Handed Fate* had been in Richard Bluecrowne's very capable ones? What if someone—Voclain or the seamen in black or even an American ship whose captain had no idea what he'd stumbled across—captured the device and decided to blast England off the map for what seemed, from that person's perspective, to be the good of all?

No, he couldn't leave the answer to anyone else; there was no trusting anyone else to do it, not even his own government. But the question had to be answered so England could not be hurt by the device. It had to be answered so a bloodthirsty prime minister or first lord couldn't use it to kill innocent people. It had to be answered so that whatever it did and whoever had it, it would not violate the principles Max wished for in his imagined world without wars. And it had to be answered so there could be no translation problems. The device seemed, impossibly, to understand English just fine, but what if really it had to extract the meaning from its instructions by main force?

"Stop." Lucy gave his arm a good shake. "Whatever you're thinking, stop. You're going to make yourself sick."

"I can't stop! I have to figure this out before— It's in the world now, don't you see? It's not a theoretical *thing* any longer. It's real. It refers to itself as *I*, for God's sake." Max covered his mouth with one hand. "Lucy, what have I—"

"Nothing yet that can't be undone," she interrupted. "The other thing about weapons is that you can break them."

"It's not a gun you can spike to keep it from firing, Lucy."

"I bet I can. You want to see me try? Just to see if it can be done? We built the thing. Surely we can fix anything I manage to harm."

Max discovered that he very much wanted to know if it could be broken. "Yes, if you please."

She nodded, took her knife from her ditty bag, and crouched beside the now mostly empty bottle. She worked a pair of the threads away from the cable with the point of the knife and flicked her wrist. The blade ricocheted with a resonant *twang*. The force of it wrenched the knife from her hand, and she ducked as it flipped through the air inches from her neck to embed itself, quivering, in the wall. Max's heart threatened to give out. "For the love of—"

Lucy, however, was merely annoyed. "Too good for my knife, are you? Let's see how you like my marlinespike." She retrieved the tool he had last seen during her failed attempt to break into Jeton's shop: a long, thin barb with a flattened tip.

"Lucy, if a knife won't do it—"

"It's a very special marlinespike." She worked the flat end between the filaments and gave the spike a practiced twist-and-jerk. This time, with a sound like a chord played on an out-of-tune guitar, a chunk of threads split and a gout of silver liquid spattered across Lucy's face. Then, before Max's eyes, the loose ends whipped toward each other and knit themselves back together again.

"*Gaah!*" Lucy sprawled backward, wiping her face with her sleeve. "It *burns!*" she howled. "Max, get the surgeon!"

He tore his eyes from the now perfectly undamaged cable and found Lucy scrubbing frantically at her skin as red welts emerged across her nose and forehead. "Oh, no, Lucy—"

"*Just get the surgeon, Max!*"

He rushed for the door. As he passed the device, the writing arm began to move again. The silver curls that formed across the tape spelled one word: *Ouch.*

Max fled.

thirty
THE DREAMER

Lucy sat as patiently as she could while the surgeon daubed her face with olive oil. "How bad is it?"

"Likely not as bad as it feels," Dr. Domanova said. "Now, have I missed any, do you think?"

"Is there one on my chin?"

"Aha. I see it, the creature." Dr. Domanova sat back and looked her over. "I'm sorry to say you shall have to endure the burning."

"I'll manage. Thank you." She gave the device a wide berth as she left the forepeak on the surgeon's heels and climbed up the ladderway.

Lucy had barely stepped out onto the weather deck when Oliver Dexter turned up, looking suspicious. "How goes your packing, Miss Bluecrowne?" He peered at her closely. "And what happened to your face?"

Before she could come up with a lie, Liao appeared at her elbow. "Lucy! Come quickly. Max left the ship, and you *know* what happens when Max leaves the ship."

"He's a landsman, Liao. He's fine when he leaves the ship." Though what the hell was he doing leaving the ship now?

"Except when he gets himself snatched, Lucy!" Liao protested, hopping with impatience.

She groaned. "Pass the word for Kendrick. I know he has far too much to do already, but he'd better come with us in case there's any trouble." She turned back to Dexter. "Apologies, sir. We shall be ready by midnight, but you know how it is with Max."

Lucy, Liao, and Kendrick caught up with him in the square where the Chapel of Saint Nicholas stood. "There," Liao said, pointing to the familiar figure climbing the gilt stairs. "Perhaps he decided to try the pilgrimage himself."

"I doubt it. Wait here, will you?" Lucy followed Max into the chapel. She found him in an alcove, looking morosely at a bank of flickering candles. "Max?"

He waved a hand at the collection of prayer cards scattered among the votives. "I don't have a card."

"Doesn't matter. We only leave them when we go church to church so that when we have none left, we know we've done the whole route." She watched Max uncertainly. "Did you come to say a prayer, Max?"

"I didn't want to be on the ship and I didn't know where to go." He scratched his head. "Is there a saint for natural philosophers?"

"I imagine so. We can ask the parson, if you like."

Max looked up at last and his face went very pale in the candlelight. He raised a hand and carefully touched her cheek, just beside a burn under her eye. "Oh, Lucy."

She forced herself not to flinch and smiled as carelessly as she could manage. "I had imagined a mess of red freckles. They must look worse than they feel."

"No, no, they're not bad at all." It was obviously a lie; fortunately

Lucy didn't much care what they looked like. "Do they hurt?" Max asked, guilt thick in his voice.

"I barely feel them," Lucy lied back.

They stood for a moment, with Lucy looking at the candles and Max looking at Lucy, until finally he spoke up again. "My father died for this device—I was ready to die for it—and now we've built it and suddenly I'm afraid I've done a terrible thing."

"If you hadn't built it, the Frenchman would've."

"I know it. And yet I wish there was a way for no one to have it at all." He looked closely at her, as if he were counting the burns. "It doesn't frighten you? I suppose not. Nothing does."

"Plenty does," she protested. Max's eyebrow went up skeptically. "Is that really what you think, that I haven't sense enough to be scared by the world's ultimate weapon?"

"I didn't mean I thought you were foolish—"

"That's what it takes to never feel afraid, Max. I haven't said anything about being afraid up until now, and I'll tell you why if you like, but I'm plenty frightened by it."

Max's eyes were wide in the half-dark. "Tell me."

Lucy turned her face up to the dimness overhead as she put her thoughts in order. "My job, it seemed to me, was to make sure you could do yours," she said, finally. "Because you hired my ship, and because my father died on this mission. I'm afraid of failing my papa, and my ship, and you."

"You mustn't be afraid of failing me," Max said fiercely. "And your memory of your father oughtn't be tied up with this mess of mine."

"Well, it is, but even failing's not what scares me most now. What scares me most now is that you might let anyone other than you decide the device's orders."

"But you're the one who suggested it!"

"Because it made sense to suggest it. It's a real option. But leaving the thing's orders to someone else means leaving it to the Admiralty or the Ministry of Defense. I trust you a thousand miles farther than I trust them."

He scoffed. "You don't trust me to walk down the street, Lucy."

"True." She smiled in spite of herself, and Max's drawn face cracked just a bit toward a smile in response. "But I do trust you with this machine of yours, ridiculous as that seems. Because I know you love England and want her to win, but I also know that when you talk about peace, it's something you want for everyone. And you're honorable, and you're not cruel, and you're not foolish enough to not be afraid, either. And I think you're the most brilliant fellow I've ever met, though I imagine that wouldn't count for much if not for all those other things." And then, because it was also true and because for some reason she felt it had to be said this very minute, she added, "I'm afraid of your device, but I hate it, too, because it means we won't be shipmates anymore. And I have loved being shipmates with you."

Max said nothing, but he was looking at her so seriously, and they were so very close to each other. As the moment stretched, two warring impulses fought for control of Lucy Bluecrowne.

Lucy being Lucy, tactical instinct won out. "Max," she said with a sigh of resignation, "I find I very badly want to kiss you right now, but I'd better tell you this stupid story first."

Max's jaw dropped.

"I know, I know," she said impatiently, "who am I and what have I done with Melusine Bluecrowne. We'll deal with that another time." At that, he actually cracked a grin, but blessedly Max didn't interrupt. "The Spinster told me a thing this morning, and all day I've been trying to work out what it means. I'm not quite there, but

I think you might find it helpful. She said . . . she said it was a matter of metal and dreams."

As quickly as she could reconstruct it, Lucy told Max the Spinster's story of the five elements and the instrument they created together. "She said it was a device capable of helping one to create great things. At first I didn't see how it was relevant, but then there was the dancing metal tree, and wheels-within-wheels . . . and Max, if you had seen that liquor before it was bottled—it was like an elixir made of pure sunset."

Max shifted at her side. "You think we're wrong about what this thing is?"

"I have no idea," Lucy answered honestly. "But I don't believe in coincidences, Max."

He sat still and silent for a moment, gone away into his own head the way he did. *"Of these is the world made,"* he murmured. It was the beginning of his father's translation. *"From the singularities is built the great engine that in turn builds the vision of the dreamer—"* Abruptly he stopped talking and looked at Lucy. "The other thing now."

She blinked, confused. "What other thing?"

"The other thing you said, Lucy." Very carefully, he put a hand to her chin where there were no burns. He leaned toward her, his breath feathering across her singed cheeks, and Lucy's heart became a sail in the wind.

Then, horribly, just as his lips were about to touch hers, in the dark beyond Max's ear Lucy saw a violet flame pop to life at the top of the big gilt cross on the altar.

She froze. "Max." His eyes flew open, and against the dark blue iris of his left eye Lucy saw the reflection of another corposant flickering somewhere behind her.

They sprang apart as more and more lights appeared. "Impossible," Lucy whispered. "In a *church*?" She wasn't quite sure why this seemed so desperately wrong, except that the whole point of churches, as far as she was concerned, was to stand against the kinds of things that fell into the broad category of *bad omens and such.*

"Outside," Max hissed. But before they could get to the entrance, the doors swung open, and silhouetted against the twilight stood two men in black uniforms.

Lucy wheeled and dragged Max back toward the nave. The other churchgoers scattered and the sounds of heavy boot heels rang on the stone floor. Then, like a thunderclap, a single word rang out: "*Stop!*"

As the command echoed through the chapel, a man in a red robe emerged from a door beside the altar. He took in the sight of Lucy and Max sprinting up the aisle with their pursuers stalking after them, took in the glowing corposants. Then he raised a hand and pointed at the men in black. "Stop where you stand, demons!"

The men in black paused and regarded the rector. Just as Lucy remembered from Fells Point, they wore smoked-glass spectacles that made it impossible to make out any details of their eyes, and both had angular faces and sand-toned skin that seemed to have a golden burnish to it. "Demons," one of them said. "I tire of being called a demon." His words were accented, but it wasn't an accent Lucy recognized.

"This is a place of sanctuary!" the rector shouted. "Get thee gone, unholy ones!"

The second man shook his head. "Unholy ones. Always these kinds of words, as if we were things to be banished like dark by a candle." He tilted his head. "Listen, Man: we are here for that one, and that one alone." He raised a thin, knobby finger and pointed at Max. "Child, you must come with us now. This game has run its course."

Lucy shoved Max behind her. "No."

"Don't be ridiculous, Lucy!" He shoved her behind himself.

"We didn't fight our way past them all those times at sea to have them take you by land! Get out of my way, Max!"

"Both of you get behind me," the rector ordered. "I will not have anyone taken by force in my chapel."

"You will not remember it afterward. It will be as if it never happened," the first man told him in an unexpectedly sympathetic tone. "But we will take the boy."

"*I say you shall not!*" the rector thundered.

"Who are you?" Lucy demanded. "You fired on the French, and you're not Americans."

The two men laughed. It was a strange, dissonant sound. "You and your nations," the first said. "Your nations, and your demons, your things holy and unholy. Different words, but always the same meanings, every time."

"But why Max?" she persisted.

The second man spoke up. "Child, you know why. Because of the thing he wishes to build." He looked to the rector again. "Stand aside, Man, and we will leave you in peace, such as you understand it."

Now Max spoke up in a shaky voice. "What do you mean, every time?"

The second man tilted his head again. "Every time the device is built."

"But it's been unknown for—it must be thousands of years!"

"No, *the record you found* has been unknown for thousands of years. It comes from one era in which the apparatus was built, but there were others. Accounts of some of those times were written down. Others were not." Even without seeing their eyes, Lucy understood that they were angry. "This is why you cannot be trusted with this machine. You know nothing of it. The only way to understand a thing is to know from whence it has come."

So nearly what the Spinster said yesterday, Lucy thought. *Who are these men?*

"But how do *you* know?" Max persisted. Lucy grabbed the back of his coat as he stepped forward, and he shook her off. "If you know, *tell* me. Help me understand!"

"We do not think we can make you understand. You have too much war in your heart, and there is too much war in your world for the device to be used for anything other than making more of it."

The rector had begun to mutter urgently in Latin. Everyone ignored him. "I don't have war in my heart!" Max protested. "I'm after peace!"

"That may be true," the second man acknowledged, "but you will not accomplish that by making a weapon. If you had chosen any other thing to make of it, perhaps—"

Wild hope blossomed on Max's face. "What do you mean, 'any other thing'?"

The first man began to press forward again. "We are wasting time, child."

"You stay back," Lucy ordered. "Max—"

"What do you mean, 'any other thing'?" Max demanded again.

"Once, it fed a multitude in the desert for forty years," the second man in black said. "In another time, it helped great artists to build tremendous monuments. But many times it has been dreamed of as a weapon. As your father dreamt of it. In those times, we have intervened."

Max's already pale face went green. *"Did you kill my father?"*

"In the times when it is dreamt of as a weapon," the man said with strange kindness, "we have stopped the dreamer. This is why your father could not be allowed to carry on, and why you must come with us. This device—the device as you dream of it—must never be built."

"But you don't know what I want to do with it," Max argued. "How could you know?"

"We know because the other child told us." And the golden-skinned man pointed one thin finger at Lucy.

"No," she gasped. "No, I didn't! I would never—"

"You did," the man told her gently. "You told us in the place called Baltimore. You did not have a choice. And we did not wish you to be angry at yourself for what you did not choose to do, so we took the memory."

The non-memory of the forgotten conversation in Fells Point hit Lucy like a kick to the chest. "But I would never have told anyone," she protested wildly. It seemed impossible—it *was* impossible. And yet even as she told herself that the strangers were lying, she realized with a sick heart that she believed them. She had betrayed Max to their pursuers in Fells Point.

Through her shame and guilt, Lucy felt Max's hand reach for hers. "Why do you get to decide what anyone does with it?" he asked.

"Because we are the only ones who have seen what it can do, and who know what has been prevented. That is why."

"That's impossible, if it all happened so long ago."

The first man in black shook his head. "It is not impossible. It is merely beyond you."

"Have we answered your questions to your satisfaction?" the other asked. "It is time to be going."

Despite their claims to know so much, the two strangers clearly didn't know the machine had already been built. "What if we give you the pieces?" Lucy suggested. "I have crew outside. They can go fetch them, and Max and I will wait here with you, as hostages, like, until they come back. Would that satisfy you?"

The two men looked at each other for a moment, as if they were having a conversation in silence. At last, the one who had spoken first shook his head. "No. The dreamer is part of the device now, and he must come with us."

"The hell he must! If it's the machine you want, take the machine!"

Max put a shaking hand on her arm. "Lucy, stop. Don't make it worse."

The man tilted his head, amused. "You would lecture me on the rightness of killing one creature to stop more destruction? We have watched your ship these many months, Child, and do not forget that you and I have spoken at length before now. Do not argue what you do not believe."

The other stepped forward, one spindly hand outstretched. "Maxwell Ault. Come." Max dropped his head, and to her horror, Lucy realized that he just might obey. She spun, searching. Aboard a ship she would know where to find a weapons locker, or at minimum a belaying pin that could be swung like a club. But in a church—

There.

She plunged past the rector, grabbed a towering candlestick, and flung it at the man approaching Max. Instantly the black-upon-black uniform went up in flames. The fiery figure flailed, crumpled. His companion gave a weird screech and rushed to his side, pulling off his uniform coat to try to smother the fire. Lucy seized Max and dragged him back down the aisle. He stumbled once as the second man grabbed for his arm, but Lucy wrenched him away and together they sprinted for the door.

thirty-one
FLIGHT

Night was deepening when at last Mr. Cascon came aboard, followed by his new recruits, and saluted the quarterdeck of the *Left-Handed Fate*. Oliver looked up from his coffee and breathed a sigh of relief. There were at least two dozen tars there, enough that they could leave Flotilla whenever they chose.

Mr. Cascon passed the volunteers off to another crewman and joined Oliver on the quarterdeck. "I believe we are manned now, sir."

"Well done! There were this many Americans wanting to ship back home?"

"Well, no, sir. These are mostly Nagspeakers. *Left-Handed Fate* or *Sinister Fury*, the barky's famous here, and I think they're eager to ship in her at least once. And they're all able seamen, no doubt of that. Only—" He broke off with a frown.

"What is it, Cascon?"

The older man hesitated, then shook his head. "I imagine I'm just overtired."

"So we can weigh anchor tomorrow? As today's Friday." There

was no way Oliver was inviting any more bad fortune by setting sail on the unluckiest day of the week.

A sudden ruckus kicked up from the dock. "The ship! The ship ahoy! Out of my way, you—the *Fate*, ahoy!" Lucy Bluecrowne plunged out of an alley with Max, Liao, and Kendrick on her heels. The four of them raced aboard and Lucy hurried to the quarterdeck. "They're in Flotilla," she panted. "The seamen in black. They're after Max, they'll find us here, we've got to—" She bent double, hands on her knees, and gulped air. "You've got to get us out of Flotilla. Put us ashore someplace else, but get us out of here."

"You want us to weigh anchor *now*?" Oliver protested. "Just like that? Can't you go to the Masthead? Talk to the Quartermaster?"

"There's no time! *They want to kill Max.* They'll be upon us ages before we can get to the Masthead! The only way is to leave Flotilla this minute." She clapped her hands twice: *chop chop.* "Yes, *now*, Mr. Dexter, do you hear? It's the only way, or we're done for. They'll kill us all if they have to."

"But it's Friday," he said in an embarrassingly small voice.

The sound of a bosun's whistle cut through the air. On the dock, the Flotilla sentry called, "The Honorable Jonquil Levinflash!"

The Quartermaster stood at the gangplank. "Permission to come aboard?"

Despite the tone of his last interview with the Quartermaster, Oliver sighed, relieved. "Permission granted."

"Nell!" Lucy rushed to meet her.

"I missed you yesterday," Nell Levinflash said, hugging her. "But sadly, I'm not here to visit." She turned to Oliver. "I've heard from the Port Admiral that a corvette called the *Marie Colette* put into the harbor today. That was the ship you claimed to have had a skirmish with, was it not? I cannot imagine they aren't here looking for you."

Oliver slumped. There didn't seem to be any alternative: unlucky Friday or no, the *Fate* had to get out of Nagspeake. He straightened. "Best respects, Miss Levinflash, and how quickly can we get a channel?"

"Immediately, Mr. Dexter." The Quartermaster pulled her own whistle from under the collar of her shirt and blew a sequence upon it. A moment later, a reply sounded from somewhere farther out in the district.

"Thank you." Oliver turned to Lucy. "Miss Bluecrowne, where shall we put you and the others ashore?"

The Quartermaster glanced at Lucy. "Why would you be put ashore anyplace else?"

"We can't stay in Flotilla now, Nell," Lucy said. "The men in the black uniforms have found us as well. What about putting us ashore at the battery? Even if the French spot the *Fate*, they would never trouble it with the city's great guns staring down at them."

"Begging your pardon, sir," Mr. Cascon said to Oliver, "but the pilot was off-watch, and I'm told he's in no condition to get us down the river."

"The pilot's *too drunk*?" Oliver asked, aghast. It took a lot for a sailor to be too drunk for anything.

"I'll kill him," Lucy fumed. "Off-watch or not."

The Quartermaster spoke up. "Excuse me, Mr. Dexter, but I can help you."

"You know of a pilot we can find nearby?" Oliver asked.

"Certainly." She grinned. "Me. I've known that river since I was a girl. And any of the Fates can vouch for my capabilities at a tiller."

"Well, there's a piece of good luck at last," Mr. Cascon said.

Oliver smiled weakly. "I suppose."

·····················

Down in the forepeak, Max paced. The device glinted in the candlelight, and the last messages it had written remained unanswered on the tape. *What am I? Ouch.*

Once, it fed a multitude in the desert for forty years, the man in black had said. *In another time, it helped great artists to build tremendous monuments. But many times it has been dreamed of as a weapon.*

Dreams and dreamers. Elements with life and dreams of their own.

And then there had been the words the other man had spoken when he had grabbed Max, making him stumble as he fled the chapel with Lucy. *We will come for you, make no mistake*, he had said, *but until then, only you can stop what you have begun. It will ask you a question. Answer with great care; you can answer only once.*

And still the silver words gleamed. *What am I?*

Lucy burst through the door. "Evidently the French are on their way as well. Dexter's putting to sea now. He'll put us off at the battery."

"All right."

"Max, how are we going to get that thing ashore?"

He pressed his hands to his face. "I have no idea."

She hesitated, then turned and departed, shouting at passing sailors as she closed the door.

Max took the writing implement from the device's arm. Instantly the machine cut loose the used paper and spat forth a fresh bit.

You are Copley, Max wrote. It was the closest he was ever going to get to a medal now. He watched the device trace over his answer, sucking the ink back up. It gave a low-pitched whirring, then began writing again.

Copley does not exist in either my standard library or my program. Please instruct in the function of a Copley.

The door opened again and Liao poked his head in. He carefully avoided looking at the device. "Did Lucy tell you we're sailing soon? And that we must get our things together?"

"Yes."

"What did you write?" Liao asked reluctantly.

"Nothing useful, I'm afraid. I suppose all I did was to give it a name."

"What name?"

"I called it Copley."

Liao considered. "It's a nice name. It makes me think of a kind of firework I know called a caprice. *Caprice* sounds a bit like *Copley*, doesn't it?"

"Something like, yes, I suppose."

Liao nodded. "It's a nice name."

They stood side by side together for a long moment, looking at the device. Then Max turned slowly, thoughtfully, to study the boy at his side. "Liao," he said, "Lucy told me a story earlier."

"Oh! Was it the one about the goat who ate the Christmas pudding, only it wasn't a Christmas pudding, it was something funnier?"

"No, not that one. Listen."

························

NELL LEVINFLASH WAS A VERY GOOD PILOT. WITH THE Quartermaster herself easing it confidently and quickly around the darkening curves and hidden shoals, the *Left-Handed Fate* slid gracefully down the river toward the Atlantic. It was full dark when the schooner emerged into the open ocean, and every hand on deck broke into applause. Nell relinquished the tiller and took a bow.

When they came within view of the lights of the battery, Oliver reached out and shook Lucy's hand. "Good luck, Miss Bluecrowne."

"Good luck, Lieutenant," she said, her voice cracking. "Be good to my ship."

Max stumbled onto the quarterdeck, looking dazed. "Good luck to you, too, Mr. Ault," Oliver said.

"Thank you," Max replied absently.

"*Sail ahoy!*"

"Where away?" Oliver turned automatically to port, toward the mouth of the bay. Sure enough, there was the *Marie Colette*, heading out into the Atlantic.

But, "Straightaway to starboard, sir," the lookout replied. "Three frigates, sir, and all flying the tricolor!"

"Beat to quarters!" Oliver whirled with a sinking heart and spotted the French ships coming from the opposite direction.

"No," Lucy whispered. "Not now, not after everything."

"Make for the battery," Nell said. "They cannot attack you under our guns!"

"We'll never get there," Oliver argued. "The corvette'll cut us off."

"You have to try. There's no other option."

She was right. Oliver shouted orders and the *Fate* raced for the protective cover of the fortress and its row of great smashing guns. But Oliver had been right, too, and the unfriendly wind and the laws of physics brought the *Marie Colette* flying down at them.

She fired a single shot across the *Fate*'s bows, and someone shouted from her deck. "The *Left-Handed Fate*, ahoy!"

Someone put a speaking trumpet into Oliver's hands. He raised it mechanically, but when he began to speak the words came easily and boomed across the water with a thousand times more confidence than he felt. "*Marie Colette*, this is Lieutenant Oliver Dexter, United States Navy, accompanied by the Quartermaster of the district of Flotilla, city of Nagspeake. You are committing a breach of local neutrality and an act of war against the United States. Stand down!"

"You are carrying cargo destined for England, which is now against United States law," came the reply. "Strike your colors or we will open fire."

"Don't—" Lucy whispered.

Oliver shot a furious look at her. "I am *not giving up the ship*, for the hundredth time! Mr. Ault, if you wish to put the pieces of your device overboard, you'd best go below and get them now. Then come back and I'll tell you where to find the ones in my cabin. Cascon! Bring her around. All guns, fire as they bear!"

The guns erupted in hellfire noise and draped the deck in smoke. Oliver heard the French ship's reply before the air cleared enough to see it. A single shot made it to the *Fate*, but that one whipped across the quarterdeck. Oliver surveyed the vessels out in the Atlantic as the smoke dissipated. Soon the *Fate* would be trapped with the *Marie Colette* on one side and the frigates on the other. There would be no fighting out of that.

The *Fate* fired again. "We think the corvette's rudder's gone, sir," the gunner reported. The crew cheered. The *Marie Colette* would have a hard time maneuvering now.

On the other side, the frigates approached in tight formation. Then came an explosion from above as the guns of the battery fired at last. The frigates weren't quite within range of the *Fate*, but they were within range of the fortress's much more powerful artillery. The dark water around the approaching ships churned into a froth.

For a moment all discipline evaporated as the deck of the *Left-Handed Fate* burst into celebration. "Man your guns!" Mr. Harrick bellowed. "That corvette hasn't gone anywhere!" As if in response to this, the fortress fired again, whipping the ocean around the *Marie Colette* into choppy white.

Amid the second wave of cheering, Nell Levinflash came forward. "Mr. Dexter."

"Yes, Miss Levinflash?" There was something amiss on deck now. Oliver couldn't quite put a finger on it, but there was something wrong with the flow of things.

"I need your attention, sir."

Oliver tore his gaze from the deck and looked at the Quartermaster. Behind her stood a dozen and a half Nagspeake tars. That was the disturbance he had sensed: eighteen sailors detaching themselves from their places.

"Back to your posts!" he shouted. "We're not out of the woods yet!"

"You don't know the half of it, mate," one of the Nagspeakers replied.

Nell Levinflash regarded Oliver calmly. "Mr. Dexter, by order of the Sovereign City of Nagspeake, I am taking charge of this ship."

"*I beg your pardon?*"

Lucy spoke up immediately. "Nell, don't, please. I could never have it on my conscience—"

Nell gave her a strained smile. "Rest easy, Lucy. I'm not taking the ship for you. The schooner and its cargo are being seized by the city. I'm very sorry."

Lucy gasped. "*What?* Why? What have we— Nell, surely there's something you can do!"

Oliver's disbelief was short-lived. "Do?" He snorted. "She's already doing it!" The clerk at the Minister's office had warned him of exactly this. *If I were in charge of a city like Nagspeake, it would have occurred to me straightaway that if I possessed such an object as the one you've described, no other country should ever be able to drag me into any sort of conflict.* "The Quartermaster wants Max's pieces. I might have seen it coming when so many of the new hands turned out to be Nagspeakers," he added, disgusted.

"Quite correct." Nell had the grace to look remorseful, not that Oliver cared.

"Nell, you can't!" Lucy protested. "Please. I know it's terrible to ask you to ignore orders—"

"Ignore them?" Nell glanced at Oliver, who was feeling just then that perhaps neglecting to mention Nell Levinflash's promotion to Lucy had been a very, very bad mistake. "You didn't tell her."

"There are no orders for her to ignore," Oliver said bitterly. "She *is* the Quartermaster."

"No!" Lucy clapped a hand to her mouth.

"I'm afraid so, love. And I really do regret it." Nell actually had the gall to reach a hand out to her.

Lucy shied away. "We were your *crewmates*. This was your *ship*!"

Nell dropped her hand. Her face hardened. "This *city* is my ship," she said coldly. "I love you, Lucy, but whatever I owed your father is outweighed by what I owe to Nagspeake." She turned to Oliver. "Give the order to stand down, Mr. Dexter."

"I suppose I'd better." But what Oliver shouted when he raised his voice was, "Shipmates! *We are betrayed!*"

Surprised, the Quartermaster reached into her jacket. Before she could draw her pistol, Lucy kicked a foot into Nell's stomach hard enough to knock her to the deck and scatter the delegation behind her.

"All hands to repel boarders!" Oliver bellowed. "Take prisoner everyone who came aboard in Flotilla!"

thirty-two
FIRE

When the sounds of the skirmish broke out overhead, Max barely paused in his work. If they had somehow been boarded, there was no time to waste.

He loaded the musical tree and the leftover cards into a bag, wishing he'd thought to take a cannonball from the weather deck before he'd come below. He hefted the bundle under his arm, opened the door of the forepeak, and stared into the face of Théodore Voclain. Behind him the consular officer, Cloutier, took a pistol from his belt. "Good evening, Monsieur Ault."

"Wait." He raised his hand. Cloutier fired, and Max's hand burst into agony. He heard someone—himself?—howl in pain, and the bag he'd been holding thudded to the floor. Max lowered his wrist, expecting to find nothing but a bloody stump, and discovered the shot had only grazed his thumb. Relief battled anguish until he realized that his thumb had been mere inches from his face when Cloutier had pulled the trigger, at which point he had to fight not to faint.

"Time is short," Cloutier said, reloading.

"Where did you come from?" Max demanded, cradling his hand.

"A small party in a little boat may easily sneak aboard when the crew is otherwise occupied. I hear you have used this ruse yourself." Voclain tossed Max a handkerchief. "Take us to the—*oh*." He shoved past Max and approached the device. With Cloutier's pistol to the back of his head and Voclain's reddening handkerchief clutched to his thumb, Max stood numbly as the other natural philosopher looked in wonder at the machine. "How beautiful it is. How does it work?"

Max blinked. "You don't expect me to—"

The consular officer cracked him across the skull with the butt of the pistol. Max clutched his head with his uninjured hand and groaned. "I will put the next bullet through your knee," Cloutier warned. "Speak up."

"But it *doesn't* work. Not yet. We hadn't—" Another cracking blow. Lights flashed before his eyes. "It's true!" Cloutier said nothing, only pressed the barrel of the pistol hard against his skull. Max sagged. "The thing attached to the arm is like a pen. You write the machine's command on the tape. The machine reads it and begins its program."

Another prod. "And is there a particular command that it requires?"

"What else?" Max answered bitterly. *"Fire."*

"So simple?" Voclain smiled, delighted. "Such an elegant thing."

"Marvel later, sir," Cloutier said. "The fighting cannot last. Whoever wins will trot the losers straight below."

Max started, confused. "Those aren't your men upstairs?"

"Nagspeake has entered the negotiations," Voclain said disgustedly. "How I hate this city."

"Will the device move?" Cloutier asked impatiently.

Voclain gave the mechanism an experimental push, and it glided along easily on its lower wheels. "It will. And it is wondrously light.

If you can convince Mr. Ault to help, he and I should be able to get it up the ladder."

"He will help or have his brains painted across the wall," Cloutier said grimly. "But do not fear, Monsieur Ault. A great poet once wrote, *It is beautiful to die.*" He recited the dreadful line as if he actually thought it might be a consolation.

"That poet was full of it," Max said under his breath. He was rewarded with another crack to the crown.

All hands were up above, fighting for ownership of the *Fate*. There was no one to challenge the little group as it maneuvered the machine up to the forward ladderway. "But what happens when we get to the weather deck?" Max asked. "You can't possibly expect to pass through that fray unchallenged."

"We have a boat and men waiting at the bows, so I hardly think we need pass through it. But even if we did, who would dare try to stop us now that we have this?" Voclain stroked the filigreed exterior of the Copley device.

"Go on," Cloutier said to Max. "When you reach the top, tell them to stand down, or they will be blown from the deck by a single shot from the very weapon they are fighting for."

Max swallowed. He took a careful hold on the device just below the writing arm and climbed awkwardly up through the hatch and onto the deck, with Voclain supporting the device from below.

As soon as he reached the deck, he let go of the machine, stood, and scanned the melee for Lucy. Bile rose in his stomach. It was like the day the ship had been taken all over again: so many dead. Then he saw her, or at least a momentary flash of her, swinging some bit of tackle from the rigging like a club.

"Lucy!" he shrieked. It was not his best quarterdeck voice, and it broke halfway through her name before the sound was absorbed by the general commotion. Then there was Cloutier's pistol against his head again. Max managed to turn just enough to see that the Frenchmen had maneuvered the device through the hatchway. Voclain held the pen in one hand, at the ready.

"Say your lines," Cloutier hissed. "Let us be done with this."

Max took a deep breath and willed his voice to carry. "The deck ahoy! The French have the weapon! *The French have the weapon!*"

....

EVERYONE TURNED TOWARD THE SHOUT. THERE AT THE FRONT OF the ship stood Max with two strangers, and between the strangers stood Max's device.

"Max!" Lucy shoved her way forward from the waist of the ship.

Cloutier leveled his pistol at her. "Stop where you are, mademoiselle. Stand down, all of you!"

Oliver stared down at the machine, unable to process what was happening. *Impossible.* Not *pieces* of a device: the thing that stood on deck was obviously the device itself. "They built it," he mumbled. "After everything, they built it right here." The betrayals just kept on coming. Suddenly he felt very small and very, very helpless.

Overhead, the deep-voiced boom of one of the battery's massive guns thudded through the night, followed by a prodigious splash mere yards from the schooner. Someone up above wanted to remind them all that the city could change its mind at any time about how much it cared that the *Fate* stayed afloat.

"*You* stand down," Nell Levinflash shouted. She aimed her own pistol at Cloutier and produced a second gun from inside her jacket. This one she pointed skyward. "One signal-flare from me and they'll put this ship on the seabed."

"Send your signal, Mademoiselle," Cloutier snarled. "With this device, we can put your *battery* on the seabed. Shall we see who is faster?"

Nell Levinflash flexed her fingers on the signal gun, but she didn't lower it.

"She needs a demonstration," Voclain said. His eyes glittered with anticipation and a strange, untamed joy. He began to write. "At long last, a demonstration," he whispered.

The device's arm began to move.

....

OLIVER LOOKED ON IN HORROR. LUCY DID THE SAME. MAX watched with a curious expression on his face, something like sadness and something like anticipation.

The arm stilled as the last bit of silvery ink disappeared into the nib of the pen. And then something new happened: all of the spheres inside the device began to whirl together, blending with the clacking of the whalebone cards and the plinking of the disc. The webwork of filaments at the top end of it began to unravel and reknit itself again in the shape of a long gun—a very elegant gun, but an extraordinary one. Oliver had said the mechanism in the tapestry looked wild; so too did the cannon it sprouted like some sort of huge, elongated, furled metal blossom.

From the ladderway behind the Frenchmen, Liao crept onto the deck and caught Max's eye, and the two of them exchanged a look that would have been entirely unreadable had anyone else noticed it. But no one did. All eyes were on the Copley device.

It fired.

thirty-three
COPLEY

I t fired; and the night became something else.

The mouth of the gun burst open and outward, so that as it discharged, it also appeared to bloom like a massive, mercury-colored flower. There was a stabbing plum-colored flash, and then an explosion with a tone completely unlike that of a proper gun: something uncontrolled, something almost musical. But there was not even the merest whiff of smoke, and Lucy's eye could pick out no projectile sailing upward against the dark sky.

Oliver turned immediately to the battery, waiting for the inevitable blast when the projectile, whatever it was, hit the ramparts. The device's gun was so small, it was hard to imagine anything it could throw doing any damage to the battery, if it managed to reach the battery at all. And yet . . . *what if?*

Voclain's eyes were wide with ecstasy as he stared at the ramparts. "At last," he whispered. "At *last.*"

Liao came to stand beside Max. Max put his arm around the boy, and the two of them gazed upward. "Anytime now," Max murmured.

There was no smashing of stone, no splashing of debris into the surf below. When the eruption happened, it did not happen at the battery, but in the sky above it. Far, far overhead, so far up that the first pinprick of light was nearly invisible among the stars.

It was small at first—just another glimmer in the firmament. Then with a rush of radiance, it became a very bright, very blue radiance that glittered for a moment before bursting into a chrysanthemum of light. But instead of fizzing out and falling in a shower of sparks, the chrysanthemum grew rapidly, increasing in size and complexity as an ever-expanding crystalline pattern wove itself out of light. The blue became blue and gold and crimson and silver and the rose of quartz and the violet of the strange corposants that had been following Max and his work all across the Atlantic.

No one, not a single person still standing aboard the *Left-Handed Fate*, moved.

Luster poured forth across the darkness overhead, spilling outward like brightly colored silk, and the night was transformed. A symphony of light illuminated the world from horizon to horizon. Infinitely varied hues flickered, blended, and burned, spinning themselves into filigreed configurations and ever-shifting arrays. An aurora grown to the size of the entire sky, a tapestry woven by a Mad Spinster in the heavens, a silent fugue of color played for an audience of stars and planets.

Liao was the first to move. As if he could not hold still for another minute without exploding himself, he burst into wild applause, jumping up and down and cheering in an amalgam of English and Mandarin. Then, before anyone could react, he bounded out from under Max's arm and hugged the Copley device. This jolted Max out of his reverie, and he yanked Liao away from the machine as the rest of the spectators began to come to their senses.

"But . . . the battery," Voclain protested.

Cloutier whirled on Max. "What went wrong?"

"Nothing went wrong," Max said. "Absolutely nothing went wrong."

Voclain grabbed the pen again. "Fire upon the battery," he muttered, writing. The arm read his instructions and the device whirred again for a second or two before replying. "*These actions are not part of Copley's program*," Voclain read, his voice thick with anger and disbelief. "What is a Copley?"

"That's Copley," Liao replied, pointing at the device. "Look at the thumping great blues! And the greens!"

"Monsieur," Cloutier said to Voclain in a warning tone. "*Do something—*"

"*Destroy* the battery," Voclain said, scrawling again. He read the machine's written response and actually snarled. "*Eliminate* the battery! *Remove* the battery!" Again and again the device wrote back the same message: *These actions are not part of Copley's program.*

"What does it think its program *is*?" Cloutier demanded.

"What is Copley's program?" Voclain hissed, writing again, and Copley spewed out inch after inch of script by way of answer. It began in Max's handwriting, followed by questions in the device's neat penmanship that were answered sometimes by Max and sometimes by fragments in a much younger hand that wrote in a combination of English words and Chinese characters.

Voclain scanned it all and turned to Max in disbelief. "Its program is *to set off fireworks*?"

"Well, fireworks as it understands them," Max replied, nodding at the ongoing phenomenon in the sky. "We did our best to explain, but it seems to have had some ideas of its own."

"The greatest weapon the world has ever seen, and you turned it into a . . . a show? A *spectacle*?" Voclain's face reddened with fury. "Undo it! Change the program!"

Max shook his head. "It can't be done. The program can only be set once."

"Then take it apart!" Cloutier snarled. "Build it again!"

"You try and take it apart," Max countered. "It defends itself."

Nell Levinflash came forward. "You mean it's not a weapon anymore? It *can't* be a weapon anymore?"

"It never *was* a weapon," Max said. "It could have been, perhaps, but that chance is gone now. Now it's just Copley, and this is what it does. This is *all* it does."

Oliver spoke up from the quarterdeck. "May I remind everyone that this schooner is a lawful prize of the United States? Whatever laws you were willing to break for this weapon—well, you see now that there *is* no weapon. So *get off my ship*." He looked around the deck, his small form somehow taller, his voice carrying more power than seemed possible from a twelve-year-old boy. "D'you hear, all of you? *Get off my ship*, and when I report this to my country, I will do my best to explain it as an unfortunate misunderstanding." He faced Nell Levinflash. "France may not care, but Nagspeake certainly does not wish the United States to declare war upon her."

The Quartermaster tightened her fingers on the handle of her signal gun. But before she could answer, Cloutier grabbed hold of Liao, lifting him right off the deck, and raised his pistol again. "We'll take the device, weapon or no. And if it's really no weapon at all, you'll let us take it."

"Liao!" Lucy screamed.

Max raised his hands, one still wrapped in the bloodstained handkerchief. "Let the boy go. I'll be your hostage."

Cloutier gave a single harsh, angry laugh. "I need a hostage I don't want to shoot on principle. In fact—" Without another word, he aimed the gun at Max and pulled the trigger.

Before anyone on the deck could move, shout, draw breath—before Max, shot at point-blank range, could even begin to buckle—a thousand corposants sprang up with an electrical crackle around the ship.

· Max, still standing, stared at the flame balanced at the end of Cloutier's pistol. Their eyes met over the tiny light. Cloutier pulled the trigger again, inches from Max's face. The little flame fluttered, but that was all.

Then the lookout's voice shouted from overhead. "The deck ahoy! Right off the starboard—there! *There!*"

On the sea to starboard Oliver could make out nothing at all but a dancing light on the surface, the reflection of some patch of illumination overhead. Except—he looked up at the sky, looked back down. The patch on the water brightened as he watched, and Oliver realized the glow was not reflecting down from above but instead was coming up from below the surface.

The glow spread until it was fifteen, then thirty feet across. Spines of blue-white light like the arms of a starfish reached out and began to turn widdershins: five arms, then ten, then fifteen, stretching until their spinning could be seen clear over on the other side of the schooner. The center of the wheel churned, and out of that churning rose the white trapezoid of a topgallant sail.

The sail lifted itself clear of the radiant froth, followed by another topgallant and a topgallant staysail, the huge rectangles of a foretopsail and a maintopsail and all the sails of a square-rigged brig. White water poured from its decks and the brig rose with remarkable speed until it rode alongside the *Left-Handed Fate* just as if it had been there all along.

"We are not often surprised." All eyes turned from the brig to

the *Fate*'s deck, and there, out of nowhere, one of the men in black stood beside Max Ault and Cloutier. His companion stood next to the device, examining it minutely. "It is a very pleasant thing, to be surprised," the first added thoughtfully, looking from Copley up into the painted heavens.

Voclain found his voice first. "No," he whispered, aghast. "We thought Jacquard had gone mad when he told us— *Who are you?*"

The man in black considered Voclain, then the four French ships surrounding the *Fate*. "We were . . . mistaken," he said. "You did not have the mind for the puzzle, that much was clear. The child, we thought, could solve it, and so we believed he was the greater danger. But we were wrong."

The man watched with interest as Cloutier brought his pistol up again and tried and failed for a third time to fire it, this time into the stranger's chest. "Yes," he said coldly. "The war in your hearts is much greater, and you have far less wisdom to temper it." His face twisted into a mockery of a smile. "Let go of this little child now."

Shaking, Cloutier lowered Liao to the deck. He scrambled to Max, who pushed him gently into Lucy's arms.

The golden-skinned man looked from Cloutier to Voclain. "You men will come with me. The war is over for you. But I promise you will see wonders."

And then, in the blink of an eye, he and the two Frenchmen vanished. A heartbeat later, two voices protesting loudly in French could be heard from the deck of the brig as a trio of crewmen there led Cloutier and Voclain below.

....

THE REMAINING MAN IN BLACK CAME TO STAND BEFORE MAX. "You answered the question well."

"Thank you." Max took a deep breath. "I'll go with you, if that's what you require. But please leave my friends to go their way."

The man smiled. It was a better approximation than his companion's effort. "There is no need for that now. There is no weapon here. You might have architected one, but you woke from one dream and entered another." He turned his face upward. "And it is a very beautiful dream."

"It wasn't only my dream," Max admitted. "A friend convinced me that even machines would rather create beautiful things than destruction, if given a choice."

"Your friend is wise," the man said. Liao smiled in Lucy's arms.

"Will you take the device, then?" Max asked.

The stranger shook his head. "Did we not tell you that it had been used to do great and important things? Of dreams such as these is the world made, after all."

Max's eyes widened as he recognized for the first time what the second line of the inscription text actually meant. "But is this great and important?" he asked, dubious. "It's beautiful, but . . . all we were trying to do was to describe fireworks."

"Look you." The stranger gestured around the ship, at all the faces still lit by the spectacle in the sky. "*Wonder* is great and important. And wonder at the visible—at what can be seen and shared, that requires no nationality or belief to experience—that is a special kind of phenomenon."

He smiled again and lifted thin, knobby hands to the stunning sky. Across the ship, heads turned heavenward as the man in black's voice rose with his arms. "A moment like this can be shared between strangers, as we share it now. It crosses all lines, makes them converge, turns enemies into wide-eyed children in the face of the miraculous. And for a moment, the battlefield stills. As this battlefield has stilled."

Something raw and aching and full of power swelled in Max's chest—a feeling so close to pain and yet so magnificent that he felt tears rising behind his eyelids. "I didn't know. I wish I had known— I wish I had meant to do this, but . . ." He choked on a laugh. "But it was just fireworks."

The man smiled again. "It does not lessen your work that you did not know how powerful it would be. Now bring to me the remaining pieces of the design. They must be scattered once more."

"But what if someone finds them again?"

"Someone will, when your dream is done. That is the nature of it."

"Couldn't you just destroy the pieces now? Then there'd be no need to worry about another weapon."

"We could," the stranger agreed. "But that is not our place. Many things have been done with this device that your world would be poorer without. There is no telling what a dreamer will build until he begins. Until we know that one who has the mind for the puzzle dreams of a weapon, we watch and wait and hope that he or she will dream of wonders instead."

....

By the time Max had come back with the bag, Dexter had taken charge of the *Fate* again. Lucy stood at the gunwale with wary eyes and folded arms as the remaining Nagspeakers were shepherded into Cloutier and Voclain's abandoned gig. Nell Levinflash called out to her once, but Lucy only turned away. Meanwhile, near the bow, Liao told the man in black about how he and Max had tried to explain fireworks to the device. The stranger was listening with every appearance of serious attention.

"When did you do that?" Lucy asked as Max came to stand at her side.

"While the ship was coming up the river. Liao said the name I'd given the thing reminded him of a firework. It gave me the beginnings of an idea." He looked down at her with a little smile. "So I told him the story the Spinster told you."

The man in black detached himself from Liao as Max came forward with his armful. "This is all of it," Max said, tipping the bag into the stranger's hands.

"Except for the recipe," Lucy put in. "You won't hurt the confectioner, will you?"

"There is no need. We are experts in forgetting, you recall."

Against all logic, Lucy snorted a laugh. "Oh, come on," she protested when Max stared at her in disbelief. "Experts in forgetting? *You recall*, meaning me, when I was the one he made forget? Oh, for the love of—it's *hilarious*."

Max groaned, but the man in the smoked spectacles tilted his head for a moment, then burst into a braying laugh. Then, still chuckling and with his arms full of Max's short life's work, he vanished.

The glowing water under the hull of the brig began to churn and the gleaming arms began to spin again. The ship sank rapidly below the surface, and in moments, the highest sails were all that remained to be seen. Then those, too, disappeared. The light under the water diminished, and all that was left was the reflection of the glory that still hung in the sky overhead.

thirty-four
PAROLE

Oliver stared along with everyone else as the brig sank beneath the waters, then he remembered that there were still four enemy ships watching. "Mr. Wooll! Mr. Harrick!" he shouted. The Fates were already rushing to clear the deck and ready themselves for further battle, but the *Marie Colette* was in no condition to fight. Her weather deck was in a state of complete disorder; half the crew stared up like mooncalves and half searched the water where the brig had vanished. The frigates were too far off for Oliver to see so clearly, but their perfect line of battle had broken down and they drifted at odd angles. None could've fired a proper broadside at the *Fate* without hitting one of its confederates.

The *Fate*'s sailing master stepped up to the quarterdeck. "Aye aye, Mr. Dexter."

Oliver lowered his telescope. "All sail, Mr. Wooll, and make for Norfolk."

Mr. Wooll glanced briefly to where Lucy stood near a weapons locker beside an exhausted Max Ault, a glowing Liao, and the silvery device. Lucy gave a single nod, and Mr. Wooll raised his knuckles to his forehead again. "Aye aye, sir. Make all sail and Norfolk it is, sir."

"Thank you." Oliver turned to the gunner. "Mr. Harrick, I don't believe we shall be pursued, but make sure we are prepared if I'm wrong, will you? And masthead," he called to the lookout, "sing out if you see anything from the frigates." Then he trooped tiredly over to the weapons locker to join Max, Lucy, and Liao. "Compliments, and may I join you?"

Lucy made a salute. "If you please, Lieutenant."

Liao scooted over to make room, and Oliver dropped onto the locker, for once not caring whether he looked more like a tired boy than a naval officer. He leaned his head back on the gunwale and for the first time allowed himself a real look at the sky. "Remarkable."

"Thumping great colors," Liao said seriously, leaning his head back, too. "Copley did a splendid job, didn't it?"

"I think everyone did a splendid job," Oliver replied. "We seem to be the only crew kept our wits about us."

"We should likely be all a-hoo as well, if not for you," Lucy said.

Oliver smiled gratefully. "Thank you."

For a long while they sat together in silence, watching the sky and listening to the sounds of the rigging and the bow-waves rushing along the hull. Oliver and Liao lay back with their heads on the gunwale. Max gazed at Lucy until she met his eyes. She held out her hand. Max took it, pulled her close, and, when she didn't punch him in the gut for that, leaned closer still and pressed a kiss to her temple.

At last Lucy spoke up again. "I apologize for breaking our parole and betraying your trust, Mr. Dexter."

"I'm sorry as well," Max said.

"It was the wrong disc, I suppose," Oliver said. "The one you gave me."

Max nodded. "It was a terrible trick to play."

"We gave our word, and we broke it again and again. I thought it was the right thing to do, but . . ." Lucy looked at the boat pulling for the battery and shook her head in disgust. "I suppose Nell thought the same thing."

Oliver said nothing for a moment. "Is it true?" he asked at last. "That the device is not a weapon, and can never be one?"

"Yes. That's why the men in black didn't take it. Or me." Max nodded skyward. "Now it is a machine for that."

"Then I suppose, technically, you did wind up observing the terms of your parole. You weren't to build a weapon, and you didn't." Oliver snorted. "At the very last minute. What is the status of your mission now, Mr. Ault?"

Max shrugged. "There is no mission any longer."

"But will you try to build another weapon?"

"No. And I couldn't, even if I wanted to. Not without everything I've given away to the men in black, and not without what's inside of Copley there."

Oliver nodded. "And you, Miss Bluecrowne? If there is no mission, what becomes of you and your crew?"

Lucy sighed. "I don't know. We can still make our way in Nagspeake. I'll probably avoid Flotilla for a bit, though. The swab. I would never have believed it of her."

"But I meant, will you go on privateering?"

Lucy made a wry face. "Without a ship?"

"Could you really not afford a ship, though?" Max asked. "Your father wasn't without means, and there's still my payment to collect."

"Perhaps I could. Perhaps I will, someday, with my own letters of marque and reprisal. But without those, I'm no privateer and neither is the *Fate*. We should be pirates, nothing more."

"Are not some pirates very dashing and heroic?" Max asked. Lucy gave him a look of utter dismay. "Have I said something wrong?"

She folded her arms. "I daresay there have been pirates who have done noble things, and I suppose they have honor of a kind, but not the sort I grew up with."

"And in the end," Oliver said, "it wouldn't be the same as sailing for one's country."

"No, it wouldn't." She reached out to run a hand along the gunwale behind them. "But then, nor would sailing in any other ship."

"A ship is a fighting machine," Liao said. "It's only home so long as you hold it. That's what you said."

"I was lying, Liao. I was trying to make you feel better. Did it help when I said it?"

"Not particularly."

"Well, I apologize, but that's why."

"I am so tired of trying to figure out how to do the right thing." Oliver watched the sails fill and glow, backlit by the sky. "I am thinking about a parole arrangement," he said at last.

There would be no justifying it to the navy, of course; but perhaps, if Lucy was willing to play along, he might at least be able to explain it to the satisfaction of whomever he finally reported to when this was all over.

"I am thinking," Oliver said slowly, "about a parole arrangement for the *Left-Handed Fate*."

Lucy looked dubiously at him. "A parole . . . for the schooner?"

"Do ships get paroled?" Max asked.

"Not usually," Lucy said, frowning. "And your navy needs ships too badly for you to let a craft like this one go."

"Yes, it does. But look around." Oliver gestured across the deck. "There are only a handful of Amaranthines left, and still, what, fifty-odd Fates?" Lucy began shaking her head. Oliver ignored her and raised his voice a touch. "And here I am, sitting between the heirs of the ship without any sort of weapon in reach."

Across the deck the crew, Amaranthines and Fates alike, were listening now, although they were trying hard not to look like it. Oliver shook his head minutely to let the remnants of his prize-crew know he was not asking for rescue.

"Absolutely not," Lucy said, raising her voice, too. "We gave our word. I've broken enough promises, thank you."

"If you were to take the ship back now—"

"Absolutely not!"

"If you were to ask my surrender," Oliver said, speaking calmly over her protests, "I should not have any choice but to hand the ship back. And when we reached Norfolk, you could send us into the harbor in one of your boats, and we should be able to report that following engagements with the French, the city of Nagspeake, and an unknown enemy, our numbers were too small to hold the ship. And as you have no miraculous weapon to carry home to England, I don't think I would lose much sleep over it."

"That's not a parole," Lucy protested. "That's us taking the schooner back!"

"I think it *is* a parole if you agree not to raid American shipping for the duration of the war."

"Lieutenant Dexter, you *need* this ship."

"Captain Bluecrowne," Oliver insisted, "you need it more."

Lucy put her hand to her mouth. For a moment no one said anything. Oliver waited, counting the stars that could now be seen dimly through the stranger colors as the aurora began, very slowly, to fade. It looked, he thought, as if the hues of a dyed cloth were beginning to run in the rain, and the stars were the pinpricks left by stitches pulled out so that the cloth could fly to pieces along with its fading color.

At length, Lucy put one shaking arm around Oliver's shoulders and leaned her damp cheek against his. "Mr. Dexter," she said in a shaking voice, "I have no right to ask you to strike your colors."

"You must," Oliver said quietly.

Lucy cleared her throat. "I have no right, but . . . but as you see—" She gave a choked little laugh. "As you see, you are quite surrounded."

Relief poured through Oliver. He reached for Lucy's hand and squeezed it hard. "I see that." He raised his voice so that it would carry properly across the deck. "Amaranthines, we are thoroughly outnumbered. Our only course is to surrender the ship." He looked at Mr. Cascon, then at the other four remaining members of his prize-crew. "Understood?"

All five lifted their knuckles to their foreheads. "Aye aye, sir," Mr. Cascon said, not bothering to hide his smile.

Lucy opened her mouth to say something, but then she wrapped both arms around Oliver instead. From across the deck, Oliver heard someone—Fate or Amaranthine, he wasn't sure which—shout, "Three cheers for Lieutenant Dexter!"

The shouts of *huzzay* rang out in succession: three shouts, repeated three times. When the cheering was done, Lucy wiped her face. "My first act as captain. Pass the word for Garvett!"

The grinning steward appeared, and Lucy asked for wine and toasted cheese.

"Perhaps we might toast Papa now," Liao suggested in a small voice when they each had a glass.

"Yes, of course. Let us toast Papa." Lucy hugged him fiercely, spilling the contents down the poor boy's back.

Max refilled her glass without comment. "To Captain Bluecrowne."

"To the *first* Captain Bluecrowne," Oliver corrected him. "I wish I had met him."

Max nodded. "You would have liked him. He would certainly have liked you."

"To Papa," Liao whispered.

Lucy's throat worked for a moment. "To Papa."

She, Max, Liao, and Oliver raised their glasses, and for a while they sat in silence as the night and the sea and the rigging murmured around them. Then they ate their picnic under the last dwindling light of Copley's aurora as the *Left-Handed Fate* swept Oliver northward, homeward at last, and night fell for a second time across the Atlantic.

Acknowledgments

This book was my husband Nathan's idea. I would never have read Patrick O'Brian's Aubrey/Maturin novels if Nathan hadn't insisted—and I took some convincing—that I would love them. (I did, desperately.) Later Nathan pointed out that a fighting ship of this era would be the perfect setting for a middle-grade novel, since children routinely went to sea at very young ages. This was standard operating procedure in the Royal Navy, and I would later learn that, at the time of the War of 1812, the young U.S. Navy considered twelve to eighteen years the optimal age range for new midshipmen. So the first and biggest thank you goes, as ever, to Nathan, who continues to be responsible for almost all my best ideas.

I would not have been able to write this book without a big support group of very dear friends. Thanks first of all to Honorary Uncle Ray Rupelli, Honorary Aunt Julie Culver, Heather Courter, and Chelsea Hesketh, who have made it possible to juggle a child and a writing career with a minimum of angst. Endless gratitude goes to Gus and the wonderful folks at Emphasis Restaurant in Bay Ridge, Brooklyn, who have graciously allowed me to use the booth by the wall socket as a branch office for the past five years, and most critically for the three years since my son was born. Thanks to the

Kickstarter backers of *Bluecrowne*, which is Lucy and Liao's first adventure in Nagspeake and the backstory of the smugglers' inn in *Greenglass House*. Writing *Bluecrowne* helped me to get to know Lucy, Liao, and the Fates so well that working on *The Left-Handed Fate* was like coming home. And cheers to Sarah McNally, Cristin Stickles, and all the wonderful folks at McNally Jackson Books for giving me a home away from home every Saturday, in addition to all the other amazing things you do for writers and readers and books and the community and each other.

My wonderful critique group (Lisa Amowitz, Heidi Ayarbe, Pippa Bayliss, Linda Budzinski, Dhonielle Clayton, Lindsay Eland, Cathy Giordano, Trish Heng, Cynthia Kennedy Henzel, and Christine Johnson) read the earliest versions of *The Left-Handed Fate* and made it better. I will be forever grateful to Ann Behar and Noa Wheeler for seeing the potential of this story and taking a leap of faith that I'd be able to deliver something worth reading. Thank you to Julia Sooy and Barry Goldblatt for bringing the book home, and to Emma Humphrey for her critical eye along the way. Thanks also to Craig Garcia; in previous books I've thanked Craig for making me a better writer, but he's also one of the best managers I ever worked for, and Lucy's philosophy as a commander is lifted pretty much directly from things Craig taught me about leadership. David Antscherl and Lucy Bellwood lent their considerable expertise in matters nautical to keep me from doing silly things with my ships and sailors, and any errors or acts of excessive whimsy I've committed here are mine alone. Finally, I have been unbelievably lucky to have been paired with remarkable illustrators over and over, and this book is no exception. A million thanks to Eliza Wheeler for bringing the *Left-Handed Fate* and her crew and the city of Nagspeake and her denizens to life so very, very beautifully.

My father and grandfather both served in the U.S. Navy. Granddad (Bud Chell Sr.) and Grandmom (the irrepressible Norma Hauswald Chell) lived in a house on the Chesapeake Bay. Granddad died when I was seventeen; Grandmom followed almost nineteen years later. My final work on the first complete draft of this book was done on Grandmom's dining table overlooking the bay just a few days before she passed away, and if even a fraction of her spirit made it into Lucy Bluecrowne, Lucy is stronger for it. *The Left-Handed Fate* is dedicated to their memories, with love—although I think Granddad would've said there isn't enough singing in it, and Grandmom would've suggested I write in a couple whiskey sours.